Four-&-Twenty
Bloodhounds

Four-&-Twenty Bloodhounds

Edited with
introductions by
Anthony Boucher

Carroll & Graf Publishers, inc.
New York

Foreword

THIS IS NOT a formal historico-critical anthology of detection. Essentially it's simply a collection of some of the best stories about some of America's best fictional detectives. None of these stories has appeared in any other anthology; most of them have never before appeared in book form; and a few have been written or rewritten especially for this volume.

You have a grand lot of fiction reading ahead of you, and I shan't blame you if you plunge right on into it. But if you are a foreword-reader and care to pause here a moment, I'll be glad of your company.

It's often been said that in each of his five stories of deductive analysis, that great pioneer Poe anticipated one or another of all the standard elements that go to make up the modern detective story, from the Locked Room to the Least Suspected Person.

It's also true that in three of the stories taken as a group Poe anticipated yet another essential item: the Series Detective. Like many another Poe discovery, this was raised to its acme and given permanence by Sir Arthur Conan Doyle in his creation of the greatest Series Detective of them all.

Doubtful though it is that any customers in the 1840's asked for the latest story about C. Auguste Dupin, it's completely certain that readers in the 1890's wanted, not the new Doyle, but the new Holmes story. And ever since then, the detective has tended to dominate his creator to the point where librarians have to keep reference lists of detectives, because the public almost never asks for a book by author. (How clever of the Queens to select the same name for detective and for auctorial pseudonym!)

That is why the emphasis in this volume is on the detective—and an odd and interesting lot of detective protagonists you'll find here, ranging from a Skid Row bum to a Senator of the United States. These are not the detectives you've seen in all the standard anthologies—the Valmonts, the Van Dusens, the Poirots, the Thorndykes, the Browns. These are, for the most part, the latest American crop—and you'll notice some interesting departures.

The pure amateur, for instance, though still present in such delightful personages as Miss Hildegarde Withers or the Troys, is much less in evidence than heretofore. Instead you'll find professional policemen, like Trant and Magruder; semi-official police consultants, like Queen and Merlini; such other officers of society as a medical examiner and a fire marshal; detectives whose professions (as various as insurance salesman and medical missionary) force them into the investigation of crime; and of course, the private eye (though not nearly so ubiquitous here as on radio and screen).

And along with the stories you'll find the official, never-before-revealed biographies of these sleuths. You'll learn strange facts about your favorite detectives: that Miss Hildegarde Withers, for instance, is fascinated by the new self-proclaimed science of dianetics, and that Solar Pons is an authority on the Cthulhu Mythos of H. P. Lovecraft. You'll learn the truth about the theatrical careers of Haila Troy and Miss Rachel Murdock, the weakness in the armor of Lieutenant Timothy Trant, the rise and fall of onetime-Lieutenant Nick Noble, the singular phone number of The Great Merlini (and the secret behind the pseudonym, "Clayton Rawson").

Bibliophiles will be entranced by the countless publications of these detectives (seemingly even more prolific than their authors), with titles ranging from An Analysis of the Coextensive Range of Malaria and Blackwater Fever in Central Africa to 500 Limericks.

Before passing you on to the stories themselves, I must pay tribute to a phenomenon without which the modern American detective short story could hardly have reached its present stage of development. A glance at copyright acknowledgments will show you how many of the stories in this volume were first published in Ellery Queen's Mystery Magazine. A glance at other contemporary periodicals will show you how little chance of publication those stories would have had before the founding of EQMM—the first, and still the only consistent market for short stories on the same level of literacy and ingenuity as the best novel-length detective stories.

I'd further like to convey my gratitude to Kenneth Macgowan, who first conceived the idea of detective Who's Who notes in one of the best of all criminous anthologies, Sleuths (Harcourt, Brace, 1931); to all of the members of MWA who contributed these stories and biographies; to all of the other members whose stories were reluctantly excised for reasons of practicable length; in particular to Lawrence G. Blochman and Ellery Queen for assistance beyond the call of MWA duty; and finally to Mystery Writers of America itself, for its indefatigable work in stimulating and safeguarding all that is best in the American detective story.

ANTHONY BOUCHER

Berkeley, California
March, 1950

Table of Contents

Good things come in threes. In 1913 Ellis Parker Butler created the first correspondence school detective, Philo Gubb. Thirty years later Percival Wilde revealed the wonderful correspondence between the Acme International Detective Correspondence School and one P. Moran. And then, to round out the triad, Verne Chute reached back into the past for the extraordinary achievements, in 1910, of Shad Arnold. Here's the first of Shad's exploits—and if the description of Ludolph Hoorn's free lunch doesn't drive you out to the icebox while you're reading it, you're a strong (and unenviable) man.

.SHADRACK ARNOLD in

Never Trust the Obvious

BY VERNE CHUTE

SHADRACK ARNOLD's beardless face tightened as he watched the portly butcher and the butcher's lone customer, the Marston kid. Since the mysterious death of Harvey Norton the week before, Shad watched everybody. Yet all six feet, six inches of him was out of its domain—by the width of Granville's dusty street. He belonged across the way where the ancient horse, hitched to Carter's grocery wagon, shook its head at the myriad flies and stamped out the minutes with monotonous regularity. It was four o'clock in the afternoon and Shad should have been starting out on his last delivery of the day.

Shad inspected several sugar-cured hams hanging on the rack. But his interest in hams was ostensible and remote; his suspi-

From *Short Stories*, Oct. 10, 1944. Copyright 1944 by *Short Stories*.

cious eyes looked past the gibbous outlines to the butcher busy at work putting up the boy's order.

Shad's unusual height, stringy yellow hair, and smoky-blue eyes would have made him conspicuous in any place other than Granville. But Granville was used to him now, had seen his rise from roustabout at Johnson's Livery Stable to delivery boy for Old Man Carter. Shad was twenty-four, weighed one hundred and twenty-eight pounds. His gaunt frame was draped with well-worn Levis, a black sateen shirt, and a cloth vest. Although his Homburg-style hat had the imprint of a St. Louis firm in it, this was an accident—the hat had blown off the head of a curious Easterner who paid a price for gaping at Shad from a train window.

Shad watched the butcher adroitly cut the last of the thick sirloin steaks and toss them on the scales. The four-pound weight went up—to stay. The butcher added a double handful of suet and began wrapping the meat in thick brown paper.

"Thirty cents," he said.

The Marston boy looked startled. "You mean, *thirty cents*? For just that?"

"I'm throwing in some liver—"

Shad watched the kid fumbling with his money, while the butcher added several thick slabs of liver to the package.

"Ma said to put in a soup-bone," said the youngster.

The butcher nodded patiently and wrapped a soup-bone in a piece of week-old *Center City Chronicle*. Only then did the kid give up his two dimes and his two nickels.

The butcher grinned. "Meat's high, kid—this is 1910! All right, 23—skiddoo!" He turned to Shad.

"Nothing," said Shad from the side of his mouth and slid out the door in the wake of the Marston kid. Shad had plenty of room to have gone out normally, but he slid out sideways—even as the great detective, Captain Ellsworth, might have done shadowing a suspect.

It was evident that the butcher had passed Shad's inspection and was no longer under suspicion. But Shad was on a hotter trail. When he spoke again, it was still from the side of his mouth, and to the Marston kid.

"I got some groceries going out for your ma," he told him. "You can ride with me."

The boy's sudden grin set his freckles to dancing. "Kin I, Shad?"

Shad nodded soberly and led the way across the street, his bean-pole shadow slanting out behind him. As his limpid eyes swept up and down the nearly deserted street he allowed a faint smile to drive the inscrutability out of his face. But it left a deeply-veiled secret behind his eyes. Granville didn't know it, but in its midst was the best private detective in Grail County, perhaps in the State!

If Shad wanted to claim his title he had the proof at hand. Reposing secretly, if not majestically, in his inside vest pocket was a diploma that could set any scoffer to shame—a gold-edged diploma from Investigators, Incorporated, St. Louis! A diploma signed by Captain Ellsworth himself.

And that wasn't all. In a felt pouch inside the hip pocket of his Levis was a pair of shiny handcuffs and a nickel-plated badge, in case he needed to make an arrest. The sixty-nine-page book that went with this paraphernalia stated emphatically on page twelve that the power of arrest was every man's prerogative. The course, fully equipped and including the sixty-nine-page book, had cost Shad a total of forty dollars. Two months' wages at Carter's.

To Shad, money well spent. No longer did he live a drab existence. Vicariously, he had rubbed elbows with the denizens of vice dens on the waterfront, had walked hand in hand with the swells. He had conducted investigations for senators, for governors, and for fine, perfumed ladies. Countless children had been rescued from the sordid hands of child-stealers and restored to grateful parents. Shad had even, when nothing of greater importance pressed, saved the pets of beautiful ladies, whose rewarding embraces he had had to fight off. On many occasions he had politely but firmly declined these beautiful ladies' offers of marriage.

Shad pulled up, rousing himself. Old Man Carter was coming out of the store with a box of groceries. Near-sighted and puffing, he wheezed at Shad, "Where you been?" Without waiting for an answer he said, "Take these groceries out to Mrs. Marston's right away. She's having Alice Wainwright and young Mr. Peaslee over to supper tonight. Stop in at the feed-barn and get her a sack of wheat for her chickens. Number Two grade. If you see her kid tell him to come home." Mr. Carter gave Shad and the wagon a cursory glance and hobbled back into the store.

"Yes, Mr. Carter," Shad called after him. He shoved the grocery box farther into the wagon bed and smiled at the Marston kid who was already climbing to the wagon seat.

As soon as he had backed the wagon away from the hitch rail, Shad looked down at the youngster. Shad's eyes were as inscrutable as Captain Ellsworth's on page one, where he was pictured questioning a suspect.

"Son," he said quietly, "who's to supper beside the school-teacher and the bank cashier? You got four pounds of steak!"

"Beefsteak's for tomorrow," said the youngster scornfully. "We wouldn't have that for company. We're having chicken. Mr. Winston, the banker, will be there."

Shad's eyes half closed. When Randolph Winston, the town's number one citizen, was present it meant the Marstons were having out-of-town company. "Who else is coming, kid?"

"Mr. Buchanan's coming in on the six o'clock. Mr. Buchanan's sheriff from over Center City way."

Shad's smoky eyes narrowed still further at this information. That was something, the sheriff coming! It meant that Mr. Marston and perhaps others hadn't been satisfied with old Doc Bayley's verdict that Harvey Norton had died of over-drinking. It meant—Shad's thin lips suddenly warped to the side.

"Who does your pa think killed Mr. Norton?" he asked.

The kid gulped, and he started to shake his head. "Hully gee—" But his eyes turned to look back along the street.

Shad let the horse shuffle to a walk, while his trained, inscrutable, photographic, deductive eyes followed the Marston kid's backwards glance.

There were only two persons back there on the sidewalk. One of them, Randolph Winston, had just come out of his bank. Mr. Winston was tall, gray-haired, with sideburns of a much earlier period than 1910. He wore a tall black hat and dark clothes, and because of his gloomy appearance had once been mistaken for the undertaker. Mr. Winston occupied the seat of honor at Granville's civic functions.

The other man on the sidewalk, oddly enough, was the town's most disreputable figure—Henry Mark. Hank Mark polished boots and shoes at his stand in front of Lever's Barbershop; he was thick of body, unkempt in appearance. His small, dark eyes were deeply set in his fleshy face, and he looked like a man with something on his mind.

Shad slapped the reins as their trailing cloud of dust caught up with them. Spurred on, the effete old horse swept on again to pull the wagon away from the cloud of dust.

Shad allowed that faint, reserved smile to seep back into his face. The Marston kid had practically pointed out the killer. Shad muttered, as if to himself, "I knew old Doc Bayley was wrong—so your old man thinks it was Hank Mark who killed Norton, huh?"

The kid squirmed in the seat, looking scared.

"Gee, Shad, I ain't saying—not one way or the other."

"Then the schoolteacher and Mr. Peaslee are just over for supper—"

"Mm-huh," said the kid. "Mr. Peaslee is sitting up with Miss Wainwright—he's got a good job at the bank with Mr. Winston —and Ma says he's going to propose to her tonight—I mean, Mr. Peaslee is to Miss Wainwright."

Shad nodded slowly. But he knew Mr. Winston would occupy the place of honor at Marston's table. *That was something.* Shad's eyes grew wistful. Some day— But after a few tentative wishes he lost interest and retreated into his own thoughts.

Shad knew he had to hurry to complete his case before the sheriff arrived. But he was on the job. On page two of Captain Ellsworth's book it said, among other things: "*A private detective owes a certain allegiance to his community. His conduct and reputation must be above reproach, and he should always keep his payments up to date.*" And there was a subheading that cautioned, "*Refrain from trusting the obvious.*"

So Shad kept his payments up to date, and he didn't trust the obvious. That was the reason he questioned the popular verdict that Harvey Norton had come to his untimely end by disobeying the doctor's orders—and drinking nearly a quart of whiskey. At least, the bottle had been nearly empty when they found Harvey Norton. The kindly old doctor had explained everything with a shake of his head. "I told poor Harvey not to touch the stuff again."

But Shad had been skeptical—and worried. If, as they said, Harvey Norton had just passed away, there would be no case. And Shad *had* to have a case. It might be years before he would have another chance!

So Shad decided on robbery as well as murder. Harvey Norton was supposed to have had a lot of money. But not in the bank. The banker testified that Norton had drawn heavily on his savings until practically nothing remained.

When Shad arrived at the Marston place he carried the wheat into the shed and the groceries into the kitchen. He came out with a quarter of a cinnamony apple pie.

On his way back to the store he took a side street, stopping in front of the Harvey Norton house. He got out, unlatched the door, and went inside. Nothing had been disturbed; it was as it had been when Norton's body was found. Shad had his badge ready in case Tom Dillon, town marshal, came snooping around.

But Tom Dillon didn't come around and Shad had his fill of his new investigation. Almost next door was the shack occupied by Hank Mark, the bootblack. The house was screened by un-trimmed trees and it was easy for Shad to get inside without being seen. His eyes popped at what he found. Hank Mark had a new suit hanging in the closet, a pair of shoes still in their box, and a new Stetson hat. And there was a new suitcase under the bed. Hank had always talked of going to California; now it seemed as though he really was going.

BY THE time Shad had put up his delivery wagon and fed his horse, the red glow of sunset was setting fire to the store windows across from Carter's. When he crossed the street, he smiled faintly, feeling a glow of pride at his own coolness.

He was on the trail of the criminal. And Hank Mark was his man! But it would take more than just apprehending Mark; the man must be forced or tricked into admitting his dastardly crime!

Randolph Winston came down the sidewalk, strolling along with regal dignity. He smiled faintly and spoke to Shad as if Shad might some day have enough money to put in his bank.

Shad spoke and hurried on. The bootblack stand was closed, so Shad hurried on toward the Paradise Bar.

Ludolph Hoorn, the Dutch proprietor, had taken no chance that a thirsty stranger might overlook his place. Each of his painted windows was covered by his sign. Another sign swung out over the sidewalk. On the wide expanse of false front was pictured an enormous schooner of frothy beer and the legend, "Biggest Beer In Town, 5c."

Shad moved up under the swinging sign and looked across the top of the batwing doors. The smell of beer tightened his nostrils. Then came the other smells, the aroma of roasted meats, of cheese, rye bread, and dill pickles.

HANK MARK was the only customer. His thick lips were almost lost in the foam of a giant-size schooner of beer. Across the bar was the portly bartender and proprietor, who was beaming at his sole customer and shining glasses that reflected the light of sunset coming over the top of the batwings.

Shad pushed inside. Mark looked around, grunted, and returned to his beer. The proprietor's beaming face turned, too. The expectant light in it went out, like a lamp being turned low. "Noddings," he said for Shad, and mournfully returned to shining his glasses.

A moment later, Hoorn said to Hank Mark: "New bickles, I gott—from St. Louis, ja!"

Shad's eyes brightened. St. Louis was the home of Investigators, Incorporated! But Shad went on studying the calendar on the side wall. Pictured on it were gay lovers on ice skates, the boy young and agile, the girl alive with vibrant youth and beauty.

There was no title or inscription under the picture other than "St. Elmo Tombstone Company, St. Louis." Beyond the calendar at the side door was another sign, "Family Entrance. No Profanity—It Might Be Your Sister."

But Shad was watching and listening, sizing up his man.

Hank Mark was talking to the bartender. "Yeah, when I get out to California I'm going to buy me a bar like this." He added, hastily, "I been saving my money."

"*Ja!* Goot." The Dutchman waved a hamlike hand toward the end of the bar. "Haff it some vree loonch, hey, Ma-a-ark?"

"I'll get to it," grumbled Mark, his sardonic eyes moving along the bar.

Both men seemed to have forgotten Shad. But Shad's eyes were missing nothing. They took in the barrellike chest of the boot-black, his bulging muscles, his scowling face. Shad was about to say his inevitable "nothing" and walk out—and then he thought of page thirteen. Page thirteen would let him stay in Hoorn's Paradise Bar until the six o'clock train came in. Page thirteen, under the heading *"Follow That Man,"* said: *"It is often necessary to follow your suspect into the lowest places, and at times, to join him in his sotten pleasures."*

Shad tightened his thin jaw and moved forward. Hank Mark shuffled to the "Free Lunch." Mark picked up two wide slices of rye bread cut fresh from a long thick loaf spread out on a bar towel. With a meat fork he speared a tender slice of roast beef from its gravy; he followed this with a thick slice of roast pork and one of boiled ham, and topped his sandwich with a piece of Wisconsin cheese and a couple of small pickled onions he speared out of their vinegar. After Mark found a hard-boiled egg that suited him he slid back to his beer, finishing it off with a gulp.

"Another one," he demanded.

"*Ja!*" The Dutchman chuckled to himself and proceeded to draw off another foaming mug of beer. His jowls vibrated to his sly mirth, and he whispered to himself, "He forgets it the bickle —*Ja!*"

Shad moved on up to the bar. He stuck a foot on the rail.

"Beer."

Proprietor Hoorn nearly dropped the glass he was filling for Mark. "Vat!" he cried, his eyes dilating with surprise. He raised his fat face so he could take in all of his new-found customer. "Peer?"

"Beer!" Shad repeated. His voice, he noticed, was firm, peremptory. Calmly, he opened his purse, selected one of the most worn five-cent pieces and laid it on the bar.

Hank Mark's contribution to this strained moment was a sneering laugh. Ludolph Hoorn quickly placed the beer before Mark and waddled back to draw Shad's. The big man's whole body worked to get the beer poured and onto the bar before his customer could change his mind. He handed it over—foamy, glistening, and cold. Looking at Shad as if he had found a long-lost brother, he waved a welcoming hand toward the free lunch.

"New bickles, I gott—St. Louis. Help yourself, my poy!"

"Better take some," sneered Hank Mark. "You'll need something to hold that beer down."

Shad said nothing. But he had beer suds on his lips and a thick sandwich in his hands when the six o'clock whistled for the crossing a mile out of town. Shad nearly choked on his beer.

The big Dutchman, concerned over his new customer, rushed up to slap him on the back.

But Hank Mark laughed scornfully. "Better weaken that beer with some water for him—"

Shad caught his breath, remaining silent. He moved to the batwings when the train bell began to sound over the building tops. He cast a surreptitious glance back at Hank Mark, then toward the station. Shad could see between two of the buildings. The tall man who got off the train shook hands with Harry Marston first, and then with Banker Randolph Winston and Marshal Tom Dillon.

Shad stood there watching them. The four men started toward the main street—and toward the Paradise Bar. As soon as Shad was sure they intended coming into the saloon, he went back to the bar. He was standing with his foot on the rail when the four men came inside.

SHAD's eyes passed up the banker and the short, stocky town marshal—and held to the tall, fine-appearing man who stood by Marston. Shad was a little disappointed. He had pictured the sheriff as a raw-boned gunman with glittering eye, a star on his chest, and a long walrus mustache which he would twist continually; instead, Sheriff Buchanan was a calm, clear-eyed businessman who nodded to the bartender and said, "Beer."

The sheriff's eyes held to Shad—but then all strangers did that, until they got used to him.

Ludolph Hoorn said, "Ja!" four times, beaming just a little more each time he said the word. Then he bustled about his job of drawing the four beers.

Shad moved back so he could see his suspect. Hank Mark had nodded to the men when they came in, and was now watching them with appraising, suspicious eyes. Shad felt into his pocket for his badge, and for his shiny handcuffs. If his knees were a trifle unsteady it was from the excitement—an Investigators, Incorporated, detective was without fear. Anyway, he would be all right in a minute—in a minute he would have their eyes popping.

"Surprise," said page fourteen, was the element for a situation like this. But Shad knew he had to work fast. The men were closing in on Hank Mark like a pack of fox hounds around its prey. Shad's eyes swerved to Banker Winston's lean face. There was a cold, sadistic pleasure in the man's eyes as he looked sideways to Hank Mark.

Harry Marston, Tom Dillon and the sheriff were raising their drinks to their lips now and talking in a low voice. Shad couldn't hear their words, but the import of those words was plain—in a moment they would arrest Hank Mark for the murder of Harvey Norton.

And they could prove nothing. Doc Bayley had already testified that Harvey Norton came to his end through overindulgence.

Shad didn't hesitate any longer. He turned to the men and said quietly, yet with confidence—according to instructions on page twenty-eight: "Gentlemen, I think you've got something there."

All eyes snapped to him. Shad's voice had sounded like a

shout in a quiet church. And now Shad was nodding to Sheriff Buchanan, in keeping with the admonition, *it is always best to recognize any duly constituted officer of the law*, and he was taking his badge from his pocket and calmly pinning it on his vest.

Shad took advantage of the surprised silence to speak directly to the visiting sheriff. "You are right in reopening the case of Harvey Norton," he smiled.

Surprise held them in those first few moments. Then the banker said thinly, "Better get back to your delivering—this is Sheriff Buchanan!"

Sheriff Buchanan put down his beer and waved his beer hand. "Wait a minute," he said, and turned back to Shad. "Who told you I was coming here to reopen the case?"

Shad gave the law officer a professional smile; it was supposed to be his part of an exchange of knowing smiles between two men who understood each other.

But the sheriff hid his part of the smile. He stepped closer to the scintillating badge on Shad's chest. "Investigators, Incorporated," he said. "Mm-mm. That's the outfit in New York, isn't it?"

"St. Louis," said Shad.

Sheriff Buchanan nodded. Then he asked, "What do you know about this case, son?"

Shad smiled with quiet dignity. "The name's Shadrack Arnold." Then he added, "I guess I know all there is to know about this case. Harvey Norton didn't die of drink, he was murdered— in cold blood. Mr. Norton had recently drawn his savings from Mr. Winston's bank—and the killer knew this."

The sheriff's gray eyes swung past Harry Marston and the town marshal to Banker Winston. "Is that correct?" he asked. "Did Norton draw all his money from your bank?"

"Why, yes," said Winston. "He was afraid of the present administration—I thought Harry Marston told you about it."

The sheriff barely nodded. "How much was it?"

"Let's see," said the banker gravely, "I believe it was about twelve hundred dollars. I believe he sent the money away—"

"Buried it," said Harry Marston, "unless—" He hesitated, then added, "Old Harvey was on the secretive side—nobody knew much about him."

Shad had been watching Hank Mark's face. There was fear in it now. His dark eyes darted from one man's face to another. He was bolting his sandwich.

Shad recklessly finished off his beer and turned his blinking eyes to the sheriff. "Harvey Norton didn't die from too much drink—he was robbed and murdered!"

Marshal Tom Dillon's red face flushed to a deeper hue. "I'm getting fed up with you, Shad." He grasped Shad's arm. "If you know so much—where's the killer now?"

But Shad was gulping most unprofessionally. The schooner of beer had been a little too much for him. He felt a sudden lightness because of it. He fought back the desire to dance. Then he heard the sheriff's calm voice, and he held to his spinning senses.

Sheriff Buchanan said, "Go ahead, son—er, I mean Mr. Shadrack. Tell us what you know."

The sheriff's words had a sobering effect on Shad. But he stood back against the bar for a moment, watching Proprietor Hoorn come out from behind it, pull down the hanging lamp and light it. Then Shad said, without looking at Hank Mark: "The killer is right here in this room."

A beer mug overturned at the bar. The sound of the beer dripping to the floor gave an edge to the silence that followed Shad's words.

They all looked at Hank Mark, who was trying to recover what was left of his third schooner of beer. Mr. Hoorn waddled up with a bar towel.

But Shad matched Sheriff Buchanan's calmness. Before the eyes of his amazed audience, he took out his nickel-plated handcuffs, smiled faintly and put them away again. But the last part of his gesture was fast—he had just remembered page twenty: *Lull your suspect's suspicion before springing your big surprise on him!*

Shad's lean features steadied. His eyes went from one man's face to another's—anywhere but on Mark's scowling features.

"The killer wanted us to believe that Old Harvey was drinking. Here's what happened. It was night and Old Harvey was reading in bed. One lamp was on the table and another light, a candle, was burning in the kitchen. The lamp burned all night and ran out of oil; the candle burned itself out, too. But the killer had sneaked inside before then and found his victim asleep."

The batwing doors made a funny sucking sound as somebody came in. Ludolph Hoorn said, "Sh-hh," and drew a schooner of beer. "New bickles, Ed—St. Louis—sh-hh."

Shad took a look at Mark's face. It seemed pasty in the light of the swinging lamp. Then Shad's eyes swung—to the small mole on Banker Winston's cheek. His eyes clung to that mole, seeming safer there than any place else in the room.

"Go on," said the sheriff.

Shad nodded, his eyes holding to the safety of Banker Winston's mole.

"After the killer smothered Mr. Norton, he hunted around and found the money. Then, to make everybody believe Mr. Norton had died drunk, he poured half of a bottle of whiskey on his clothes. Mr. Norton's clothes were still wet from the whiskey the next day, but nobody noticed it but me. Everybody thought Old Harvey had just drunk too much."

Shad pulled up then, his eyes chilled, remorseless. He waited for the question page thirty said would follow the gasps of the listeners.

The question came—from Sheriff Buchanan. "How do you know all this?"

THIS was the moment! In this moment, said Captain Ellsworth, the case would be successfully consummated, or would fail. If the detective was sure of his man, yet had nothing really tangible —now was the time to bluff. Whatever the detective said now would be justifiable, providing it was the means of trapping the killer.

"Speak up, Shad!" cried Harry Marston. "Who did it?"

"I'll tell you," cried Shad. His eyes kept away from Hank Mark, held valiantly to that mole on Banker Winston's cheek. Shad's eyes were hot and accusing when he blurted at that mole: "I saw him do it! I was looking through the window when it happened!"

A wild gasp followed Shad's words. A wilder voice shouted: "It's a lie! A dirty lie!"

They looked at Hank Mark. But it wasn't Hank Mark who had screamed.

The man who had screamed was standing back from them all now. *Banker Randolph Winston.*

His trembling hand wiped across his white lips as if trying to recall his fateful words. He glared at Shad, his cold eyes bitter, full of hatred. He might have faced it even then, but he didn't— he turned and ran from the saloon.

The sheriff caught Marshal Dillon's arm. "Better get after him. The banker's your man!"

For moments after the marshal surged out the door the men stared at each other in silence. Then the sheriff smiled. "Plain enough, isn't it? That twelve hundred dollars Harvey Norton was supposed to have drawn from the bank probably never left it. And we'll probably find that Mr. Randolph Winston needed that amount to clear himself with the bank examiners."

Shad stood there, his mouth partly open. It took all the teachings of Captain Ellsworth to keep him from blurting out that he hadn't meant to accuse the banker, that he was just staring at him to keep from looking at Hank Mark.

But Sheriff Buchanan was full of praise.

"Detective Shadrack, you saved the County of Grail a lot of money. From the way things looked, you might even have saved an innocent man's life." He cast an apologetic glance toward Hank Mark and then turned back to Shad. "Randolph Winston was the last man we suspected. Shad, I'm proud to be associated with you on this case." The big lawman held out his hand.

"Thank—thank you, sir," stuttered Shad as the sheriff shook his hand. Then Shad's bewildered eyes turned toward Hank Mark.

Hank was grinning at him. It was a grateful sort of grin. Then the man was raising his hand to Proprietor Hoorn. "Draw two," he said. "One for me and one for my friend, Shad."

Shad took a deep breath and watched the sheriff turn to Marston. The lawman's eyes twinkled when he whispered, "We'll be one short at the supper table—unless you've got a new number one citizen in Granville."

Harry Marston grinned. "Shad," he said, "how about you coming out to our place for supper?"

Shad flushed. This *was something*. Yet he took one more deep breath and said, "Thanks, Mr. Marston. Some other time. Tonight I'm having some lunch with Hank."

"Ach," sighed Proprietor Hoorn. Then he beamed happily and dry washed his fat hands. "New bickles, I gott—St. Louis."

from DETECTIVE WHO'S WHO

ARNOLD, Shadrack, private detective, Correspondence School License Number 10007; Investigators, Incorporated, St. Louis, Mo.; b. May 19, 1886; s. ———(?) and Sarawell Jane A., unmarried housekeeper, who deserted him four times, the last time successfully. Granville Grammar Sch., plus four extra years in eighth grade. Livery stable roustabout, 1905–08. Delivery boy, Carter's Grocery, 1908–10. Private detective, complete with badge, handcuffs, and diploma, 1910—. Home: 129 First St., Granville. No party affiliations; when asked if he were a Republican or a Democrat, said he was a Methodist.

*The Locked Room and analogous Impossible Situations at-
tract, at least in America, peculiar specialists. The cleverest
Locked Room of recent years was solved by the business
manager of a health cultist, and earlier openers of the way
include a magician, a nun, and a United States Senator.
Meet Senator Brooks U. Banner in an "impossible" case
which the Great Merlini might well envy him.*

SEN. BROOKS U. BANNER in

Death by Black Magic

BY JOSEPH COMMINGS

PELTING rain shrouded the old Abbey Theater on West 46th
Street on the night that the Great Xanthe was strangled. But
U. S. Senator Banner had no foreboding of murder as he scurried
under the dripping marquee and out of the rain that was hitting
the sidewalk like .45's. The capacious wraprascal hung soggily on
his titanic shoulders as he pounded on the boarded-up panels of
the lobby doors. When he took his fist away there were no
sounds save those of the punishing rain and the thin distant bleat
of a taxi horn on Broadway.

A light flickered behind the crack. "Who is it?" asked a voice.

"The Clutching Claw!" said Banner with a jovial laugh.

"Oh," said the voice, recognizing the familiar chuckle.

The light blinked out and Banner heard the racket of a metal
bar being removed and the rasp of a key in a long-unused lock.
The lobby door creaked back and he saw Xanthe Oberlin's white
face and white hair against the velvet blackness. It looked like a
disembodied head.

From *Ten Detective Aces*, Nov., 1948. Copyright 1948 by Ace Periodicals.

Banner moved in out of the wet and turned on his own pocket flashlight. Xanthe rebarred the door and locked it with a snick of the tarnished key.

Banner said, "You're keeping the place tighter than the cork on a champagne bottle."

Xanthe showed his pearly smile. "Why should we be disturbed?" His leanness, his dark clothes, and the shadows made him look six-and-a-half feet tall. He loomed over Banner's own six-feet-three.

Banner drew out a kettle-sized hunting-case watch. "Eight forty-five. Right on the button."

They walked past musty plush drapes hanging in tatters on brass rails and down the aisle of the theater.

Banner was at once overcome by the eerie atmosphere of decay. The great chandelier was grim with dust and looked down with a thousand eyeless sockets. The whole place needed an airing.

The footlights and the overhead stage lights were the only illumination. The stage was bright with a canary-yellow backdrop and side curtains. The house was empty except for one girl sitting in an aisle seat in the orchestra. When they reached her row she looked up at them and smiled. She was knitting an afghan and she was so quiet you could hear a stitch drop.

She was Xanthe's daughter, Konstanz. She was twenty-one. Her hair was a black cloud and she had her father's eyes. But while his eyes were merely piercing, hers were great round black-centered orbs. They disturbed you. Her small red mouth, against a lime-white skin, disturbed you, too.

BANNER greeted her with relish and seated himself down beside her. The chair squeaked rustily. Then he unbuttoned his wrap-rascal and dumped a bundle of yellowed newspapers tied with an old shoelace on the rat-chewed upholstery. Konstanz stared in astonishment at the fifteen-year-old date-line. Banner flung off his coat, spattering raindrops like a Saint Bernard shaking itself.

Xanthe said in his smooth beguiling voice, "Shall we look at the cabinet, Senator?"

"I'm r'aring to go, X. Where is it? Backstage?"

"Yes." Xanthe took long strides toward the ramp that led to the stage. Banner followed him, brushing a cobweb off his jowl. "Give me a hand, please, Senator. It isn't very heavy, but it's too awkward for one man."

It was just inside the wings. Together they carried it to midstage. It was a plain wooden cabinet, seven feet tall. It stood on four stout legs, lifting it a foot off the floor. The top was open. The side that faced the audience was curtained. The curtain was drawn back revealing a lot of nothing inside.

Xanthe grinned. "We shall try it for the first time tonight. The Chinese Cabinet of the Great Xanthe!"

Konstanz had joined them on the stage. Banner rapped the sides of the cabinet, then the back and bottom. He was certain there were no sliding panels or trick openings.

Xanthe was still grinning. "Next, Senator, I'll show you its possibilities. Do you mind sitting in the audience?"

Banner clambered off the stage. Xanthe turned to Konstanz. "When I go inside the cabinet, I want you to pull the curtain across, my child. Then step back about ten feet. Are you all set, Senator?"

Banner had lowered himself into a groaning seat in the thirteenth row. "Shoot the works, professor," he said.

Xanthe bowed his head at Konstanz and stepped firmly inside. He stood there with plenty of room on all sides. He waved a hand through the open top. "Do nothing till I give the word." Konstanz took hold of the cabinet curtain and yanked it sharply.

There was a tinkle of silver rings and a red dragon breathing flame appeared embroidered on the fully exposed curtain.

Konstanz turned and walked to the footlights. Slim and bedeviling, she stood motionless in a brown wool dress, dainty black suède pumps, and prettily filled nylons. She had left her knitting on her seat and her arms hung naturally at her sides. *She has stage presence*, thought Banner, *just like her old man*. Her profile was to Banner, his eyes glued to the drawn curtain.

Banner glanced at his watch. Eight fifty-five.

There was a long silence. Banner heard the rats scuttling behind the scenery and the lash of the rain on the roof. Somewhere a leak dripped stealthily.

Then he heard whisperings come from the stage—from the cabinet—swift whisperings. There were other small sounds, but that might have been the rats.

There was silence again.

Konstanz had never moved. The cabinet had her magnetized.

Banner got weary of waiting. He looked at his watch again. It was almost five past nine. He got up and trudged toward the stage. Konstanz turned her head and looked at him with puzzled amusement and casually shrugged her shoulders.

Banner said, "Ready or not, X, we're opening up."

There was utter silence from the box.

Banner reached his hand across the red dragon and the curtain shot back on its silver rings.

Xanthe was in there, but he was crumpled on the floor and his face was as purple as a ripe grape. Konstanz' silence made Banner glance once quickly over his shoulder to see if she was still with him.

Banner eyed the livid lump on Xanthe's temple. He reached in and lifted Xanthe's chin. He saw the deep red marks of thumbs on either side of the windpipe. He stooped, listened for heart beats, and felt for a pulse. There wasn't any.

He spun around to face Konstanz.

Her eyes were huge. "Daddy?"

"Honey," he said, "there's nothing we can do. He's dead. Strangled."

IT REALLY started late that morning in the dining room of the Sphinx Club on Fifth Avenue. As you step through its black oak doors, the past masters of necromancy frisk you with their eyes from portraits on the walls: Houdini, Herman the Great, Thurston, Blackstone, Keller. Banner was the focus of these painted canvas eyes as he trotted into the dining room shod in soiled white sneakers. He was at once hailed to a table at which four people sat.

Banner's sapphire-blue eyes gleamed. "How have you been, X?" The magician's eloquent hands with the silver wishbone ring rose to shake his. "Konstanz! How come you do to me like you do?" She was entrancing in a woolly pull-over and a pencil-slim gray skirt.

"Sit down, Senator," invited Xanthe. He was clean and comfortable in loose English-made tweeds. Four hundred years ago he would have been burned at the stake as a sorcerer. Today he earned a healthy living doing the same job. "Had breakfast? No? Have it with us."

Banner shanghaied a chair from another table and joined them. He ordered a slice of ham as big as a life raft, fried eggs with their eyes shining, and coffee fresh enough to talk back to you. While this was going on he was being introduced to the other two people.

Nedra Russell was in her middle twenties. She sat very erect and tall. She had olive-green eyes, crocus-blond hair, and one of those thin haggard faces that can be made tormentingly attractive. She nervously twisted a rhinestone bracelet on her left wrist. For a living she designed costumes.

Konstanz said, "I've known Nedra ever so long."

"Four years," smiled Nedra.

The man with them was Lawrence Creek. He was as heavy as Banner, but he didn't have the reach. He dressed like a chief pallbearer and wore a scarab tie-pin in his foulard. As soon as Banner got his nose into action he ticketed Creek as "the man with the nice stink." Creek wore *Tzigane*, a perfume that cost forty-five dollars an ounce.

Xanthe said, "Mr. Creek is a magician, too."

Banner grinned at him. "How's tricks, cousin?"

Creek took ten seconds before replying, and all the while he stared at Banner as if the family honor of the Creeks had been dragged through the muck. Banner was to learn that Creek always gave a delayed action response, no matter what you said to him. This time his answer was something incoherent.

"Senator," said Xanthe as Banner sliced a wedge of ham, "you're vitally interested in magic, aren't you?"

"Interested! I have been ever since I first broke down the secret of taking off a shirt with a vest still on. Did you ever see my cocktail shaker? I fill it with water, but if you call for beer, it pours beer, if you call for wine, it pours wine. And so forth."

He paused and stuck his hand into the bulging, junk-filled pocket of his sack-like frock coat. He searched for a minute, then held up a banana. With a childishly gleeful chuckle he peeled the banana by pulling down a zipper.

"I like to startle people by dipping my hand in water, then shaking their hand. Mine'll be as dry as a mummy's. It's been dusted with lycopodium, of course. I'll say I'm—"

Xanthe interrupted politely. "Senator, you're known to be much more than that. You've solved murders by your shrewd observation of tricks. You're keen to catch an error. I want you to see my Chinese Cabinet. It'll be featured in my new show at the Abbey Theater next month."

Banner paused in his eating. "The Abbey?"

XANTHE smiled his professionally superior smile. "You know the Abbey, don't you, with its haunted reputation? There hasn't been a performance of any kind on its stage in fifteen years. Well, it's an ideal background for magic, isn't it? I'm keeping it just as it is. Cleaning away the dust, that's all. I'm leaving all the spiders and the rust and the old programs on the floor and the general appearance of rot."

"That is a brainstorm," said Banner.

"Is the Abbey authentically haunted?" asked Creek. "I mean ghosts."

Xanthe nodded earnestly. "Yes. There's a weird murder connected with its closing."

"Tell us," said Nedra. "We'll have time for the story." There was a queer tightness in her voice and her jaded eyes were boring into the wizard's smooth placid face. Konstanz gazed at her father with great devotion.

Xanthe said in a low emotionless voice, "Fifteen years ago *Othello* was enjoying a run at the Abbey. Remember the Simmondses? They were a man-and-wife starring team. Simmonds played the Moor and his wife Desdemona. In every way they lived the parts created by Shakespeare. Simmonds was jealous, just as Othello was. He was suspicious of her. He thought she was in love with another actor in the cast, the one who played Iago.

"The final fatal performance was on a raw blustery night in early December. In the last act, you remember, Othello is so convinced of his wife's infidelity that he strangles her on her couch before the audience. Simmonds got his hands on her throat in this scene and it looked too damn' real. He held her longer than the action called for. Then he rose laughing and stared out at the audience like a madman. At that moment all the stage lights went out. They were out for about twelve seconds, then they all came on again. Simmonds wasn't on the stage. *He had vanished into thin air!*"

"A trap door?" suggested Banner.

"No," said Xanthe. "The stage has a grave-trap, but at a rehearsal one of the players fell through it, injuring himself, so it had been nailed up from underneath because there was no use for it. These nails had never been tampered with.

"Now! The wings were jammed with players, scene shifters, prop men. They all swore that Simmonds did not pass through the wings. The man stationed at the stage door was positive that nobody left the theater by that exit. Ushers were in all the aisles in the audience. There was a faint glow from the fire exit lights. Simmonds never came up the aisles. Several people were standing in the lobby. They took oath that he never passed out that way. He couldn't have gone far unnoticed. He still wore the black robes of Othello.

"When they found Mrs. Simmonds strangled, every door was doubly guarded. Every person in the audience and every actor backstage left the theater in single file through a sieve of police. Simmonds never left disguised as someone else. When the police searched each nook and cranny later there was no trace of him. He was not in the theater, yet he had never left it. He literally dissolved into thin air during the twelve seconds the lights were out."

Creek said, "There was no hint of him in later years?"

XANTHE shook his white head. "None. Not the slightest trace. Every time the police think of the case they have the shudders."

"The Simmondses had a child, hadn't they?" said Nedra. "What became of it?"

"I'm not sure," said Xanthe. "I believe it was adopted by some professional family." He turned his sharp black eyes to Banner. "All this brings me to my Chinese Cabinet. It's never been worked quite like this before. I do it entirely without assistance of any kind. I want you to see its first rehearsal tonight at the Abbey. If it has a flaw, you'll spot it. How do you stand, Senator?"

Banner picked his teeth with his raccoon-bone toothpick. "Abracadabra is my meat."

"Konstanz will be there." Xanthe turned to Creek. "And you, my friend?"

Creek took his customary ten seconds before replying. "Sorry, Xanthe. I'm putting on a show myself tonight. Some amateur magicians in a loft . . ."

"I'll come," said Nedra enthusiastically.

Xanthe smiled and shook his head. "Must I remind you of your own work, Nedra? The costume designs for the Raja stunt. They must be ready tomorrow at the latest."

Nedra frowned. "How utterly disappointing."

"Before you go to the studio, Nedra, you'd better give it a ring and see if everything's ready for you. The number is Ravenswood 7-1149."

"Yes," she said.

"There'll only be three of us?" said Banner.

Xanthe nodded slowly. He seemed to be watching Creek the way a starved robin watches a worm.

Nedra got up and gathered her things. "I'll call the studio now," she said. "All right?"

"Yes," said Xanthe. And he repeated the phone number.

THAT'S what had happened this morning at the Sphinx Club. Now they were in the empty theater staring in bewilderment at the magician's dead body. Banner drew the curtain on the conjurer.

"Dead!" cried Konstanz with a dry sob. "But there was nothing the matter with him. He can't be."

"He was strangled," repeated Banner grimly, "while I sat there watching. Someone got into that box and I haven't the least idea how." He took her arm and led her to the wings. She was quivering, her muscles taut. "How did your dad operate the cabinet, Konstanz?"

"I don't know, Senator. It was his secret. Nobody knew."

"Wait." He trotted back to the cabinet and returned with two tarnished keys on a bright new ring. Hooking her arm, he guided her behind the scenes.

He used his flashlight against the dark. A fuzzy spider landed on his sleeve and he flipped it off. He peered through a jungle of fly-ropes at a large prop table cluttered with magical apparatus. Among the objects was a nickel-plated revolver. On the floor beside the table lay an aluminum ladder; it had black felt pads on both ends. Banner hefted the ladder. It weighed next to nothing.

The flashlight illumined a railing eaten up with iron mould, and several concrete steps. There was a sign saying in cracked paint:

DRESSING ROOMS

Konstanz followed him up the steps and along a passage to the first door. It was christened *Dressing Room 1*. A gold paper star had been pasted on the door a long time ago; its rays were curling up like a starfish with the cramps. The brass doorknob was green with neglect. Banner turned it and the door went back silently—oiled hinges.

They walked in and listened to the rain hammering furiously at the window. Banner tried the light switch, but the results were sterile.

He played the flash over the mirrored make-up table, seeing himself looming in it and a pallid-faced girl peeking over his shoulder. The cold cream, the eyebrow pencil, and the grease-paint of fifteen years ago were still there. There was also a dusty-looking rabbit's foot. In a corner of the dressing room was a

Punch and Judy outfit. The puppets were flung over the lip of the stage. Punch in the act of strangling Judy, and the Hangman over to one side watching them.

"This was Mr. Simmonds' room," said Konstanz with shocking unexpectedness.

Banner gasped. "Were those dolls like that the night Simmonds—?"

"Dad did that," she said hoarsely.

"Great sense of humor."

A drop of water sparkled on the floor. Banner's light followed other drops to a clothes closet. He trotted to it and wrenched it open. Clothes hung in there; clothes with a fresh smell as if they had just been worn. A raincoat, a soft hat, a jacket, a pair of pants. The raincoat glistened. Banner stretched out and touched it. It was wet.

The clothes were big enough to fit an average sized man. The hat was soggy and the cuffs of the pants damp.

"Someone took off his clothes in here," said Konstanz.

"For what reason? To walk around in these drafts in his ectoplasm?"

Konstanz didn't answer.

Banner closed the closet. They went to *Dressing Room 2.* Except for the remains of occupation years ago, there was nothing for them. From the floor of *Dressing Room 3* Banner picked up a program with heel marks stamped on it. He read the names of the cast with some curiosity. He stopped for a long time at the line:

IAGO . . . . *Xanthe Oberlin*

He shoved it at her. "Did you know that?"

She shook her head dumbly. Then she said, "Simmonds strangled his wife and disappeared. Tonight my father was strangled." Her breast heaved and her teeth chattered. *"Simmonds has come back!"*

HE THREW his arm about her shoulders to steady her. "I heard whispering in the cabinet after your father went in. I couldn't make it out. Could you?"

"I'm sure I heard him say, 'My God, what are you doing here?'"

Banner wheeled suddenly. "I'm going to look at the stage doors."

They found first the loading door, through which scenery was brought into the theater. It was locked and rusted tight. At the end of a streaky walled passage they found the regular stage door. It was locked and bolted from the inside.

Returning to the stage, Banner let his eye speculate on the dim steel frame outline of the bridge or catwalk that ran above the stage, masked from the audience by the teaser curtain.

He said, "It would be better if you didn't go near the cabinet, Konstanz, while I'm gone."

"Where are you going?" she questioned, panicky.

"To try all the doors."

He went up one side of the auditorium, trying the fire exits, and down the other. All were fastened with rusty iron chains on the inside. He had left Konstanz sitting by the footlights in a rickety chair, listening to his footfalls trail away in the balcony as he proceeded, rattling chains like a big fat ghost. He entered the lobby, following the beam of his flashlight. The lobby doors were locked and barred, as Xanthe had left them.

"By thunder," he muttered, "nobody has used any of the exits. This is giving me the willies."

He bumped open the door of the manager's office and fell over furniture undermined by termites. A phone was on a desk and he prayed it was in working order. The phone number uppermost in his mind was the one Xanthe had mentioned that morning, Ravenswood 7-1149.

He put the receiver to his ear and heard the hum. He dialed the number. In a moment he heard a woman say, "Hello?"

It was Nedra Russell.

"This is Senator Banner," he said. "Still working at the studio?"

"Yes," she answered. "Is the show over? Where are you calling from, Senator?"

"The Abbey Theater. We've seen an act tonight that wasn't on the program. Somebody killed Xanthe."

The wire went dead. Then: "Who killed him?"

"I don't know."

"Who else is there?"

"Only Konstanz and myself. Just the two of us. We're as lonesome as a pair of polecats. Drop whatever you're doing and join us."

"Of course I'll be there." She hung up.

Banner dialed again and got a loft building.

A man answered. "Lawrence Creek?" "No," said the man, "he can't come to the phone. He's performing. How long? Since eight-thirty. Of course he's been on the stage all the time. He's got three hundred people to prove it. Disappearing acts? No, he hasn't disappeared. He's been doing card-and-coin tricks and mind reading. Penny ante stuff. . . . The Abbey Theater? I don't know about that. What? All right, all right! Don't get your liver in an uproar. I'll tell him it's the cops."

Banner dialed a third time—Police Headquarters.

He was in the motion of hanging up when he heard pistol shots pound the dank air four times and then Konstanz' voice hysterically calling him.

BANNER charged down the center aisle. Konstanz stood in the orchestra pit, shivering and holding the nickel-plated revolver in her hand. Its muzzle smoked.

"Hey, June bug! No fair packing a pistol."

"Look!" she cried, pointing at the stage. "Look!"

Banner raised his eyes. A yellow human skull with a jagged crack in its cranium leered at him over the footlights from in front of the cabinet.

"Lawsy!" he bellowed. "How'd that come there?"

Konstanz swallowed several times. "After you left me," she said shakily, "I sat near the wings. Then I thought I heard a muffled voice somewhere backstage. I felt riveted to the chair, but finally I got up and peeked into the wings. I gathered enough courage to slip up to the prop table and pick up the pistol. It was very quiet then. I had begun to think my ears were misbehaving when suddenly at the top of those concrete steps I saw the flicker of a light crawl along the wall. I knew it wasn't you. I fired I don't know how many times. I don't know whether I hit—"

Banner had taken the gun out of her limp hand. He ejected two remaining rounds. "You didn't hit anything. These're blanks."

"The next thing I heard," she hurried on, "was a thump on the stage. I rushed back. That horrible skull was rolling to a stop, wheeling its hollow eyes at me. I screamed for you." She tore at his sleeve with pink nails. "Take me home, Senator, please, please. I can't stand it any longer."

"Leave?" he said. "When things are beginning to make sense?"

"Sense!" she cried.

"Come here and Uncle Remus'll read you a bedtime story." He let her follow him to the seat he had dumped his old newspapers on. He picked up the top one. "I spent the afternoon at a half-dozen press offices cudgeling editors to let me have fifteen-year-old newspapers containing accounts of the Simmonds murder. First, there's a description of Simmonds. He's one hundred and fifty pounds, five feet ten, tow-headed, gray-eyed, athletic."

"Those wet clothes in the dressing room would fit him," murmured Konstanz.

"I think so. Listen to what the chief electrician named Rock has to say: 'Before the last show Simmonds came to me and told me he was going to include a new effect in the night's performance. He gave me ten dollars for my part. And when a big star like that gives orders, you snap to. Even if you think it sounds screwy. He told me to pull the master switch on the control board so as to black the stage for about fifteen seconds as soon as he rose from the couch after strangling Desdemona. He gave me a song and dance about a psychological wrinkle he was working into the act. I realize now that he wanted darkness so that he could escape after murdering his wife. Please believe that I was in no way his accomplice knowingly. . . .'

"The inspector asked him if he noticed anything unusual during the interval the lights were out. 'Something that turned out to be no account, inspector. I thought I heard a noise of something landing lightly behind my switchboard. But when I looked later all that was there were some sandbags at the end of a rope.'"

Banner let the paper slide out of his hand. There was a satisfied smirk on his face. He jogged onto the stage again and wrestled one of the baby spotlights out of the wings. He aimed it straight up at the vaulting roof above the stage and flicked the switch.

The spot cut a swath in the blackness. He swept the dome as if hunting for enemy aircraft. Then he grunted. "Back in the limelight, brother. Konstanz!"

She stood close and squinted up at what was spotlighted.

THE wood-beamed gridiron was a hundred feet above the stage. High up among a tangle of rigging and flies hung something else. It was like a huge black bat, sleeping feet upward.

"Oh, my gosh!" she gasped. "What's that?"

"That," said Banner, feeling a chill, "is the murderer."

Then someone began to thump the lobby doors.

Konstanz clung to Banner like a barnacle while he unlocked the way for Lawrence Creek.

"What's going on?" snapped Creek, bringing in with him a gust of weather and a whiff of expensive *Tzigane*.

"We're opening a chamber of horrors. You're welcome, Creek."

As they went down the aisle, Banner told him the story in headline phrases. Creek was rattled by the time he saw the way the stage was set. Then he remembered he should show dignity and poise and he took Konstanz aside to comfort her.

The lobby doors got a rubdown with nightsticks. Banner let in the police. Captain Roberts, a walking gingersnap, was in charge of the homicide detail. Banner told him to put men at the lobby and stage doors before he did anything else. He added that a woman named Nedra Russell would show up at any time and to let her in.

When Roberts saw the thing hung away up on the gridiron, he ordered it taken down.

"How, captain?" asked a detective.

"Easy," said Banner. "Stand clear."

He went behind the switchboard. There were four sandbags there, each weighing about fifty pounds. These were tied to the end of a rope that stretched upward into nothingness. Banner's large claspknife began to hack the rope. It came asunder. The rope, released from the sandbags, shot upward out of sight. He heard a yell from those on the stage and a loud crash of something loose falling heavily.

Banner viewed the junk heap of half rotted clothes and yellow bones. "Put up your handcuffs, Roberts. Othello's in no condition to resist arrest. . . . *Simmonds never left the stage after he killed Desdemona!*"

"He's been hanging there for fifteen years?" gasped Roberts.

Banner nodded. "Simmonds planned to escape all right. He rigged up that rope, a pulley, and some sandbags that outweighed him. He tipped the beam at one hundred and fifty. The bags are at least two hundred. The bags were balanced somewhere up above so that they would pitch downward at a yank from the rope. The other end of the rope reached to the floorboards of the stage. Simmonds concealed it among the drapes. When the lights went out he dived for the rope and stuck his foot in a loop. In his rush, he missed his grip and the upgoing rope flipped him over backwards. Stunned, he shot up feet first. When he came to, everyone was searching for him. He couldn't untangle himself without help. He couldn't cry for help or they'd nab him for murder. So he hung there till he died."

"Heavens," breathed Roberts.

"Tonight," said Banner, "the disturbance produced by the sound of the four shots that Konstanz fired jarred the skeleton's skull loose."

"That's all fine and dandy," said Roberts. "You've solved a mystery that's been plaguing us for years. But what about tonight? Simmonds' *ghost* didn't kill Xanthe!"

Nedra Russell came down the aisle from the lobby. She wore a dull black Persian lamb wrap over a black evening gown. Her eyes roved excitedly. Banner had her meet Captain Roberts, then he had them all take front row seats. In the meantime Xanthe's body had been removed from the cabinet by the medical men.

"First of all," said Banner, "I'll want a man who knows how to fly scenery. Somebody who's had experience in it. It looks complicated."

Roberts urged a blue-coated sergeant forward.

BANNER sent the sergeant up to the fly floor, then he himself disappeared behind the scenes. Next they heard his voice saying, "You can't see me. I'm behind the teaser curtain on the catwalk above the stage. I'm going to lower the aluminum ladder I'm carrying down through the open top of the cabinet."

They saw one end of the ladder slowly descend until it rested on the floor of the Chinese Cabinet. Banner appeared from above, like an untidy archangel, coming down the ladder. Halfway down he stopped.

"I've instructed the sergeant to experiment with the drops. Okay, Chuck, I'm ready!"

A Spanish patio scene started to come down in front of Banner's nose.

Banner sneezed. "Not that, Chuck. Try again."

Several more varied scenes were lowered.

Captain Roberts was getting restless. "This ain't even funny," he snorted.

He heard Banner shout, "This is it!" And he looked up to find Banner without a head. Slowly dissolving, Banner became only the lower half of a man. Then only his shoes were left. Then the rest of the ladder vanished and there was nothing left but the Chinese cabinet and the canary-yellow drapes.

"My gosh!" howled Roberts. "I'm seeing things!"

Banner stepped into sight out of the cabinet.

He said, "It's done with a drop that's a huge mirror. The top of the mirror is tilted at an angle enough to reflect the drapes on the upper front of the stage. These drapes are identical with the ones hanging behind the cabinet. The murderer was hidden behind that looking-glass drop-scene when he entered the cabinet!"

Roberts dashed onto the stage to examine the mirror, front and back. "Amazing," he muttered. "Yet easily rigged up with a winch."

Banner went down into the audience and whispered to Konstanz in a voice that did not carry more than six inches, "Go to the manager's office, wait five minutes, then call this number." He gave her the number.

Puzzled, she left her seat and walked up the aisle.

"Captain," said Banner, "have those two men who're guarding front and back doors come to Dressing Room One toot sweet. Better leave replacements."

Roberts issued orders. He was on the Senator's coat-tail when Banner reached the dressing room.

"It's still raining," said Banner.

"There's been no letup."

Banner frowned at the phone on the make-up table. The number on the handset dial was Longacre 4–3281.

As Roberts' two men entered, the phone bell sounded with a purr so muffled that it could not be heard outside the room. Banner looked at the bell box. The bell's hammer had been padded with felt. Banner snatched up the receiver. He heard: "This is Konstanz Oberlin speaking. Senator Banner told me to—"

"That's enough, lambsy," said Banner. He replaced the phone. He swung on the nearer cop. "Were you watching the lobby door?"

"Yes, sir."

"Have you let in a woman in black?"

"I have not."

Banner wheeled on the other. "Did she get in through stage door?"

"No, sir."

"I didn't think so," said Banner. "Her coat would have glistened, even if she'd only crossed the sidewalk from a taxi. Instead it was dull. *She hadn't been out in the rain!*"

Roberts was standing flat-footed. "What's this?"

Banner tried to be patient. "Arrest Nedra Russell! She killed Xanthe! And don't ask her why she wore an evening gown to work. Look at the shoes its skirt is covering up."

"IN A WAY," said Banner later, "both crimes were alike. The killer escaped by going up. . . . You've got to understand Xanthe; the vanity of the supreme artist. He wanted to foster the illusion that the trick of the cabinet depended on him alone. He didn't want us to know that he needed someone's help, so he prepared the alibi for Nedra. That was the purpose of the hocuspocus about the phone number—her alibi. What's more, he knew that if he could dupe *me*, he'd really be pulling off something.

"He went about it painstakingly, the way he performed his stunts. That little skit about Nedra's staying at the 'studio' to design costumes was put on for my benefit. Xanthe repeated the Ravenswood number twice so that it would stick in my mind in the event I wanted to check on Nedra's not being in the theater. If I called that number, she would answer—seemingly from her studio—and I wouldn't know she was helping Xanthe.

"Sometime before I arrived tonight, Xanthe secretly let Nedra in through the stage door, locking and bolting it after her. Her wrap and evening gown were in *Dressing Room One*. She was wearing a man's suit under a raincoat, and a soft hat. This was necessary, for she had to have suitable clothing to climb around the rigging backstage in order to get that aluminum ladder down to X in the cabinet.

"Okey-doke. The trick was working beautifully. Nedra operated the winch that let down the screening mirror and Xanthe was ready to vanish from the cabinet—all of which was supposed to leave me dumfounded in my seat. Nedra appeared on the catwalk above him and lowered the ladder, blocking his exit. We heard them whispering. X was annoyed. She had some excuse about something going wrong.

"Then she brained him and, dropping into the cabinet, strangled him. You don't have to be strong to strangle somebody who's unconscious. Prolonged pressure is enough. When she was sure he was dead she skinned up the ladder again, pulled it up after her, carted it backstage, and worked the winch to raise the mirror into the drops, where it hung concealed. She darted back to *Dressing Room One* and changed clothes, putting on her gown and wrap. She had to keep out of our way as we prowled around in the rooms. But that wasn't very hard.

"The only time she was nearly caught was when I phoned the 'studio,' really *Dressing Room One*. The Ravenswood number changed to Longacre was more of X's foresightedness. He had written that phony number on the dial to throw me off about Nedra's whereabouts during the act. Konstanz heard her answer my ring and fired a blank pistol at her as she left the dressing room. After the police came, Nedra pretended to enter through the lobby. It looked so obvious that she thought we'd never question the cop on guard."

Captain Roberts said, "You were right about her shoes. She was wearing rubber-soled sports. Not the kind at all that goes with an evening gown."

"There were no shoes in the closet. I knew that although the killer changed clothes, he was still wearing the same shoes. Has Nedra told you about the motive?"

Roberts shook his head. "She's as mum as that skull."

Banner chuckled. "That's no more than likely. The skull belongs to her father. She's the Simmondses' child that was left parentless by the Abbey murder fifteen years ago. By coincidence she became chummy with Konstanz. She didn't know that Xanthe was the Iago who instilled the jealousy in her father until she came here a few days ago to help prepare the theater for the show. She saw X's name billed on a program. She said to herself, 'That's the man who made my father kill my beloved mother.' The same murderous streak that was in her father was in Nedra. . . . You'll see if I'm not right!"

FROM DETECTIVE WHO'S WHO

BANNER, Brooks Urban, U. S. Senator; b. Utica, N. Y., 1894; s. Orson and Griselda B.; m. Minnie Waycross (now deceased); no children. Orphaned at age of four, raised in orphanage; grad. Cornell U., Albany Law School. Sec. Lieut., Infantry, World War I. Hobo; furniture salesman; auctioneer; barker for sideshow spiritualist; ward boss; county sheriff of Manhattan; U. S. Senator. Recreations: Tinkers with old locks and mechanical toys; collects childish magic tricks, such as banana with zipper on it; has wide basic knowledge of magical illusions; reads comic books; sporting enthusiast; has trunk full of press clippings covering quarter-century of crime; delights in solving locked-room murders. Organizations: Sphinx Club (magicians); Criminal Bar Ass'n. Address: 91 Morningside Drive, New York City.

*One of the rarest items in the crime field is the short short
detective story—neither a skeletal puzzle nor a tricksy frag-
ment of biter-bit irony, but a legitimate job of honest detection in a thousand words. Which makes this adroit
Brannon story a collector's item and a model of succinct
technique.*

JIM BURGESS IN

The Perfect Secretary

BY W. T. BRANNON

"WHAT makes you think it's murder?" Tom Wall asked curiously.

Detective Jim Burgess poked at the portable typewriter. "It's
too clean for suicide," he drawled. "Not a print in the joint."

"What about the note?"

"Fake," said Burgess. "A big shot like Oehler dictates all his
letters. If he was going to write a suicide note, he'd use his fountain pen, not a typewriter."

"Why you think it's the dame?"

"I gotta hunch, is all."

"You can't pin it on her with a hunch," Tom said.

"I can try. Go bring her in."

When Tom came in with the red-haired girl, Burgess was still
poking at the typewriter.

"Show the lady to a seat," Jim said.

She wore an off-the-face hat and a mink coat. Pretty expensive
for a secretary, Jim thought. And she had on too much make-up.
A vain effort to cover a sleepless night, he guessed, looking at the
drawn lines in her face.

"You Martha Hawkins?" he asked. "Oehler's personal secretary?"

"Yes."

"Worked for him long?"

"About six months."

"I get it. Saw you around the office and liked your looks."

The girl flushed. "I was under the impression that he liked my work."

"Yeah? Well, skip it. When was the last time you saw him alive?"

"Yesterday afternoon when I took some letters."

"Write a lot of letters for him?"

"Of course. That was my job."

"Yeah, sure." Burgess leaned back in his chair, stuck his thumbs in his vest. "You go out to dinner with him last night?"

"No."

"Another dame, huh?"

"I don't know."

"He took her up to his room, didn't he?"

"I don't know."

"You had a room across the hall, didn't you?"

"Yes."

"See the dame when she left?"

"I told you I didn't see her."

"Oh, all right." Burgess waved an arm. "You didn't go in his room last night, did you?"

"Of course not!"

"You always had a separate room when you went on a business trip with Oehler?"

"Certainly! What do you mean?"

"Nothing. The guy must've reformed."

"I don't understand—"

"Maybe not. But it's something new for Oehler to have a hall separating him from his woman." He picked up a pencil and began tapping it on the desk. "You know anybody that might want to kill him?"

"Kill him? Why, I thought he—"

"Suicide? Naw, murder."

She said nothing, but watched nervously while he tapped the pencil on the desk.

"Funny thing," said Burgess, "but I guess I had you all wrong. I figured you shot him."

The girl bit her lip, as if to keep down the crimson flush of anger. Then she said defiantly, "Why should I murder him?"

Jim Burgess shrugged, reached for a sheet of paper on the desk. "I never could account for all the crazy things a jealous woman will do."

She leaned closer as he laid the sheet of paper on the desk in front of her, began drawing a circle with his pencil.

"What's that?" she asked.

"Oh, that. Wanta see it?" He grinned. "Guess I oughtn't to be drawing pictures on it." He let it slide over where she could see it more closely, continued the circular movement of the pencil.

"Oehler wrote a funny letter, huh?"

She didn't answer. Her face was very pale, as if a ghost had suddenly appeared. Terror was in her eyes.

"You don't know this other woman's name, do you?"

"N-no."

"I don't s'pose her initials would be M. H., huh?"

"No!" She reached out suddenly for the letter, but he snatched it from her grasp.

"All right, sister!" he said, with an abrupt change of tone. "Let's quit fooling."

Her gaze was fixed on the letter. She looked at it, shocked, as if she couldn't believe her eyes.

"I shot him," she said, in a tired voice. "I was so mad I couldn't see. I went in and shot him as soon as—as she left. Then I went back to my own room to cool off. I was scared to death. So I tried to make it look like suicide. I put the gun in his hand. I typed the note and wiped off everything with a towel. Then I went back to my room and waited—"

"The perfect secretary," said Burgess, "always puts her initials in the lower left-hand corner of every letter."

Later, after the confession had been signed and the girl had been taken away, Tom Wall said, "Gosh, I didn't see those initials."

"Naw," said Jim Burgess. "Neither did I." He had folded the paper in his hand. He struck a match and held it to a corner of the sheet.

Tom Wall looked on in astonishment. "Jim! You're burning the evidence."

"Naw," said Jim. "This is not evidence." He opened his desk drawer, pulled out a sealed envelope, and a box of Benton Oehler's personal stationery. "There's the note she typed." He grinned. "But, hell, I know how to use a typewriter."

FROM DETECTIVE WHO'S WHO

BURGESS, James, police detective; b. Clearwater, Ind., 1918. Hobbies: sports, gadgets of all kinds. Clubs: Clearwater Optimists, Police Athletic League, Clearwater Kennel Club. Professional Societies: Midwest Chapter, Mystery Writers of America (Associate Member); Indiana Police Association. Publications: *Detective Story Magazine; Ellery Queen's Mystery Magazine; Mammoth Mystery Magazine; Ellery Queen's Mystery Magazine* (foreign editions); *Uge Revyen* (Copenhagen). Office: Police Headquarters, Clearwater, Ind. Residence: 329 South Wood St., Clearwater, Ind.

Search in and out and round about and you'll discover
never another man so versed in every aspect of the Locked
(or to be more precise, the Inaccessible) Room as Dr.
Gideon Fell. But in this story—of all Mr. Carr's work possibly the specimen most influenced by his idol (and mine
and, I trust, yours) G. K. Chesterton—the two-caned enor-
mity of a doctor finds that solving a Locked Room is not
enough to solve the problem which it encloses. . . .

DR. GIDEON FELL IN

The Wrong Problem

BY JOHN DICKSON CARR

AT THE Detectives' Club it is still told how Dr. Fell went
down into the valley in Somerset that evening and of the man
with whom he talked in the twilight by the lake, and of murder
that came up as though from the lake itself. The truth about the
crime has long been known, but one question must always be
asked at the end of it.

The village of Grayling Dene lay a mile away towards the sunset. And the rear windows of the house looked out towards it.
This was a long gabled house of red brick, lying in a hollow of
the shaggy hills, and its bricks had darkened like an old painting.
No lights showed inside, although the lawns were in good order
and the hedges trimmed.

Behind the house there was a long gleam of water in the sunset, for the ornamental lake—some yards across—stretched al-

From *Dr. Fell, Detective*, N. Y.: Mercury, 1947. Copyright 1942, 1947
by The American Mercury, Inc. Reprinted with the permission of the author and
Ellery Queen's Mystery Magazine.

most to the windows. In the middle of the lake, on an artificial island, stood a summerhouse. A faint breeze had begun to stir, despite the heat, and the valley was alive with a conference of leaves.

The last light showed that all the windows of the house, except one, had little lozenge-shaped panes. The one exception was a window high up in a gable, the highest in the house, looking out over the road to Grayling Dene. It was barred.

Dusk had almost become darkness when two men came down over the crest of the hill. One was large and lean. The other, who wore a shovel-hat, was large and immensely stout, and he loomed even more vast against the skyline by reason of the great dark cloak billowing out behind him. Even at that distance you might hear the chuckles that animated his several chins and ran down the ridges of his waistcoat. The two travelers were engaged (as usual) in a violent argument. At intervals the larger one would stop and hold forth oratorically for some minutes, flourishing his cane. But, as they came down past the lake and the blind house, both of them stopped.

"There's an example," said Superintendent Hadley. "Say what you like, it's a bit too lonely for me. Give me the town—"

"We are not alone," said Dr. Fell.

The whole place had seemed so deserted that Hadley felt a slight start when he saw a man standing at the edge of the lake. Against the reddish glow on the water they could make out that it was a small man in neat dark clothes and a white linen hat. He seemed to be stooping forward, peering out across the water. The wind went rustling again, and the man turned around.

"I don't see any swans," he said. "Can you see any swans?" The quiet water was empty.

"No," said Dr. Fell, with the same gravity. "Should there be any?"

"There should be one," answered the little man, nodding. "Dead. With blood on its neck. Floating there."

"Killed?" asked Dr. Fell, after a pause. He has said afterwards that it seemed a foolish thing to say; but that it seemed appropriate to that time between the lights of the day and the brain.

"Oh, yes," replied the little man, nodding again. "Killed, like others—human beings. Eye, ear, and throat. Or perhaps I should say ear, eye, and throat, to get them in order."

Hadley spoke with some sharpness.

"I hope we're not trespassing. We knew the land was enclosed, of course, but they told us that the owners were away and wouldn't mind if we took a short cut. Fell, don't you think we'd better—?"

"I beg your pardon," said the little man, in a voice of such cool sanity that Hadley turned round again. From what they could see in the gloom, he had a good face, a quiet face, a somewhat ascetic face; and he was smiling. "I beg your pardon," he repeated in a curiously apologetic tone. "I should not have said that. You see, I have been far too long with it. I have been trying to find the real answer of thirty years. As for the trespassing, myself, I do not own this land, although I lived here once. There is, or used to be, a bench here somewhere. Can I detain you for a little while?"

Hadley never quite realized afterwards how it came about. But such was the spell of the hour, or of the place, or of the sincere, serious little man in the white linen hat, that it seemed no time at all before the little man was sitting on a rusty iron chair beside the darkening lake, speaking as though to his fingers.

"I am Joseph Lessing," he said, in the same apologetic tone. "If you have not heard of me, I don't suppose you will have heard of my stepfather. But at one time he was rather famous as an eye, ear, and throat specialist. Dr. Harvey Lessing, his name was.

"In those days we—I mean the family—always came down here to spend our summer holidays. It is rather difficult to make biographical details clear. Perhaps I had better do it with dates, as though the matter were really important, like a history book. There were four children. Three of them were Dr. Lessing's children by his first wife, who died in 1899. I was the stepson. He married my mother when I was seventeen, in 1901. I regret to say that *she* died three years later. Dr. Lessing was a kindly man, but he was very unfortunate in the choice of his wives."

The little man appeared to be smiling sadly.

"We were an ordinary, contented, and happy group, in spite of Brownrigg's cynicism. Brownrigg was the eldest. Eye, ear, and throat pursued us: he was a dentist. I think he is dead now. He was a stout man, smiling a good deal, and his face had a shine like pale butter. He was an athlete run to seed; he used to claim that he could draw teeth with his fingers. By the way, he was very fond of walnuts. I always seem to remember him sitting between two silver candlesticks at the table, smiling, with a heap of shells in front of him, and a little sharp nut-pick in his hand.

"Harvey Junior was the next. They were right to call him Junior; he was of the striding sort, brisk and high-colored and likable. He never sat down in a chair without first turning it the wrong way round. He always said 'Ho, my lads!' when he came into a room, and he never went out of it without leaving the door open so that he could come back in again. Above everything, he was nearly always on the water. We had a skiff and a punt for our little lake—would you believe that it is ten feet deep? Junior always dressed for the part as solemnly as though he had been on the Thames, wearing a red-and-white striped blazer and a straw hat of the sort that used to be called a boater. I say he was nearly always on the water: but not, of course, after tea. That was when Dr. Lessing went to take his afternoon nap in the summerhouse."

The summerhouse, in its sheath of vines, was almost invisible now. But they all looked at it, very suggestive in the middle of the lake.

"The third child was the girl, Martha. She was almost my own age, and I was very fond of her."

Joseph Lessing pressed his hands together.

"I am not going to introduce an unnecessary love story, gentlemen," he said. "As a matter of fact, Martha was engaged to a young man who had a commission in a line regiment, and she was expecting him down here any day when—the things happened. Arthur Somers, his name was. I knew him well; I was his confidant in the family.

"I want to emphasize what a hot, pleasant summer it was. The place looked then much as it does now, except that I think it was

greener then. I was glad to get away from the city. In accordance
with Dr. Lessing's passion for 'useful employment,' I had been
put to work in the optical department of a jeweler's. I was always
skillful with my hands. I dare say I was a spindly, snappish, suspicious lad, but they were all very good to me after my mother
died, except butter-faced Brownrigg, perhaps. But for me that
summer centers around Martha, with her brown hair piled up on
the top of her head, in a white dress with puffed shoulders, playing croquet on a green lawn, and laughing. I told you it was a
long while ago.

"On the afternoon of the fifteenth of August we had all intended to be out. Even Brownrigg had intended to go out after
a sort of lunch-tea that we had at two o'clock in the afternoon.
Look to your right, gentlemen. You see that bow window in the
middle of the house, overhanging the lake? There was where the
table was set.

"Dr. Lessing was the first to leave the table. He was going out
early for his nap in the summerhouse. It was a very hot afternoon,
as drowsy as the sound of a lawn mower. The sun baked the old
bricks and made a flat blaze on the water. Junior had knocked
together a sort of miniature landing-stage at the side of the lake
—it was just about where we are sitting now—and the punt and
the rowing-boat were lying there.

"From the open windows we could all see Dr. Lessing going
down to the landing-stage with the sun on his bald spot. He had
a pillow in one hand and a book in the other. He took the rowing-
boat; he could never manage the punt properly, and it irritated
a man of his dignity to try.

"Martha was the next to leave. She laughed and ran away, as
she always did. Then Junior said, 'Cheerio, chaps'—or whatever
the expression was then—and strode out leaving the door open.
I went shortly afterwards. Junior had asked Brownrigg whether
he intended to go out, and Brownrigg had said yes. But he remained, being lazy, with a pile of walnut shells in front of him.
Though he moved back from the table to get out of the glare, he
lounged there all afternoon in view of the lake.

"Of course, what Brownrigg said or thought might not have been important. But it happened that a gardener named Robinson had taken it into his head to trim some hedges on this side of the house. He had a full view of the lake. And all that afternoon nothing stirred. The summerhouse, as you can see, has two doors, one facing toward the house, the other in the opposite direction. These openings were closed by sun-blinds, striped red and white like Junior's blazer, so that you could not see inside. But all the afternoon the summerhouse remained dead, showing up against the fiery water and that clump of trees at the far side of the lake. No boat put out. No one went in to swim. There was not so much as a ripple, any more than might have been caused by the swans (we had two of them), or by the spring that fed the lake.

"By six o'clock we were all back in the house. When there began to be a few shadows, I think something in the *emptiness* of the afternoon alarmed us. Dr. Lessing should have been there, demanding something. He was not there. We halloo'd for him, but he did not answer. The rowing-boat remained tied up by the summerhouse. Then Brownrigg, in his cool fetch-and-run fashion, told me to go out and wake up the old party. I pointed out that there was only the punt, and that I was a rotten hand at punting, and that whenever I tried it I only went 'round in circles or upset the boat. But Junior said, 'Come-along-old-chap-you-shall-improve-your-punting-I'll-give-you-a-hand.'

"I have never forgotten how long it took us to get out there while I staggered at the punt-pole, and Junior lent a hand.

"Dr. Lessing lay easily on his left side, almost on his stomach, on a long wicker settee. His face was very nearly into the pillow, so that you could not see much except a wisp of sandy side-whisker. His right hand hung down to the floor, the fingers trailing into the pages of *Three Men in a Boat*.

"We first noticed that there seemed to be some—that is, something that had come out of his ear. More we did not know, except that he was dead, and in fact the weapon has never been found. He died in his sleep. The doctor later told us that the wound had been made by some round sharp-pointed instrument, thicker than a hat-pin but not so thick as a lead-pencil, which had been driven through the right ear into the brain."

Joseph Lessing paused. A mighty swish of wind uprose in the trees beyond the lake, and their tops ruffled under clear starlight. The little man sat nodding to himself in the iron chair. They could see his white hat move.

"Yes?" prompted Dr. Fell in an almost casual tone. Dr. Fell was sitting back, a great bandit-shape in cloak and shovel-hat. He seemed to be blinking curiously at Lessing over his eyeglasses. "And whom did they suspect?"

"They suspected me," said the little man.

"You see," he went on, in the same apologetic tone, "I was the only one in the group who could swim. It was my one accomplishment. It is too dark to show you now but I won a little medal by it, and I have kept it on my watch-chain ever since I received it as a boy."

"But you said," cried Hadley, "that nobody—"

"I will explain," said the other, "if you do not interrupt me. Of course, the police believed that the motive must have been money. Dr. Lessing was a wealthy man, and his money was divided almost equally among us. I told you he was always very good to me.

"First they tried to find out where everyone had been in the afternoon. Brownrigg had been sitting, or said he had been sitting, in the dining room. But there was the gardener to prove that not he or anyone else had gone out on the lake. Martha (it was foolish, of course, but they investigated even Martha) had been with a friend of hers—I forget her name now—who came for her in the phaeton and took her away to play croquet. Junior had no alibi, since he had been for a country walk. But," said Lessing, quite simply, "everybody knew *he* would never do a thing like that. I was the changeling, or perhaps I mean ugly duckling, and I admit I was an unpleasant, sarcastic lad.

"This is how Inspector Deering thought I had committed the murder. First, he thought, I had made sure everybody would be away from the house that afternoon. Thus, later, when the crime was discovered, it would be assumed by everyone that the murderer had simply gone out in the punt and come back again. Everybody knew that I could not possibly manage a punt alone. You see?

"Next, the inspector thought, I had come down to the clump of trees across the lake, in line with the summerhouse and the dining room windows. It is shallow there, and there are reeds. He thought that I had taken off my clothes over a bathing suit. He thought that I had crept into the water under cover of the reeds, and that I had simply swum out to the summerhouse under water.

"Twenty-odd yards under water, I admit, are not much to a good swimmer. They thought that Brownrigg could not see me come up out of the water, because the thickness of the summerhouse was between. Robinson had a full view of the lake, but he could not see that one part at the back of the summerhouse. Nor, on the other hand, could I see them. They thought that I had crawled under the sun-blind with the weapon in the breast of my bathing suit. Any wetness I might have left would soon be dried by the intense heat. That, I think, was how they believed I had killed the old man who befriended me."

The little man's voice grew petulant and dazed.

"I told them I did not do it," he said with a hopeful air. "Over and over again I told them I did not do it. But I do not think they believed me. That is why for all these years I have wondered. . . .

"It was Brownrigg's idea. They had me before a sort of family council in the library, as though I had stolen jam. Martha was weeping, but I think she was weeping with plain fear. She never stood up well in a crisis, Martha didn't; she turned pettish and even looked softer. All the same, it is not pleasant to think of a murderer coming up to you as you doze in the afternoon heat. Junior, the good fellow, attempted to take my side and call for fair play; but I could see the idea in his face. Brownrigg presided, silkily, and smiled down his nose.

"'We have either got to believe you killed him,' Brownrigg said, 'or believe in the supernatural. Is the lake haunted? No; I think we may safely discard that.' He pointed his finger at me. 'You damned young snake, you are lazy and wanted that money.'

"But, you see, I had one very strong hold over them—and I used it. I admit it was unscrupulous, but I was trying to demonstrate my innocence and we are told that the devil must be fought with fire. At mention of this hold, even Brownrigg's jowls shook. Brownrigg was a dentist, Harvey was studying medicine. What hold? That is the whole point. Nevertheless, it was not what the family thought I had to fear, it was what Inspector Deering thought.

"They did not arrest me yet, because there was not enough evidence, but every night I feared it would come the next day. Those days after the funeral were too warm; and suspicion acted like woolen underwear under the heat. Martha's tantrums got on even Junior's nerves. Once I thought Brownrigg was going to hit her. She very badly needed her fiancé, Arthur Somers; but, though he wrote that he might be there any day, he still could not get leave of absence from his colonel.

"And then the lake got more food.

"Look at the house, gentlemen. I wonder if the light is strong enough for you to see it from here? Look at the house—the highest window there—under the gable. You see?"

There was a pause, filled with the tumult of the leaves.

"It's got bars," said Hadley.

"Yes," assented the little man. "I must describe the room. It is a little square room. It has one door and one window. At the time I speak of, there was no furniture at all in it. The furniture had been taken out some years before, because it was rather a special kind of furniture. Since then it had been locked up. The key was kept in a box in Dr. Lessing's room; but, of course, nobody ever went up there. One of Dr. Lessing's wives had died there in a certain condition. I told you he had bad luck with his wives. They had not even dared to have a glass window."

Sharply, the little man struck a match. The brief flame seemed to bring his face up towards them out of the dark. They saw that he had a pipe in his left hand. But the flame showed little except the gentle upward turn of his eyes, and the fact that his whitish hair (of such coarse texture that it seemed whitewashed) was worn rather long.

"On the afternoon of the twenty-second of August, we had an unexpected visit from the family solicitor. There was no one to receive him except myself. Brownrigg had locked himself up in his room at the front with a bottle of whiskey; he was drunk or said he was drunk. Junior was out. We had been trying to occupy our minds for the past week, but Junior could not have his boating or I my workshop; this was thought not decent. I believe it was thought that the most decent thing was to get drunk. For some days Martha had been ailing. She was not ill enough to go to bed, but she was lying on a long chair in her bedroom.

"I looked into the room just before I went downstairs to see the solicitor. The room was muffled up with shutters and velvet curtains, as all the rooms decently were. You may imagine that it was very hot in there. Martha was lying back in the chair with a smelling-bottle, and there was a white-globed lamp burning on a little round table beside her. I remember that her white dress looked starchy; her hair was piled up on top of her head and she wore a little gold watch on her breast. Also, her eyelids were so puffed that they seemed almost Oriental. When I asked her how she was, she began to cry and concluded by throwing a book at me.

"So I went on downstairs. I was talking to the solicitor when it took place. We were in the library, which is at the front of the house, and in consequence we could not hear distinctly. But we heard something. That was why we went upstairs—and even the solicitor ran. Martha was not in her own bedroom. We found out where she was from the fact that the door to the garret-stairs was open.

"It was even more intolerably hot up under the roof. The door to the barred room stood halfway open. Just outside stood a housemaid (her name, I think, was Jane Dawson) leaning against the jamb and shaking like the ribbons on her cap. All sound had dried up in her throat, but she pointed inside.

"I told you it was a little, bare, dirty brown room. The low sun made a blaze through the window, and made shadows of the bars across Martha's white dress. Martha lay nearly in the middle of the room, with her heel twisted under her as though she had turned 'round before she fell. I lifted her up and tried to talk to her; but a rounded sharp-pointed thing, somewhat thicker than a hat-pin, had been driven through the right eye into the brain.

"Yet there was nobody else in the room.

"The maid told a straight story. She had seen Martha come out of Dr. Lessing's bedroom downstairs. Martha was running, running as well as she could in those skirts; once she stumbled, and the maid thought that she was sobbing. Jane Dawson said that Martha made for the garret door as though the devil were after her. Jane Dawson, wishing anything rather than to be alone in the dark hall, followed her. She saw Martha come up here and unlock the door of the little brown room. When Martha ran inside, the maid thought that she did not attempt to close the door; but that it appeared to swing shut after her. You see?

"Whatever had frightened Martha, Jane Dawson did not dare follow her in—for a few seconds, at least, and afterwards it was too late. The maid could never afterwards describe exactly the sort of sound Martha made. It was something that startled the birds out of the vines and set the swans flapping on the lake. But the maid presently saw straight enough to push the door with one finger and peep round the edge.

"Except for Martha, the room was empty.

"Hence the three of us now looked at each other. The maid's story was not to be shaken in any way, and we all knew she was a truthful witness. Even the police did not doubt her. She said she had seen Martha go into that room, but that she had seen nobody come out of it. She never took her eyes off the door—it was not likely that she would. But when she peeped in to see what had happened, there was nobody except Martha in the room. That was easily established, because there was no place where anyone could have been. Could she have been blinded by the light? No. Could anyone have slipped past her? No. She almost shook her hair loose by her vehemence on this point.

"The window, I need scarcely tell you, was inaccessible. Its bars were firmly set, no farther apart than the breadth of your hand, and in any case the window could not have been reached. There was no way out of the room except the door or the window; and no—what is the word I want?—no mechanical device in it. Our friend Inspector Deering made certain of that. One thing I suppose I should mention. Despite the condition of the walls and ceiling, the floor of the room was swept clean. Martha's white dress with the puffed shoulders had scarcely any dirt when she lay there; it was as white as her face.

"This murder was incredible. I do not mean merely that it was incredible with regard to its physical circumstances, but also that there was Martha dead—on a holiday. Possibly she seemed all the more dead because we had never known her well when she was alive. She was (to me, at least) a laugh, a few coquetries, a pair of brown eyes. You felt her absence more than you would have felt that of a more vital person. And—on a holiday with that warm sun, and the tennis-net ready to be put up.

"That evening I walked with Junior here in the dusk by the lake. He was trying to express some of this. He appeared dazed. He did not know why Martha had gone up to that little brown room, and he kept endlessly asking why. He could not even seem to accustom himself to the idea that our holidays were interrupted, much less interrupted by the murders of his father and his sister.

"There was a reddish light on the lake; the trees stood up against it like black lace, and we were walking near that clump by the reeds. The thing I remember most vividly is Junior's face. He had his hat on the back of his head, as he usually did. He was staring down past the reeds, where the water lapped faintly, as though the lake itself were the evil genius and kept its secret. When he spoke I hardly recognized his voice.

" 'God,' he said, 'but it's in the air!'

"There was something white floating by the reeds, very slowly turning 'round with a snaky discolored talon coming out from it along the water, the talon was the head of a swan, and the swan was dead of a gash across the neck that had very nearly severed it.

"We fished it out with a boathook," explained the little man as though with an afterthought. And then he was silent.

On the long iron bench Dr. Fell's cape shifted a little; Hadley could hear him wheezing with quiet anger, like a boiling kettle.

"I thought so," rumbled Dr. Fell. He added more sharply: "Look here, this tomfoolery has got to stop."

"I beg your pardon?" said Joseph Lessing, evidently startled.

"With your kind permission," said Dr. Fell, and Hadley has later said that he was never more glad to see that cane flourished or hear that common-sense voice grow fiery with controversy, "with your kind permission, I should like to ask you a question. Will you swear to me by anything you hold sacred (if you have anything, which I rather doubt) that you do not know the real answer?"

"Yes," replied the other seriously, and nodded.

For a little space, Dr. Fell was silent. Then he spoke argumentatively. "I will ask you another question, then. Did you ever shoot an arrow into the air?"

Hadley turned 'round. "I hear the call of mumbo-jumbo," said Hadley with grim feeling. "Hold on, now! You don't think that girl was killed by somebody shooting an arrow into the air, do you?"

"Oh, no," said Dr. Fell in a more meditative tone. He looked at Lessing. "I mean it figuratively—like the boy in the verse. Did you ever throw a stone when you were a boy? Did you ever throw a stone, not to hit anything, but for the sheer joy of firing it? Did you ever climb trees? Did you ever like to play pirate and dress up and wave a sword? I don't think so. That's why you live in a dreary, rarefied light; that's why you dislike romance and sentiment and good whiskey and all the noblest things of this world; and it is also why you do not see the unreasonableness of several things in this case.

"To begin with, birds do not commonly rise up in a great cloud from the vines because someone cries out. With the hopping and always-whooping Junior about the premises, I should imagine the birds were used to it. Still less do swans leap up out of the water and flap their wings because of a cry from far away; swans are not so sensitive. But did you ever see a boy throw a stone at a wall? Did you ever see a boy throw a stone at the water? Birds and swans would have been outraged only if something had *struck* both the wall and the water: something, in short, which fell from that barred window.

"Now, frightened women do not in their terror rush up to a garret, especially a garret with such associations. They go downstairs, where there is protection. Martha Lessing was not frightened. She went up to that room for some purpose. What purpose? She could not have been going to get anything, for there was nothing in the room to be got. What could have been on her mind? The only thing we know to have been on her mind was a frantic wish for her fiancé to get there. She had been expecting him for weeks. It is a singular thing about that room— but its window is the highest in the house, and commands the only good clear view of the road to the village.

"Now suppose someone had told her that he thought, he rather *thought*, he had glimpsed Arthur Somers coming up the road from the village. It was a long way off, of course, and the someone admitted he might have been mistaken in thinking so. . . .

"H'm, yes. The trap was all set, you see. Martha Lessing waited only long enough to get the key out of the box in her father's room, and she sobbed with relief. But, when she got to the room, there was a strong sun pouring through the bars straight into her face—and the road to the village is a long way off. That, I believe, was the trap. For on the window-ledge of that room (which nobody ever used, and which someone had swept so that there should be no footprints) this someone conveniently placed a pair of—eh, Hadley?"

"Field-glasses," said Hadley, and got up in the gloom.

"Still," argued Dr. Fell, wheezing argumentatively, "there would be one nuisance. Take a pair of field-glasses, and try to use them in a window where the bars are set more closely than the breadth of your hand. The bars get in the way—wherever you turn you bump into them; they confuse sight and irritate you; and, in addition, there is a strong sun to complicate matters. In your impatience, I think you would turn the glasses sideways and pass them out through the bars. Then, holding them firmly against one bar with your hands through the bars on either side, you would look through the eyepieces.

"But," said Dr. Fell, with a ferocious geniality, "those were no ordinary glasses. Martha Lessing had noticed before that the lenses were blurred. Now that they were in position, she tried to adjust the focus by turning the little wheel in the middle. And as she turned the wheel, like a trigger of a pistol it released the spring mechanism and a sharp steel point shot out from the right-hand lens into her eye. She dropped the glasses, which were outside the window. The weight of them tore the point from her eye; and it was this object, falling, which gashed and broke the neck of the swan just before it disappeared into the water below."

He paused. He had taken out a cigar, but he did not light it.

"Busy solicitors do not usually come to a house 'unexpectedly.' They are summoned. Brownrigg was drunk and Junior absent; there was no one at the back of the house to see the glasses fall. For this time the murderer had to have a respectable alibi. Young Martha, the only one who could have been gulled into such a trap, had to be sacrificed—to avert the arrest which had been threatening someone ever since the police found out how Dr. Lessing really had been murdered.

"There was only one man who admittedly did speak with Martha Lessing only a few minutes before she was murdered. There was only one man who was employed as optician at a jeweler's, and admits he had his 'workshop' here. There was only one man skillful enough with his hands—" Dr. Fell paused, wheezing, and turned to Lessing. "I wonder they didn't arrest you."

"They did," said the little man, nodding. "You see, I was released from Broadmoor only a month ago."

There was a sudden rasp and crackle as he struck another match.

"You—" bellowed Hadley, and stopped. "So it was your mother who died in that room? Then what the hell do you mean by keeping us here with this pack of nightmares?"

"No," said the other peevishly. "You do not understand. I

never wanted to know who killed Dr. Lessing or poor Martha. You have got hold of the wrong problem. And yet I tried to tell you what the problem was.

"You see, it was not my mother who died mad. It was theirs— Brownrigg's and Harvey's and Martha's. That was why they were so desperately anxious to think I was guilty, for they could not face the alternative. Didn't I tell you I had a hold over them, a hold that made even Brownrigg shake, and that I used it? Do you think they wouldn't have had me clapped into jail straightaway if it had been my mother who was mad? Eh?

"Of course," he explained apologetically, "at the trial they had to swear it was my mother who was mad; for I threatened to tell the truth in open court if they didn't. Otherwise I should have been hanged, you see. Only Brownrigg and Junior were left. Brownrigg was a dentist, Junior was to be a doctor, and if it had been known— But that is not the point. That is not the problem. Their mother was mad, but they were harmless. I killed Dr. Lessing. I killed Martha. Yes, I am quite sane. Why did I do it, all those years ago? Why? Is there no rational pattern in the scheme of things, and no answer to the bedeviled of the earth?"

The match curled to a red ember, winked and went out. Clearest of all they remembered the coarse hair that was like whitewash on the black, the eyes, and the curiously suggestive hands. Then Joseph Lessing got up from the chair. The last they saw of him was his white hat bobbing and flickering across the lawn under the blowing trees.

FROM DETECTIVE WHO'S WHO

FELL, Gideon, retired; formerly schoolmaster, journalist, and historian; b. Staveney Manor, Garth, Lincolnshire, 1884; sec. s. Sir Digby and Lady F.; grad., Eton and Balliol, Harvard (U. S. A.), B.A., M.A., (Oxon.), Ph.D., (Harvard), LL.D., (Edinburgh). Fellow of Royal Historical Society. Grand Cross of Legion of Honor (France). Publications: *Romances of the Seventeenth Century* (Smith, 1922); *The Drinking Customs of England from the Earliest Days* (Crippen & Wainwright, 1946). Clubs: Garrick, Savage, Detection. Hobbies: Reading and detection of crime. Present address: 13, Round-Pond Place, Hampstead, London, N.W. 3.

Doctors, lawyers, and others intimately connected with death have often functioned as detectives; but never to my knowledge, outside of one series of stories in the lamented Detective Fiction Weekly, has a case been solved by the man closest to the corpse—the mortician. Here is one of the neatest (if least profitable) jobs of undertaker Mortimer Death.

MORTIMER DEATH IN

Too Late for Murder

BY KEN CROSSEN

It's maybe an hour after lunch and Matson and me are in the back room at headquarters playing cards. We usually play five hundred rummy but today nothing would do Matson but he's got to teach me this gin rummy they play out in Hollywood. Matson, as you probably know, is a Detective, First Grade, and tags along with me on homicide cases. He ain't much on brains but when it comes to a fight, I'd rather have Matson than a whole regiment of marines. I ain't going much for this gin rummy even if it is the thing to play, being fifty cents out, so I'm tickled when the phone rings.

"Sergeant Stuart speaking," I says into the phone.

"I hate to interrupt your card game, sergeant," Lieutenant France says sarcastically, "but there's a rumor around that you're paid a salary to catch murderers, and who am I to call people liars. If you've got a few minutes of time, there's a case you might look into."

From *Detective Fiction Weekly*, June 14, 1941. Copyright 1941 by Munsey.

This is my superior officer speaking. He always seems to be sore at me about something. Now it's because I won ten bucks from him in a poker game at the last smoker. If it wasn't for him being such a sorehead I'd probably have been a lieutenant a long time ago.

"Matson and me are always eager to do our duty," I says with dignity. "What's up?"

"Some guy called up a few minutes ago," Lieutenant France says, "and started yelling something about being murdered. They switched the call to me and began tracing it. The guy kept on yelling over and over again that he's being murdered and I can't get him to make any sense. Then all of a sudden he stops talking and the receiver is hung up. But the operator got the call traced before he hung up. It came from a phone listed to George Barnard in a private house uptown. A swell section, too. The operator's been trying to call the number since then but gets a busy signal all the time. So you and Matson better jump in a car and run up there."

"It would help some if you gave us the address," I says, "me and Matson not being what you'd call clairvoyant."

"None of your cheap wisecracks, sergeant," he snaps. That's the trouble with the guy; he ain't got a sense of humor. Anyway, he gives me an address which is in a swanky part of town not far from Park Avenue.

"And don't stop to pick any daisies along the way," he says after I repeat the address to him to prove I got it right.

"It's the wrong time of year for daisies," I says, hanging up before he can answer.

"Some guy calls up and tells the looey he's being bumped off," I tells Matson, "so we got to sprint out there and check up on it. He's probably got indigestion and thinks somebody's trying to poison him. Come on."

"You owe me fifty cents," Matson says.

Can you imagine that? Here's a guy maybe dying and he's thinking about half a buck! You'd think I was going to cheat him out of it. It's a good thing he don't remember the two bits I lost to him last week.

"Here's your pound of flesh, Simon Legree," I says, tossing over the fifty-cent piece.

"It was Shylock who wanted his pound of flesh."

"Okay, it was Shylock. What's the difference if it was maybe even Uncle Tom? Let's go."

So WE go out and climb in a squad car. Matson drives, opening the siren up, and I got to say this for him: he's one of the best drivers on the force. In no time at all we're pulling up in front of the address, one of them old brownstone fronts. A house like that really cost potatoes in the old days.

We get out of the squad car and walk up to the front door. I push the buzzer and then wait, thinking maybe we're going to have to bust the front door down.

"Hey, look, sarge," Matson says, tugging at my sleeve. "Look down the block there."

I take a look and there on the corner is a big house, with a sign in front which says: *Mortimer Death, Mortician.*

Yeah, that's right, he's the guy that kind of helped me out on a couple of cases. No kidding, that's his real name—Mortimer Death! He's a little, short, fat man with the most cheerful puss I ever see on a guy. He really is an undertaker but he ain't so successful. I guess it's partly because of his name and partly because he looks so damn cheerful nobody wants him puttering over the remains of their Aunt Sadie. So he's got a lot of time on his hands and he gets interested in crime. I let him hang around on a few cases because I like the little guy, and anyway the help he gives me don't do me no harm down at HQ.

"We'll have to drop in and say hello, as soon as we clean this up," I says, giving the bell another strong push.

I don't even get time to get my thumb off the button when the door opens and the one of these flunkies with striped pants opens the door. He looks just like these butlers in movies. I figure right off if there's any dirty work underfoot, he's the lad. I don't read detective stories and see movies for nothing.

"Yes?" he says, only it sounds like "Ya-a-a-s?"

"We want to see this George Barnard," I tells him.

He looks kind of startled at that and I can see where my first impression of the guy is right.

"I'm afraid that is quite impossible," he says. "Mr. Barnard is dead."

I got to hand it to him, he's a cool customer.

"Yeah, that's the reason we're here," I says. "He called and said somebody was trying to bump him off but I guess we're too late to save him. We're the homicide men."

"I'm afraid there has been some mistake," the butler says, like he was talking to a grocery boy who brought the wrong order.

"You're damn right there has been," I says. "The mistake was in bumping the guy off. One side, chum, and we'll get the thing cleared up right away."

"But," he says, "he couldn't have just phoned you. Mr. Barnard expired shortly after eight this morning. He had a heart attack early last night but Dr. Hislop was unable to save him."

"Well, we'll just—wait a minute! What was that you said?"

"I said Mr. Barnard passed on shortly after eight this morning, so he couldn't have phoned you."

"What is this, a gag?" I says. "Somebody called from here and said they was being murdered. Who else lives in the house?"

"Only Mr. Barnard's son, Daniel. He is, however, in the best of health, although naturally grieved over the demise of his father."

"Well, we'll just take a look around anyway," I says.

"Such action is extremely unseemly, officer, in face of events," the butler fellow says with a frown.

"So it's unseemly," I says. "Do you move or do I slug you?"

"HERE, here—what's going on?" another voice says from back of the butler.

"I'm going on," I says. "There's something phony around this joint."

Still another figure has appeared at the door and I blink with surprise as I see who it is. It's Mortimer Death, the little undertaker I was telling you about. He's all decked out in a frock coat and striped pants and he's wearing his usual cheerful grin.

"Ah, greetings, Sergeant Stuart," he says. "Hello, Matson."

"What the hell are you doing here?" I asks.

"I have been called in to take care of the deceased," he says, looking so damned happy I catch myself grinning back at him.

"You know these men, Mr.—ah—Death?" the heavy-set guy beside him asks. He's wearing nose glasses, with a big black ribbon, and he's got the kind of an expression that you can just imagine the guy being happy because he discovers somebody's got a new incurable disease. So I figure that he must be the sawbones. When Mortimer answers him I see I'm right.

"Yes indeed, Dr. Hislop," Mortimer Death says. "They are connected with the police department, in the homicide division. Although I don't quite understand what they are doing here. Is something wrong, sergeant?"

I'm getting tired of standing out on the steps like maybe I'm singing Christmas carols, so I shove the butler to one side and Matson and me step inside. Then I tells them the story that somebody calls from this house and says he's being murdered and that ever since then we get a busy signal on the phone. I can see by the way Mortimer Death's eyes are brightening up that he's already getting more interested in what I'm saying than in getting the old man fitted into a box.

"Nonsense, sergeant," the doc says when I've finished. "No one made such a call from here and no one here has been using the phone at all, so your story of the line being busy is preposterous. You must have made a mistake."

"We don't make mistakes; other people do," I says. "In the meantime I want to see the stiff and then I want to talk to the son and this here flunky."

"I won't have the police barging in on the natural grief of this home," the doc says, getting sore.

The way I look at it, docs must be sort of unhealthy. They're always getting upset about things. "Sure," I says, "but I'm barging anyway."

"I'll report you, sergeant. I'll see that you're demoted if you don't leave this house immediately."

"Get wise to yourself, doc. We're cops, see, not the local boy's club selling tickets to a raffle. Our operator says that call came from here and we're going to look around even if I have to have Matson here put the slug on you."

"It might be advisable to permit them to look around," Mortimer Death says to the doc who is beginning to look like he is coming down with the Russian measles. "I'm sure that Sergeant Stuart will be most discreet and will have the proper respect for filial sorrow."

"Very well," the doc says. "I suppose you're right. Perhaps I was a bit hasty, sergeant, but it's been a very trying night."

"That's okay, pal," I says. "Live and forget, that's my motto. Where's the stiff?"

"This way," he says and steps ahead towards a room to the right. Mortimer Death follows and me and Matson trail along.

WE GO into this big room which is so filled with flowers that you'd think it was a greenhouse, only they don't have corpses laid out in greenhouses. Yeah, the old guy is laid out as nice as you please, with his hands folded across his chest. Only his face ain't so peaceful, being sort of screwed up as though he had indigestion.

"Looks like he wasn't too happy about dying," I says pleasantly, deciding there ain't no use being grim about this business. The doc and Matson and even Mortimer Death, who usually laughs at my little sallies, pretend to be shocked at this but I guess it's only because they think that's proper.

"There is often considerable pain with heart trouble," the doc says, "and Mr. Barnard suffered a great deal before passing on. In fact, we had to give a narcotic injection to soothe his last few moments."

"Who's 'we'?"

"Dr. Fullan, who assists me in my practice. He was here until shortly after Mr. Barnard died."

"You here all night, doc?" I asks.

"Not straight through. But I was back at six this morning and have been here since."

"You're sure the old boy kicked off about eight?"

"Positive," he says. "It was just a few minutes past."

"Looks like he'd have had trouble calling us right after lunch then," I admits, "but—"

"Look, sarge," Matson says, nudging me and nodding towards the corner of the room. I see what he means right off. There's a phone on the desk there and the receiver is off the hook, lying on the desk. That's the reason the police operator gets a busy signal every time he calls.

"There's the reason for the busy signal all right," I says, "but now the question is who called up and said he was being murdered?"

"I declare," the doc says, going over and replacing the receiver. "I must have left the receiver off when I called Mr.—ah—Death here." It's beginning to tickle me the way he keeps stumbling over Mortimer's name. I bet he wishes he had called an undertaker named Smith.

"How'd you come to call Mortimer here?" I asks, remembering that Mortimer practically never gets any business.

"Why, I merely looked in the classified phone book and picked the nearest mortician. Mr.—ah—Death is only a few doors from here."

"Uh-huh," I says. "Going to give the old boy a good send off with a fur-lined box and all, Mortimer?"

"Not exactly," he says. "It seems that it was Mr. Barnard's wish to be cremated, so I am making the arrangements for that."

"Yeah?" I says, getting skeptical again. The way I figure, nobody in their right mind is going to want to be burned up after they've kicked off. "Any chance that maybe he was poisoned instead of having ticker trouble?" I asks Mortimer.

"I RESENT that," the doc says indignantly. Like I told you these sawbones are always touchy as an old maid.

"Okay, okay. Where's the son?"

"You'll probably find him in the library," the doc says stiffly.

"If you don't mind, I think I'll accompany you," Mortimer says. I can see he's already forgot all about the business of Mr. Barnard's remains.

"Sure," I says. So the three of us leave the room and after blundering into the kitchen and scaring the hell out of some old crow there, we find the library and there is some pale-faced young fellow, with thin, blond hair. He's kind of sickly-looking and don't appear to be grieving near as much as you might think. This library is big enough to be part of Grand Central Station and the way it's fixed up I can see that it cost a pretty penny to set up housekeeping in this joint.

"You Daniel Barnard?" I asks him.

"Yes," he says. "What can I do for you, my good man?"

Can you imagine him giving me that "good man" stuff? I can see right away that he's feeling pretty chipper considering his old man is stiffer than a board.

"I'm the cops," I says. "What do you know about the murder of your father?" I figure I'll catch him off guard.

"Afraid you're barking up the wrong tree, Sherlock," he says. "The old man died of heart failure."

"You don't seem to be put out much?"

"Not much," he admits frankly. "We were never what you could call clubby."

"And I suppose his death'll mean that you inherit a lot of potatoes?" I says, looking significantly around the room.

"Wrong again," he says. "The old man lost practically all of his money in the last couple of years. All that's left are his insurance policies."

"For how much?" Mortimer Death asks. I notice Matson looking at the books along the wall. A hell of a detective he is.

"I believe about three-quarters of a million," the young fellow says.

"That's *all* that's left, huh?" I mutters.

"Who is the beneficiary?" Mortimer asks.

"Myself."

"Hmm," Mortimer says. I see he's through asking questions so I start up again.

"We got a call at headquarters about an hour ago from here. Some man said he was being murdered. What do you know about that?"

"Maybe it was the old man's ghost," he says flippantly. "They might be making it too hot for him now."

"Did you make that call?" I asks, ignoring his manners. The things us cops have to put up with.

"No."

"Who around here could have done it?"

"Anybody could have," he says, "although I doubt if they did. I'm sure that Dr. Hislop wouldn't think of playing such a practical joke. I'm sure I didn't, and I don't think that Roberts would."

"Who's Roberts?"

"The butler."

"That guy, huh?" I says. "I'm glad you mentioned him. How long has he been working here?"

"About twenty years. Why?"

"He don't look exactly kosher to me. Do you think he might have bumped your father off?"

"That's ridiculous. In the first place Roberts wouldn't bump, as you call it, a fly off and besides my father died of heart trouble. Don't you cops have anything else to do but run around playing charades?"

"I NEVER touch them myself," I says, "and don't try giving me any of your lip. Somebody called headquarters from here and I'm going to find out who it was."

"It was probably from another number and some poor man is being murdered while you're wasting time here."

"It was from here," I says, beginning to get a little tired of everybody hinting the cops make mistakes like that. I look over at Mortimer Death, only he ain't there no more. I look over towards the books but he ain't with Matson either.

"If you're looking for your fat friend," young Barnard says, "he took a run-out powder on you several minutes ago. I guess he was getting as bored with your monologue as I am."

It ain't like him to run out like that but then I think maybe he suddenly remembers he's got a customer in the next room. Of course in a business like his you don't have to worry about the customer taking his business elsewhere. Anyway I turn back to the business at hand.

"This here Roberts," I says, "he looks to me like an ugly customer. Kind of moody, ain't he?"

"You might say that," the young fellow admits, although I can see he don't want to admit anything to me. "But that doesn't mean he's vicious."

"Them is famous last words," I says. "You leave the detecting to us coppers, brother. We get paid for it."

"I was wondering what they paid you for," he says.

I ignore the crack, figure that'll burn him up more than answering it. "If you cash in all these insurance policies, you'd keep this Roberts on, wouldn't you?"

"Of course."

"A pretty soft job for him. The way I look at it, maybe he did something in the last day or two and the old man threatens to fire him. He sees this easy job slipping away, but he knows if the old boy kicks off, he's got a job with you. So he takes advantage of this heart attack. Doc Hislop—and that's a hell of a name if you ask me—admits he wasn't here all the time. It would have been a cinch for Roberts to slip in and give your father a couple extra shots of strychnine. That's what they give these heart patients, so there'd probably be plenty of it around. And nobody's any the wiser because the doc is expecting his ticker to fold up any minute anyway."

"A very nice theory," the young man says, "except you forget that my father died a little past eight this morning and you say your phone call didn't come through until a little after lunch time."

"I got that all figured," I says. "What happened was he wasn't really dead this morning, only unconscious from the poison Roberts had slipped him. But the doc thinks he's off. Later on the old boy—I mean your father—comes to, realizes he's been poisoned, and calls us up. He manages to get back to his bed and then dies. You see how it all fits?"

"I'm beginning to see that you're nuts," he says.

"The trouble is you laymen don't understand the fine points of this business," I says with dignity. "Matson, I want you to go out and collar this here butler. We're taking him down to headquarters—"

THAT's as far as I get when the door to the library busts open and in comes some old party, dressed in a baggy old suit of clothes and a shaggy hat on his gray hair. He looks like some bum out of the gutter. Right behind him is Mortimer Death holding a gun on the old party.

The minute they enter the young guy lets out a squawk you could have heard down to Union Square and looks like he's going to maybe faint. Me, I don't like the way Mortimer Death is waving that gun around.

"Here," I says, "where'd you get that gun?"

"I'm sorry, sergeant," he says, "but I took the liberty of borrowing yours, thinking I might need it."

I grab at my holster and damned if it ain't empty. He's picked the gun out while I was talking.

"You can't do that," I says. "It ain't legal and besides how would it look if the papers got hold of the story that you swiped a cop's gun?"

"They won't," he says. "Here is one of your culprits."

"What do you mean, one of my culprits?"

"This gentleman," he says, indicating the old party with the muzzle of the gun, "is Mr. George Barnard and you can charge him with murder—although I think it was just his idea and Dr. Hislop did the actual murdering."

"Hey, wait a minute," I says. "Remember, it's Barnard that's dead. You mean he murdered himself?"

"No, sergeant. The corpse inside is that of someone they picked up for the job. Mr. Barnard has been very much alive all the time."

"And you said that was your father in there, huh?" I says, swinging around on the young fellow.

"I said nothing of the kind," he says weakly. "I—I took it for granted that it was my father. Dr. Hislop said so. I had no particular desire to see him after death, so I never entered the room."

"I'm sure that is quite correct, sergeant," Mortimer Death says. "I believe they relied on the fact that the son wouldn't care to see his father's body and it was probably easy to keep the butler from entering."

"Now wait a minute," I says. "What's this you're trying to tell me?"

"I was sure that you were correct about the phone call," Mortimer goes on, "so I began to speculate on what was going on. As soon as I heard that Mr. Barnard had lost all of his money but was heavily insured, it occurred to me that perhaps he wasn't even dead.

"I immediately saw an easy way the switch could have been accomplished. Dr. Hislop and his assistant, who is the victim they've picked, arrive here early in the morning after having set up the business of the heart attack. Later the assistant—now Mr. Barnard—leaves. Then the doctor kills off the victim, makes out the death certificate, and has the body cremated. The son here unwittingly collects the insurance. The father lets him know that he's alive and he wants most of the money. If the son doesn't come across, he's implicated in the fraud.

"The victim spoils the plan by reviving long enough to get to the phone and call the police. But Dr. Hislop catches him and is forewarned. He'd already explained this morning that the father had died at eight so he sticks to his story and tries to bluff it through.

"When I got suspicious I looked in the phone book and failed to find any Dr. Fullan listed. Yet Hislop claimed that was the name of his assistant. Acting on a hunch, I run out to Dr. Hislop's office, which is only a couple of blocks from here, and did a rather neat job of burglary. Sure enough I found Mr. Barnard there and, with a little persuasion, he verified the story as I've given it to you. I suggest you better get Dr. Hislop—"

"A VERY pretty story, Mr.—ah—Death," a new voice says from back of Mortimer. It's the doc, who's slipped in without being noticed while we're all listening to the story. He's got a gun in his hand.

"It's too bad," he goes on, "that you have to spoil what was otherwise a perfect and lucrative scheme. Fortunately, I am not of a vindictive nature or I should probably kill you all before leaving. As it is, I shall only temporarily disable you until we can make our escape. George, will you take the gun from Mr.—ah—Death's hands and render each of our guests unconscious with the butt of it."

Maybe because me and Mortimer Death always do all the talking, you've forgotten about Matson. Evidently, doc has. That's a mistake. Like I told you, Matson ain't never got much to say but action is his long suit.

About this time he slings one of them heavy books through the air and follows after it. The book catches the doc square in the puss, knocking him off balance. The gun goes off, tearing a hole in a picture on the wall, and then Matson has planted one just under the doc's first molar. The doc flies one way and his fancy nose glasses the other way. Matson scoops up the gun and the party's over.

Remember how in the very beginning I'm telling you I don't like this doc's looks? At least, I meant to. I tell you they have to get up pretty early in the morning to fool Sergeant Stuart. And when I get a little help from Mortimer Death, like in this case, I'm damn near unbeatable.

It's only two hours since the call came into headquarters and here I am with the whole thing sewed up. This George Barnard is a weak sister and when we get down to Centre Street he spills the whole story to a police stenographer and it's all over but the frying. Looks like the pale-faced young fellow is still going to collect that three-quarters of a million potatoes in insurance. Even Lieutenant France had to admit that I'd done a good job.

But I got to laugh when I think about the case. This old party which they bumped off—and they did it with strychnine just like I said—to pass off as Barnard was a guy they pick up in the Bowery, so he gets planted in Potter's Field.

Get it? Here is the first real piece of business that Mortimer Death gets in maybe six months and he helps me knock himself out of it. Since the old party ain't got any potatoes, of course all the fuss is off and the county officials do the job.

But Mortimer don't seem put out any. Like I told you he's got a yen for fooling around with crime—it's getting so that fixing stiffs is only his hobby—and he's as happy over the solution of this business as some kid that's just got his Junior G-Man badge in the morning mail. Can you beat it?

FROM DETECTIVE WHO'S WHO

DEATH, Mortimer, mortician; b. Cleveland, Ohio, Sept. 12, 1915; s. Alaster and Karen Mortimer D.; no siblings; m. Barbara Goldner, April 21, 1947. Descended from Aylmer Mort, foot soldier, army Edward II; family motto: *Sanguis Dicet.* Educ.: Columbia U., N. Y. Sch. of Embalming; post-graduate work, Harvard U. in dermasurgery. Licensed mortician, New York City, 1938. Due to extreme interest in crime, and perhaps to unpleasant associations with name, the Death Funeral Parlor did not prosper. Business sold 1945 and Mortimer Death moved to California where, in partnership with Gelasius Muratori, he opened The Enchanted Vale Crematorium. First became interested in crime through reading Sherlock Holmes stories. Interest became active when discovered evidence of murder while preparing body for burial. Publications: *The Use of Vascular Injections in Autopsies; The Viscera; From Oil of Lavender to Formaldehyde; Dermasurgery and Crime; An Undertaker Looks at Murder; Criminology for the Embalmer.* Consulting editor, *National Funeral Directors Pharmaceutical, Anatomical, and Chemical Lexicon* (1948). Editor, *Crime in the Crematorium* (1950). Hobbies: Criminology, card tricks, collecting examples of zeugma. Ambition: To visit all radio vice presidents in his professional capacity. Res.: 938½ Third Street, Santa Monica, Cal.

Matthew Head is noted as one of the most perceptive and
ironic of modern American mystery novelists; and his medical missionary, Dr. Mary Finney, is as original and living a
detective as has appeared in many years. But neither author nor character has ever been associated with the short
story—which is why MWA takes particular pleasure in
bringing to you, for the first time anywhere, this biting
short story rearrangement of facts encountered by Dr. Finney in one of her novel-length adventures.

DR. MARY FINNEY IN

Three Strips of Flesh

BY MATTHEW HEAD

THE BODY of Gérôme de l'Andréneau, with the neck broken
and three strips of flesh peeled off the back of the shoulders, was
found at the tip of a spectacular promontory near the limits of
the Congo-Ruzi station. Although there was other money on
the body, the murder or murderers had robbed it of exactly one
franc.

The Congo-Ruzi was a private agricultural experimental station in a remote part of the Kivu, in the Belgian Congo, and it
was in a hell of a bad way even before the murder of its director.
I happened to be there because I was making an inspection of
the station in connection with an American government loan
they had applied for during the war.

I had rather liked this Gérôme de l'Andréneau—a tall, still
good-looking man of the fading matinee idol type, who was utterly lost in the Congo, and so lousy a manager that he had re-

duced the station to such an extremity that there wasn't a chance of giving them the loan.

Gérôme was survived by several people who for one reason or another might have liked the idea of his being dead, including his wife and her lover, and his assistant manager who did all the work for half the salary, and a very large group of natives. As for the wife, Jacqueline, from the minute I met her I knew that if she wasn't a nymph she was close to it, and although she obviously didn't bite her nails, which were about an inch-and-a-half long, she was pretty well chewed up inside. You couldn't help feeling sorry for her in a way, since it can't be much fun being a woman who has never lived for anything but her looks and the pleasure of attracting men, when she finds herself on the verge of middle age isolated a hundred miles from the nearest village and a couple of thousand miles from a really first-rate cosmetics counter. With Gérôme dead she could have sold the station for what it was worth, which was still something, and got back to the source of supply of men and war paint.

I've no way of being certain that Jacqueline had a lover at the station, a big handsome young fellow named Henri Debuc, except that Jacqueline and Henri were both people of tremendous sexual vitality, that neither one of them gave any indication of being particularly strait-laced, that they had an awful lot of spare time on their hands, and that the isolation of the Congo-Ruzi station was just one step beyond the old cast-up-on-a-desert-island-together deal. And although I personally wouldn't have killed a jack rabbit for the privilege of running off with Jacqueline, I could see how Henri might have looked at things differently, especially if the setup involved a release from the desperate ennui of his position.

Gérôme gave a party for me the night I arrived at the station, with all the white population of the station—six—there, plus two white visitors. I arrived late, with Henri, since I was being put up at his cottage, and after we had said polite things in the hallway to Gérôme and Jacqueline we went on into the living room. This was two days before the murder. They were talking about a killing which had occurred some time before, when a

local tribe, the M'bukus, had done away with a white overseer.
A large, carroty-haired, plain-faced woman about fifty years old
was gesturing with a pair of big freckled hands and speaking in
English with a strong Middle-Western accent.

"My God, César," she was saying, "I don't see how you can
say it. You saw him as well as I did, lying there with his throat
cut from ear to ear and half the flesh stripped off his back. If it
wasn't for my medical oath, I wouldn't touch another of your
goddam M'bukus with a ten-foot hypodermic."

Jacqueline interrupted to introduce me around; she was
dressed in a slinky kind of hostess gown that was threadbare in
spots, but in her own affected way she had a certain amount of
style. The carroty-haired American, I learned, was Dr. Mary Finney, a medical missionary who had hit the Congo-Ruzi the day
before on her semiannual visit to the native village near by.

"Don't let us interrupt you, Miss Finney," I said. "What's a
goddam M'buku?"

"Have I been swearing again?" asked Miss Finney.

"You know you have, Mary Finney," said a small mousy
woman at her side. This was her partner, Miss Emily Collins.
Miss Finney always said that since Emily ran the soul and hymn
department, the two of them represented the flesh and the spirit
between them.

"Every time I swear, Emily bursts into tears," said Miss Finney.

"I do not," said Emily.

"You do too," said Miss Finney, and Miss Collins gave it up.

Henri stepped into the breach. "My houseboy's a M'buku," he
said to me, "the one who took care of your things. They're the
leading tribe around here. Miss Finney hasn't much to say for
them."

"They're the meanest blacks in the Congo, I'll say that much
for them," Miss Finney told him.

"But that boy doesn't strike me as being mean," I said. I felt
sorry for Miss Collins, who was fiddling nervously with the hem
of her skirt and looking pretty well squashed. She had a pallid,
grainy face with light brown eyes and scanty hair crimped in some
kind of patent waver. "Oh, yes, I know that boy," she said. "Al-

bert. Albert Nkodio. He's a member of the village mission. Albert's been a very faithful boy."

Miss Finney grunted.

"He's been a very syphilitic boy," she said. "You needn't worry, though, Henri—I gave him that examination this morning and you just keep on giving him the injections."

Miss Collins coughed daintily and nervously, took the tiniest sip of her drink, set it down on the table by her side, and pulled at her hem.

"Emily," said Miss Finney, "if you pull that damn skirt one more time you're going to have it right down off your neck. After the things we've done the last twenty-five years I should think you could take a little reference to syphilis without fidgeting. You've got a chronic case of New England girlhood, that's what you've got." She added as an afterthought, "I'd rather have syphilis."

Miss Collins coughed again and glanced meaningfully at somebody I haven't mentioned yet, an extraordinarily pretty young girl named Gabrielle.

"Oh, that," said Miss Finney. All this had been in English. She said in French, "Gaby, did you understand what we were saying?"

Gaby said in English, "Not very much of it." She had a very strong and very delightful accent. She was, I'd have guessed, only about sixteen, perhaps at most a year or two older. She had naturally that wonderful combination of tawny skin and blond hair that the girls in California work toward with sun and chemicals. Her father was the assistant manager who did all the work for half the salary, César Boutegourde, such a short fat bald little typical *père de famille* that I always thought of him as Papa Boutegourde, and his plump wife, with nothing left of what must have been real beauty except her great luminous eyes, as Mama. They were sitting protectively on either side of Gaby. Papa was a violent Walloon, but Mama's family were Flemings, so Gaby had learned at home to slip easily from French to Flemish. She spoke French to Gérôme and Jacqueline and Henri, and English to Miss Finney and Miss Collins and me, and later I heard her chatter in Lingala to the natives, and she used all of these, shifting from one to another without any difficulty or hesitation. She had grown up doing it.

There was a short silence, and I realized that I was looking directly across the room at Gabrielle's breasts where they began to swell above the low, square-cut neckline of her dress, and that everybody else in the room was looking at me doing it.

I said quickly, "These M'bukus. I've heard of them somewhere."

Miss Finney grinned at me and said, "Maybe you've heard of the M'buku Rebellion."

I hadn't, but I said I had. Miss Finney grinned at me again and said, "César thinks of it as his own little rebellion. It was on one of the station's fields, not forty miles from here."

Papa Boutegourde opened his mouth, but Miss Finney said, "Let me tell it. It's a fine bloody story. You see, Mr. Tolliver," she said to me, and then, "Oh, for goodness' sake, what's your first name?"

"Hooper."

"Well, Hoopie, you see, this nasty little Duclerc was subadministrator or something, and after the natives had worked out their road tax—they all pay a road tax in labor—he kept them working on his own plantation, and no pay."

"And a gun and whip to back him up, remember that," said Papa Boutegourde.

"All right, a gun and whip to back him up. I guess there was a lot to be said for the natives," admitted Miss Finney. "But he made his mistake when he hired a couple of Kitusis to stand guard."

Papa Boutegourde interrupted. "The Kitusis had always warred on the M'bukus, but even in the old days the M'bukus wouldn't eat Kitusi flesh because they regarded the Kitusis as inferiors, but when Duclerc hired—"

"*I* started this," Miss Finney broke in. "I know you know everything about native history and customs, César, but I'm trying to get to the bloody part. Hoopie's a tourist. *Well*," she said with relish, "it was the most excitement this place ever saw. Three

M'bukus got the Kitusis, then they went on and got Duclerc. Damn fool, if he hadn't hired the Kitusis he'd have got away with it. White men are still sort of demigods out here, but not when they play with Kitusis. They dragged Duclerc out of his house into the bush and cut his throat and took three strips of flesh off the back of his shoulders. I suppose," she said, "they cut his throat first. I know they ate the flesh."

Miss Collins moaned faintly. "*Mary!*" she breathed.

"That's all," said Miss Finney. "It's a nice story for tourists and happens to be true into the bargain. They got one of the M'bukus alive and hanged him right there on the plantation."

"They did?" I said. "In a place like this, who acts as hangman?"

There was an uncomfortable pause. Then Papa Boutegourde said hesitantly, "They—asked me to, but I couldn't bring myself to it." He paused again, then said, "Gérôme was—brave enough."

"I hanged him," Gérôme said, with a smile. He indicated a coin that hung on his watch chain. "A souvenir," he said. "Perhaps a rather grim souvenir. One franc. My fee. They paid me one franc, to make it legal." He smiled again, not at all uncomfortably, and said, "It was only a native, of course, but still, I can say I hanged a man."

Jacqueline said sharply, "If you have quite succeeded in ruining our appetites—" then she pulled herself together, smiled at us around the room, and said to me, "Mr. Tolliver, will you take me in to dinner?"

By rights Papa Boutegourde should have sat at Jacqueline's left, but Henri was there instead, and Jacqueline was so much more interested in him than in me that I paid my attention mostly to Gaby on my other side. Sitting close to her I looked for a single flaw in her skin; it wasn't there. She had on some lipstick and I think a little darkening on her eyelashes, but beyond that she wasn't made up, and didn't need to be. We talked about nothing much, but always knowing what we really would have liked to talk about, then all of a sudden she said to me,

"Do you like my dress?"

"I do. It's a very pretty dress."

"I made it myself. We have to do so many things for ourselves out here." She looked directly at me and smiled and said in a lower voice, "Before I came tonight I cut the neck lower. Mama is furious. But you like it, don't you?"

She took me so by surprise that I stammered like a fool. She smiled again and turned calmly from me with a faint air of dismissal and said to Henri, across the table, "I haven't seen you for so long, Henri. You are not looking well." Jacqueline looked at her with hatred, then turned to me and began talking about New York. Gaby kept her calm air all through dinner, but I noticed something else. Under the shield of the table she would clench her napkin or twist it in her fingers. Then she would stop, but before long she would be at it again, her hands twisting and clenching until the napkin was moist and crumpled all over.

Two days later I had finished my inspection of the station, and I was sitting up late with Papa Boutegourde in the Boutegourdes' house (the houses on the station were separated as much as half a mile, in the interest of some kind of privacy), and we were winding up the checking of some figures I had to take with me when I left the next morning. It must have been nearly two; Mama and Gaby had excused themselves long ago, and I was getting worried, because things were stretching out and I was afraid that Gaby would get sick of waiting for me out on the promontory, where we were going to say good-by.

Papa and I were in a small room, a kind of study, or we would have heard Jacqueline as she came stumbling and gasping across the station grounds. We heard her burst into the living room and ran in there; she was horrible to see and hear. She was trying to talk in a strange, thickened voice, but a kind of idiot laughing or sobbing would break through and she would go off into hysterics. There were remains of make-up smeared over her face, and her hair was sticking out in every direction. She had on something that looked like red crepe lounging pajamas; they were ripped and snagged all over, and spotted with dust and stains of moisture. We got her onto the sofa and she lay there looking thin and slippery-boned, writhing like an eel and twitching, and clutching at Papa Boutegourde's bathrobe while she screamed with laughter or choked with sobs.

"You'll have to hit her to get her out of that," I said. Jacqueline sat straight up. "*Rape!*" she screeched, and fell flat on her back again and went into peal after peal of laughter, twisting her fingers together until you would think they would never straighten out again.

"They hurt me!" she whimpered. She began screaming again. "Oh, Gérôme, my poor Gérôme! Where's Gérôme? What did they do to you, Gérôme? Oh, Gérô-o-o-o-ome!" and her voice went off into a long howl. Then she collapsed and lay there heaving, with hiccoughs jerking out of her.

Mama Boutegourde appeared in the room in bathrobe and pigtails, wild-eyed. "*Brandy!*" yelled Papa Boutegourde, and Mama disappeared. She reappeared with a glass and a bottle, and Papa pressed the glass of brandy against Jacqueline's lips, but she moaned and made bubbly and snuffly noises into the glass so that the brandy spilled over.

"If she won't drink it, throw it on her," I said.

Jacqueline whimpered and downed the brandy in a couple of gulps.

"You've got to find Gérôme," she said, fairly normally, but still in that strange, thick voice. It gave me the feeling you get when the dentist stuffs the little wads of gauze under your lip while he's working on you. Jacqueline was quiet enough now so that I could see that her mouth didn't look funny only because the lipstick was smeared. It was bruised and swollen on one side, and the bluish flush spread on up into her cheek.

"*Regardez-ça!*" cried Madame Boutegourde suddenly. She had lifted one of Jacqueline's hands to chafe the wrist, and the loose sleeve had slid back to the elbow. Her wrist was bruised. You could see the finger marks, and when Madame Boutegourde pushed the sleeve on up to the shoulder, there they were again, on the upper arm.

"They hurt me," Jacqueline moaned. "Gérôme! Oh, please, they've got him; go find him, César!" Now she lay back on the pillow and began crying in a helpless, despairing kind of way that would have been heart-rending in anybody else. "You all hate me," she said, "and you won't help me. Oh, Gérôme, Gérôme!"

When we finally got the story out of her, it went like this:

She had gone to her room to change into the pajamas earlier that night, and had expected Gérôme to follow her. When he didn't appear she had gone back into the living room. Gérôme was standing petrified, facing two natives she had never seen before. She had not heard them come in, she had heard no sound at all; they had simply appeared out of thin air, and she had entered to face the terrifying tableau. Gérôme spoke to the natives in French, asking them what they wanted. They had answered briefly in their own tongue, but neither Jacqueline nor Gérôme could understand a word.

Jacqueline remembered Gérôme's pistol in their bedroom. She turned to leave the room but one of the natives was upon her in an instant, grabbing her from behind by the arms near the shoulder and making the bruises we had seen. Gérôme had turned to attack the native. The second native jumped across the room and felled Gérôme with a blow. Gérôme lay still on the concrete floor. Jacqueline had screamed. The second native stepped over Gérôme's body and grabbed both her wrists in one hand. "He was big, big! A great black brute of a thing—" and she displayed to us her two small bruised wrists that he had clamped in his one great hand. He had put the other over her mouth. She had fainted.

When she came to, both natives had Gérôme's body and were carrying it out of the room. She had crawled across the floor toward them on her hands and knees. Then rising to her knees she had beat at one of them with her fists. He freed one hand and hit her in the mouth, saying something in his language. She didn't know how long she was unconscious this time. When she came to she was alone. She was half crazy with terror; she hadn't even remembered that she could have driven the car. She had run all the way to the Boutegourdes', falling down, running into bushes. She remembered it only as one remembers a nightmare. The rest we knew.

Mama Boutegourde went to get towels and water for some

kind of repair job on Jacqueline, but instead, we heard her shriek from the other end of the house. She appeared in the doorway looking like the last acts of all the Greek tragedies rolled into one. "She's gone!" she screamed. "She's not there! Her bed—her window—" Mama Boutegourde fell into a chair and began giving a good imitation of what Jacqueline had just been doing.

I said to Papa Boutegourde, "I know where Gaby is. I'll go get her." Papa Boutegourde looked as if the last semblance of reason had been snatched from his universe. I went out, to keep—in a way—my late date with Gaby.

You reached the promontory through a bush path that was used as a short cut between points on the station. I had been along it before, with Gaby, but tonight I kept going off the path and into the thick masses of foliage which bounded it. I had a flashlight, and in any case you couldn't stray far, simply because of the thickness of those foliage walls, so I blundered through at a good rate of speed, with things swishing and crackling around and under my feet, and my face and hands getting scratched; but I didn't have to go far before I found Gaby there, cowering as far off the path as she could press herself into the tangled growth. My light picked her out, half crouching and pressing herself backward, her eyes wide and her lips drawing back from her teeth. She was so still that she looked like one of those night photographs of wild animals, where the animals trip off their own flash.

Her voice came out in a croak. "Don't touch me," she said. "Don't touch me." She kept saying it.

"It's Hoop, Gaby," I said. She didn't move or change expression. I turned the light up into my own face, so she could see.

I heard her cry come out like something giving way under pressure. Before I got the light back onto her she had flung herself on me, both hands clutching the front of my shirt. I put both arms around her to keep her from falling, and she let go of my shirt and flung her arms around me too. We stood there pressed close together and I could feel the current of her fear, like an actual emanation from her body. She tried to talk but I couldn't get the words, then she began to relax and tremble, and finally she stopped trembling and let her head drop against me and began to cry. I could feel her going limp and I knew she was all right now.

She told me what I could hardly believe, that he was there; then she led me along the path until we came to the clearing on the promontory where we had been supposed to meet. I remember how he looked in the beam of the flashlight. I could see the gash in his throat and I saw his shirt ripped half off his back and his back dark with blood, but it wasn't until I had taken Gabrielle home and Miss Finney had come back and examined him that we saw how the strips of flesh had been peeled off his shoulder.

I won't go into the embarrassment of seeing Papa and Mama Boutegourde and having to admit that I was meeting Gabrielle on the promontory. As far as good Belgian parents are concerned, murder is a less heinous crime. But I will summarize Gaby's story as she told it to her mother and father and Miss Finney:

She had gone out to the promontory and waited there for me, she didn't know how long, until she had heard the sound of someone coming. Since she couldn't be certain it would be me, and since the footsteps seemed oddly slow and heavy, she had run back into the edge of the bush, and had seen one figure come out onto the promontory, bent over under the weight of what he carried on his back. He had thrown his weight onto the ground. The body was long and thin and in white pants and shirt; she had recognized it as Gérôme's. She could see the other figure in not much more than silhouette, but she could tell it was a native. She had shut her eyes when she saw that he had a knife, and what he was doing to the body, after ripping off the shirt; she was afraid she would faint, and concentrated everything on staying conscious and quiet. She didn't know how long it took until the native left, going down the path into the valley toward the native village; she didn't remember how long it had taken her to go back along the path when she saw my light in the distance. She thought it was a native, with a light he had stolen; either a native concerned with Gérôme's murder, or the same native she had seen, doubling back. She had told him not to touch her, and then had recognized me when I turned the flash on myself. She showed me Gérôme's body, as I have told, and I took her back to her house.

Miss Finney listened to this story of Gaby's that night. It was close to dawn when we left the Boutegourdes' house, because among other things Miss Finney had had to administer sedative injections to Mama Boutegourde and Jacqueline.

As we drove along the station roads to her guest house, Miss Finney said to me, "Hoop—what exactly did Gaby say, when you flashed that light on her?"

"Just what she said she said," I told her. "She just kept saying, 'Don't touch me, don't touch me,' over and over again."

"Those her exact words?"

"You asked me, I told you. Yes."

"Strange," said Miss Finney. "If she didn't know it was you, why did she speak in English?"

I felt myself flushing in the dark. "Sorry," I said. "She did say it in French, now that I think of it."

"Goddammit," said Miss Finney, "when I say exact words I mean exact words."

"All right then, her exact words were 'Ne me touchez pas.' "

"Exactly," said Miss Finney. "According to her story she thought you were a native, so she said to you 'Ne me touchez pas.' "

"Get to the point," I said.

"Lord Almighty, Hoop!" said Miss Finney. "She spoke in French! In French! Gabrielle never spoke to the natives in French. She was one of those Congo babies who have black boys for nursemaids and have to be spanked into speaking French. They always pick up Lingala first and they'd rather speak it, it's easier. She translates back and forth like a breeze. It's second nature to her to speak their own tongue to the natives. Most of them wouldn't understand anything else anyhow. She didn't think you were a native—she thought you were a white man, a French-speaking white man. She didn't see a native out there with Gérôme's body—she saw a white man. She didn't see him go down the path to the village, she saw him go back in the direction of the station, the way he had come. When she saw that light bobbing through the bush she thought he was coming back for something, taking the short cut. When the light flashed on her she thought there was a murderer behind it—a white man! She didn't think it was a native. If she had, do you know what she'd have said? She'd have said 'Koba! Koba-du-bai! Koba-du-bai!' My God, does that sound like Ne me touchez pas to you?"

"All right, all right," I said, feeling sick about what was coming next.

"But then she pops up with this rigmarole about a native," Miss Finney went on, "because she saw that white man and what he was doing to that body and she knew why he was doing it, and why he was laying him out on the path to the village like that, to make it look like a fancy M'buku revenge on Gérôme for that hanging job he did. But she loved Henri. She might not have wanted him to touch her, not there in the bush or ever again, but she couldn't bring herself to give him away. If you don't know she loved Henri you're blind. What else could happen—a young healthy girl who never sees any man at all, stuck out here, and Henri as handsome as he is? If he hadn't been tied up with Jacqueline—and I guess you think he is just the way I do—they might have fallen in love. Of course, she loved him."

"All right, she loved him," I said, "but this white man she saw. It happens I've been with Mr. Boutegourde all evening so he's out, but you didn't know that and you jump at Henri right away. Why couldn't you suspect Boutegourde?"

"Oh, my God, Hoop," Miss Finney said in despair, "why wouldn't I suspect Santa Claus? And anyhow, she'd have spoken in Flemish if she'd thought it was her father."

"I'm finished," I said meekly enough. "And what are you going to do now?"

Miss Finney was quiet for a moment. She sighed heavily, and said, "I don't know exactly. I know from the bruises on Jacqueline's arms and wrists and mouth that she was being beat up pretty badly. I don't think those bruises were planted on purpose. It's hard to do something like that to yourself or to someone else deliberately, even to conceal a murder. The only man around here I can think of who'd have reason to beat Jacqueline up was Gérôme. The only reason Gérôme would beat her up right now, with you, an important stranger on the place, would be that something unexpected had happened that cracked him up. And the most unexpected thing that could happen to Gérôme, poor dope that he was, would be to find Jacqueline and Henri together. I think he did. I think he grabbed her, hit her in the face, and so on, and I think Henri tried to stop him and killed him by accident. His neck was broken. And I think it was Jacqueline's idea to fake this native vengeance on the body. Then by the time she had run half a mile and fallen down a few times and showed up bruised and genuinely half hysterical at the Boutegourdes', she could put on a pretty convincing show. And all Henri has to say is that he slept through the whole thing. Do you think that holds water?"

It held a little too much water. Henri's suicide, some weeks later, was accompanied by a written confession.

FROM DETECTIVE WHO'S WHO

FINNEY, Mary, physician and surgeon, medical missionary; b. Ft. Scott, Kansas, 1892; d. Robert Spencer and Alice (Harrington) F.; A.B., U. of Kans., 1912; M.D., 1916. Went to Belgian Congo (1918) with Emily Collins, missionary, with whom she is cofounder of numerous missions and hospitals for natives in Kivu area. Author: *An Analysis of the Co-* *extensive Range of Malaria and Blackwater Fever in Central Africa*, 1936; numerous articles on tropical maladies, pub. in American, Belgian, French medical journals. Awarded *Médaille d'Honneur* from Belgian Congo for distinguished contribution to native welfare, 1945. Home: Kivu-Bashongo Mission, via Costermansville, Congo-Belge, Africa.

Lillian de la Torre's transcriptions of the deductions of Dr. Sam: Johnson, detector, have been unanimously acclaimed as unique blends of meticulous period re-creation with the best elements of modern crime fiction. Yet one of the most distinguished of these stories has never before appeared in a fiction collection, but only in Miss de la Torre's anthology of fact-crime, Villainy Detected. Here then, for the first time to most fiction readers, MWA's oldest sleuth (in point of birthdate) investigates one of history's greatest puzzles, the Canning Wonder.

DR. SAM: JOHNSON IN

The Disappearing Servant Wench

BY LILLIAN DE LA TORRE

ELIZABETH CANNING went from her Friends between nine and ten on *Monday Night*, being New Year's Night; betwixt *Houndsditch & Bishopsgate*, fresh-colour'd, pitted with y* Smallpox, high Forehead, light Eyebrows, about five foot high, well-set, had on a purple masquerade-stuff Gown, black stuff Petticoat, a white Chip Hat bound round with green, white Apron and Handkerchief, blue Stockings, and leather Shoes. Any Coachman, who remembers taking up such a Person, and can give any Account where she is, shall have Two Guineas Reward, to be paid by Mrs. *Canning*, in *Aldermanbury Postern*, Sawyer, which will greatly satisfy her Mother.

THESE LINES were roughly printed in the form of a handbill. My friend Dr. Sam: Johnson, *detector* of crime and chicane, produced the dog's-eared scrap of paper from the accumulations

From *Villainy Detected*, N. Y.: Appleton, 1947. Copyright 1947 by Lillian de la Torre.

in his untidy book-garret in his house in Johnson's Court. I perused it with care.

"Pray, sir," I ventured, "have you still, in April, hopes of finding the girl? Sure the thing is all too plain. The lass hath been caught up and carried off by some rakish fellow, and now ten to one she plies a shameful trade by Covent Garden, and shames to return to her mother."

"No, sir, there you are out. The girl has returned to her home long since."

"Why then, sir, the girl has told her tale, and there's an end on't."

"Yes, sir, the girl has told her tale indeed, and thence arises the puzzle."

"Pray tell it me."

"Why, thus, sir: 'Twas King Charles's Martyrdom Eve, eight and twenty days after that fatal New Year's Day, and the Sawyer's 'prentice was just upon locking the door for the night, when there comes a faint knocking. 'Tis Elizabeth Canning! She is sodden, and starving, and exhausted and blue, and her clothes are gone. Good lack, cries Goody Canning, Bet, what has happened to you? And Bet tells her tale. Stay, you shall hear it as she told it in Bow Street."

From a mass of old printed papers my bulky friend drew a thin pamphlet, and from it began to read out in his sonorous voice:

"The INFORMATION of *Elizabeth Canning* of *Aldermanbury Postern, London*, Spinster.

"This Informant, upon her Oath, saith, that on Monday, the First Day of January last past, she, this Informant, went to see her Uncle and Aunt, who live at Salt-Petre Bank, near Rosemary-Lane, in the County of Middlesex, and continued with them until the Evening; and saith, That upon her Return home, about Half an Hour after Nine, being opposite Bethlehem-gate in Moorfields, she, this Informant, was seized by two men (whose Names are unknown to her, this Informant) who both had brown Bob-wigs on, and drab-coloured Great-coats; one of whom held her, this Informant, whilst the other, feloniously and vio-

lently, took from her one Shaving Hat, one Stuff Gown, and one
Linen Apron, which she had on; and also, Half a Guinea in Gold,
and three Shillings in Silver; and then he that held her threatened
to do for this Informant. And this Informant saith, That, immediately after, they, the same two Men, violently took hold of her,
and dragged her up into the Gravel-walk that leads down to the
said Gate, and about the Middle thereof, he the said Man, that
first held her, gave her, with his Fist, a very violent Blow upon
the right Temple, which threw her into a Fit, and deprived her
of her Senses (which Fits, she, this Informant, saith she is accustomed and subject to, upon being frighted, and that they often
continue for six or seven Hours. . . .")

"Stay, stay, sir," I implored, "for here is such a foyson of this
Informant, and the said Informant, as carries me back to the
Court of Session, whence I am newly a truant; so pray, sir, give
me the straight of the story without circumlocution."

"Well, then, sir: Bet Canning told a horrid tale, how these
pandours in bob-wigs snatched her up by Bedlam Gate, and carried her off in her fit. They carried her off to a bawdyhouse in the
suburbs, said Bet; and there an old woman took her by the hand,
and My dear, says she, will you go our way? For if you do, you
shall have fine clothes. No, says Bet. Straightway the old woman
takes up a carving-knife, and cuts the lace of the girl's stays, which
the men in bob-wigs had overlooked, and takes them from her.
Then she feels of the girl's petticoats. These are of no use, says
she, I'll give you them. With that she gives the girl a great slap
in the chops, and turns her up a pair of stairs, half-naked as she
was, into a kind of loft or shuffleboard room. There, said Betty,
she found some old mouldy bread and a broken jug full of water;
but for which, and a penny minced pye which she happened to
have by her, she had starved to death. For eight-and-twenty days
no soul came nigh her. On the five-and-twentieth day the bread
was all gone. On the seven-and-twentieth day she ate her minced
pye; and on the eight-and-twentieth day she broke out at the
window and ran away home."

"Sure, sir," I cried, "these were no Christians, but heathen
Turks, so to misuse a poor innocent girl!"

"Yet you will allow, sir, that 'tis an excess of Christianity, thus to suffer for eight-and-twenty days an unnecessary martyrdom; for she who can break out at a window on the eight-and-twentieth day of fasting, might have done so with less fatigue on the first."

"Heathen Turks," I reiterated hotly, "and I heartily wish they may have been laid by the heels."

"As to Turks, Bozzy, you are not so far out; and as to laying by the heels, they were so. And a precious crew they proved to be, being the old bawd, Susannah Wells by name, and a parcel of gipsies, her lodgers. They carried the girl to the suburbs to identify the people and the place. This is the house, says Bet; this is the shuffleboard room; and these are the miscreants, says she, pointing at the gipsies. It was the old gipsy woman cut my stays; and I think, says she, I *think* the gipsy man her son was one of the men in bob-wigs; while as to the two gipsy wenches her daughters, though they laughed at me they did nothing to me. As to the old bawd, I don't know that ever I saw her in my life before."

"I hope," cried I, "that the whole precious crew have long since had their just deserts."

"No, sir," replied my friend coolly, " 'tis true, the world was once of your mind; Wells was branded in the hand, and the old gipsy woman was to hang for the stays. But the old woman found friends, who have so managed that she had the King's pardon, and placed the girl in the dock in her stead."

"Upon what charge?" I cried.

"Upon a charge of perjury."

"Monstrous!" I exclaimed angrily. "How mean you, friends? The publican of some ale-house under a hedge?"

"No, sir," replied Dr. Johnson. "I will name but one: the Lord Mayor of London."

I gaped.

"You have wished to see the sights of London," remarked my friend. "Here is one you are not to pass by. The girl takes her trial today."

Now it was clear why my friend had caused me to hear the girl's story. The curtain was about to rise on a new act of the drama.

"Will you come, sir?"

"No, sir. I am too old and too thick in the middle to batter my way into the press at the Old Bailey."

I was young and spry. I clapped on my three-cornered hat and made off down Fleet Street to the Sessions House in the ancient street known as the Old Bailey.

Before I had turned the corner a muttering sound told me of the crowd that was milling uneasily in the paved court-yard. I was not to be daunted. I butted and pushed my way until I stood, half-suffocated, under the balcony and close by the dock.

On the long bench at the front sat the Justices of Oyer and Terminer, the lawyers in robes, the aldermen with their chains of office about their necks. On the floor before them a spry man with his big-wig pushed back was talking in brisk tenor tones. But I had no eyes for them.

On the raised platform of the dock, clinging to the rail that fenced it, stood the girl. She was a stocky chit, no higher than five feet, drest in a clean linnen gown. She wore buckled shoes and a decent lawn kerchief, and her plain cap was fastened under her chin. The light fell on her pink, expressionless face. The spry lawyer was describing her in unflattering terms as a liar for profit; but the large blue eyes never flickered. Elizabeth Canning looked at him as if he weren't there at all.

Then her eyes shifted, and I followed her gaze. Seated to one side, in a large armed chair, sat the most hideous old hag I had ever had the misfortune to see. She was bent, and tremulous, and swarthy. Swathing clouts half-hid a face like a night-mare. She had a great frog's mouth smeared all over the lower half of her face. Her chin was aflame with the purple scars of an old disease, and her swarthy hooked nose jutted over all. This was Mary Squires, the gipsy beldame. She was attended by a sparkling dark girl and a trim-built young gipsy man.

I could not read the stolid girl's expression as she looked at her enemy. It held neither indignation nor remorse, but something more like puzzlement.

For ten mortal hours I stood on my feet as the gipsy's witnesses followed one another on the stand.

"How is it with Canning?" asked Dr. Johnson as I supped with him. "Is she cast?"

"No, sir," I replied. "There are prosecution witnesses still to come, spare the defence; for length this trial bids fair to make history."

"Pray, how will it go?"

"Sir," I replied, "ill, I fear. Here have been forty witnesses come up from Dorset to swear an alibi for yonder gipsy hag. She was strolling, they will stand to it, through the Dorset market-towns peddling such smuggled goods as she might come by in the sea-ports. Here has been a most respectable witness, an exciseman, who will swear it, that they lay in the excise office at Abbotsbury on the very night. Here have been landlords of inns from Abbotsbury to London to trace them on their way, bar only a four-days' journey from Coombe to Basingstoke. They came to Enfield full three weeks after Canning absconded. How 'tis managed I know not, but the girl is devoted to doom."

A knocking interrupted my discourse. The knocker proved to be a heavy-set red-faced man. He was accompanied by a younger man, a spindle-shanked sandy fellow with a long nose. Between them they supported a weeping woman. The woman was fortyish, and ample to overflowing.

The sandy young man burst immediately into speech.

"Robert Scarrat, hartshorn-rasper, at your service, sir, which I rasps hartshorn on a piece basis for Mrs. Waller of Old 'Change, and her son is tenant to Mrs. Canning here."

The weeping woman snuffled and confirmed the hartshorn-rasper with a nod.

"This here," the nervous strident tones hurried on, "is by name John Wintlebury, as is landlord of the Weavers Arms, and Bet Canning was a servant in his house."

" 'Tis a good wench," rumbled the publican.

"Nevertheless they have contrived her ruin among them," cried the woman, "and will transport her to the plantations—unless you, sir, would undertake to clear up the matter."

"You must tell me," replied my friend, "what they are saying about her."

" 'Tis never true that I hid her for my gain," cried out the weeping mother, smearing her bleared eyes with a thick finger, "for I never had rest, day nor night, for wondering where she was. Mostly I thought her dead in Houndsditch, sir, or catched up by some rakish young fellow. I had dreams and wandering thoughts, and I prayed day and night to have a vision of her. But the cunning man said—"

"The cunning man?"

"A mere piece of woman's folly, sir," muttered the innkeeper, but Mrs. Canning paid him no mind.

"The cunning man in the Old Bailey. I went to him to have news of her, he had a black wig over his face."

"What said he?"

"Not a word, sir, only wrote, scribble, scribble, scribble along. He said, an old black woman had my daughter, and she would return soon."

"Ay," chimed in the hartshorn-rasper, his prominent hazel eyes rolling with superstitious awe, "is't not strange, sir?"

Mrs. Canning shuddered, and sobbed harder than ever. The landlord laid his hand on the woman's arm.

"Be easy, ma'am," he said gently, "for we know Bet's a good girl, and Dr. Johnson will soon make the matter clear. No need to take the hystericks over it."

The woman moaned. Scarrat took up the tale.

"Nor 'tis not true," he went on, "that I went off with the girl for my pleasure, for she was unknown to me."

"Ay," seconded the landlord, "for all the time she lived in my house, she was modest and shy, and would scarce so much as go to the door to speak to a man; and though Mr. Scarrat frequented the house, they never exchanged a word."

"And," cried the spindly man, growing hot, "as to my forging this tale, out of revenge against the bawd, 'tis false as Hell, though indeed I owe the creature no kindness."

"A notorious woman," said Wintlebury, "I knew of her infamous brothel when I lived and courted in Hertford."

"Oh, pray, pray, Dr. Johnson," sobbed out the weeping mother, "will not you help us?"

"Do, sir," I seconded. "Could you but see the vile face of the gipsy hag, you would rush to the girl's defence."

"As to faces," replied my friend, "there's no art to find in them the mind's construction; and as to helping, if I must come down to the Old Bailey, 'twill not do."

The fat woman gave a howl and fell to the floor in a paroxysm. There was instant confusion. The fat friend and the thin one fell to slapping her wrists, while I applied under her snubby nose the hartshorn-bottle which was perhaps the fruit of Mr. Scarrat's endeavours.

When she had gasped and sat up, I turned to my kindly friend.

"Pray give your assistance," I begged. "I will be your deputy to the Old Bailey."

My friend accepted of my offer, and the friends of Canning departed in better cheer.

ONLY the fame of my companion gained us access to the gipsy. She sat in the best room of the White Horse, in the Haymarket, and regarded us sardonically with black, beady eyes. She was surrounded by a court of Dorsetshire fishermen, King's landwaiters, and gipsies in leather breeches. Her pretty daughter sat hand in hand with a tall man in fustian; I recognized with a start one of the principal witnesses for the prosecution, a cordwainer of Dorset. A black-browed little raisin of a man turned out to be the girl's uncle, Samuel Squires, a landwaiter of the customs right here in London and a gipsy of considerable influence.

Dr. Johnson ran a lowering eye over the motley crew; the men of the customs particularly took his eye. Then he waved them all away, and to my relief they went.

"Now, ma'am," says Dr. Johnson, "out with it. There's more in this than meets the eye."

The beady eyes measured him.

"I will confess," said the rusty voice.

I thrilled to my toes. The girl was saved!

"I'll confess. Though I have passed myself for a strolling pedlar, I am in reality—"

Dr. Johnson leaned forward.

"I am in reality—a *witch*. I can be present at *two* places at one time," whispered the old beldame with hoarse and ostentatious caution, "and though all these people saw me in Dorset, I nevertheless carried Canning to Enfield on my *broom-stick—*"

Dr. Johnson cut short her triumphant cackle by rising to his feet.

"Have a care, ma'am," he said angrily, "I am not to be trifled with."

The old hag leaned back and laughed in his face.

"I know you are no witch," my friend went on grimly, "but I will tell you what you are."

He spoke three words in her ear. Her face changed. She looked at him with more respect.

"Ah," she said, "I see you are in the councils of the great."

"I can see a church by daylight," he replied as we withdrew.

I made off, being engaged to dine with some ladies in St. James's, but Dr. Johnson turned into the tap-room and lingered.

"Alack, Mr. Boswell," he told me when again we met. "Alas for Bet Canning, the rusticks are honest. I had their story over a can of ale, and with such a wealth of detail as can scarce be forgery. The honest cordwainer loves the gipsy wench; he dallied eight days in their company at Abbotsbury, and when they departed he followed them on the road. There are landlords to swear to them all, and the things they saw and the meals they ate. So rich is the tale, it must be more than mendacious invention."

"Yet who pays," I cried, "who pays the scot of the poor gipsy pedlar and her forty witnesses at the White Horse in the Haymarket? Who keeps them in victuals and gin?"

"My Lord Mayor, 'tis said," replied my companion. "But come, Mr. Boswell, let me know your mind: shall we push forward and uncover the truth, wherever it lies? Or shall we leave Bet Canning to her luck with the jury?"

"Let us wait," I replied uneasily, "and see."

I FILLED the days of waiting in the court-room of the Old Bailey, where each day the girl sat in the dock with her wrists crossed before her, and looked on without expression while witnesses called her liar or martyr.

"How goes the trial, Bozzy?" demanded my friend as I returned bedraggled from another day's session.

"Ill, for the girl, ill," I replied dejectedly. "You may know how ill, when I tell you that the Lord Mayor was pelted by the resentful Canningite rabble as he came away from the Sessions-house. The girl has been made to appear a liar. Before the sitting Aldermen, so he has sworn, she described her prison to be little, square, and dark. Then they took her to Enfield; when it appeared that the room she swore to was long and light, with many other contradictions. I know not what to think."

"A starved girl, after long imprisonment, may surely exhibit some confusion," suggested Dr. Johnson thoughtfully.

"There is more," I replied. "From Enfield came many witnesses, who swore that they visited her supposed prison during that month, and saw there no such person as Elizabeth Canning."

"What said the girl to this?"

"Never a word, save once. 'Twas a son of Wells's testified, he stepped into the shuffleboard room to lay by his tools, for he is a carpenter, and there was no soul there save the labouring man that lodged there. Bet Canning leaned forward, and scanned him closely. She frowned, and looked him up and down. *I never saw him before, as I know of,* says she."

"Why did she so?"

"Who can tell? 'Tis a strange wench. Just so, by the evidence, did she comport herself when they took her to Enfield: would not be sure of the gipsy man, could not be sure she had ever seen Wells. Only the gipsy woman she swore to without hesitation. They report strange things of the girl, too, in Wells's loft. *Do you remember that six-foot nest of drawers?* says they. *I never saw it before,* says Miss. *Do you remember the hay and the saddles stored up here?* says they. She scratches her head. *I will not swear,* says she, *but there is more hay. As to the saddles, I remember one only. But there was a grate,* says she. *O no,* says they, *look for yourself. There's no grate and never has been: look at the cob-*

webs. There was a grate, says she, and from it I took the rags I wore when I fled. There was never a grate, says they."

"Is it so!" cried my venerable friend. "Here is no liar, but one trying to speak the truth. Bozzy, we must save this girl!"

I stared. The evidence, that had shaken my faith in the girl, had spoken quite otherwise to him. It had spoken with such clear moral force and conviction that it stirred his great bulk, and brought it next morning into the court-room of the Old Bailey.

He cleared his way through the press like a bailiff, with jerks of his sturdy oak staff. We were in time to hear the defence begin. The crowd murmured in sympathy as Bet's sad story was repeated by her friends as they had heard it from her on that Monday in January. All her natural functions were suspended, related the apothecary in sepulchral tones, the whole time of her imprisonment; she was very faint and weak, and the black-and-blue marks never went off for a month afterwards. My venerable friend shook his head from side to side, and clicked his tongue.

Burning glances of sympathy were levelled at the abused girl where she sat impassive in the dock as the story was told. They changed to looks of triumph as the defence brought aces out of their sleeves—a witness who had seen the girl led past his turnpike, in tears, by a pair of ruffians; three persons who had seen the bedraggled creature returning in the misty evening.

Dr. Johnson, seated on a bench with his chin on his staff, frowned and shook his head.

"How can this help?" he muttered. "The girl swore she was dragged off in a fit. Now we find she walked by the turnpike. Where is truth to be found?"

The defence rested.

It was three o'clock the next morning when I knocked up my friend.

"The girl is cast!" I told him. "She will be transported."

"Cast!" exclaimed my friend. "What this girl has been, I know not; but she is no perjurer."

A double knock announced a later walker than I. Again it was John Wintlebury and Robert Scarrat.

"You must help us!" cried the hartshorn-rasper. "Can you give us no hope?"

"Only this, that the girl is innocent," replied my friend. "I will do what I can. Where is the girl?"

"Alack," exclaimed the volatile Scarrat, "in Newgate."

"Then we must have her out."

That was easier said than done, but Johnson managed it. Scarrat carried the request. Meanwhile, off went the black boy Francis to the White Horse. He came back with a note:

> "She says she will come, if only to laugh.
> Ma: Squires"

THE old gipsy woman herself was not far behind. Next to arrive was Mother Wells. She came supported by the carpenter son. My friend received his curious callers with solemn dignity, and offered them cakes and port. The wrinkled old bawd guzzled hers with coarse greed.

It was still dark night when a sedan-chair turned into Johnson's Court. It was attended by two turnkeys and followed by our friends, once again supporting between them the high-strung matron. All three tenderly extracted from the chair the stocky person of Elizabeth Canning, and so she was assisted up the stair.

Dr. Johnson took her hand.

"Do not be afraid, my dear."

"I am not afraid," said Bet Canning.

She looked levelly at the hideous old gipsy hag, then at the bawd. The latter wiped a drool of port off her chin. Dr. Johnson handed the girl to a chair, her friends found places, and a hush fell as everyone in the room looked toward my learned friend.

"My dear," said Dr. Johnson, addressing himself to the girl, "there are those who think you are lying. I do not think you are lying."

"Thank you, sir."

The gipsy beldame, a mere huddle of rags except for her bright black eyes, snorted.

"But, my dear," my friend continued quietly, "there is much that is dark, much that you have not been able to tell us."

"I have told," said Bet Canning clearly, "all that I know."

"We must look further, then. There is one in this cause," said Dr. Johnson, "who seemed a knowledgeable man."

I leaned forward.

"Who?"

"The cunning man," replied my learned friend solemnly. "He knew where Elizabeth was, and he wrote it down, scribble, scribble, scribble along. He was right. I would have consulted him myself, but he is not to be found. There is no conjurer in the Old Bailey."

"I saw him there myself," cried Mrs. Canning. "He had his wig over his face; and when he lighted up the candles, he frighted me, and I could not stay for more."

"Well, well, he is gone away from thence, he is no longer to be consulted. We must make do without him."

He produced a leather case, which being opened revealed a gleaming polished disk of some black substance.

"This," said Dr. Johnson solemnly, "is the famous Black Stone of Dr. Dee the alchemist. I had it of Mr. Walpole against this night's purpose. Into it," he lowered his sonorous voice another pitch, "the alchemist used to call his spirits, and they revealed the truth to him."

Nobody spoke.

Dr. Johnson extinguished the candles, all but one, which gleamed fitfully on the table, accentuating rather than piercing the darkness. For a moment there was dead silence.

"Before the spirits speak," said Dr. Johnson, "has no one a word to tell us?"

I heard somebody gasp. The old gipsy was shaking and muttering to herself, it might have been a charm or an incantation. Mrs. Canning was crying again, in long shuddering gasps, and the hartshorn-rasper was twitching where he sat. Only the stolid inn-keeper and the cynical old bawd preserved an unbroken calm.

Elizabeth Canning's gaze caught and hung on the gleaming speculum. Her plain face was white as paper.

"Pray, my girl," said Dr. Johnson gently, "look into the magick stone of Dr. Dee, and tell us what you see."

"I see nothing," she faltered.

"You will see the truth," said my friend. "Look well, and tell us what you see."

The girl stared into the polished surface, scarcely seeming to breathe. Her eyes contracted to pin-points. She sat rigid.

"It is the night of January 1," breathed my friend in the silence. "Do you see Elizabeth Canning?"

"I see her."

The voice was tight and high, and seemed to come from a long way off.

"I see Elizabeth Canning. She is walking between two men, and weeping. It is a road, with water in it. Now they turn into a house, there is an old woman there."

"Swarthy and black?"

"No, grey and wrinkled. She takes away her clothes, and puts her into a room."

"Without any furniture?"

"No," replied the trance-like voice. "No, it is the best bedroom. The door opens, and the man comes in. Now Elizabeth can see his face. It is he. It is the same man who wanted Elizabeth to do the bad thing, always and always he was at her elbow saying it to her, and she would not. Now he is here to do it, and Elizabeth cannot help herself."

In a violent shudder the dreaming voice died away. For a moment there was silence in the room.

"Here," muttered Wintlebury finally, "you must stop this, sir, you've bewitched the girl to her hurt. Who knows what she'll say?"

"She'll say the truth," said Dr. Johnson sharply. "Be silent, sir, and listen."

He spoke soothingly to the rigid girl.

"It is the eve of King Charles's Martyrdom. Do you see Elizabeth Canning?"

"I see her."

"Where is she?"

"She is in the loft. The wicked man has left her behind, they have taken away her clothes, she cannot eat for shame. Because she would not do the bad thing with other men, they have beaten her and thrust her into the loft. She wants to go home, but she does not know where home is. She has forgotten her name. She has forgotten everything. She is very wretched."

Again the level voice died away.

"And then?"

The polished disk gleamed in the candlelight. The girl's eyes were like pin-points.

"And then she hears her name spoken, and she knows it is hers. She looks down into the kitchen and sees the ugly-face gipsy. She is hungry and cold and afraid. The minced pye is still in the pocket of her torn petticoat; it is stale and dry, but she eats it. She takes an old rag from the fireplace to wrap herself in, and breaks out at the window, and runs away home."

"But the grate?" I struck in.

"A saw across the fireplace," said a quiet voice in my ear. It was the young carpenter. "My cross-cut saw."

"She runs away home. They ask where she has been for four weeks; but she has forgotten. Only it seems to her that she was somewhere hungry and cold, and she has been somehow harmed, the ugly-face woman must have done it, and her clothes are gone; so she tells them as best she can what must have happened, and they believe her, and are very angry. Even the man who did the bad thing to her, he is angry too, and wants the gipsy hanged. Elizabeth has forgotten what he did to her; she thinks he is her friend."

"The man," Dr. Johnson leaned forward gently, "who was the man?"

"That's enough of this flummery," came an angry voice. "Can't you see that the girl is mad?"

A rough hand struck aside the magick speculum of Dr. Dee. Elizabeth Canning looked up into an out-thrust face, somehow distorted in the flickering light of the candle from below, and recoiled with scream after scream of terror. Then the candle flame was struck out, and footsteps clattered on the stair.

"Let him go," said Dr. Johnson. "Mr. John Wintlebury is not

the first to enforce his desires on a virtuous serving-wench, and I fear there's no law to touch him."

"I'll touch him," cried the hartshorn-rasper violently. "I'll— I'll rasp him!"

He held the shuddering girl tight against his shoulder. He touched her pale hair.

"She's not mad, sir?" he pleaded.

"Not the least in the world," replied my friend, "yet hers is a strange affliction. The learned call it the catalepsy. One so afflicted may preach, or prophesy, or fast without hunger, or cut his flesh with knives, and not feel it; or fall unconscious and lie as the dead; or believe the body's functions to be pretermitted; or they may upon great suffering or shame forget who they are, and wander homeless until they remember. It was Mr. John Wintlebury's good luck that the wronged girl forgot him and the wrong he did her, and even herself, for very shame."

"And my bad luck," croaked the gipsy crone, "for the story that came from her disturbed mind put me into jeopardy of my life."

"You were never in jeopardy, being what you are," returned Dr. Johnson.

"What are you?" I burst out uncontrollably.

"A customs spy," replied the old witch, "and a good one, young man. Who'd ever suspect the old gipsy beggar when she came nosing about the barns? I knew every smugglers' lay on that coast. O no, me Lord Treasurer wouldn't have let the old gipsy woman hang. 'Twas but a few nights lying hard in gaol; he could not move openly in the matter, for fear of betraying me and mine to the smugglers. In the end me Lord Mayor had his orders, and I was enlarged."

"And Mother Wells?" I touched flint and steel to the candle.

"It all happened," my friend replied, "of course, in her house of assignation; it was she who beat the girl when she would not go the way of the house."

I advanced the candle toward the old bawd's corner. The lees of her port were there in the glass, but the old woman was gone.

"Upon her," remarked Dr. Johnson, "justice has been done. You will remember that, although Mary Squires was pardoned, Susannah Wells has been branded on the hand for her part in the work."

Elizabeth Canning's sobs had died away, and she lay in a sleep like death against the hartshorn-rasper's shoulder.

"When she awakes," he asked, "will she remember?"

"I cannot say," replied my learned friend. "Perhaps she will remember everything. If not, you must tell her, gently, over and over, until the two times join into one in her mind and she no longer has those agonizing moments of trying to remember, like the time in the loft, or in the dock when she struggled to remember the young carpenter."

He pulled aside the heavy curtains and let in the dawn.

"Tomorrow," he said, "I will wait upon the Secretary of State."

The sun was up as the sleepy turnkeys rouzed to help lift the unconscious girl back into the sedan-chair. My benevolent friend followed it with his eyes to the mouth of the court.

"The issue of this night's sitting," he remarked with a half-smile, "has exceeded expectation. I reasoned that someone close to the girl knew where she was, else why the cunning man with the muffled face, who must write his predictions? Clearly his face and his voice were known. I brought her friends together, and produced a conjuration of my own. I hoped that superstition would affright one of them, and even that the girl might take courage and 'see' in the speculum what perhaps she had been frighted from telling. I never guessed that so strange is the mind in a catalepsy that it will see truly, as it were in a sleep, what it has forgotten in waking.

FROM DETECTIVE WHO'S WHO

JOHNSON, Sam: author, lexicographer, detector; b. Lichfield, England, Sept. 18, 1709; s. Michael and Sarah (Ford) J.; educ., Lichfield Grammar Sch.; Pembroke College, Oxford; M.A., Oxon., 1755; LL.D., Trinity C., Dublin, 1765; LL.D., Oxon., 1775; m. Elizabeth Jervis Porter, July 9, 1735. Detected: the Cock Lane ghost, 1762; the wax-works cadaver, 1763; the Flying Highwayman,

1763; the disappearing servant wench, 17—; the Monboddo ape-boy, 1773; the frantick rebel, 1777; etc., etc. Publications: *The Rambler*, 1750–52; *A Dictionary of the English Language*, 1755; *Rasselas*, 1759; *Lives of the Poets*, 1781; etc., etc. Clubs: Ivy Lane, Literary, Essex Head. Recreations: chymical experimentation; rolling down hill; glazing china; travelling rapidly in a post-chaise with a pretty woman, "rode harder at a fox chace than anybody." Address: No. 8, Bolt Court, Fleet Street, London, England.

Somewhere in the scale of detection between the netsuke-collecting amateur and the sadistic, venal professional, falls the man from an allied profession—shrewd, hard, but human—who is forced into detection as part of his own business. That allied profession is often the Bar, which numbers among its ornaments Scott Jordan—whose practice should bring him as much as it's bringing the reprint publishers.

SCOTT JORDAN IN

Widow in Waiting

BY HAROLD Q. MASUR

THE LADY'S HUSBAND, it seems, was indulging in a little extra-curricular activity, though why a man should stray from the fireside with such nice homework around was more than I could figure.

The homework sat in the red leather client's chair across my desk, taking me in with turquoise eyes that moved languorously under canopied lashes. Red hair framed a regal face with a faintly amused mouth. She was wearing one of those knitted outfits that clung to her figure like a coat of paint. It was a figure that could raise a man's temperature to fever pitch.

She was Mrs. Ivy Strickland, out of Park Avenue by way of Hackensack, calm, assured, and a little careless about dumping her ashes in the tray.

"I know Claude is seeing another woman," she said in a deep contralto. "I've been aware of it for some time."

From *Dime Detective*, November, 1949. Copyright 1949 by Popular Publications, Inc.

"How?" I asked politely.

"Oh—" she waved airily— "a woman can tell."

I looked at the man beside her. "You know how I feel about divorce cases, Owen."

"Sure," he said. "But everybody makes exceptions."

"This is a bad time for it. They're cracking down on lawyers and crooked detectives."

He smiled. "Exactly. That's why we want a lawyer with an unimpeachable reputation. Everyone knows that Scott Jordan wouldn't touch a case tainted with suspicion."

It was oil out of the can and he knew it. He knew, too, that it would be hard for me to refuse. Owen Lang was an accountant, a tax expert. We'd worked together on some rebate cases and he'd brought some good clients into the office. You have to take the bad with the good. He probably thought he was doing me a favor by bringing Mrs. Strickland in.

"Another thing," he said, "money is a minor consideration. Mrs. Strickland won't quibble about a fee. Charge whatever you think it's worth."

The money helped clinch it. Some rapid rationalization helped, too. Getting a woman her freedom from a no-good husband is really an act of benevolence, I thought.

"Okay," I said. "Let's have the facts."

His smile widened. Owen was a handsome party in a rugged, loose-jointed way. "It's the usual triangle, Scott. Claude Strickland and his secretary."

"How do you know?"

"Mrs. Strickland's been following them. They meet once a week in the Hotel Boncourt, Wednesday nights usually."

"This is Wednesday," I said.

He nodded. "Exactly."

"You mean, tonight?"

"Why not?" Mrs. Strickland asked. "The sooner, the better."

"Are you certain he'll be there?"

"Yes. He phoned he'd be home late. *Business.*" The last word was accompanied by a contemptuous snort.

"Good enough," I said. "There'll be a raid."

"You know what he looks like?" Owen asked.

"Who doesn't?" I said.

Claude Strickland had been a big name back in the heyday of silent flickers. He'd even starred in a few talkies after the movies found a tongue. But it hadn't panned out. His voice spoiled it. He came through the amplifiers sounding like an Italian coloratura.

So he'd severed his relations with the production end of the business and entered the exhibiting end, buying a chain of houses with a man named Balado. Strickland & Balado. Two first-run palaces and a dozen neighborhood grinds.

"Will you want a retainer?" Mrs. Strickland asked.

"Yes," I said, testing her. "Five hundred dollars."

She scribbled the check without debate. "May I volunteer some information? Claude usually reserves the same room every week. Number 725."

"And he usually gets there about ten," Owen said.

All this was nice to know because it simplified the job. I accepted the check and I divided a smile between them and we all stood up and I convoyed them to the door and through the anteroom.

IT SEEMED like the architects had searched for a musty smell and then built the Boncourt around it. Or maybe the structure was just old. From its revolving door to its Philippine mahogany desk a silk-thin rug rambled across an acre of chandelier-illuminated lobby. Potted palms drooped here and there. Ancient inhabitants drowsed in faded chairs. It was all as calm and as peaceful as a game of whist with your maiden aunt.

Shortly after ten o'clock I stepped into the elevator. It was one of those open-front, iron-grille cages. Max Turner was at my heels. Max was a private detective who had helped me on a number of jobs. He had an anonymous face and a card-index memory. He was one of the best leg-men in the business. A young assistant of his was trailing along as a witness.

The hallway was wide enough for a brace of elephants and Number 725 was at the end of the corridor.

I didn't bother with a skeleton key. There is a certain type of lock that generally yields to a simple trick. You turn the knob, put your shoulder tight against the door, and heave sharply. If you have the weight, if you have the knack, it springs the latch and sends the door flying.

I didn't like what I was doing. Neither does the daredevil who hangs by his toes from an airplane at four thousand feet. But that was his job and this was mine.

I followed the formula. The trick worked fine and the door flew open. Momentum carried me halfway into the room. Sudden shock stopped me short.

The charge didn't surprise Claude Strickland. Nothing would surprise him any more. He was through with all of that.

He lay crossways on the floor, wearing glen-plaid and a chestful of black hair that looked like a sleeveless sweater bought in a bargain basement. One side of his classic profile was intact. The other side was something else. It was the face of a blind steer who'd charged into a brick silo.

I jumped back and blocked the door. I straight-armed Max Turner into the corridor. "Go home," I said, in an off-key voice.

"What?" He looked at me dumbly.

"It's all off," I said. "A bust. Go home."

Perplexity wrinkled his forehead. "What's the matter with you, counselor?"

"Max," I said, swallowing hard, "it's better this way, believe me. Don't argue. Bail out. You didn't see anything. You didn't hear anything. You don't know anything. Get lost, Max, please."

I closed the door in his face. Why drag Max into it? He was an innocent bystander. No need for him to spend the night down at headquarters trying to explain something he knew nothing about.

I turned and had another look at Claude Strickland.

The gun was in his right hand. It had been fired into the side of his head. Powder gas had chased the bullet into the wound, expanding and tearing out a ragged hole. Blood stained the whole side of his face.

I looked at the gun, but I didn't touch it. A .32 Colt Banker's

Special, short, snout-nosed, lethal. An elephant gun might have done worse damage but it couldn't have made him any deader.

It was supposed to look like suicide.

Only somebody had bungled.

It wasn't suicide. Not with the gun in his right hand and the bullet hole in his left temple. Mrs. Strickland wouldn't need any divorce now. A good thing I had cashed her check that afternoon.

I made a quick survey. The room held three doors. Two closets and one door leading into the bathroom. It was one of those adjoining bathrooms, shared by the room on the other side, privacy being insured by a door locked with a hook and eyelet device.

I went back and reached a reluctant hand for the telephone. . . .

You can skip the next two hours, what with the lab boys, the medical examiner, and the D.A.'s assistant. Then I was alone with Detective-Lieutenant Nola.

Nola was a slender man, dark-skinned and dapper, with quiet brooding eyes, a quick mind, and the tough core of a betel nut. He sat on the edge of the bed and said. "Okay, Jordan. I'm listening."

"You heard me tell it to the D.A."

"You didn't tell all of it, boy. You were holding back. Pull the plug and let it spill."

Lying to Nola would get me about as far as a wide-eyed anarchist at a banker's convention, so I opened the bag and dumped it into his lap.

He made a distasteful mouth. "A divorce raid. You! I'm surprised, Jordan." He folded a hand over his chin. "Any ideas?"

"Yes. This job was pulled by an amateur, some Nervous Nellie in a hurry to kill and clear out. Bad planning, bad execution. Witness the gun on one side and the bullet hole in the other."

"No trace of the girl when you got here?"

"None. What does the desk clerk say?"

"Strickland was alone when he checked in."

"Maybe the girl was supposed to meet him here."

"Maybe. You know her name?"

I shook my head. "The widow probably does."

"The widow is at an opera party. We can't locate her." He regarded me steadily. "What do you know about her?"

"Dynamite, lieutenant. Thirty years younger than the deceased and really constructed."

"An old man and a young wife. That means she married him for his dough." His bottom lip bulged thoughtfully. "It shapes up peculiar. Why would she divorce him just because of this?" His gesture embraced the room.

"There's her pride," I said. "There's alimony. Or a cash settlement. And could be there's another boy friend."

"Okay. Okay." He turned wearily and headed for the door.

I followed him to the elevator. He was silent all the way down. When we reached the street he paused to deliver a brief but trenchant lecture on steering clear of police business, emphasizing each point with a rigid finger jabbing my breastbone.

Then he ducked into a squad car parked at the curb. The driver kicked it over and took it past a red light as if he were color blind, splitting traffic in half.

STEER clear, Nola had said. But he wasn't fooling me. I wasn't out of the woods yet—not by a long shot.

I patronized the nearest telephone booth and dialed Owen Lang. He was home. "Well, Scott, how did it go?"

I ignored the question. "Owen, I need some information."

"Shoot."

"Who's the auditor for Strickland & Balado?"

"Me."

"Is the firm solvent?"

He hesitated. "Well, Scott, it's no secret. They're on the rocks."

"Will they sink?"

"Looks that way. Unless one of them suffers a heart attack. There's partnership insurance—one hundred thousand dollars' worth. Plus double indemnity except in the case of suicide."

"I see. Give me a line on Strickland's secretary."

He laughed briefly. "That, Jordan! Nice, isn't she? Name's Violet O'Hara. Lives at the Milton. But you won't get to first base, boy. I know. I tried— Say, what is this? Why all the questions?"

I had pumped him dry, so I mumbled an excuse and broke the connections and vacated the booth. . . .

Louis Balado had an apartment on Central Park South. He was a man who had a finger in many pies. We knew each other casually from some corporate reorganization meetings. Recognition and surprise mingled on his face when he opened the door.

"Good evening," I said. "Business. May I come in?"

He piloted me into a wide living room and planted his feet apart on a camel's hair rug and lifted bushy eyebrows over questioning eyes. A thick man built low to the ground, with tiered chins and a forehead that reached all the way back to a horseshoe fringe of sparse hair, with a face dyed ox-blood by unrestricted scotches.

I said, "So you're in business by yourself now."

"I beg your pardon."

"The partnership, Strickland & Balado—it's finished."

A double wrinkle of puzzlement dented the bridge of his nose. "What are you talking about?"

"A corpse," I said. "A corpse with a bullet-hole in his head. I'm talking about murder. The murder of Claude Strickland."

His mouth fell open and he groped at a chair for support. A gasp caught at his throat. This, I thought, is acting in the grand tradition. Stanislavsky and the Moscow Art Theatre. He worked his voice into a squeak.

"Strickland dead! How? When? Where?"

I answered categorically. "Shot. Tonight. In a hotel room."

Louis Balado sank back against a nest of pillows on the sofa. He swallowed enormously. "Who—who did it?"

"That's what I aim to find out." I towered over him. "I'm looking for motive. I think I found motive. You were his partner in an almost bankrupt business. There was insurance—a hundred thousand dollars' worth. How's that for a nice fat slice of motive?"

His fingers flattened across his chest. He smiled at me like a man with the mumps. "Me? You think I killed Strickland?"

"Why not?"

He shook his head. "But there was another policy, the same amount, for his wife."

"So what? You still had a business to protect. And you probably knew where he could be found tonight."

"You're wrong, Jordan." His tongue rubbed over parched lips. "A hundred thousand dollars wouldn't be enough. It would just about buy out the wife's interest."

"Two hundred thousand," I corrected. "Double indemnity for death by violence."

His hands shooed at invisible insects. "Only in the case of murder. Not if it was suicide. Strickland did it him—" Balado broke off, snapping his jaw shut. He looked as if he'd swallowed a baseball. He shriveled back against the sofa, frightened.

I reached down and collected a handful of velvet smoking jacket and pulled him close.

"How did you know about suicide?"

He made incoherent noises and his eyeballs floated in quick moisture. I shook him.

"Nobody said anything about suicide, Mr. Balado. Yet you know. You know because you were there."

His lips moved soundlessly.

"Talk," I growled. "How did you know?"

His mouth opened and then, suddenly, the telephone was ringing. I listened to it for a moment. I released him. "Go ahead and answer the thing."

The telephone was in the bedroom. He stumbled through a door on the right. The ringing died when he lifted the receiver. "Hello," I heard him say. "Hello, this is Balado speaking."

And that was all he said. Whoever was on the other end of the line did most of the talking, did it all, in fact. Not another syllable came out of Balado. More than a full minute passed before I got it. Then I catapulted toward the bedroom. But it was too late. He was gone. The handset dangled off the night table at the end of its cord. I yanked at doors until I found one that led through a hallway out of the apartment. The hallway was deserted.

The bonehead! How far did he think he could get?

It must have been panic that sent him flying. Or maybe he needed a little time to think.

I took the elevator down, but the doorman hadn't seen him. I sighed and flagged a cruising cab and told the driver to take me to the Milton.

VIOLET O'HARA answered my knock. She was something to see— a slender girl, with dark hair and pale face, and enormous eyes that were trying hard to look casual. They weren't succeeding. They were moist and apprehensive.

I rode her backwards into the room and closed the door, not giving her time to think. "All right, Miss O'Hara, what happened tonight?"

"Tonight?"

"At the Boncourt."

"I—I'm afraid I don't understand."

I shook my head. "That won't wash, miss. It's too late to play innocent. We know all about it, about Strickland and the divorce, about you, too. Everybody's clearing their skirts and talking. Don't get left behind."

Her lips trembled. A pair of tears glistened in her eyes. The hard core that had formed inside me began to melt.

"Did you kill him?" I asked gently.

"No. . . . Oh, no, no."

"But you were with him tonight."

She took a deep breath that shivered on the way down. Her eyes searched mine and seemed to find confidence. "Yes," she nodded. "I was with him."

"Were you in love with Strickland?"

"Oh, no. It wasn't like that at all."

"Suppose you tell me how it was."

She selected her words carefully. "Mr. Strickland asked me to do him a favor. He said he was going to get a divorce and he needed help."

"You knew they were staging a raid?"

"I—I guess so."

"You weren't afraid of besmirching your reputation?"

Her eyes were wide and innocent. "He said my name would never come into it."

"Why you?"

"He didn't know anyone else."

"So you went."

"Yes. I liked Mr. Strickland. He'd been very kind to me. He loaned me money once when my mother needed medical treatment. He was unhappy and I wanted to help him. His wife was running around with another man. They had decided on a divorce and this was the least I could do."

"Go on from there. What happened?"

The recollection was painful. "I went to the Boncourt. I got there at seven o'clock. Mr. Strickland was waiting for me. He'd been drinking from a pocket flask he always carries and he was a little drunk. He offered me some. I don't like liquor. But he was very insistent. So I had a drop." She covered her eyes with her hands.

"Things grew hazy. Something happened to me. I think I fell asleep. The next thing I remember I was sitting up, staring at him." Her voice went down to a flat, awed whisper. "He was dead. He'd been shot and the gun was in my lap. I didn't know how it got there. I was very frightened. I—I was afraid they'd blame me."

I said quietly, "So you put the gun in his hand to make it look like he had committed suicide."

She nodded, wordless.

"Now, tell me—" I started, but the doorbell rang, cutting me off.

Violet O'Hara went rigid. She clutched at my sleeve, sudden fear warping her mouth. Her eyes appealed to me beseechingly.

I loosened her fingers gently. "Go see who it is."

She went to the door and opened it and two men stepped inside.

"Headquarters, miss," one of them said. "You're wanted downtown."

She turned slowly, perplexity joining the fear on her face. Her finger aimed at me. "But this man says he's a policeman, too."

The plain-clothes man put a pair of hard eyes straight at me.

"She's mistaken," I said. "She drew the conclusion herself."

"You'd better come along with us too. . . ."

Everybody was deployed around Lieutenant Nola's office. Ivy Strickland sat tear-stained on a straight-backed chair. Owen Lang was folded-armed soberness behind her. A thick-necked cop held Louis Balado vertical in front of the desk. Violet O'Hara stood there, looking pale and resigned.

"Jordan," Nola said coldly, "didn't I tell you to stay out of it?"

"How could I, lieutenant? I was in it up to my neck. Where did you find Balado?"

"In his apartment. Why?"

"He must have sneaked back. He ran away from me."

Nola was a man driven to exasperation, but containing himself with difficulty. "So you were there, too?"

"Yes, sir."

"And maybe you solved the case," he said sarcastically.

"Yes, sir."

His jaw dropped and then his eyes narrowed skeptically. "Well, who is the killer, then?"

"A question first," I said, and looked at Balado. "How did you know about suicide?"

HE LAID his ears back like a mule and his eyes went stubborn. He wasn't talking. Nothing could make him talk.

It was Violet O'Hara who spoke. "I told him," she said. "I phoned him when I left the Boncourt. I had to tell someone and I thought Mr. Balado ought to know." The picture focused for me when I saw how he looked at her, like she was Joan of Arc. Louis Balado, short, fat, and balding, was carrying the torch for Violet, and nobody on heaven's green footstool could make him say anything that hurt her.

"That clears the decks," I said. "Now we're stripped for action." I faced Nola. "Has Strickland been posted yet?"

"Tomorrow morning. But I don't need the Medical Examiner to tell me what killed him."

"Sure," I said. "He was killed by a bullet through the head.

But if they're not careless, if they do a thorough autopsy, they'll find he has a stomach full of chloral hydrate, commonly known as knockout drops. Mr. Strickland drank a Mickey Finn out of his own flask."

"How do you know?"

"Deduction. Violet O'Hara drank from the same flask and fell asleep. Precisely as contrived—which gave the killer a chance to enter the room, shut off Strickland's meter with a bullet, impress Violet's fingerprints on the gun, and then fade. It almost worked, too. Except for one uncalculated hitch.

"Violet hates liquor. So she took only a small sip from the flask and woke up too soon. She recognized the picture and tried to rearrange it. But she was walking on eggs, panicky, and she planted the gun in the wrong hand."

Nola's palms pressed flat to the desk. "Whittle it down. Who?"

"Owen Lang," I said.

Ivy Strickland gasped. Her fingers were a bowknot of distress at her throat, and she stared at the accountant, appalled.

Lang stood rigid, trying to smile, if you can call the horrible distortion of his lips a smile.

"Untangle it, Jordan," Nola said.

"It figures. Balado wouldn't do it. He's crazy about Violet. He'd never frame her. Mrs. Strickland didn't do it. She was at an opera party. I didn't do it. So who's left? Only Lang."

"The motive?" Nola asked tightly.

I crossed two fingers. "Lang and Mrs. Strickland. Like that. She had a boy friend. He's it. She was getting her divorce to marry him. But it's just as easy to marry a woman with money as one who's broke. She wouldn't get any settlement from her husband. He was strapped. But she did stand to collect plenty if he died. And twice as much if he died the hard way. Only it would have to be done soon because after the divorce he would probably change his beneficiary."

Owen Lang laughed once, hoarsely. "The man's crazy."

"Am I? Who suggested that I reach the Boncourt at ten? You did, friend. But Violet got there at seven. You needed that interval to complete your operations. You knew exactly when she'd be there, because you mounted and staged the whole production. And I was sucked into the deal, thinking it was on the level."

"Words," he croaked. "Only words. You have no proof."

He was clutching at straws. He was fighting a losing battle. He knew it and I knew it.

"We can get what proof we need," I said. "We'll check the person who registered for the adjoining room at the Boncourt. I'll bet the handwriting is yours, even if the name isn't. You were in that room, waiting for the moment. You stuck a card between the door and the jamb and lifted the hook out of its eyelet. That's why you selected the Boncourt. You knew the setup and how easy it would be. Then you went in and did what you had to do.

"And there's the flask, too. It's missing. You didn't want the police to find it. You took it away and I'll bet it's still hidden somewhere in your apartment. If that doesn't wrap it up, Nola can locate your source of chloral hydrate. You're sewed up tight, friend. You're hooked and you'll never wriggle off."

I guess he believed me. His head bowed down and he put his face in his fingers and began to tremble.

I turned around and went over to Balado, whose arm was over Violet O'Hara's shoulder. "It's all right," I said. "I'll take her home. She's got a lot to forget."

I figured I could help more than he could.

FROM DETECTIVE WHO'S WHO

JORDAN, Scott, attorney at law; b. New York City, Jan. 29, 1917; s. William (d. 1929) and Barbara (d. 1930) J.; living relatives, Lucy Jordan, aunt, age 70, Larchmont, N. Y. Educ., Bordentown Military Institute, New York U., B.S.; N. Y. U. Sch. of Law, J.D. Formerly U. S. Postal Inspector, 1939–42. U. S. Army, Captain, O.S.S., 1942–45. Private practice of law, 1945. Home: Hotel Drummond, New York City. Office: Rockefeller Plaza, New York City. Further biographical details, chronicled by Harold Q. Masur in *Bury Me Deep* (Simon and Schuster, 1947); *Suddenly a Corpse* (Simon and Schuster, 1949), *You Can't Live Forever* (Simon and Schuster, 1951).

My friend and neighbor Peek-a-boo Pennington looks at once wistful and embittered when anyone mentions the adventures of book and radio Private Eyes; his own life as California's most publicized private detective is nothing like that. He'd probably enjoy this exploit of Johnny Liddell; it's one of the few occasions in the annals of the hard-boiled school upon which the Private Eye winds up in precisely the jam he's asking for.

JOHNNY LIDDELL IN

Slay upon Delivery

BY FRANK KANE

JOHNNY LIDDELL shifted the jigger to his left hand, swung around to peer into the swirling smoke of the Club Madrid bar. He downed the thick brown liquid, wiped the back of his hand across his mouth. He fumbled through his jacket pocket, came up with a handful of change, and dumped it on the damp bar. The bartender nodded good-night as Liddell shouldered his way through the incoming crowd toward the street.

The air felt fresh and clean after the thickness of the club. Johnny shuddered slightly, drew his jacket closer around him. He was annoyed by the feeling of apprehension that had clung to him throughout the evening. He decided to walk it off.

It was at the entrance to the park that it happened. A slight fog, almost reminiscent of the clouds of smoke at the Club Madrid, had come up from nowhere. Passers-by were ghoulish shapes behind an opaque curtain.

From *Crack Detective*, October, 1946. Copyright 1946 by Columbia Publications, Inc.

Liddell dug a limp cigarette from his pocket, hung it from the corner of his mouth. He was moodily contemplating the burning end of a match when the girl bumped into him. He had a fleeting glance at a small, pert face, corn yellow hair, and wide blue eyes.

He dropped the match and grabbed her as she stumbled.

"I—I'm sorry," she murmured. Liddell wondered idly as to the origin of the faint accent that slurred her words. "I'm very careless!"

He grinned. "Think nothing of it," he said. "That's the first good thing that's happened to me today."

The girl looked over her shoulder as though expecting to see some fearsome thing there. "I need help," she said. "Will you help me?"

Johnny looked into the wide, serious eyes searching for evidence of a rib. "What kind of help?" he asked.

He felt a square package being pushed into his hand. "I want someone to hold this for me until tomorrow," she said. "It's very important to me. My—my life may depend upon it." Her eyes were very serious, her tones scared.

Liddell held the package for a moment, then slipped it into his jacket pocket. "Sure. I'll hold it for you, but if you're in any danger, why not let me come along and take care of you?"

The girl shook her head. "That would make it only worse. They would know I suspect them," she said. "That would be like signing my own death warrant." She caught him by the arm. "You will keep that for twenty-four hours?" she pleaded.

He nodded. "What then?"

"I'll meet you here tomorrow night at ten o'clock." The eyes were beseeching. "You will not fail me?" Suddenly the girl stiffened. She perched her head on one side as though listening to something Liddell could not hear. "They're coming," she said in a frightened voice, and before he could stop her she had glided into the fog.

"Wait a minute. I want to talk to you," Johnny called after her. He tried to follow, but her slim form had disappeared. He listened for signs of the noise that had frightened her. Then, with a shrug he gave it up.

Johnny Liddell wandered through the fog, then hit back to the Club Madrid. He leaned on the bar with an ease born of long experience and watched with a jaundiced eye as the bartender made wide, round damp circles with a wet rag. He downed the drink in front of him and poured another shot from a bottle with a cognac label.

He had just finished his second drink when a tall, lean individual in a dark blue suit took his place beside him.

"Harris, special agent of the F. B. I.," the man introduced himself in a low voice. He opened his hand to show F. B. I. identification against his palm. "We'd like to have a talk with you."

Johnny Liddell grunted. "What about?"

"You'll be told by the agent in charge," he was informed.

Johnny Liddell poured himself another drink, tossed it off. "And if I'm not in a talkative mood?" He wiped his mouth with the back of his hand.

The man in the dark suit grinned mirthlessly. "We'll have that talk, anyway."

Liddell tried to outstare the operative for a minute, then grinned. "Okay, chum," he said. "You talked me into it." He led the way toward the door, the man in the dark suit at his heel.

The agent in charge of the F. B. I. Field Office was a new one to Johnny. He showed no signs of knowing the private detective.

"We've information that you're in possession of papers that were stolen from a United States diplomatic pouch," his voice was low, each word clipped and precise.

Liddell looked from the agent in charge back to the man in the dark suit who had escorted him there. "What kind of a pipe dream is this?" he asked. "I'm Johnny Liddell. I've done a lot of work for and with your outfit. I don't get this pitch."

The agent in charge failed to be impressed. "We have some reason to believe that you are in possession of a small package containing these papers," he said. "If we are mistaken you are free to go with our apologies. At any rate you will not object to a search?"

"Of course not—" Liddell's hand started automatically for his jacket pocket, then froze as it encountered the square outline of the package. He pulled it out, then tossed it on the table. "Outside of this I can account for everything in my pockets," he added.

The agent in charge picked up the package, turned it over curiously. "And this?"

"I don't know," Johnny shrugged, pulled a battered cigarette from a paper package, stuck it in his mouth. "A girl stopped me tonight and asked me to hold it for her."

The edges of the F. B. I. man's thin lips twitched upwards. "And you don't know what's in it?" A note of disbelief colored the question.

Liddell pinched his long nose between his thumb and forefinger. "I haven't opened it, if that's what you mean. And the babe didn't have time to tell me what was in it."

"I see." The agent said it as if he didn't see but was willing to pass the matter by. "You understand, Mr. Liddell, that if this package happens to contain what we suspect it contains that you will be held?"

Johnny Liddell growled deep in his chest. "That's crazy," he said. "Why don't you check up on me? Call your Washington office. Call anybody who knows anything about this district. They'll vouch for me." He crushed the cigarette angrily in an ashtray. "Brad Baxter who used to run this outfit will tell you I'm okay."

The man behind the desk drummed his fingers on the desk pad. He stared at Liddell unblinkingly, then lifted a direct wire telephone from its cradle. He spoke into it in a low voice, seemed puzzled by what the instrument told him in return. After a moment he returned the phone to its hook.

"Apparently the home office is satisfied with your reputation, Liddell," he said. "It may be that there's been a mistake made. If so, I'll be the first to apologize. If not," he shrugged unpleasantly, "I'll be looking forward to seeing you again."

Johnny grabbed his hat from the end of the desk where it lay and jammed it down on his head. "You'll be seeing me again, all right," he promised ominously. "Only, next time I'll have somebody to introduce to you."

He could feel the G-man's eyes on his back as he stamped toward the door and slammed it after him. In his mind's eye he was recalling the face of the girl feature by feature and photographing it in his memory. He had an uncomfortable feeling that she wasn't going to keep her date for the following evening—but he was just as sure that he would be seeing her again. Soon.

JOHNNY Liddell watched disconsolately as Sally Herley, ace feature writer for the *Express*, elbowed her way through the crowd at the bar and carved herself a place alongside him.

"Hello, Sherlock," she greeted him. "Did you order me a rye and soda? Or do I have to beg?" She winked at the bartender as he pushed the drink over to her.

Johnny growled under his breath, dumped a handful of silver on the bar. "The way these barkeeps baby dames these days," he mourned. "Guess I'll have to take my business to McSorley's."

Sally nodded her head in mock seriousness. "Now I know it's a big favor he's getting ready to ask," she commented. "The more he raps women, the bigger the favor. Rationalization, I guess they call it." She kept her eyes averted from the private dick, took a deep sip of her drink. "Okay, Johnny. Spill."

Liddell grunted. "Wonderful institution, women," he said. "It takes a woman to get you into trouble and it takes another one to get you out of trouble."

The girl reached over, speared a cigarette from the pack on the bar in front of Johnny. "Uh-huh," she said. "Now suppose you cut the philosophy and tell me what you really want."

Liddell scratched a match across the top of the bar, held the light for the reporter. "What's the name of the guy on your paper that wrote those undercover articles a couple of months ago?"

"You mean Leigh Devon? The fellow who exposed the Falange secret society set-up?"

"That's the guy," Liddell nodded. "Didn't he have a stoolie in that outfit to get the dirt for him?"

The girl stared at the fine gray ash on the end of the cigarette, then dumped it floorward. "Yeah, but it would be worth the guy's life if it got out," she said. "He was a member in good standing of the society. Why?"

Johnny poured himself a jigger of cognac. "I want to meet him," he said.

The girl shook her head. "No can do, Johnny," she said. "Ask me something easy."

He drained his glass without looking up. "I got to meet him," he said in the same flat tone. "Something more important than his life is at stake—my reputation."

Sally grinned. "You're kidding?"

The private dick picked the girl's cigarette up from the edge of the bar where it perched precariously, took a deep drag. "If you can fix it, maybe I can fix it for you to scoop the town." He looked up into the girl's eyes. He knew by the sudden flash of interest that the fix was in.

Sally Herley masked her large eyes with thick lashes, then, "What kind of a story, Johnny?"

"The kind that any real newshound would give a right arm to run under his by-line," he assured her.

The girl picked up her cigarette, regarded the crimson stain left by her lipstick morosely. "Leigh Devon would be awful mad," she reflected. "It would have to be an awful good story."

Johnny Liddell shrugged. "Maybe I ought to dump it into Devon's lap, then," he said. "I just thought you'd like to pull something off."

Sally dropped the cigarette to the floor, ground it out with her toe. "You know—I really think you're rat enough to do it, too."

Liddell grinned and nodded. "Sure. What do you say?"

"You win, Sherlock," Sally Herley wrinkled her nose up into a grimace. "But it ain't gonna be easy. This guy is pretty skittish. You know they play rough with squealers when they catch up with them."

"Sure, sure," Liddell growled. "I don't care if they skin him and use his hide for a parlor rug—just as long as it happens after I get what I want to know."

The girl seemed convinced. "Okay, Johnny," she said. "I'll play. You be at Nick's Downtown Bar. Know the place?" He nodded. "Be there at eight tomorrow night. There's a phone booth in the rear of the joint, and right next to it a door. There'll be a guy waiting for you inside that little room."

NICK's Downtown Bar didn't get much of a night play. A bored bartender stood gossiping with a race track sport at the end of the bar while an overdressed blonde worked what appeared to be a very tired businessman at the other end.

Johnny Liddell glanced at the old-fashioned clock on the wall as he came in. It was exactly on the hour—what hour the clock failed to say. The hour hand had long since gone to its reward and so great was the reverence in which it had been held that it had never been replaced.

The private dick headed directly for the little door next to the phone booth. None of the occupants of Nick's Downtown Bar paid him a second glance. As he placed his hand on the door-knob, he let his other hand dip into his jacket pocket. The handle of the automatic felt cold to his touch.

As the door swung open, a dark man at a rickety table inside glanced up. The hollows in his cheeks combined with the poor lighting to give his face an almost Oriental cast. He fixed Liddell with an unwavering glare. The smallness of his pupils told their own story.

"This pew's taken, chum," he croaked. "Find yourself another roost." As though he had lost interest, his eyes slid off Johnny and resumed an unblinking contemplation of the table top.

Liddell stepped in and closed the door behind him. "I got a date with a friend," he said. "Name's Johnny Liddell."

The pinpoint pupils again focused on the private dick. "Who's the friend?" the frog-like voice croaked out again.

Johnny shrugged. "That's not important. Matter of fact I don't know his name and I don't want to." He stood above the thin man in the chair. "He's a friend of a guy named Leigh Devon, and he was going to do me a favor."

The man in the chair nodded. "Sit down." He watched without apparent interest as Liddell turned one of the unpainted chairs around and straddled it. "What can I do for you?"

Liddell reached for the button on the wall. "Drink?"

The thin man shook his head.

"On the junk, eh?" Johnny Liddell grunted. "I read someplace that that kind of coke and rum don't mix." He changed his mind about the button. "I'm looking for a girl."

The thin man stared unblinkingly. "That ain't my racket, mister," he said. "You must be looking for some other guy." He started to pull himself out of his chair, but Liddell halted him with a wave of his hand.

"A special girl," he said, "a girl you probably have bumped into in your—er—business connections. It's very important that I locate her."

"Describe her to me," the other man directed.

Liddell squinted ceilingward. In his mind's eye he was summoning a memory. "Let's see, now. She's about five-foot-four. Got a small round face, kind of pretty. Corn-colored hair that she wore long, blue eyes that look like she was born yesterday, and—"

"Daisy LeFevre," the thin man interrupted.

Johnny Liddell paused. "What'd you say?"

"Daisy LeFevre," the thin man repeated without a change of inflection. "She's been working with Antonini. What do you want to know about her?" His eyes showed no interest, seemed looking at something far in back of the private dick's head.

"Where can I find her?"

For the first time the other man's dead eyes seemed to flicker. With apparent difficulty they focused on Liddell's face. "It ain't healthy to go looking her up," he warned.

Liddell scowled. "When I want advice on my health I see my own doc. Don't let it worry you. Tell me where to find her, let me worry from there in."

The other man shrugged, rubbed the back of his hand across his mouth. "She shows at the Breakers down on Water Street every night at about ten—"

Johnny pulled himself out of the chair. "The Breakers, eh? What would a babe like that be doing in a flop-house like the Breakers?"

"You asked me, and I told you," the toneless voice countered. "Now I'll tell you something you didn't ask. Don't go near there; it mightn't be healthy."

Liddell walked toward the door. "You ought to put that to music and sing it. It might sound better."

The thin man shrugged. "I was only thinking about Antonini and that knife of his. He gets a lot of fun out of it—and he knows how to use it."

Johnny opened the door. "He's welcome to his fun," he flung back over his shoulder. "There's a lot of meat here—and no points. Only, he's got to come and get it."

He slammed the door behind him, stepped into the telephone booth. He dialed the number of the F. B. I. Field Office and scowled as the metallic click indicated that the number was being rung. Suddenly the ringing stopped, a voice cut in. "F. B. I. Field Office. Brewster, agent in charge, speaking."

He stuck his mouth close to the instrument. "This is Johnny Liddell."

"Who?" the metallic voice wanted to know.

"Liddell. The guy you were going to send in front of the firing squad last night. The male Mata Hari. Remember me?"

The voice on the other end seemed to lose interest. "Oh, yes, the private detective. What can I do for you, Liddell?"

Liddell swallowed an obvious, if impolite, retort. "I've dug up that girl for you, the one who gave me the package. You can pick her up at—"

"Oh, that," the F. B. I. man said. "Skip it. We owe you an apology. There was nothing incriminating in that package. Nothing at all."

Johnny Liddell felt the hairs on his neck beginning to rise. "You mean you don't want her for anything?"

"No," the voice on the other end of the wire informed him blandly. "It was all a mistake; I hope we didn't inconvenience you too much."

Johnny Liddell said three very impolite words, slammed the receiver on the hook. He stood for a moment in the dimness of the phone booth, then stamped toward the bar. The barkeep was still engrossed in conversation with his sole customer.

Liddell started to order a drink, then changed his mind. He headed for the door, found a cab, told the driver Club Madrid, and settled back in the cushions to really give himself over to some inspired swearing.

The Club Madrid was swirling with its usual man-made fog of smoke. Johnny Liddell made out the shape of Sally Herley at the far end of the bar. He wandered down, found a vacant barstool at her side, slid onto it.

"How'd you do, Sherlock?" the girl reporter wanted to know.

"Just ducky," Liddell growled, trying to catch the eye of the man behind the stick. He finally made the grade, ordered a cognac. "Turns out that the dame they wanted isn't wanted." He accepted the jigger of dark brown liquid, smelled it experimentally. "I don't get the pitch, but it sounds like people are playing games with me, and I don't like it."

Somewhere behind the bar, a telephone pealed.

Sally Herley took a sip from her drink, leaned an elbow on the bar. "You don't make sense. You know that, don't you?"

Liddell drained his glass, set it back on the bar. "Neither does anything else. First I—"

The bartender cut in. "It's a call for you, Johnny," he said.

"What's the matter? Move your office over here?"

Johnny scowled at him, pulled the receiver out of his hand. "Hello?" he barked into the mouthpiece.

A thin, undistinguishable voice answered him. "Hello, Liddell. This is a friend. You're interested in a blonde. If I was you, I'd find some other blonde to get interested in."

"Who is this?" Johnny Liddell roared. People all along the bar stopped with drinks halfway to their mouths to stare.

"This is a guy who's going to be one of your pallbearers if you keep getting interested in that particular blonde," the voice said. The warning was punctuated by the click of a receiver.

Liddell looked into the mouthpiece as though in that way he could see the face of his late caller. Then, handing the receiver back to the bartender, he told Sally sourly, "That does it." He indicated to the bartender a refill. "Those monkeys know where I'm going to be before I do."

"Who was it, Johnny?"

He shrugged. "Some guy who wants me to lay off a case I don't even know I'm on," he growled. "Only, I'm gonna find out awful fast. What time you got, Sally?"

The reporter consulted a tiny baguette watch on her wrist.

"According to this it's about nine-forty, but don't hold me to it. Why?"

Johnny Liddell swallowed his drink with a gulp, poured a fistful of silver on the bar. "I got a date at ten. I just remembered."

Sally Herley started to wiggle off her stool. "Wait for baby," she squealed. "Don't forget our bargain. I get the story."

"When there's a story, you get it," he promised. "Only, there's no story yet."

"Then where you going?" the girl asked suspiciously.

"The Breakers down on Water Street," Johnny Liddell told her. "Want to make something out of it? It's another case. A case you wouldn't be interested in—a guy who ran away from home. See?"

Sally Herley settled back on her barstool. "Oh," she said. She watched the private dick shoulder his way toward the door, but before he had reached it, she was already on her way to the telephone booth, fumbling in the mysterious depths of her voluminous handbag for a nickel.

THE Breakers was every bit as Liddell had remembered it to be. He sat at a corner table with a glass of foul-tasting beer in front of him and cursed himself for a gullible fool. The blonde girl wasn't going to show up here, he told himself. He could hardly reconcile her cool, blue-eyed blonde beauty with the squalor and noise of this waterfront tavern.

He glanced at the clock on the wall. It was almost ten-twenty, and there had been no sign of anybody but the usual run of waterfront rats and bedraggled, beer-soaked women in the place. He fumbled in his pocket for some change, and froze.

She was coming in the door.

She looked exactly as he remembered her in his mind's eye. She was even wearing the clothes she had worn that night he met her. She walked into the place, then with never a glance to either side, made her way to the staircase at the far side of the barroom. The fact that few patrons even gave her a second look was a dead giveaway that she was no stranger to the place. He waited until she had climbed the stairs and passed completely from sight. Then, dropping enough change on the table to pay for his drinks, he followed her.

The decrepit stairs creaked with each step, and every moment Liddell was expecting to be challenged. Yet, when he reached the top of the flight there was no one in sight. A row of closed doors, the Breakers' "private rooms," faced him. A thin sliver of light came from under the door of the third room from the stairs.

Johnny Liddell walked silently to the door, applied his ear. He could not distinguish the words, but at least two voices were audible. Suddenly, he felt the sharp jab of a gun muzzle in his back. He started to straighten up, then froze.

"Don't move, chum," a hard voice advised him. "I just as soon burn you down as not."

Liddell recognized the wisdom of the advice and made no attempt to straighten up. He felt the other man reach past him and push open the door.

"You can hear a lot better when the door's open, chum," the voice said.

Inside the room, the blonde and a tall, dark, sleek man stared at him in amazement.

"Where'd he come from, Rossi?" the sleek man growled.

"Listening at the door, Antonini," the unseen man with the gun told him. The gun was jammed deep into Liddell's ribs. "Inside, chum."

Johnny accepted the invitation, heard the door close behind him. The sleek man walked over to him.

"Who are you?" he wanted to know.

Liddell looked past him at the blonde girl. She made no attempt to avoid his glance. "I'm the world's prize sucker," he said.

The man addressed as Antonini pulled a long, wicked-looking knife from a specially constructed sheath. "I asked who you were, bud."

Before Johnny Liddell could answer, the blonde girl walked over. She placed her hand on Antonini's arm. "We don't have time, Antonini," she said. "Don't forget. Tonight's the big night. We mustn't fail."

ANTONINI looked regretfully at Johnny Liddell as he returned the knife to its sheath. "I got to go away, bud. But hang around until I get back. You and me could have some fun together. Don't go 'way."

"You mean I got a choice?" Johnny growled.

The dark man turned on his heel, walked back to the table, took a black Homburg and adjusted it at a rakish angle. "Get as fresh as you like, bud," he grinned, exposing the brown stumps of his teeth. "You fresh guys always scream the loudest."

The man holding the gun in Johnny Liddell's ribs was uninterested in the by-play. "What do I do with this fat lug, Antonini? Do you want him or don't you want him?"

The girl's crisp voice cut the gunman short. "Tie him up and toss him in the closet. Antonini and I are late as it is."

Liddell was thinking of an appropriate retort when the gun butt caught him behind the ear. He felt himself slipping toward the floor, then suddenly a dark chasm yawned and he hurtled into it.

What seemed hours later it was still dark, but he wasn't in any chasm. From the various smells that he could distinguish, he concluded he was in the closet the girl spoke of. His hands were tied tight enough behind his back to cause little pins and needles to run up and down his spine.

Then he heard it again, the voice that he thought was part of his dream. It was Sally Herley's voice, and she was calling his name. It seemed nearer. Johnny pounded on the closet door with the heel of his shoe. In the confined space it resounded like the crack of doom.

After a few seconds the closet door was thrown open. The sudden flood of light temporarily blinded him but he heard Sally Herley's voice.

"Johnny," she shrilled. "Are you all right, Johnny?"

Another familiar voice cut through the semi-fog. Brad Baxter, the former agent in charge of the F. B. I. office. "Sure he's all right, Sally," Baxter was saying. "He was hit on the head, wasn't he?"

In less than ten minutes, Johnny Liddell was sitting on a stool, ruefully massaging the tender spot behind his ear. He fixed the F. B. I. man with a baleful stare. "A fine time for you to show up," he growled. "Why weren't you around the other night when that Brewster guy who took your place practically accused me of being a spy?"

Baxter grinned. "Never mind that, Johnny," he said. "What happened here tonight?"

Johnny Liddell grunted. "Never mind that, he says. Plenty happened here, tonight." He looked around the room. "What've you got to drink for a guy on the verge of a collapse?"

"Water," Baxter told him.

"Thanks. I'll collapse someplace else." He glared at Sally. "What are you doing here, Newshawk?"

Sally Herley looked at the F. B. I. man for support. "Can you imagine that? I follow him and save his life and he's mad because I'm here."

Baxter cut her short. "What happened here tonight, Johnny?"

Johnny shook his head experimentally, then winced. "I walked in on this blonde babe and some guy named Antonini. They were in a hurry or he would have carved me up, I gather. Anyway, the babe said tonight was the big night, and she didn't look like she was on the verge of learning the facts of life."

Baxter caught the private dick's shoulder in a crushing grip. "You sure about that?" he asked.

"Sure I'm sure," Liddell grunted. "I can still hear."

Baxter signaled to the other two G-men who had stayed in the background and started for the door.

"Hey, wait a minute," Johnny protested. "Where you G-guys going?"

Baxter paused with his hand on the knob. "I've got a hunch that tonight we're going to lay our hands on the top guy in a spy ring."

Johnny Liddell weaved to the door after him. "In that case, you're not going without me. I own shares in this corporation, and I'm going to collect my dividends—personally."

THE big black sedan was parked inconspicuously in the shadow of a large warehouse. Inside it, Johnny Liddell, the F. B. I. man Baxter, and his two assistants watched the small ramshackle hut on the beach. Sally Herley sat passively on the front seat, scratching notes in her pad.

"What are we supposed to be doing?" Liddell wanted to know. "I thought we were going to knock off a couple of spies."

"We are," Baxter assured him. "We're—" He broke off, then pointed to the hut. A small American flag was being hoisted on a flagpole on the roof.

"Funny time to be raising a flag," Liddell grunted.

"That flag contains a secret aerial," Baxter explained. "This is what we've been waiting for. Let's go, men."

The doors of the black sedan were opened noiselessly and the three F. B. I. men led the way across the sand to the hut. Johnny followed with Sally Herley. At the side of the hut, Baxter raised his hand for silence, then listened. From somewhere came the regular beat of a wireless sender. Baxter gave the signal and the two G-men threw their shoulders against the door. It swung open with an anguished creak.

Inside the room, the man Liddell recognized as Antonini was sitting at a bench in front of a large radio. He was sending a message, his hand poised over the key. He froze at the sight of the gun in Baxter's hand. Then, like a flash, he went for his inside breast pocket.

Johnny Liddell had just a glimpse of the blonde girl as she

struck. The gun came down with a sharp blow that beat Antonini to his knees, then flat on his face. Without a word, the girl took his place at the radio and started sending.

Liddell caught Baxter's arm. "That's the dame," he said. "She's a spy. Don't let her send that story—" He started toward the bench, but the G-man restrained him.

The blonde girl continued to send, then finally laid down her earphones and disconnected the sender. She picked up the revolver with which she had beaten Antonini down and smashed the instrument.

"Is everybody nuts?" Johnny demanded. "I tell you the dame's dangerous. She's the one who—"

The blonde came over and caught Johnny Liddell's arm. "We all owe you an apology, Johnny," she smiled. "Don't we, chief?"

Baxter grinned. "We sure do."

Liddell sought out a chair and sank into it. "Now I know that sock on the head's affected me." He watched with mouth agape as the blonde lighted a cigarette and stuck it between his lips.

"I'm not a spy," she told him. "I'm Elsie Martin, a member of the U. S. Security Corps assigned to counterespionage. My job was to get Antonini." She indicated the still unconscious figure. "And I got him."

Johnny took several deep drags on the cigarette, filled the air with metal-blue smoke. "But why drag me into it?"

"I'm sorry about that, Johnny," the girl said seriously. "I had some awfully important stuff to get to headquarters, but I couldn't take a chance on bringing it in, so I passed it off on you. Then I notified Baxter and he sent a man out to pick you up—"

Baxter nodded. "Naturally, when they brought you in, I couldn't be there, so I let Brewster handle your case. If I was there, you would have insisted on knowing what was in the package, and we were more anxious to keep you out of the case than to get you into it."

"Then it was your office who tried to warn me off?"

"It wasn't a very good idea," Baxter admitted, "but we were so close to having it wrapped up that we didn't want anybody messing it."

Sally Herley looked up from her notes long enough to ask, "If you knew this Antonini was a spy, why didn't you just up and grab him?"

"It was more complicated than that, Sal," Baxter explained. "Antonini was the only one who knew the call letters to reach the Falange intelligence station. We had to give him a chance to reach them before we grabbed him. We let him contact the base, then Elsie took over and sent the message we wanted sent."

Liddell dropped his cigarette to the floor, crushed it with his foot.

The blonde girl laughed. "They don't have to draw you a blueprint, do they, Johnny?"

Johnny Liddell laughed ruefully. "Oh, I catch on fast. I'm a detective, remember?"

Sally Herley chuckled. She refused to stop chuckling even under Liddell's most baleful glare. "I just thought of a good lead for this yarn," she said. "*Johnny Liddell, famous detective, traps the F. B. I. in espionage plot!*"

FROM DETECTIVE WHO'S WHO

LIDDELL, Johnny, private investigator; b. N. Y. C., July 19, 1921; s. late John and late Ann (Carter) L.; attended pub. schs.; College, City of N. Y.; FBI police college; unmarried; feature writer, crime expert, *New York Dispatch*, 1930–36; licensed private detective, N. Y. 1936; Acme Agency, N. Y., 1936–1950. Principal cases chronicled by Frank Kane, *About Face* (Mystery House, 1947); *Green Light for Death* (Ives Washburn, 1949); *Slay Ride* (Ives Washburn, 1950); *The Dead Wait* (in preparation, Ives Washburn, 1951); numerous short stories, *Crack Detective*, etc. Manager and chief operative, Johnny Liddell, Private Investigations, 50 West 42nd Street, New York. Home: New York City.

*As the detective story moves closer to the suspense novel
and the tale of pure terror, it's inevitable that detectives
should arise whose sensitivity fits them to cope with nu-
ances of madness and evil as well as with the cold facts of
the laboratory. Meet Inspector Magruder . . . and one of
the most fascinating of modern murderers.*

INSPECTOR MAGRUDER IN

The Finger Man

BY JEROME & HAROLD PRINCE

SHARP FOCUS in the green, gray, blue, black, blinking, wide,
dull, staring irises of many eyes; long rows of spikes, parallel,
crowded, rust-veined, jutting from a block of wood; and a man's
naked foot, trousers rolled, hovering over the spikes, up, down,
foot on the spikes, muscles bulging, balanced on the spikes, skin,
taut, whole, and the other foot, naked, too, over the spikes, down
hard on the spikes, muscles, beating, moving, on the spikes, walking, one foot after another, across the board, skin unbroken—
and a leap, the thud of heels on thick carpet, palms cracking
against palms, tinkling of ice in tall glasses, woman-murmurs,
deeper grunts of praise . . . and then a man's cheek, and the
point of a hatpin, dancing, moving, steel-gray, swiftly, deep into
the cheek, creasing the skin, point of the hatpin, bloodless, glint-
ing high on the opposite side of his face; and the women, crowding about him (pin withdrawn, skin unbroken), chattering, ap-
plauding, men, dinner-jacketed, voices louder than necessary,

From *Ellery Queen's Mystery Magazine*, Jan., 1950. Copyright 1944 by The
American Mercury, Inc. Reprinted with the permission of the authors and *Ellery
Queen's Mystery Magazine*.

taking his hand, patting him on the back, and he, flushed, grinning, answering questions, Jane saying to him, how wonderful it
was, what a pity it was over, was it really over, was it, he, nodding,
saying yes, regretfully yes, Jane coaxing, please, Don, please the
others coaxing, come on, Gallegher, be a sport, he, shaking his
head, Jane, wheedling, please, the others urging, please; all right,
but you must be quiet—this is going to be hypnosis and you
must be quiet; they, forming a circle around him now, seated,
standing, leaning, backs against the bar, an empty armchair beside him, he, glancing from face to face, asking for a volunteer,
they, smiling, no, don't count on us, he, trying again, shrugging,
turning to Jane, I can't go on without   will I do? A
little man, standing head as high as Gallegher's shoulder, dinner
jacket hanging badly, face, clean-shaven, few angles, and Jane,
oh-ing feminine delight (you just watch this, her eyes were telling her guests), whispering, wonderful, wonderful; and the little
man, head back, now, against the soft cushion of the chair, lights
dimming about him, Gallegher, eyes, a pencil, in front of him, a
long thin pencil, growing longer, and the room, trembling, gray
as in dreams, and then Gallegher, pointing to where the Dali
hung over solid wall, saying, you see that doorway, go through
that doorway, and, they, opening the circle for him, grinning, the
little man walking, rapidly, toward the wall, the picture toppling,
his body pushing against the wall, pushing again, grins into
laughter, pushing again, and Gallegher, finally calling him off,
directing him back to the center of the room, saying, shine Robinson's shoes, and the little man, kneeling in front of the seated
Robinson, whipping his handkerchief over Robinson's shoe tips,
Robinson, speech liquor-thick, deriding, the others, crowding
about, giggling, he, wiping the sides of the shoes, straightening
the shoelaces, and Gallegher, beside him now, snapping his fingers, saying incisively, that will be all   the little man,
staring, shaking away bewilderment, Robinson above him, explaining, youth-cruel, handkerchief into a ball, falling to the
floor, laughter surrounding him, Robinson, fumbling in his pockets, spraying the carpet with copper coins, the laughter rising, he,
on his feet, nostrils dilating, pudgy hands clenched into fists,

stepping toward Robinson, in front of him: Robinson, standing; and the little man, pushing his way out of the group, walking to the bar, watching, the little man asking for a drink, Jane whispering earnestly to Robinson, the young man, nodding, Jane saying, good boy, Robinson toddling to the bar, slinging one arm over the little man's shoulder, saying, all in fun, can't you take a joke, swallowing a Manhattan, another, the little man, edging away, Robinson following him, repeating blurred apologies, the little man, trying to smile, finally saying, all right, forget it, and Robinson, happy, clapping him on the back, shouting for a dozen more rounds all on one tray, and they, breaking into small groups, talking, Jane at the piano, the younger set around her, Gallegher at the bar, lecturing informally, Jane beginning to play jazz, the little man walking away from the bar, a couple dancing, Jane beating it out with her left hand, they, crowding about the piano, deep gut-bucket blues, *oh sweet má-má now don't you let me dów-aún*, Harlem rhythm jumping, *oh sweet má-má now don't you let me*   at the bar, Robinson had collapsed.

The room in motion, discords on the piano, Gallegher holding Robinson's head, the doctor elbowing his way through, stethoscope over the heart, eyelids bent back, Jane, saying, hushed, is he dead, the doctor, bending closely over the body, searching for a wound, Jane: is he dead, the doctor, looking up, puzzled, Gallegher, saying, he's not dead—but he must go to a hospital, the doctor, nodding, walking to the phone, Jane, following, grabbing him by the arm, saying, then what's wrong with him—what's happened, the doctor, stopping, uneasy, hesitating for a moment, beginning to say

Gallegher said, "He had too much to drink. Isn't that so, Doctor?"

The doctor looked at Gallegher. He said,
"Yes."

THEN, Gallegher, outside, Central Park opposite, green-black, walking, north, into the Seventies, and the little man, waiting, walking beside him now, saying,
"I'm glad you know."

Spray-gun rain, cold, halos around the lamp-posts,

"My name is Hoffman," the little man said. "You'd be sur-prised how much I had to pay to get in."

Two steps to Gallegher's one, half a block in silence, then, popping, like a broken blown-up paper bag,

"I had to see you."

Cross-town traffic bending into the Avenue, red light blinking into green, tires screeching on the asphalt; softly, Hoffman,

"I need your help."

An old two-decker bustled by like a frightened old lady. Gal-legher nodded. Then the Frick Museum was beside, soon behind them, and Hoffman was talking, words leap-frogging at first, then freely, night-phrases, jagged, Gallegher, looking straight ahead of him, saying little, above them: the white-on-black edge of a right angle sign, jutting: E. 83 ST., and Gallegher, stopping, leaning on his cane, listening, cars passing like the ticks of a clock,

"I live here," Gallegher said. Then slowly, "I'm sorry . . . really. I can't help you."

The little man said, "I don't understand. You've helped others."

Gallegher said, "Oh, I see. You've read my books."

"Over and over. That's why— There's no one else."

Gallegher said, "I can give you some advice . . . if you want it. Why don't you see a psychiatrist?"

"Psychiatrist? I told you I've tried everything. I went. It was like tonight in the chair. He said I talked. A lot, he said. I don't know. I don't want to go back."

Gallegher shrugged. He held out his hand.

"There's nothing I can do, believe me." Then, kindly, "Good night."

Hoffman took his hand.

"Good night."

The little man stood where he was, alone, his face puckering, baby-fashion, spasms moving his tightened lips, drops of mois-ture forming in the corners of his eyes. He blew his nose. Then he moved away from the apartment house, into a side street: a candy store at the corner, a telephone booth; then out into the

street again, dimout dark, collar up against the wind, face turned
away from the Avenue, elevator-heels clicking, his shadow, in
front of him, growing longer, reaching out for the darkness, light
from the Avenue snake-slithering down the center of the gutter,
the sound of leather on concrete, sharp and rhythmic, growing
fainter . . . then the little man's rain-soaked shoes beating on a
stone step, doorbell shrilling, a crack widening in the doorway,
behind it: auburn hair tumbling, a young girl's throat; Sam! and
light splashing on the sidewalk, rain pecking at the closing door,
his coat, flung on a table, hat, spinning to rest beside it, and she,
two steps above the living room, looking down at him from the
foyer, head in his hands, panting,

"Sam, what on earth are you doing here at this hour?"

He said, "Where's Dave? I'm in pain—the whole left side of
my face. Where's Dave?"

She said, "Dave had to go to the lab. Somebody called." Then,
"You are sick," crossing over to him. "You're green."

He said, "Who called?"

"A patient. Dave never tells me who. He should be home
soon." She looked at the clock. "He should be home now. I
called there a half hour ago. Nobody answered. He must be on
his way." She said, "I'm jittery."

She lit a cigarette, threw her head back, inhaled. Then she
squashed the cigarette. "Wait a minute." She left the room, returned with a wet washrag. She bent over him, placing the rag on
his forehead. He could feel the edge of her dressing gown brushing against his cheek.

He breathed, "Bernice . . ."

"Do you feel any better?"

"Bernice . . . you're lovely."

She burlesqued her surprise, saying, "At your age." She lit another cigarette, saw it tremble, ground it out. The door was behind, Hoffman in front of her. She turned her head swiftly. The
door was still closed. Hoffman was leaning forward. The washrag
was lying on an end table beside him. His forehead glistened.

Hoffman said, "I'm not so old. Forty-three isn't so old."

She tapped a cigarette package. It was empty. She tossed it aside. The clock was electric; it was never wrong.

Hoffman said, "I know what you think of me, Bernice. All of you think the same. Bernice . . . I'm not what I seem."

She was listening for the sound of an automobile's brakes, or for hurried footsteps.

"Bernice . . . suppose, suppose that I had power, so powerful that I could—"

She shrilled, "Don't be silly."

His mouth moved awkwardly; then he sank back in his chair, his eyes lowered. She was on her feet, walking (the door, the clock, the clock, the door), pulling up the window blind, letting it sag, slowly. Up the street, she could hear a couple quarreling. There was no other noise.

She said, "I'm sorry, Sam. But you can be such an ass at times. Oh, my God, you're green again."

He looked at, then he looked away from, her. She thought: He's pouting—Dave will put him out—he'll thank Dave for putting him out. It was ten after one. She looked again. It was ten after one. She picked up the phone. She heard the mechanism buzz a dozen times at the other end of the wire before she hung up. The couple up the street were quiet. Hoffman was sitting stiffly, his head still averted, saying nothing. She drummed on the window sill with her fingers. She said,

"Oh, my God, Sam. I didn't mean to hurt your feelings. Can't you talk?"

He refused to look at her. She snapped the radio on, viciously. The tubes began to warm, humming. The telephone bell screamed. Hoffman was standing. Bernice ran past him. The receiver was against her ear.

The radio said, "Do you know, I used to be a fighter in a candy store."

Bernice said, "Yes. This is Mrs. David Simon. What is it?"

The radio was amazed. "A fighter in a candy store?"

Bernice said, "This is Mrs. David Simon. What is it? Please."

"Yeah, yeah," the radio answered. "I used to box candy."

Bernice let the phone slip back in its cradle. There was no blood left in her face. Her lips were moving, but she made no sound. *Dave's dead,* she was trying to say.

Hoffman had begun to walk up the steps to the foyer. The muscles around his mouth were twitching.

HOFFMAN, the room like a pan shot: French windows opening on a terrace, books from ceiling to floor, a map in a black glass frame, medieval distortions, on the mantelpiece: two ivory lions, between them a shelf of books, author: GALLEGHER, GAL-LEGHER, GALLEGHER, and below, in front of the fireplace, behind a desk, rubber tip of a pencil tapping, Gallegher, head thrown back, Hoffman forgotten, the words of the review of his latest book sweeping through his brain, *Out of this great seminal period of American life, with the realities of a mature scientific and industrial epoch giving the lie to those starry-eyed Utopians of the turn of the century, there emerges a man whose exuberant romanticism may well be the expression of a new decade. In his own lifetime, still young, he has already become a legend—the incomparable Gallegher, heir to the traditions of Mungo Park, Richard Burton, and Marco Polo. In a gay prose, noted for Gal-*legher, the review still in his hand, rising abruptly, Hoffman wanting to speak, Gallegher, gesturing for a moment's time, lean-ing against the terrace doors, frowning, *It is to be feared that Gallegher, like Saltus or Bierce or Poe before him, works too often with the ersatz; but unlike the others, he has not the refuge of fiction or antique biography to sustain him. To him, the esoteric and the occult have always been the factual concomi-tants of strange places and alien shores; but the war has brought disenchantment: ancient Gods vanish and the medicine man wears a silk hat when the Marines land with Coca-Cola and the Saturday Evening Post. Later, one will be forced to decide that behind the brilliant façade of his style, the bric-a-brac of preten-tious folklore and old wives' tales, there is little except a bibulous and brooding imagination. What happens—and what does not happen—in the Moluccas, happens—or does not happen—in Times Square.* Gallegher, flushing, suddenly impatient, testily,

"Look here, Hoffman, there are a few points that need clarification. I'm not a witch doctor. What you saw at the party were tricks anybody can learn. I'd like to believe you—"

Hoffman said, "There was another last night."

The light behind him, full on Hoffman's face, Hoffman, eyes dog-soft, quietly,

"Before the party, I had dinner with an old friend. He's a doctor. Dave Simon?" Gallegher shaking his head, no. "He joked about my wanting to see you. I can't—I couldn't stand that. We quarreled. I knew what it would mean. I thought maybe you would help—then you left me—I went to his home. I wanted to apologize. I wanted to do something. I thought maybe I could stop it."

Gallegher, behind the desk again, the morning papers in front of him, sheets turning rapidly,

"I couldn't."

Stopping, reading, marking the outline of a column in blue pencil, setting the paper aside, picking up another, searching, Hoffman,

"His laboratory blew up. He was in it. . . . Have you found it there, too?"

Gallegher nodding, making a note, nodding yes, Hoffman,

"Please cure me."

Looking up, Gallegher, Hoffman, no expression on their faces, Hoffman, Gallegher; then, carefully, like drops from a burette,

"You knew all the while, Mr. Gallegher. Maybe you were afraid to admit it, even to yourself, but I have that power. It doesn't matter who he is, or what he does to me—if he angers me, my anger brings death . . . and he doesn't wait long for it to come," right hand spanning the side of his face, eyes closed, head swaying softly, almost to himself, "I know five have died already. God only knows how many more there were. . . . It isn't suicide, Mr. Gallegher—you know it isn't accident. That's only the way it happens. I get so angry, I can't talk . . . or see . . . everything is all upside-down. And then my power kills them."

After a while, Gallegher said, "Come back tomorrow. At four."

HOFFMAN returned—to find Gallegher almost boyish in his enthusiasm. (There was a chance—he may have found it, here, after all, on his own doorstep, murder, undiscoverable, following hard on Hoffman's anger, done by the unseen.) And for the next few days Hoffman was treated in a manner calculated to break down his mental barriers; and he responded, talking freely, while Gallegher, informal, jotted down what he was told in a queer admixture of abbreviations and shorthand. We must get the facts first, Gallegher had said; but as the days passed and his notebook filled, he realized that Hoffman could do no more than merely embellish the story he had told him that night after the party; and he could see in Hoffman's eyes the beginnings of a lack of confidence, and the doubt that this method of catharsis by suggestion would ever cure him. Gallagher said then: We can't cure yet, but we can prevent. Let's try to remove the source of irritation. Quit your business for a while, stay home, read light books, stay away from people—above all, stay away from crowds. When you come here each day, since you can't drive, take a taxi. . . . Hoffman smiled at that, promised, and came back to sessions that were beginning to grow empty, until he suggested to Gallegher that, perhaps, others had been able, in some lesser measure, to duplicate his power consciously, and that if he knew their willful techniques, he could put his finger on his own unconscious parallel actions, and, knowing them, eliminate them—and Gallegher accepted with alacrity. After that—and a week had already passed—the daily conferences became lectures, with Gallegher picking from his memory all the cases of the power of the will over matter, and Hoffman, humble, attentive, finding no analogies, leaving each night at six, unsatisfied, but confident that tomorrow must bring an end to it all.

By the close of the third week, Gallegher's knowledge had approached the exhaustion point, and he was irritable from the dysphoria that comes with the unfulfillment of half-formulated hopes. Several times that day, he was on the verge of telling Hoffman that he had never really known of a case that could not be explained naturally, but instead he repeated what they had talked about yesterday and the day before; and when the stuttering session was over, Hoffman said thanks and good-by, obsequious as always, and still hopeful.

It was just after six, Gallegher saw, and there was an appointment at six-thirty that he was eager to keep. He hurried downstairs, but neither he nor the doorman could find an empty cab. He decided against telephoning a garage, and walked east toward Lexington Avenue, then a few blocks north to the subway: kiosk, hot tunnel smell, a newsboy shouting, voice dwarf-thin, office girls, sweaty, complaining, whining sounds, jostling Gallegher, down the stairs, a small landing, at right angles to it: another flight of stairs, steep, below him: the station, people massed, two long lines converging on a booth, nickels spewed from a glass arch, turnstiles clicking, crowd-murmur, Gallegher, stopping, finding a coin, waiting on the platform   steel noises pouring from the tunnel, louder, a briefcase, insect-face of the rushing train, the crowd, mass-moving toward the edge of the platform, a briefcase, swinging, dropping, legs against it, an old man, stumbling, many eyes: dull then wide, many mouths: gaping, the old man falling, scream, screams, a subway guard catching the old man, train at rest, crowd funneling toward the doors, the guard, picking up the briefcase, flinging it at a man entering the train, shouting, redfaced, *You damn fool, you're in such a hurry to get in, you might have killed somebody,* doors snapping shut, train shuddering, Gallegher, looking down from the landing: a little man in the train, face squeezed against a glass window, the train moving slowly,

Gallegher shouted.   moving faster,

Gallegher waved and shouted.   the little man, making no sign, the train, a blur of yellow and black, a blast of wind, the crowd-murmur swelling, empty tracks.

Gallegher turned and walked up the steps to the street. Apparently, Hoffman had not seen him. . . .

NEAR by, Gallegher found a small French restaurant. He telephoned Inspector Magruder. Magruder said he'd have the information for him by tomorrow afternoon, would that be soon enough? ·Gallegher said, yes, thanks, then ordered a bottle of Chablis and cold duck. He drank a good deal of the wine, but ate so little that the proprietor, mock-irate, stood over him, scolding. Gallegher made the necessary remarks, then left, walking across Central Park, then down through the Mall. At Fifty-ninth and Eighth, he remembered the two tickets in his pocket: MADISON SQUARE GARDEN, HOCKEY, SIDE ARENA, BOX. He decided to use one.

When he took his seat, the game had already started. Across the ice, two players were throwing punches at each other, hitting the air, looking clumsy. Gallegher thought: *He'll want to kill me now.* . . . The puck was in play again; no pattern: blues, reds, yellows, streaking up and down the ice. . . . *I think he saw me. It's not without its irony: after all these years on the other side of the world, writing about it, never truly believing, wanting to, perhaps hoping, and now, here, home, in New York.* . . . The tall player wearing number seven took a short pass, body-shifted, slipped by his guard and drove hard for the goal. . . . *Stay away from crowds, Hoffman, I told him, above all stay away from crowds. I'll do that, Mr. Gallegher. But if he had gone tonight— rush hour, the Eighty-sixth Street station—he must have gone other nights. Mr. Gallegher, you've written how out in the East they make their minds control things, won't you tell me how it's done? The subway—people, tired, unhappy, anger flaring easily. He didn't come to me to be cured.* . . . Skates flinging sprays of snow, players tangling on the ice, a red light over the cage flashing, and a woman next to him, bobbing up and down, shouting, "Oh, you Billy-Boy! Oh, you wonderful man!" . . . *He came to me to learn how to use his power. He must know I know—other nights at six* . . . The crowd was on its feet. . . . *The subway is his proving ground.* . . . Then he saw the puck coming. He put his hand to his face. When he took it away, it was covered with blood.

Across the street to the Polyclinic, surgery, white gauze swathing his head, pulse: one hundred and thirty, hypodermic: barbital derivative, deep sleep; then home, noon, behind his desk, refusing to move, waiting, leaving his food untouched, forbidding the maid to bring in knives or forks, not bathing, the hour hand, slow, no one in to see him, his mind made up, no telephone calls answered, the maid, always at least three feet from him, he, watching the clock, having the maid remove the letter opener, the fountain pens; and, at four, Hoffman, coming across the room, swaggering, one elbow leaning on the desk, gay,

"I'm sorry to hear about your," pausing melodrama-fashion, "accident."

Gallegher saying nothing,

"Look here, Gallegher," Hoffman, "we're getting nowhere, and to me, time is money. You're not helping me, so I'm going to tell you what you're going to do. You've got publishers, you've got outlets—you're going to write me up. They'll read about me all over the world and—who knows?—maybe somebody will be able to help."

Gallegher breathing hard,

"No."

Hoffman, smiling indulgently, sitting on the desk, feet dangling,

"Why not?"

"You're a liar."

Color rising in Hoffman's face, draining, Hoffman, moving off the desk, looking down at Gallegher, a row of sweat-drops on Hoffman's forehead, Hoffman, apologetic,

"I'm sorry to have troubled you."

Leaving, turning,

"Send me a bill—I'll pay you more than you ask."

Hoffman gone, and Gallegher, leaning back in his chair, not believing it, then grinning, bubbling over, saying to the long-chinned man who had just come in,

"It's the damndest thing. All I wanted to do was bring it to a head—have it out with him face to face—and he collapsed like a pricked balloon. It was a hoax all the time."

The man, gesturing his bewilderment, saying,

"I wouldn't know. You, Gallegher? I'm Kuchatsky," badge flashing, "Homicide. Inspector Magruder sent me up with some info for you."

"Oh, yes. . . . I don't need it now," the brandy bottle in his hand, breaking the seal, "Say thanks to Magruder anyway," picking the two glasses from the desk top. "Have a drink with me," and Kuchatsky pleased, accepting, then remembering, saying doubtfully,

"But the chief isn't going to be happy. If he says do something —Well, you know the chief."

And Gallegher, amused, brown liquid gurgling, handing Kuchatsky a glass, pouring for himself, Gallegher,

"I'll listen."

Kuchatsky sipping, then putting down his glass hurriedly, a dirty-brown notebook, tiny, lost in his wrestler-hand, partially reading,

"In the last three weeks, there were sixty-three deaths by suicide or accident in the metropolitan area."

Gallegher, lifting his glass, inhaling the bouquet, placid, Kuchatsky,

"Of these sixty-three, one—a sixteen-year-old girl—died on the Eighty-sixth Street subway station at six-fifteen P.M. two weeks ago," tumbler to Gallegher's lips, tilting, "and nine more of them —three men and six women—used the Eighty-sixth Street subway station without fail every week-day between the hours of six and seven P.M. before their deaths."

Suddenly, the brandy odor seemed strange. The glass slipped from Gallegher's fingers. A wet spot was growing on the rug.

"That's a hell of a thing," said Kuchatsky, "wasting good liquor."

Gallegher's rooms, Gallegher, Magruder, alone, Magruder, tobacco pouch, pipe bowl scooping within it, tip of his nail, wooden match flaring, lighting his pipe slowly.

"Do you know Freudenberger?" he asked.

Gallegher lifted his eyes and said, "Yes, well. He's one of the old guard psychoanalysts—studied with Freud under Charcot. He's one of the few practitioners in this country who still uses hypnosis as a therapeutic."

Magruder nodded, handed Gallegher a sheaf of typewritten paper stapled together.

Magruder said, "He treated Hoffman—just once. What you're reading is a transcript of Hoffman's monologue under his hypnosis."

Gallegher read it. When he had finished, he said,

"It's just what he told me."

Magruder said, "Yes, I know." Then: "I asked Freudenberger what he thought of it. He told me it might mean one of many things, or all of them—a strong mother fixation, frustrations, an abnormal yearning for power—recognition. He said that the four deaths mentioned in the manuscript were probably wish-fulfillments without any true factual basis. We traced back. Freudenberger was wrong."

There were blue dabs under Gallegher's eyes. He looked like a man who hadn't slept for a long time, and who knew he wouldn't sleep for a long time again.

"When Hoffman was seven," Magruder said, "his nurse—whom he probably had reason to hate—fell down a flight of stairs and broke her neck. He was found kicking the corpse in the face. His father had him sent to a private sanitarium for observation. The sanitarium was located here in New York. There was a girl inmate, Alice—the Alice of the manuscript—who hazed Hoffman. She was later found dead in a sewer. She had been playing with Hoffman and some other children in a restricted street opposite the sanitarium and had fallen down an open manhole. The house physicians, though, found no traces of homicidal mania, and when his father died, he was released in his mother's care. She took care of him, good care of him—and then she died three years ago. He almost immediately proposed marriage to his secretary—that's the Edith. She refused and was found one morning at the bottom of a staircase in his office building. The fall had broken her neck—just as it had his nurse's."

Magruder saw the bones white under Gallegher's cheeks. He

mixed a drink. He watched Gallegher gulp it down. Then he said, "He was fond of this Nelson he mentions. Nelson was his junior partner. He blackmailed Hoffman for some minor infraction of the moral code. Nelson committed suicide by leaping from the terrace of Hoffman's penthouse apartment. Then, with Nelson and Edith dead, he turned his affections to Bernice Simon. Bernice Simon was married. You know what happened to her husband. And, by the by—Robinson? The drunk at the party?" Gallegher nodded. "He was poisoned. They found acetone and traces of carbon tetrachloride. It seems he swallowed some cleaning fluid. That doctor who treated him first told me he thought so, but that you browbeat him. Why did you do that?"

Without tone, "I just thought he was drunk."

Magruder said, "So Hoffman was telling the truth. We know definitely of five deaths by accident or suicide that followed quarrels with him. But we've found no physical evidence at all that connects Hoffman with the commisson of any of these deaths."

Gallegher snapped, "How could you expect to? The power he has doesn't leave fingerprints."

Magruder sucked on his pipe. He said slowly,

"I've been on the force for thirty years. I've seen queerer things. I'm not disagreeing, but it strikes me—doesn't it strike you—that there are a few aspects of this affair that don't quite mesh with your ideas? Here's what I mean: I think of the supernatural as something infallible. Yet this power of his doesn't always work. Robinson is still alive. So is that old man you saw stumble on the subway station. So are you—and I think he'd like to see you dead."

Gallegher's voice was tired. "I explained all that. He hasn't full control of his power. At first, it was entirely unconscious. He came to me to learn how to use it."

Magruder said, "You're probably quite right. But there *is* another way of looking at it. That night you saw him in the subway, he saw you. He also saw the papers the next morning. He knew that you would think he had directed that wild puck to hit you, and that you were about to be murdered by his power.

So he came—and offered you a bargain. What he said, in essence, was this: give me publicity and I'll give you back your life. Being hit by a puck was a dramatic accident, but if you had slipped on a banana peel and he had known about it, he would have behaved the same way. What he was after all the time was recognition, some type of fame at any cost—and the power that comes with it. Because of your position in the literary world, you could give him that—and with a certain amount of dignity: he wouldn't be a freak. Remember—under hypnosis, he said he flew over tall buildings. Freudenberger pointed out to me that that's a well-known dream symbol for the desire for power. It all fits together."

Gallegher rubbed his temples, his eyes closing. Then he looked at Magruder. He said, meaning: please don't treat me like a child, "You know it doesn't. Because he came to me to learn, ten people who used the Eighty-sixth Street subway station died. Magruder, that wasn't coincidence."

"You're right. It couldn't be coincidence. We know that Hoffman used that subway every night at six after he left you. There may have been quarrels—we think so; we can't be sure. But there is a possibility that what happened in the subway had nothing to do with his power. . . . No, Gallegher, I'm not trying to kid you. Listen to me: After you had been hit by the puck, he visited you. You had decided to force the issue, insult him, and battle for your life by matching your will against his then and there. I can understand that, knowing your background—your nerves were shot, you'd been hurt. You did insult him. You called him a liar. He folded. The word 'liar' frightened him. Was that because he realized you knew he had been using the subway? That couldn't be the lie. If I'm right, he was capitalizing on that very knowledge of yours to force you to terms. He had been lying all along about something else, and he thought you had discovered it—something so important that he was willing to give up his plans for obtaining publicity through you, and to offer you more money than you asked for—in order to keep it quiet."

Gallegher shook his head. He said hopelessly, "What could he have been lying about?"

Magruder said, "I don't know—except that it may have been

connected with his activities in the subway and elsewhere. He's being tailed. Kuchatsky is watching his apartment through binoculars. We're not making too much progress. But if I'm right about his psychopathic desire for publicity, I'll be able to find out." He paused. Then: "I know how you feel about this, Gallegher, but you'll have to co-operate for your own good. We'll give you all the protection necessary, but do this for me: Call Hoffman, apologize, be nice to him. Tell him you'd like him to meet a friend of yours. Stress this: that this friend is a great authority on the occult, with wide influence, and a wider audience. Ask for an appointment at his penthouse."

Gallegher's face went stiff and blank. After a while, he said, "All right—as long as I'm free of fear again."

A PENTHOUSE terrace, the street twenty stories below it, one side: masonry, windows, a door swinging open; three sides, around the edge of the terrace: bamboo sticks, close together, neck high, rooted in concrete, perennials, green, weaving around, between them, through the door: Gallegher, a tall man beside him, blue serge suit, string of a polka dot tie hanging from a shapeless white collar, hair, chemical-black, close-cropped as a cinema Prussian's, features, good-looking, hard-boiled fashion, intelligent; and Gallegher acknowledging the welcome,

"This is my friend who is a student of the occult. Mr. Hoffman —Mr. Magruder—Mr. Magruder—Mr. Hoffman."

Hands stretched, pressed, and Gallegher, leaving them, nerve-gnawed facial muscles relaxing, March wind, soft, gusts from the Hudson, yards away from him: standing, Hoffman, Magruder, talking,

"Mr. Hoffman just told me a very interesting story. It's about a man who has a power which brings death to whoever angers him. You know, Gallegher," meaning: why did you waste my time bringing me here, "I don't put much stock in that sort of thing any more."

Hoffman, nostrils thin, sucking his lower lip, sitting not far from Gallegher now, looking up at Magruder, eyes frosting, Magruder, turning to Hoffman, glib,

"A few months ago, I went up to a small town in Maine to

investigate a series of so-called devil deaths at the local inn. The town was in a panic—until the police chemist discovered that the innkeeper was putting roach paste in the soup," laughing, businessman fashion, loud, hollow, and Hoffman, face wooden, staring coldly in front of him, Magruder,

"Oh, say, Hoffman, I didn't mean to hurt your feelings. It's only that after all these years, I'm a bit disillusioned. I'll tell you something, though—I think more of a murderer than I do of a man with supernatural powers. I think it's a finer thing to be a criminal genius *yourself* than merely to be the instrument of something beyond you."

Hoffman, eyes like white buttons, then narrow as a camera slit, body taut as the hair of a bomb sight,

"Do you?"

"I'm writing a book about it."

Surging to his feet, eyes racing back and forth over Magruder's face, smile: a rictus, then vanishing, suddenly calm,

"I know a man—he's not a criminal, Mr. Magruder, mind you that, he's not a criminal—but I think you would appreciate his life's work."

Walking slowly up and down, then turning to Magruder, Magruder, absorbed, Gallegher watching Hoffman, Hoffman, so slowly that Gallegher counted watch-ticks between the words,

"This man was told when he was a child," to Magruder, "told by God," Magruder, nodding, understanding, pace accelerating now, "that he was to single out the transgressors for Divine judgment."

Hoffman waiting, Gallegher shifting his eyes, Magruder nodding, go ahead, go ahead, Hoffman, excitement tumbling the words,

"But God said to him: you're human, you can make mistakes. Prepare the execution. *I'll* accept or reject. *I'll* be the executioner —not you."

Gestures frenetic now, eyes glowing, Magruder, Gallegher, Magruder saying softly,

"I'm sorry, I don't understand."

And Hoffman, laughing, explosive, one syllable,

"Oh, it's simple and it's wonderful. Suppose this man knew of

an evil woman. Before she walked down a flight of stairs, he
would place a small toy on the top of the stairs—a roller skate, a
toy elephant on wheels. If God didn't want her, she would see
the toy. If he wanted her, she would fall and break her neck. . . .
I know that a child was once marked by him—oh, long ago. She
was playing blind man's bluff in the street with her hand over
her eyes. He removed the manhole cover. God accepted her," face
close to Magruder's, words machine-gunned, whispering, "He
opened the Bunsen burners in a doctor's laboratory. God wanted
this doctor. The doctor came into the laboratory with a lighted
cigar in his hand."

Eyes like aircraft flares,

"He found evil where people congregate: theaters, ball parks,
museums—but he liked the subway best of all. He dropped his
briefcase on the platform once. She stumbled. The train cut her
head off, right at the base of the neck. Sometimes there were
difficulties: he had to follow the men and women he marked in
the subway. There was a carpenter. He followed him to his shop,
loosened the head of his hammer. God wanted him—and the
hammer-head struck him in the temple. . . . Tomorrow perhaps, or the next day, he'll go to a night club he knows. He'll
drop a match in the fireproof decorations. If God accepts—"
a voice uncertain, walking more slowly, standing still, "He put
cleaning fluid in a cocktail at the bar. The man drank it—but he
didn't die. The other man smelled the bitter almonds over the
brandy," Hoffman, suddenly pale, "God rejects, too," sitting,
his body an empty sack, shivering, biting the underside of his
index finger, his chin quivering like an infant's,

"But nobody would admire that man. They'd call it murder.
Nobody would understand that man."

Magruder saying,

"I would. I'd like to meet him."

And Gallegher, bitterly,

"A page from Krafft-Ebing."

Hoffman, eyeballs lost in the corners of their sockets, grin in-
cipient, to Gallegher,

"Maybe . . . that's where I read it."

And Magruder, expiration of air, soft, almost whistle-sound,

"For a moment there," disappointment, "you almost had me believing you knew this man."

Then, Hoffman, looking up, smile: experimental, soon natural, bustling to his feet,

"Gallegher! Come here to the edge of the terrace. The Hudson is beautiful. You've never seen such a view."

Gallegher shaking his head, no, not a chance, pressing his body firmly to his chair, Magruder, catching his eye, motioning him to go, Gallegher hesitating, Magruder insistent, Gallegher, walking, close to the bamboo fence, his body leaning against it, then: leaves dancing away from the broken bamboo fence, the street below him, bamboo sticks floating downward, a hand hurting his shoulder, street turning into blue sky, Magruder flinging him back on the terrace floor, two men above him, swaying together, Magruder's voice,

". . . binoculars . . . we saw you cut through the bottom of those poles," a panting Hoffman, quiet now, handcuffs on his wrists . . .

Gallegher rose. Hoffman smiled at him, then turned to Magruder,

"You see," the little man said, "this one, God did not accept."

FROM DETECTIVE WHO'S WHO

MAGRUDER, John Bankhead, police inspector; b. N. Y. C., March 19, 1897; s. Daniel and Edith (Fields) M.; educ., pub. schs., N. Y. C.; B.S., College, City of N. Y., 1917; M.A. (Psych.), Columbia U., 1918; LL.B. Bklyn. Law Sch., 1921. Admitted N. Y. Bar, 1921. Patrolman, Police Dept., N. Y. C., 1922–1928; successively sgt., lieut., capt., 1928–1941; deputy inspector, 1941–1943; inspector, 1943. Gained national prominence during basketball scandal, 1941. Member: Phi Beta Kappa; American Bar Assn.; N. Y. Med. Legal Soc. Author: *Psychological Clues and the Law of Evidence,* 1940; *A New Tool for the Criminologist: The Dream,* 1950. Contrib. to treatise on criminology (edited by E. G. Hervey), 1944; *Journ. of Criminology;* law reviews; other periodicals. Hobby: Basketball. Home: 1500 Ft. Washington Ave., N. Y. C.

John Marshall is a private detective who's married. He's too happily monogamous to belong to the standard Private Eye school; besides, he is generally sober and never vicious. And yet, though his wife takes a strong interest in his cases, he's too much of a hard-working professional to fit into the Bright Young Couple pattern. You'll simply have to call him Likable Straight, as he is in this hitherto unpublished story.

JOHN & SUZY MARSHALL IN

Start from Scratch

BY JAMES M. FOX

IT WAS an early Sunday evening late in March when Frank Brownell phoned me. He is Los Angeles branch manager for the Mutual Life and Indemnity Insurance Society of Boston, Massachusetts, which happens to be my only substantial annual retainer client, a fact he likes to bear in mind.

"There's been a little accident," he told me jovially, over the background clink of dishes and murmur of voices in his dining room. "They had it on the six o'clock news just now. Man named William Radford fell off the ski tow at Evergreen and broke his silly neck. One of our policyholders. We're on him for only five, straight life, not much better than burial insurance these days. It just goes to show. Always the guy who doesn't believe in it, turns out he needs it bad."

"Who's the beneficiary?" I asked him.

"His wife, if I remember. It's a pretty old policy, I haven't looked at it for some time. Radford-Bix, music publishers, office on the Strip, big showplace down in Palos Verdes. You better check the deal, Marshall. Once over lightly. The company doesn't like accidents very much, and five is still money."

I gathered the policy was one of those with half a dozen lines in fine print stipulating that the insured agrees to be nice and not fall off any ski tows or subway platforms or kitchen tables either. I told Frank he'd have my report in the morning, hung up, and went into the bedroom to change from bathrobe and swimming trunks into slacks and a sports jacket. In Southern California, even a private dick can sometimes manage to spend an afternoon relaxing with his wife on the patio under the avocado tree.

Suzy deserted her dishpan and came running out of the kitchen to peek in on me expectantly.

"Johnny, are we going somewhere?"

"One of Brownell's little routine jobs. I'd go tomorrow, only they might've cleaned things up too good by then. Feel like a ride in the moonlight, pussycat?"

She was already dabbing on lipstick and rushing a comb through her lush disarray of gleaming auburn curls. She was wearing a suit of heavy Kelly green corduroy lounging pajamas, anklets, and saddleshoes. "Can I go like this?"

"Better grab your old squirrel coat and a couple of rugs," I recommended, surveying her with my fondest grin.

It took us a minute to wake up the Packard, and half an hour through the usual messy post-cocktail traffic on Sunset Boulevard to hit Glendale and the Angeles Crest Highway. From the moment we climbed out of the sweltering coastal valley smog, the night air acquired a crisp tang and the peculiar glassy translucence of early spring in the mountains that made a feeble yellow mockery of our headlights.

Mt. Evergreen, 8,520 feet, towers over the road to Big Pines a few miles beyond Devil's Canyon. It is just one of half a dozen primitive but easily accessible snowspots in the county, within two hours' driving of Los Angeles. Scoop out a parking lot, throw a few logs together into cabins, rig up a cable tow to the peak, and you're all set for the college trade. We pulled into the parking lot at nine-thirty sharp, noting with surprise that we shared it with some twenty other cars and that the cabins and the mountainside itself bristled with lights. Snow glittered in patches under the pine trees and crunched frostily underfoot—old, dirty snow, gravel-stained and boulder-studded, packed hard by feet and tires and quick changes of temperature.

The jukebox in the cabin lodge had Woody Herman jiving away on *Blue Skies*, and a briskly roaring fire under the chimney, but only a handful of customers. A small group of local rustics clustered around one end of the soft drink bar; a girl in ski pants sat with two men in a booth, staring dull-eyed into her cup of hot chocolate. Behind the bar a white-haired, weather-beaten oldster in bleached khaki jeans that were several sizes too big for him tinkered clumsily with the coffee machine. He came over for our orders and looked without interest at my card.

"Accident!" he said, sniffing his contempt.

Suzy said indignantly: "Well, what about it? You had one last year, didn't you? Woman fell off the tow and broke both legs. They closed you up for a month, I remember."

He glared at her. "Last year, I take over. Slow down machine, put straps on all seats, yet. The tow, she is safe. The man, he rides her many times. Always I tell him use straps, he is laughing at me. Today maybe he is sick, maybe he is just fed up, so he jumps. So okay, is tow operator's fault. Comes police, comes trouble, comes the insurance." He sniffed again, louder.

"German, are you?" I inquired.

He shook his head wearily and said: "Swiss. My son, Anton, five years in U. S. Army. Now he runs ski school for me. You wait for him, mister. He's up there now with police."

"What are they looking for?"

The old man shrugged and turned away. We left the bar and went out on the tow's loading platform. The cable ran up on slender steel pylons at a steep angle, just over the treetops, until it vanished from sight where the mountainslope shifted its angle of incline. The tow was stationary, of course, but one of its seats, suspended from the cable by a short steel bar, was conveniently at the platform. I sat in it, wiggled around, and tried the safety belt. Even without this your living room armchair might have been more comfortable, but not much less dangerous, unless you wanted to play games on the way up.

Torches and flashlights on the mountains were moving down and converging upon us. Men were shouting to each other, sliding and crashing through the underbrush. They were having rough going.

We strolled back into the lodge to wait. The little blonde in ski pants was still staring into her cup, and the men with her had not moved. One of them was quite young, hardly more than a boy; he wore a faded UCLA sweater and the cuffs of his frayed gray flannels were tucked into heavy squaretoed boots. He seemed absorbed in the construction of a bridge across the sugarbowl out of half a dozen soda straws. The other man was older, small and swarthy, leaning back in his outside seat, contemplating his empty beerglass with an air of detached boredom. I suddenly recognized him and showed him two fingers across the room. He grinned back at me and came over to our booth, without taking more than one eye off his companions.

"What cooks, Garcia?" I asked him.

He shook hands with us, ceremoniously, and tucked his own back into a pocket of his neatly brushed imitation camel-hair.

"We got a funny one," he told me, screwing up his nose to show me how funny.

"No kidding!"

"Yeah. Seems like this guy Radford . . . Oh-oh!" He scampered back to his booth. The door had flown open with a crash, and a bunch of uniformed sheriff's deputies came stamping in on the heels of a dapper little man, attired in a badly scuffed and dirt-raked mackinaw, who carried a long parcel tenderly wrapped in an army blanket.

Suzy had a grip on my arm and let fly at him with a shriek past my ear. "Yoo-hoo, Dave! Here we are!"

Lieutenant David Hogan, Confidential Squad, shot us a quick scowl before he allowed himself to approach.

"I might of known," he admitted sardonically.

"Relax, Dave," I said. "This is one of Brownell's babies. We're just checking."

"Now ain't that a shame?" His narrow, clear blue eyes glinted at us. "No luck, Johnny. Radford was murdered."

I stared at him, thoughtfully. Suzy caught her breath and said: "Dave, how? Those tow seats are singles, more than a hundred feet apart. He must've been up there all by himself . . ."

"Oh, sure. Fifty yards up, over the canyon. No snow where he came down. Smashed to bits, he was. Just the same, we found the bullet hole, after we took him downtown."

"Think of that!" I said, properly impressed. "Who done it, teacher?"

He refreshed his scowl and jerked his head at Sergeant Garcia's booth. "Another juvenile case we got. Them crazy kids, always copying each other, figuring they can get away with it. Radford's, stepdaughter and the boyfriend. The way I hear, he was kind of decent, only he'd promised his wife when she died that for her brat there wouldn't be any quick marriage to some busted college boy like this Jeff Morris. So today when he comes to col-lect them after they been up there skiing, they're waiting for him with a rifle."

"Dave, how perfectly horrid. Are you sure?"

My sweet little wife and self-elected helpmate, edging up to the rescue. I said hurriedly: "Well, nice to see you, lieutenant. Drop in soon when you're not too busy, huh? Guess we better blow now, sugar, it's getting late."

"But Johnny, your report. . . . You know Frank, always complaining about how you don't give him the facts and every-thing."

"It's in the bag," said Hogan. "Stick around if you want to."

He stalked off, washing his hands of us, and sat down behind a table with the bundle before him. His deputies had cleared the room by this time and were standing around, chewing gum and hitching their belts. Garcia caught a nod and beckoned to his charges. They came out and sat down meekly at Hogan's table, watching him with eyes that were dumbly apprehensive, almost expressionless.

"Tell me again," he invited them, conversationally. "Better

get it right this time. Start from scratch, when you left home this morning and all."

The Morris boy said: "I got to Jean's place about ten. Her dad was supposed to come with us, but he'd changed his mind. He said for us to go ahead, he'd pick us up around four-thirty so he could ride the tow a couple of times and take us to dinner afterwards. We drove out in my car, got in at twelve, had a hamburger in here, and went up to the ski. When Mr. Radford didn't show by five, we looked for him at the terminal and they told us he'd had an accident. So we came right down on the tow, but the ambulance had already left. The patrol car officers were there and told us to wait." He hesitated, glanced at the girl beside him and added half-defiantly: "We're still waiting. . . ."

"That how it was, Miss Ludlow?" Hogan asked mildly.

She was playing with her handkerchief and did not look up. "Yes," she said. "That's how it was." She made it sound cool and disinterested, as if all this fuss did not really concern her.

"Any friends with you up there?" Hogan inquired.

"We didn't see anybody we know," Jeff Morris said. "We were alone most of the time, on the south slope. The trails on this side were closed. Not much snow left."

"Yeah, we know. You're supposed to be kind of hot, though, ain't you? You could of made it down them closed trails and up again, both of you?"

"I guess so. We wouldn't've had much fun, doing that."

"Going steady, you two?"

The girl twitched slightly. The boy flushed and said stiffly: "We're engaged to be married, if that's what you mean. I've told you that before."

"Uh-huh. You did, at that. How old are you, Miss Ludlow?"

This time she looked up at him.

"Sixteen," she admitted briefly.

Jeff Morris suddenly stiffened. "What's the idea, lieutenant?" he asked in a tight voice. "We haven't done anything. Why can't you just leave us alone?"

Hogan ignored him and started to unwrap the bundle. He took

his time about it, carefully picking the knots on the string and taking out the blanket folds one by one, with the queasy precision of a striptease queen who has been told the man from the License Commissioner's office is in the house. He made me curious enough to get up for a peek over his shoulder. The rifle was a Remington Sportsman, with a twenty-power Lyman Supertarget scope squatting on the barrel, quite a fancy piece of .22 popgun. Except for a little mud and a few dried pine needles here and there, it was in pretty good shape.

For a while nobody made any comment. The room was so quiet it made the logs burning in the fireplace sound like an artillery barrage three miles away. The kids were staring at the gun, and the rest of us were staring at them. It was hard to tell how they were taking it. They looked scared, all right.

"Yours, ain't it?" Hogan suggested casually.

The boy nodded, licking his lips. "Where did you find it?" he asked, fighting the croak in his voice.

Hogan promptly called him a jerk with two heads, both of them rubber, and proceeded to tell him where and why and what else, winding up with a forcefully worded invitation to quit stalling. He didn't have much luck with it. The kids just sat tight, holding hands and looking bewildered. It took him twenty minutes to lose his temper and decide to get the show on the road.

On the way back to our car, the little woman was on the verge of tears.

"Johnny, it's too *preposterous!* They're mere children, they *couldn't* have. . . . These juvenile delinquent cases you read about are only horrible exceptions, but they've confused Dave to a point where he can't *think* any more. What are we going to do?"

"It's a pretty strong case, honeybun. Dave didn't go off half-cocked. He found out right away about Morris being a sniper in the army and still a first-class amateur target shot. And about the girl giving him this rifle for a birthday present three months ago. He kept it in his locker at the Glenview Country Club range. They could've sneaked it out of there early this morning while nobody was looking. Leave it in his car, go up on the tow, come down the closed trail, pick up the gun, lug it back to the canyon, and they were all set. Afterwards all they needed was to hide the gun in a tree, where Dave found it, and get back up the trail to the terminal platform. Some bright young lad in the coroner's department spotted the bullet hole and they were out of luck. With a fifty-yard drop to the rocks, consider the odds against that happening."

"And you call yourself a detective!" she said indignantly.

"Well, what of it? Our client is Mutual Indemnity. All they care is whether Radford jumped or not."

"John Marshall, if you're going to be a goon and let them try that sweet young couple for murder, so help me I'll get after the real killer myself!"

She was grinding one dainty little spike heel into the muddy snow of the parking lot and her eyes were flashing green danger signals. The lot was almost empty now; the cavalcade of police cars had dwindled to a distant roar and a string of winking rear lights down the highway. Two uniformed deputies had been left behind. They were worrying over a big maroon Cadillac town car and an elderly Plymouth coupe, parked side by side a few yards away.

"Need a hand, boys?" I asked.

One of them said no, they needed keys. The Caddy was Radford's, the coupe belonged to the Morris boy. They'd been ordered to take both cars down to the Hall of Justice, but in the heat of departure someone had overlooked the fact that Radford's keys were with the rest of his effects at the morgue. As for the Plymouth's key, it was traveling down the road in Sergeant Garcia's pocket.

I kept my face straight somehow, and showed them how to fix the ignition wiring behind the coil. We had a little trouble starting the coupe, which was just about ready for Freddy, a battered old wreck with a leaky fuel-pump. The town car was a very different proposition, brand new, sleek and shiny, engine purring like a sleepy tomcat. Its only flaw seemed to be a six-inch horizontal scratch on the belly of its right rear fender, with flakes of fresh white paint still clinging. The registration slip on the steering column supplied the owner's name and address: William J. Radford, 9116 West Loma Vista Boulevard.

The deputies pulled out and I went back to my own troubles. The little woman sat waiting for me in stony silence. We hit the road and started rolling back to town. It was getting late; the radio had only disk-jockeys to offer. We were passing Red Box Gap before I could make up my mind.

"Okay, cherry pie. You win. This is liable to take us all night, though."

"I don't mind."

"It's only because I noticed something funny. I think maybe we ought to check it."

"Darling, you're wonderful. I'm sorry I called you names. . . ."

Nine thousand one hundred and sixteen West Loma Vista turned out to be a small but fairly new and well-appointed colonial mansion in the Playa del Rey sector; apparently Radford had moved since the death of his wife, two facts our Mr. Brownell seemed to be unaware of. The house was in darkness and stayed that way after five minutes of my leaning on the doorbell, but somewhere in the backyard a dog had been rattling its chain and bellowing its heart out from the moment of our arrival until finally lights snapped on in the garage, followed by footsteps and a scolding voice. The dog subsided and a man wearing slippers and a pair of black uniform trousers with suspenders dangling appeared in the driveway.

"Yes, sir, can I help you?"

"Have the police been here yet?" I asked him.

He stiffened and looked at us for a long time.

"No, sir," he said at last, sounding even more gravely courteous than before. "May I inquire why you should expect them to come?"

"There has been a little trouble," I told him. "Mr. Radford and Miss Ludlow won't be home tonight. Does anyone else in the family live here?"

"No, sir." He hesitated. "If the matter is serious, perhaps you'd care to communicate with Mr. Calvin. Mr. Calvin Radford, that is, the master's brother." He mentioned a West Los Angeles address.

"We'll go right over," I promised. "Any other servants here?"

"There's a Negro houseman who sleeps out," he told me. "Is there anything I can do, sir? Grimes is the name."

"You're Mr. Radford's chauffeur, aren't you? Why weren't you driving him today?"

"I'm sure I don't know, sir. Usually on Sundays the master has me drive Miss Ludlow, her fiancé, and himself out to the mountains, but at breakfast this morning he informed me he had changed his plans and he sent me off for the day."

"Didn't tell you where he was going?"

"No, sir, he did not. Excuse me, may I ask . . ."

"Sorry, Grimes, I can't tell you any more right now," I said. "Just one more thing I'd like to know, though. Did you graze a fence post with the car recently? There's a scratch and a streak of white paint on the right rear fender I happened to notice."

"Absolutely not, sir. I washed the car last night, Saturday night that is, and it had no scratches anywhere, I'm sure. Both the master and myself are always most careful."

"We're getting someplace," I told Suzy as we pulled away. "The old gentleman had something on his mind this morning and went visiting. The visit upset him so much he hit the gate on his way out."

She was almost dancing with excitement. "Darling, of course! He knew something was wrong, that's why he sent the children off by themselves and dismissed the chauffeur. Or maybe the man he had an appointment with told him to come alone. . . ."

"It may have been a woman," I reminded her. "His brother might know."

Calvin Radford's residence proved to be a magnificent English villa on Dumont Avenue, a few blocks from the big Sawtelle Hospital reservation. The driveway swept into an acre of stylishly-landscaped grounds between two pillars of solid black marble. Lights were on in the hall and behind open living room curtains. The Filipino who admitted us looked spruce and wide awake in his starched white monkey-jacket. I gave him my card, and he returned almost immediately to show us into a den cheerfully paneled in lemon birch, the walls lined with bookshelves and sporting two enormous elk-hunting trophies and a stuffed blue marlin.

The man who come forward to greet us must have been in his early fifties, but he was the cleancut, comfortably exercised, intelligently professional type that could pass for fifteen years younger in a quiet suit of tweeds, even at three o'clock in the morning. He offered me a strong, capable hand, gave the little woman a bow and the inevitable quick doubletake of masculine interest, and waved us into chairs around the fireplace.

"You're private investigators for the insurance company? Good Lord, you people don't waste any time, do you?"

"I see you've heard the bad news," I said.

"God, yes. The sheriff's office called me hours ago. I went straight down to identify my brother, and while I was there they brought in my niece and her young man, but they wouldn't let me talk to them, not even as Bill's attorney, or perhaps because of that. What a ghastly thing to happen! Believe me, Marshall, I still have trouble keeping my wits about me. Those kids are innocent, of course, I hope you realize that. Jean worshiped my brother, he was the only father she'd ever known—her own died of alcohol poisoning when she was two years old."

"If they're innocent, how do you think it happened, Mr. Radford?" I asked him.

"My dear fellow, I haven't the faintest idea. Perhaps they took the rifle to go squirrel-hunting, and an unlucky shot caught my brother just as he was going up to meet them. Or it may have been a stray bullet from some other hunter's gun. But for Jeff and Jean to lay for him like that, deliberately, that's quite out of the question, I assure you."

"Morris is said to be an expert marksman," I pointed out. "And I'm willing to bet you any amount they'll match the fatal bullet with his rifle."

"Mr. Radford, what sort of man was your brother?" Suzy intervened hurriedly. "Did he have any enemies that you know of?"

The Filipino came cat-footing in, deposited a silver tray with a bottle of Canadian Club and the makings on the hammered bronze coffee table between us, and padded out again.

"Bill was a prince," said our host. His hand holding the ice tongs shook a little and he made a visible effort to steady himself. "They don't come any better, Mrs. Marshall. I know it must sound rather fatuous, but he was almost too good for this world. People were forever taking advantage of him, playing on his sympathy, cheating him left and right. After his wife's death it got so bad he finally had to ask me to take over the management of his personal estate—he was a wealthy man, but his army of false friends and hangers-on would have sucked him dry by now. I am not talking about the children, mind you. Jean has never lacked anything, but she's young and her tastes are simple. As for Jeff, I'm convinced the boy has never been impressed by her money. If anything, it has frightened him a bit, and I remember him telling me once that he was worried about how he could provide for her well enough to avoid any embarrassing attempts on my brother's part to contribute financially to their menage."

"Your brother would have approved an early marriage?" I asked.

"No. He did not believe in the idea, in principle. He liked Jeff, but he wanted the kids to wait, at least until Jean was through college. They'd agreed to that. It wasn't really an issue, so far as I know."

Suzy said: "Mr. Radford, we think your brother went to see someone this morning, before he drove out to Evergreen, and that they had a fight. Do you have any idea who it might have been and what they could have been quarreling about? It seems a little odd, because he dismissed his chauffeur and went by himself, as if he wanted to keep the visit a secret."

"Good Lord, that certainly is unusual." He frowned at us, obviously disturbed. "It doesn't sound like Bill at all. Normally, he'd come to me if there were anything troubling him, but there's been nothing of the sort for months. I'll think about it, and I'll go over his papers and things in the morning."

"Woman stuff?" I suggested.

"Oh dear, no. Definitely not."

"Well, if you're sure," I said doubtfully.

He brushed the point aside and said: "I realize it's impossible, but I wish you two were free to investigate this distressing affair on behalf of the estate, Marshall, rather than on behalf of the insurance people. Of course I'm going to do everything in my power to help my niece and young Morris. If there must be a trial, I'll represent them and get Giesler or some other first-rate counsel to assist. You'll keep in touch with me, won't you?"

We promised him we would and took our leave. In the car I suddenly remembered Frank Brownell telling me about Radford being a music publisher. Radford-Bix sounded like a partnership. We almost went back to ask Calvin about it, but instead we turned into an all-night filling station on Wilshire and consulted the telephone directory. It listed *Bix, Chas. W., ofc 9400 Sunset bl., r. 2132 N. Cresc Hts bl.* The publishing company's office address checked.

Mr. Charles W. Bix's residence on North Crescent Heights Boulevard proved to be the Baltimore Arms, a massive six-story pile of stucco and glass brick, carefully labeled "No Solicitors No Dogs" in black paint and "No Vacancies" in dainty blue neon. Anyone could walk into the cool Mexican tiled lobby and find "No Service." The usual row of letterbox inscriptions placed our man in Apt. 26.

We climbed the stairs to the second floor and gave 26's buzzer button a play. The occupant seemed to be a remarkably light sleeper, because the door opened in something under twenty seconds. Blinking at us through a pair of heavy tortoise-shell glasses was a short fat party in violently purple-striped silk pajamas and a fancy canary mandarin robe, conspicuously initialed.

If you think a man would need excellent nerves to show himself in that kind of getup, this one would have fooled you. We didn't actually hear his knees knocking, but only because we didn't bother to listen.

"Y-yes? Wh-what is it, please?"

"Mr. Bix? Sorry to wake you up, but we'd like to talk to you." It sounded a little snappier than I had intended.

"Wh-what about? Who are you?"

I showed him my card and told him, "This is urgent. It's about your partner."

His expression would have been the same if I had whisked out a knife and held the point against his bulging stomach.

"Detectives . . ." he mumbled. "But he agreed—"

"Who agreed what, Mr. Bix?" I inquired sharply.

He stiffened and moved back. "Come in, please." We obliged and found ourselves in a pleasant enough bachelor's living room, slightly overdecorated in Swedish modern. The bourbon bottle on the coffee table was a dead soldier; the lonely glass beside it and the big majolica ashtray loaded with butts testified to an evening of solitary contemplation.

"If you'll pardon me for just one moment, folks," said our host, suddenly sounding brisk and hearty. He gave us a sickly grimace apparently intended to pass for a smile of apology and backed away from us into the next room, gently closing the door behind him.

We were left staring at each other.

"Johnny, something's wrong! Maybe we shouldn't have let him . . ."

"He can't go anywhere. There's no service door or anything. I looked."

The shot didn't make much noise, hardly more than a B-movie heroine defending her virtue, but it shattered the apartment's primly peaceful atmosphere as effectively as the crack of doom. We just about broke each other's ribs trying to get in together. Mr. Charles W. Bix was kneeling by the bed, slumped forward in an attitude of prayer, his head buried in a pillow which was burning merrily away and producing a streamer of pungent, dirty blue smoke. He had fixed himself up with his own private service door.

I snatched a water pitcher off the dresser and dealt with the fire. The little .25 automatic was covered by the mess of wet feathers, ashes, and blood. It was one of those situations that freeze your teeth, but solid. We got out of there, back into the living room, almost as fast as we'd come in.

Women have better stomachs, for some reason. "Johnny, such

a break! As good as a confession, nearly. Let's hurry and call Dave."

"Uh-uh."

"Why not? Don't you see he must've done it and thought we came to arrest him?"

"It doesn't fit," I explained, patiently. "Bix was in trouble, but not that much. There was an agreement of some kind that would've saved his bacon. Sounds like a business deal. Our turning up at this hour of the night made him think he'd been crossed."

"But darling . . ."

"Radford wasn't here this morning. No fence post."

"Maybe they met at the office."

"No. We drove by there on the way up here."

She looked at me, tired and exasperated. "What'll we do?"

"Go downtown, see Dave. Maybe he's got some new dope that'll check with all this."

We made it to the car with no questions asked. The Baltimore Arms could get along without worrying about its tenants shooting off guns at five o'clock in the morning. Dawn was already breaking slowly behind the foothills and foreshortening the beam of our headlights. Driving east, we had Hollywood Boulevard all to ourselves, but at the Sierra Bonita intersection a couple of drunks in a small gray convertible going sixty miles an hour plowed through the stop sign and scurried across, almost taking my radiator nose with them.

"Johnny, look!"

I saw it, all right. Screaming brakes had jerked us to a full stop at the corner, and there right beside us, surrounded by a neatly-landscaped garden plot, fenced-in and served by a dinky little driveway of its own, stood one of those trim California adobe office bungalows.

Maybe you think that finger-of-Fate stuff is a lot of bunk, but this one I'll guarantee. The picket fence had a sturdy white post on each side of the driveway exit, and the one that would be on your right coming out bore a fresh six-inch scar at about the height of an average automobile fender. The black iron shingles suspended from a miniature gallows behind it said, in Ye Olde English gold lettering, *Calvin Radford, Counselor at Law*.

LIEUTENANT DAVID HOGAN growled, "You figure a little thing like that's this guy's motive, maybe?"

"I never thought to ask him," I said. "But he told me he was managing his brother's estate, so if they did have a fight Sunday morning you guess what it was likely to be about. He knew his brother was a slow, careful driver, so all he had to do was get into his car and beat him by twenty minutes or so out to Evergreen. If you take the trouble to inquire, I bet you'll find he's a member of the Glenview Country Club himself, and that he could've sneaked the rifle out of Jeff Morris' locker any time Saturday night or early Sunday. Framing the kids was a double cinch, because if the girl were convicted as an accomplice, she couldn't inherit from the old man—he would, as next of kin. Even if she got out of it somehow, he'd be able to sit on the estate as her guardian for at least five years."

Hogan grunted skeptically. Suzy said: "Dave, don't be stubborn. You can't lose anything. You didn't get a confession after working on those poor children for all this time, and you told us yourself the paraffin test on their hands was negative."

"With a new rifle the gas won't leak," he told her morosely. "So the test being negative don't mean a thing. We got enough on our suspects to convict 'em three times over. Whyn't you two go on home and leave off bending my ear with your screwy ideas? I'll see about this Bix angle the minute I get a report from Higgins and Garcia. They should be out there now."

The rifle was on his desk before him, and I had a better chance to inspect it closely than before at the lodge. There was dusting powder on it now, in six or seven spots where they'd photographed the Morris boy's fingerprints, but what interested me was a faint scratch near the muzzle, hardly more than a hairline about three-eighths of an inch long. I lifted the barrel, and found two more on the other side just like it.

"Your ballistics man see this?" I asked Hogan.

He nodded indifferently and said, "They're just scratches,

from where it got scraped in the car or on a rock or something."

"Listen, you'd better find another expert. Those were made by the adapter bolt of a British-type silencer. I've seen plenty of them before, when I was in G-2 during the war. The adapter slips over your muzzle, and the silencer itself screws on to it. We borrowed scores of them, for some of the Ranger details and O.S.S. personnel, but they were originally designed for hunting purposes. Calvin Radford hunts; he's got some very pretty trophies in his den. He must've taken his own silencer along, so he wouldn't be spotted by the noise if anyone else were on the trail or riding the tow."

Hogan studied the Remington's barrel through a magnifier, scowling dubiously.

"You're sure of this, are you?" he demanded.

Driving out with us on Wilshire, he insisted he was coming along for the ride only, just to see we didn't get into any more jams. "We got nothing to go on, except the guy didn't tell you he saw his brother yesterday morning. That don't prove nothing. I can't get a search warrant on that kind of evidence. He'd of dumped the muffler by now anyway."

"Not likely," I said confidently. "They're expensive and hard to come by, and still harder to get rid of. Even if he wanted to. They're big and they look odd, you can't just throw one away. The chances are it would be found and brought in. Almost the only safe method would be taking it a mile out into the Pacific and dropping it overboard."

He grunted some more and kept to himself for the rest of the journey. We made it to the corner of Wilshire and Dumont by six-thirty. The morning sun was already warm and bright, and receiving eager tribute from the birds in Calvin Radford's handsome garden, but the street was quiet and deserted, the house asleep. I parked out of sight on a filling station lot. The yawning attendant watched us without curiosity as we clustered around his coinbox phone.

The connection buzzed a couple of dozen times before I got the Filipino houseboy, but he put Calvin on the wire almost right away.

"Oh yes, Marshall. You have news?"

"We promised we'd keep in touch with you," I reminded him. "We haven't turned up anything so far, but at headquarters Lieutenant Hogan told us only a few minutes ago that he isn't quite satisfied with the case against Miss Ludlow and young Morris. He said he's made a list of everybody who knew your brother, and he's going out to check their cars."

"Splendid! Then he must have some definite idea about what to look for?"

"Of course," I lied cheerfully. "He didn't tell us what it was, but we think we know. The County Highway Department is testing several new road surfacing materials, and last week they laid out a short experimental stretch of one on Angeles Crest, about three miles east of Red Box Gap. It's a special mixture of asphalt and decomposed granite, and we heard it's not satisfactory at all. Too soft, sticks to tires. But it'll make a swell clue if they find traces of it on somebody's car."

"I see. Good Lord, you people certainly know your stuff these days! I do hope it works, Marshall. Good of you to call. Let me hear the minute there are further developments, won't you?"

I told him that would be a pleasure and hooked the receiver, ever so gently. Hogan sniffed, and Suzy grabbed his arm and pulled him out of the filling station's office. We crossed the boulevard and found an alley leading around the back of Radford's villa, screened by a row of flowering jacarandas. The garage fronted on a small flagstone plaza and was carefully padlocked. We waited behind it, and in less than five minutes there were footsteps from the house, the padlock clicked, and the garage door groaned open. A starter whined briefly and brought its engine to roaring life.

Hogan moved, but I caught his shoulder.

"Not yet! He'll take it out into the light first, to see for himself. . . ."

Gears clashed and the car rolled slowly out on the plaza. The handbrake rattled, a door clicked shut and nothing remained except the idling engine's steady, hollow thrum.

When we walked around the garage, Calvin Radford was

squatting on his heels, anxiously inspecting the left front tire of a heavy new Chrysler sedan. He got up fast and the blood jumped to his face, but his voice was firmly under control, calm and icy. "Is this silly game supposed to be the latest in Hollywood police procedures?"

"You play pretty good," said Hogan. "Care to show me that silencer of yours? We'd kind of like to make a few tests with it in the lab, downtown. Funny stuff, cordite gas—leaves a deposit you can identify the make of cartridge by."

"My dear man, please don't be absurd. I've never even seen a silencer, much less owned one. You're welcome to search the house, if you wish, although I'm quite sure you hold no warrant to do so."

For a minute the four of us just stood there, glowering at each other. Then my ears caught something in the air that sounded faintly out of tune.

"That motor's pretty noisy, for such a nice new expensive buggy," I mentioned casually.

It wasn't really, the noise didn't amount to worse than a slight wheezy overtone; but it didn't belong, it meant something. Out of one corner of my left eye, I saw Radford's face change expression when I reached for the Chrysler's hood-catch under the dashboard. Suzy caught her breath, but Hogan wasn't asleep at the switch. He had Radford's collar and a knee in his back, two jumps before I needed to worry.

We found it in the air-cleaner, a long fat greasy black cylinder still screwed on its adapter bolt, just big enough to interfere a little with the intake filter. The lettering stamped on one side said Parker-Hale Sound Moderator, Birmingham, England, and quoted the patent numbers. By that time Hogan had fixed him up with the nippers, reluctantly.

The payoff, such as it was, we caught upon our return to the Hall of Justice, where we found Garcia waiting for us with a funny gleam in his eyes.

"Hey, lieutenant, that guy Bix—he's been spilling company dough to the bookies all right, but his partner says he'd given him a week to make good on it."

"His partner?"

"Yeah. Guy named William B. Radford, lives down in Palos Verdes. No relation to the guy that got bumped. He's waiting in your office now."

Hogan raised his bushy eyebrows at us. "You wanna talk to him?"

The little woman and I looked at each other. I could see she was having trouble deciding between laughing and crying. I shook my head at Hogan and put my arm around her to take her back to the car. There was nothing more in this for us: People *will* go around using each other's names. I figured Frank Brownell would be pleased when I told him his customer didn't seem to need life insurance so badly after all.

FROM DETECTIVE WHO'S WHO

MARSHALL, John Conger, private investigator; b. Cleveland, Ohio, July 10, 1916; grad., Cornell U., 1938; m. Suzanne Willet, July 31, 1938, Washington, D. C. Volunteered active service Nat. Guard, ROTC commission, March 15, 1939; attached to G2–IV, May 2, 1939; overseas in Europe, April 18, 1942 to August 6, 1945; honorably discharged, rank of Major, Counterintelligence Corps, August 19, 1945. Awarded Purple Heart; Silver Star; French Croix de Guerre; Dutch MWO 3rd Class. Moved to California, August 25, 1945. Private Investigator's License No. 2952A issued by the State of Calif., Oct. 2, 1945. Hobbies: Hunting; fishing; small firearms; dogs. Member: Cornell Alumni pistol team; Westwood Country Club; Hollywood Athletic Club. 6130 North Broxton Avenue, Westwood, California. Telephone: ARizona 4–2323.

FROM DETECTIVE WHO'S WHO

MARSHALL, Suzanne Willet; b. Montgomery, Alabama, Oct. 20, 1918; moved to Washington D. C., 1925; grad., Radford, 1938; m. John C. Marshall, July 31, 1938. Joined War Dept. under Civil Service, June 10, 1939; overseas in Europe, March 12, 1943 to June 29, 1945, attached Code Room, SHAEF. Moved to Calif. as per above. Occupation: Housewife; husband's general factotum; gadfly.

The lamentably few short stories about The Great Merlini are familiar to all devotees through Ellery Queen's annual award collections; but many Merlini aficionados may not know that their hero's appearances have not been restricted to novels and short stories. He has also starred in a jigsaw puzzle, and in a series of prize-contest puzzle stories. Two of these we bring you here, with their solutions printed upside down. Do not turn this book without matching wits with the Mephistophelean Master of Mystification and Magic!

THE GREAT MERLINI IN

The Clues of the Tattooed Man & the Broken Legs

BY CLAYTON RAWSON

THE GREAT MERLINI looked at his watch for the umpteenth time just as Inspector Gavigan's car pulled up before the Hotel Astor.

"I've got a good notion to turn you into a rabbit," the magician said as he got in. "I've been waiting here for you ever since eleven o'clock."

"You're a mind-reader," Gavigan said in a tired voice. "You should know why we're late."

"I see," Merlini said. "Murder."

"I've seen you make better guesses," Gavigan said gloomily.

"It's murder, all right. But it's also attempted suicide, a gambling charge, a vanishing man, a nine-foot giant, a . . ." His voice trailed off as though he didn't believe it himself.

"And dope, too," Merlini said. "Gavigan, you've been hitting the pipe."

The inspector growled. "Brady, you tell him. I'm a nervous wreck."

Brady seemed just as glum. "Well, it's like this. We get a phone call at eleven-forty from a guy who says his wife has been murdered. He's in a phone booth in the lobby near the Garden. We step on the gas getting up there because he sounds like he might have suicide in mind. He does. We find a commotion in the drugstore off the lobby and the druggist is scrapping with a tall, skinny guy who bought a bottle of sleeping tablets and then started to eat them like they was peanuts. So we send the Professor down to Bellevue to keep a date with a stomach pump."

"A professor?" Merlini asked. "What of—romance languages, mathematics, nuclear physics—?"

"I never heard any worse guesses," Brady replied. "His name's Professor Vox. The circus opened at the Garden this week and he's a ventriloquist in the side show. So we go upstairs and before we can get into room 816 where the body is we have to wade through a crap game that is going on in the corridor outside—a cowboy, a juggler, and three acrobats. I know then I won't like the case and a minute later I'm positive—the ventriloquist's wife is a snake-charmer. And she has been strangled with a piece of cloth a foot wide and about twenty feet long."

"And that," Merlini put in, "gives you a Hindu as a suspect."

"Wrong again. It's a turban all right, but it belongs to a little fat guy who is billed as Mohammed the Magician but whose real name is Jimmy O'Reilly and who makes up like a Hindu with greasepaint. What's more, he has taken it on the lam and so we figure as soon as we catch him the case is solved. But then we question the crap players. And we find that their game starts at eleven, that Zelda, the Snake-Charmer, goes into her room a few minutes later, and that the magician never goes near her room at all."

"Maybe," Merlini said, producing a lighted cigarette from thin air, "he was already there—waiting."

"I hope not because this is on the eighth floor, the only window is locked on the inside, the crap players insist he didn't leave by the only door, and the only way out is to vanish into thin air."

"It's a good trick," Merlini said noncommittally—"if you can do it."

"Yeah," Brady went on even more glumly. "And pinning it on him in court would be a good trick too, because what happens next is that the crap players all agree there was one guy who went into the murder room between the time they last saw the snake-charmer and the time we show up. He goes in at eleven-fifteen, stays for maybe ten minutes, and comes out again. They swear his identification is a cinch because his face looks like a crazy quilt. He is Tinto—The Tattooed Man.

"And he's also missing. We send out a call to have him picked up. And while we wait we turn up two more hot suspects—both guys who are scared to death of snakes and hate the snake-charmer because she sometimes gets funny and leaves a snake or two in their rooms for a joke. They both look like I feel at this point—definitely not normal. One is Major Little, a midget who is almost so small he could have walked past that crap game without being noticed—only not quite. The other is a guy who is about as noticeable as an elephant; he's a beefy nine-foot giant named Goliath.

"So now we got murder, attempted suicide, a crap game, a vanishing magician, two freaks with motives and no alibis—they claim they were asleep—and a walking picture gallery who is the only guy who could have done it. Two minutes later Tinto walks in—a tall, underfed-looking egg with a face like a WPA post-office mural. And he says he had a date to meet Zelda in front of the Hotel Astor at a quarter to eleven and waited there over an hour—only she didn't show up. He can't prove it and four witnesses say different. So we charge him."

"Well," Merlini said, "your excuse for keeping me waiting is one I haven't heard before—I'll give you that. There's one little thing I don't like about it though."

"One little thing!" Gavigan exploded. "My God! All of it is—" He stopped abruptly. "Okay, I'll bite. What didn't you like?"

"Your skepticism concerning Tinto's story. I think he was in front of the Hotel Astor at the time of the murder—just as he claims."

"Oh, you do, do you?" Gavigan said darkly. Then suddenly he blinked. "So that's it! Now we got a magician as a material witness. You saw him there at the time of the murder—while you were waiting for me."

Merlini nodded. "Yes, I did. But why so unhappy about it? That should tell you who killed Zelda. It's obvious that . . ."

Who do you think murdered Zelda, the Snake-Charmer? Was it

> Tinto the Tattooed Man
> Professor Vox the Ventriloquist
> Mohammed the Magician
> Major Little the Midget
> Goliath the Giant

And what are your reasons?

Author's Solution to

THE CLUE OF THE TATTOOED MAN

by CLAYTON RAWSON

"Since I myself saw Tinto at the Hotel Astor at the time of the murder," Merlini explained, "it's obvious that the tattooed man seen by the crap players was a phony. In other words, someone was impersonating Tinto—imitating his facial peculiarities the same way Jimmy O'Reilly imitates a Hindu—with greasepaint.

"Who? Well, Brady described Tinto as 'tall and underfed' and that eliminates the fat little magician, the midget, and the hefty nine-foot giant. It leaves only the 'tall, skinny' Professor Vox.

"The motive—his discovery that Tinto was dating his wife— is also obvious.

"There's another way of pinning the guilt on Professor Vox. Since the crap players swore that the tattooed man was 'the only guy' to go into and out of the murder room before the cops arrived, how come Vox knew his wife was dead? Answer: only if he were the counterfeit tattooed man—therefore, only if he were the murderer."

THE CLUE OF THE BROKEN LEGS

by CLAYTON RAWSON

INSPECTOR GAVIGAN knelt in the glare of the police emergency light and replaced the automatic on the floor beside the body of Jorge Lasko, theatrical producer.

"His own gun," he said. "Two shots fired. One hit Lasko; the other smashed the only light in the room to smithereens. Brady, is there a phone in this place?"

The sergeant nodded. "Yeah, it's downstairs in the library."

"Get on it," Gavigan ordered. "Find out what's keeping Merlini, and then bring those three suspects in here again."

The Great Merlini's voice came from the doorway behind them. "You won't need to phone, Brady. The marines have landed." Walking in, he added, "Did you say 'three suspects,' inspector?"

Gavigan nodded. "Harold Kingsley, the novelist whose best-seller Lasko was adapting for production this fall; Dorothy Dawn, the famous star who's on leave from Hollywood to play the lead; and Marie Lasko, the victim's daughter."

"And Dorothy," Merlini said, "is also the ex-wife Lasko divorced six months ago."

"Which," the inspector added, "probably gives her a motive. And Marie inherits her father's fortune, although I don't see why she'd want to kill him for it; she owns the world-famous Lasko Parfums, Inc. As for Kingsley . . ." Gavigan scowled.

Merlini was looking at the overturned wheel chair and the body beside it. "Plaster casts on both legs," he said. "How did that happen?"

"Auto accident a few weeks ago," Gavigan explained. "He's only been out of bed a day or two but insisted on being wheeled into his study here at five o'clock to do some work on the play script. He also apparently had some business to transact with a blackmailer. I found a record among his papers of some mysterious one-thousand-dollar cash payments extending over the last six months." The inspector pointed to the scattered hundred-dollar bills on the floor near the corpse. "There's just an even grand there. It looks to me like Lasko was making a payoff, an argument developed, Lasko drew a gun, and the blackmailer jumped him. In the struggle the wheel chair tipped over and Lasko was shot."

Gavigan turned to a heavy-set individual who leaned against the wall chewing thoughtfully on an unlit cigar. "This is Dan Foyle, Merlini. A private 'op' who works for Acme. Dan, tell him what you found."

"Well," Foyle said, talking around his cigar. "Lasko's an Acme client: we got him his divorce evidence. He phoned me tonight just as I was leaving the office shortly after five and asked me to be out here at eight o'clock. He said: 'I'm going to talk to someone who's threatened to kill me. Come in through the kitchen and up the back stairs to the study. And bring a gun.'

"I got here fifteen minutes ahead of time, but it wasn't soon enough. I was just crossing the lawn when I heard the first shot. I started running. Then there's another shot and I see the light in the study go out. Up here I find the door open, and inside, in the moonlight by the French window, I see the body and a man standing by it. I covered him just as he decides to take it on the lam and heads for the window. I told him to put his hands up. He jumped a foot and was so scared he nearly—"

A tall, blond man, one of the three persons Brady had ushered into the room as Foyle was speaking, said coldly, "Who wouldn't be startled? I heard shots, entered a dark room to find a body, and then turned to discover a man I'd never seen before barking at me over a gun."

"Kingsley," Gavigan said, "I'm not satisfied with your story at all. You say you were downstairs when you heard the first shot, that you ran up, heard the second shot as you reached the top of the stairs, and that no one came out through the study door before you got to it."

The novelist nodded. "That's correct. I opened the door, pushed the light switch just inside without result, and saw the overturned wheel chair. I went across and found Lasko—dead." Kingsley looked at the private detective. "But I had no intention of leaving by the window. It was locked on the inside, and I went toward it because I heard someone outside trying to get in."

"Everybody," Gavigan growled, "tried to get in. And you want me to believe nobody ever went out—that Lasko's murderer vanished into thin air like a soap bubble. Miss Dawn, how long had you been out there on the sundeck?"

Miss Dawn's tone of voice said that she didn't like cops—not even inspectors. "Ten minutes," she said frostily. "I told you that before. And don't ask me again if anyone came out through that window. No one did. You might try asking something important. Such as where Mr. Kingsley was when he heard that first shot."

The novelist frowned. "I was in the library reading."

Miss Dawn smiled. "You never told me you could read Braille, my dear."

"Braille? I can't. Why—"

"I could see the library windows from the sundeck. They were dark. There were no lights there at all!"

"Well, Kingsley," Gavigan said, "that eliminates our invisible man. You were in here with Lasko. You're the only person who could possibly—"

Marie Lasko spoke suddenly, her voice tense and angry. "Just a minute, inspector. Harold was in the library. I know. You see— I was with him."

Dorothy Dawn smiled again. "Reading aloud to you, I suppose —in the dark?"

"Don't look now, inspector," Merlini said, "but that invisible man is back again."

"No!" Gavigan growled. "Don't give me that." He faced his three suspects. "Somebody is lying like hell. And I'm going to find out—"

"I know who's lying," Merlini said. "I'll demonstrate. Which one of you people called the police?"

It was Marie Lasko who answered. "I did. Harold told me to stay in the library, but when I heard the second shot I followed him upstairs." She indicated Foyle. "And this man told me to phone Spring 7-3100. I went down again to the library and did so."

"You see, inspector?" Merlini said. "Together with Lasko's broken legs, that tells you who has been lying and explains the mystery of the vanishing blackmailer."

The inspector scowled. "Oh, it does, does it?"

Who killed Jorge Lasko, the theatrical producer?
And what are your reasons?

Author's Solution to
THE CLUE OF THE BROKEN LEGS
by CLAYTON RAWSON

"After disarming and shooting Lasko," Merlini explained, "the blackmailer had to vanish. And with Miss Dawn on the sundeck outside the window and running footsteps approaching the only door, that was something of a trick. His first step was to shoot out the light, thus insuring that it couldn't be turned on again too soon. Then he dropped the gun by the body and flattened himself against the wall by the door. After Kingsley ran in, he merely stepped into the doorway behind him, pretended he'd just arrived, and—"

Foyle shook his head. "Theories are a dime a dozen."

"All right," Merlini said. "Here are some facts. Fact Number One: the other suspects are all in the high income tax brackets, leaving you as the only decent candidate for the blackmailer role. Fact Number Two: the blackmail payments began six months ago when you got Lasko his divorce evidence and discovered something that—"

"The D.A.," Foyle said, "will need a hell of a lot more than that."

"The best," Merlini smiled, "is yet to come. When you had to explain your presence here, you couldn't very well admit you came to blackmail Lasko. So—Fact Number Three—you said he'd phoned and asked for protection. But the telephone, as Brady and Marie both clearly stated, is *downstairs in the library.* At shortly after five, when you claim Lasko phoned you, he was confined with two broken legs to a wheel chair in his study *on the second floor.* And that puts you, Mr. Foyle, in a chair of a different kind."

FROM DETECTIVE WHO'S WHO

MERLINI, The Great, magician; b. Barnum & Bailey circus car en route through Illinois; s. Victor and Edna (Bradna) M.; educ. at intervals, Ohio, Heidelberg, Brooklyn, Paris, Beirut; m. Mary Cordona, Jan. 2, 1919; children— Michael, 1922; Roberta, 1925. Carnival and circus magician, 1917–20; Keith Circuit, 1921–28; full evening show, 1929–38; world tour, 1935–36; magic dealer, 1939——. Theatrical productions: appeared in *Magic on Broadway, Musical Magic, Impossibly Yours;* produced: *Now You See It*—; motion pictures: *Miracles For Sale;* series of short features: *Nothing Is Impossible;* currently starring: *The Great Merlini* television show. Inventor, numerous magic illusions, notably famed Sawing a Woman in Four. Publications: *Legerdemainiacs; The Psychology of Deception; Sleight of Hand for Experts; Magicians of the Underworld;* currently conducts column, "Merlini's Magic," in *Hugard's Magic Monthly;*
co-author with Ross Harte under pseudonym Clayton Rawson: *Death From a Top Hat; The Footprints on the Ceiling; The Headless Lady; No Coffin For the Corpse.*

Decorations: Sacred Order of White Elephant, presented at command performance by Maharajah of Saringapatam. Clubs: Society of American Magicians; Circus Fans Club; Lambs Club; Explorers Club; Mystery Writers of America, Inc.; honorary member, N. Y. Homicide Squad; British Magic Circle; Associated Wizards of Aberdeen; Calcutta Conjurers Club; Société des Prestidigitateurs; Magischer Verein; Gl'Illusionisti; Sociedad de Magia; Banshee Club; Honorary Medicine Man, Bantu Tribe, Lower Congo. Hobbies: Mrs. Merlini; chess; table tennis; firewalking; collecting historical magic apparatus, posters, playbills, books relating to magic, spiritualism, witchcraft. Home address: 13½ Washington Sq., N. Office: The Magic Shop, Times Square. Tel.: MEphisto 7–1313.

*Miss Rachel Murdock made her debut in D. B. Olsen's
novels as a purely subsidiary figure; but her precise blend of
reality and quaintness so tickled the popular fancy that her
creator was forced to give her starring roles. Still more interesting than Miss Rachel (more interesting, even, than
her cat Samantha) has been the curious, disturbing atmosphere of most of her cases, as in this tragedy of the man
who liked fuzzy, fluffy things.*

MISS RACHEL MURDOCK IN

The Fuzzy Things

BY D. B. OLSEN

THE man took the long slim package from his coat pocket,
put it on the table, and unwrapped it with hands that shook. He
was a big man and there was something peculiarly childish about
his fear. He was like a little boy afraid of the dark. "This came
today—the second inside a week. You can see where the chocolates have been tampered with. The other box had strychnine
in it."

Miss Rachel Murdock lifted one from its paper nest and examined the under side. There had been a picked-out hole refilled
unskillfully with a chocolate mixture, unlike the coating put on
by the candy maker. More like cake frosting, she thought.

"This wasn't addressed to you?"

"No. To my wife and her little girl, my stepdaughter." He
took out a white handkerchief and mopped his forehead. "It was
quite by accident that I noticed the tampering in the first box
and kept Jenny from sampling one of them. She loves candy and

From *Detective Story*, Mar., 1948 (as *Murder Walks a Strange Path*).
Copyright 1948 by Street & Smith.

we've spoiled her with it. My wife wasn't inclined to be afraid, but I had the filling tested just to be safe. All the candy was poisoned."

Miss Rachel pulled her lacy shawl closer as if she were suddenly cold. Her cat, a big black fluffy cat with amazingly green eyes, had been sleeping in her lap and, feeling the shiver, looked up. Miss Rachel said, "You went to the police, of course?"

"Oh, yes. Right away." He hesitated, staring at the open box. "I know I have to be completely frank if you're to help us. My wife didn't want me to go to the police and she absolutely forbade me to mention the man we suspect of sending the candy. She's sure that she can handle him. She doesn't know I've come to you. It was getting this second box, the inhuman boldness of it, that woke me up, that brought me here."

"This man you suspect—is it the child's father?"

He looked up, startled. "How did you know?"

"I just guessed," she admitted. "You'd better tell me about him."

They were seated in Miss Rachel's tiny parlor. Several unfinished bits of knitting lay about. Miss Jennifer, the elder and more sensible in her own opinion, had decided that it might settle Miss Rachel's nerves to be taught to knit; and Miss Rachel was realizing with relief that all she had needed had been some mystery to meddle with. Like this one, unpleasant as it was.

The big man with the childish fear in his eyes spoke slowly as if thinking out what he must say. "My wife married a man about whom she knew almost nothing. They met at a resort, Arrowhead, and because she was young and inexperienced she was impressed by his looks and his money. He had plenty of money. He was a counterfeiter."

The cat had gone back to sleep. The room was quiet, full of afternoon sunlight and the clean smell of the new wool Miss Rachel was supposed to be knitting on.

"When the law caught up with him a few months after their marriage, and he was sent to prison, she almost went insane. She bore their child alone, on charity. I would have helped, of course, but she didn't let me know. She worked, trained herself for a secretary, and came to me for a job. I'd been a friend of the family—I'm a lot older than she is, of course—but when we realized we were in love I helped her get a divorce and we were married. We've been very happy for nearly five years. You see, he's been where he couldn't hurt us, behind prison bars."

"And he's out now? Recently?"

"Two weeks, and already he's at work." His glance toward the open box of candy was savage and afraid.

She shook her head at the simplicity of his problem. "The police won't have any trouble tracing his purchase of the poison, or his mailing the package."

An expression of defeat settled about his mouth. "I'm hamstrung. She grows hysterical at the idea of setting the police after him."

"She still cares for him, then. Or pities him," Miss Rachel murmured thoughtfully.

"No one could love a crook like that. It's pity, of course."

Miss Rachel, from the advantage of her seventy years, reflected that he had a good deal to learn about women. Women *could* love the most awful crooks. Her own Aunt Lily, the one who had been a chorus girl in the nineties, had loved a confidence man who had, at the desperate end, run away on the money he got from hocking Aunt Lily's clothes, including her tights. Miss Rachel asked carefully, "Does anyone else know the truth?"

He hesitated a second. "My sister Dorothy. She lives with us. She's devoted to the child. Her terror over the poisoned candy is even greater than mine."

"Just what is it you wish me to do?"

"Try to convince my wife that she must, for the child's sake, turn this man in to the police. I suggest that you come for a day or two, this week-end, perhaps. In addition to convincing my wife of Jenny's danger, you may intercept some new attempt, something that we might not catch until it was too late." He clenched his hands together; the veins in his wrists stood out. "This man is an infernally clever criminal. He was a counterfeiter of the utmost skill and shrewdness. Only the slip of a subordinate finally gave him away."

"How strange, then," Miss Rachel pointed out, "that he works this attempted murder so openly, so clumsily."

He checked what he had been about to say. Some new thought, a strange fear, seemed to show for an instant in his eyes. Then he shook his head. "He's all the more dangerous. Like a mad animal. Will you come?"

"Oh, yes, I'll come."

He started to wrap up the package.

"Leave the chocolates, will you, please?"

His hand stumbled over their handling of the box. The contents spilled out suddenly into a heap upon the rug. In a seeming attempt to back away, his foot came down and crushed the candy into one lump of chocolate. He stood looking-down at it blankly. "Damn it, I've spoiled them all."

Miss Rachel was looking at him calmly. "It's all right. We'll clean the rug." Her cat jumped to the floor and went to the crushed chocolates and sniffed with a delicate disdain. "I knew you were nosy," Miss Rachel scolded, pulling Samantha away, "but not downright stupid."

He was at the door, mopping perspiration again with the white handkerchief. "When will you come? Soon?"

"I'll be at your house tonight for dinner."

"Good. I'll see that the guest room is ready. I'm—I'm sorry about your rug."

"Don't worry about it."

Through the curtains at the window, she watched him walk down the steps, across the sidewalk and get into the long gray car at the curb. The air of nervousness seemed to have passed into dejection. The final glance he gave the house hadn't much hope in it.

He had come just after lunch, given his name as Thackley and his business with Miss Rachel as private. Miss Jennifer had been dressed to go out—it was the day for the Ladies' Aid meeting— and she had cautioned Miss Rachel before leaving that there must not be any more horrors.

Miss Rachel had peeped into the hall where Mr. Thackley waited. "He doesn't look like such a horror, Jennifer."

"You know what I mean," said Jennifer darkly. "Don't get off the subject."

The interview had started by Mr. Thackley saying that he needed help and didn't quite know how to get it. At first mention of the attempted poisoning, Miss Rachel had suggested a private guard. Mr. Thackley had explained, "It's not violence I fear. I can take care of anything like that. I need someone with an acute, wary intelligence." Miss Rachel had nodded graciously at the compliment. Then he had brought out the chocolates.

Miss Rachel called her housekeeper. "We've had an accident on the carpet. Will you get the most of it into a clean box and take it downtown to the police laboratories with a note?"

Miss Rachel had an old friend in the laboratory. She sat down and wrote briefly. Then she packed a small suitcase, called a cab, and picked up her cat. The cat looked eagerly at the door; she liked to travel.

"When my sister comes, tell her I'll be away for a day or two. Tell her I had a chance to . . . ah . . . go to the Wisteria Festival."

The housekeeper shook her head. No one was going to believe that story, least of all Miss Jennifer, who would get hopping mad at the idea of Rachel being involved in a new "horror."

The Thackley home was high on a bluff above the shore near Malibu. The cab pulled up through a long drive bordered with pink asters and blue lantana, to a massive door in a stark white wall. Miss Rachel stood on dark-red tiles and rang the bell. Below was the panorama of the sea, the headlands which fell away toward Santa Monica, the far blue smudge of Catalina Island. The air held a smell of roses and blossoming sage and the wet tang of the Pacific. The door opened silently. A woman looked out at her.

She was a tall woman, well over forty, with tight graying hair, sharp cheekbones, eyes of a peculiar metallic greenish-blue. The color, Miss Rachel recalled, of Mr. Thackley's eyes also. This must be his sister Dorothy. There seemed to be a starved look to her, somehow; something denied, taken away, snatched from her grasp. Not food. Love, perhaps. Miss Rachel smiled into the grim eyes. "I'm Miss Murdock. Your brother asked me to come."

The woman opened the door and showed a long sunny hall. "Come in, won't you? I'm Miss Thackley; guess you saw the resemblance. People do. May I take your cat?"

Miss Rachel decided to experiment. She tried to put Samantha into Dorothy's arms. The cat let fuzz grow up along her back; she put claws into Miss Rachel's bosom and clung, stubborn and unfriendly. "She'll take a little while to get used to you."

Dorothy Thackley took the rebuff indifferently. "I'm not much for cats, anyway. Here, let me take your bag. I'll show you your room."

On the stairs, Miss Rachel asked, "How much of my coming did your brother explain?"

"All of it," said Dorothy flatly. "I wanted him to go to the police with the truth at once—no reflection on your ability, of course—but we pay taxes and we might as well get some return for them. The police know how to handle fiends like *him*." Her heavy sensible shoes made a loud thumping on the polished stairs. "Our little Jenny—she's all we have. We can't be too careful." The starved, lonely quality was in her voice now. There was a yearning note when she mentioned the child's name.

She took Miss Rachel into a large simple bedroom. "We're very plain here, for all the size of the place," she explained. "We do all our own housekeeping. We got used to it during the war." She stopped in the act of opening the closet. "Here's our little Jenny now. Such a tease, she hid in here to see you."

Jenny came out of the closet. She was about six, a small girl with bright brown pigtails, merry eyes, a blue pinafore and white barefoot sandals. The effect she gave was of someone small and warm-hearted and very dearly loved. She came close and put a gently inquisitive hand on Samantha's head and said shyly, "Does he mind if I pet him? He's so soft. Like feathers."

"Her name is Samantha and she seems to like you very much," said Miss Rachel. She managed, without seeming to, to get a look at Dorothy while the child made a fuss over the cat. The woman's angular face seemed wistful, the greenish eyes more lonely than before.

Jenny put her ear against Samantha's and crooned softly.

It occurred to Miss Rachel that Jenny would be easy to love; and that sometimes love is a jealous emotion.

"May I take her to my room?" Jenny begged. "I'll give her my mouse to play with."

But Dorothy came forward firmly. "No, no, Jenny. Leave Miss Murdock's cat be. We have to wash for dinner now."

The child went, but regretfully. Fixing herself for dinner, Miss Rachel was thoughtful.

THE dinner table had been set in a corner of the open patio, where bougainvillæa on a trellis made a shade. A young woman who had been putting yellow plates out upon the redwood surface turned as Miss Rachel came out of the house. She was very slender; her hair was the lively shining brown of Jenny's pigtails, curling softly to her shoulders; but her eyes were not merry and friendly as Jenny's were. They settled on Miss Rachel, examined her with displeasure and reserve. She put out a hand as if with effort. "I'm Mrs. Thackley."

"How do you do?" said Miss Rachel, finding the hand cool and unresponsive.

Mrs. Thackley's voice went on stiffly, "I hadn't been informed of my husband's visit to you, and your coming here, until a few minutes ago. As the wife, and supposed hostess of this home, you'd think I might know a bit more of who is invited here, wouldn't you?"

She was very young to be Mr. Thackley's wife, probably not more than twenty-three or four. Her air of importance, of anger, gave her the look of a little girl who is playing at keeping house. Only the harsh displeasure in her eyes was adult and real, and made Miss Rachel acutely uncomfortable.

"I'm sorry if my coming has upset you," Miss Rachel murmured quietly. She waited courteously to be told to go away.

The girl's face turned pink. "I don't mean to seem rude. I—I guess you came because of Jenny."

"Yes, that's why I came. I can't imagine anyone vicious enough to try to poison a child."

"It happened," said Mrs. Thackley quickly. "I mean, it was true. The candy came by mail and it had been opened and poison put in it."

"For you alone, perhaps?"

She shook her head. "I don't care for candy. Jenny loves it."

"The handwriting on the package—"

"Had been disguised," Mrs. Thackley broke in bitterly. "He'd know so well how to do that. He had a thousand different ways of writing his own name."

"He was clever," Miss Rachel suggested.

"As the devil from hell."

The garden was quiet. There was a single blue jay in the bougainvillæa vine. He had his eye on the basket of crackers in the center of the table. At Miss Rachel's feet, Samantha had opened her green eyes very wide. She had never been able to catch a jay, but this one might be different.

"You had word from him when he was released from prison?"

Mrs. Thackley moved a plate nervously. "He wasn't in prison, not during the last year. He was in an honor camp in the mountains. He didn't write to me, but to Jenny. He sent a short note that he wanted to see her and that he had a surprise for her. Then the candy came, the first box that Ray had analyzed." She moved to the other side of the table, covering what may have been a shudder.

"You didn't feel that you should tell the whole story to the police?"

The hands touching a yellow plate grew very still. "No. I—I feel that he'll straighten out. It's a kind of insanity. He's been shut up all these years, concentrating upon Jenny, upon me. His letters, the few he wrote that I opened, ignored my second marriage. But this blindness to the truth, his refusal to acknowledge that he has lost me, will pass. I want him to have the chance to get back to reality."

Jenny ran out into the patio. She wore a clean pinafore and her face and hands were shining. She scurried toward the cat. At this moment, feeling Samantha's attention off him, the jay swooped for the table. The cat leaped from under Jenny's hands.

There was a wild flutter of blue. Then Samantha was standing alone, looking foolish and embarrassed, and the jay was in the vine with a cracker. A single big blue feather lay beside the table. Jenny pounced on it, held it by the quill and rubbed the downy part against her cheek. Her eyes laughed at Miss Rachel. "Feathers feel so good!" she chirped.

Her mother seized the feather and tore it apart as though something about it enraged her. "Nasty! Off that dirty bird! And just before dinner! Go wash your hands again."

Jenny went in soberly and Miss Rachel saw that Dorothy Thackley met her in the hall.

THE MEAL went off quietly, under an air of restraint. When the dishes had been cleared, Mr. and Mrs. Thackley went into the living room to read. Dorothy Thackley and Jenny put on aprons and hurried to the kitchen. Miss Rachel tried to get interested in a book. She thought Mr. Thackley might wish to talk things over in the presence of his wife. When nothing happened, she decided that the kitchen might be livelier.

Jenny was on a stool, washing dishes at the sink. Dorothy was drying. There were laughter and splashings, and, on Dorothy's part, a wistful air of hoping the closeness, the fun, might never end.

"Jenny likes fuzzy soft things," Miss Rachel remarked, stroking her cat. She was in a kitchen chair, Samantha on her lap. "I remember how Samantha was as a kitten. Like a ball of wool."

Jenny smiled, turning from the sink. But Dorothy's face had stiffened, grown a little pale.

"I have a fuzzy ball," said Jenny. "When I'm through with the dishes I'll bring it for your cat."

The three of them went out into the patio when the dishes were done. The fuzzy ball was blue. In the pale twilight Jenny rolled the ball to and fro among the flowers and shrubbery and the cat ran after it, a little lazily, for Samantha had not been a kitten for a long time. Miss Rachel and Dorothy sat on one of the redwood benches beside the table. The fading light shone in Dorothy's anxious eyes as they followed the child.

Love can be like a cage, Miss Rachel thought. It can be too close, too possessive, suffocating. She was conscious that the evening air was growing chill, that the wind off the sea felt damp and salty. She had hoped that the woman beside her might talk about the problem which had brought her here, but Dorothy's attention seemed absorbed. She suddenly stood up, tense. The little girl had run out of sight behind a white brick wall. "Jenny, don't go far!"

There was an instant of utter blank silence during which Miss Rachel realized that it was almost dark. The light had faded, stars were out, and Jenny had disappeared behind a wall and now there was nothing. She rose, as Dorothy had, with sudden fear.

There came a scream, thin and terrified and childish.

Dorothy ran with a pounding hurry, Miss Rachel with the lightness of a wraith. They reached the garage at the same moment and found Jenny at its side door, staring in, shaking with fright. "There's a man inside!" Jenny shrieked. "He's on a rope!"

They stood as if rooted while inside in the deep gloom the body of the hanged man swung slowly around and around at the end of a rope tied to the rafters. Dorothy, though she was the bigger and sturdier of the two, clung to the door, her face gone sick. Miss Rachel had turned pale, but remained composed. She went in and had a look.

"Come out! Don't touch him! Oh, it's terrible!" cried Dorothy's voice.

Jenny said wonderingly, "She's very brave, isn't she?"

Miss Rachel touched the man's hand softly. "He's quite cold. There's nothing we can do for him." She looked into the dead man's face, not shudderingly but with quiet composure, and then at the dropped stuff about his feet. From among other things, little odd-colored stones and pressed fluffy flowers and bunches of downy leaves, she drew forth a small toy-man made of round knots of wood, on his head a crude mounting of feathers. The painted features on the knot forming the head had a look of humor, of wanting to be friendly. As she studied the toy a sudden expression of anger came into Miss Rachel's usually mild features. "I never believed it," she said half-aloud.

Dorothy Thackley had turned from the door, shielding the child from sight of the hanging figure. "What did you say?"

"I want you to get the police on the telephone at once," said Miss Rachel firmly. "I'll stay here until they arrive."

"But—but a lady shouldn't—" Dorothy's bulging greenish eyes seemed to take in for the first time the smallness, the frailness of Miss Rachel's figure. "You're so tiny, so helpless."

"I've got guts, though," Miss Rachel declared. She could practically hear Jennifer swoon, even at this distance.

As if spurred by this unusual declaration, Dorothy hurried away. Miss Rachel spent the next few minutes switching on the garage lights, taking one more painful look at the man who hung from the rafters, and picking up odds and ends from the floor. The dead man had been extremely handsome; even the sort of death he had endured had not erased the dark good looks, the even features, the exciting pirate dare-deviltry. The stuff upon the floor had the look of little treasures gathered for a child.

"It's what they are, of course," said Rachel to her cat, who followed her about with an air of walking softly so as not to be heard. Since her embarrassing failure with the jay, Samantha had been very quiet. Miss Rachel studied a leaf whose underside was golden and downy. "These were things he had picked up at the honor camp for his child. Bird feathers and bright stones, a toy-man he made of oak galls. A little Indian man for Jenny." The anger returned to burn deep in her eyes. "And so, of course, he didn't send the candy. I never believed he had."

She looked up suddenly toward the door, realizing the appearance there of Mr. Thackley.

He had the gasping, horrified look of someone who comes up from under a wave which has almost drowned him. "This is—is frightful! I didn't dream when I asked you here that there'd be anything like this."

"Probably not," Miss Rachel agreed coolly. "But he's here, though. Can your wife identify him?"

Mrs. Thackley glided forward from the darkness outside. She had put on a black coat, buttoned it high at the neck as if she were chilled. "It's Ted, Jenny's father. I couldn't ever forget how he looked, that clever inhuman slyness." She turned and clung to

Mr. Thackley's coat, burying her face against his shoulder. "Did he come to kill Jenny and me? Did he lose his nerve at the last and commit suicide?"

Mr. Thackley's gaze avoided Miss Rachel's searching one. He put his arms about his wife clumsily, uncertainly. "It seems as if he had. At the end, perhaps, he woke up and saw what a monstrous thing he had planned. He couldn't face the knowledge of his own evil. Perhaps we should be glad. Jenny will be safe now. He won't send any more packages."

Miss Rachel had found a small crushed box from which the feathers and leaves had fallen. She straightened the cardboard, put in carefully all the things Jenny's father had brought with him. To Mr. Thackley she said quietly, "You might prepare yourself for other possibilities. The man may not be a suicide."

"Eh?" He peered at her from above his wife's bent shining head. "Not killed himself? Nonsense!"

"The police will decide, of course. My own theory is that he may have been knocked out or drugged, then hanged here to give the impression of suicide. Perhaps the real sender of that poisoned candy feared to be exposed."

Mrs. Thackley twisted away from her husband, raised her head starkly to look into his eyes. "You told me over and over that he must have sent it."

Mr. Thackley's mouth worked; an aching fright blazed in his face. "I—I thought he must have. Why would anyone else?"

Miss Rachel had put the lid on the small box. "Several reasons have occurred to me. Shall we go into the house? I hear the police siren; they'll want this place to themselves."

WHILE they waited for the police investigation to be completed, Miss Rachel made a telephone call. Her friend at the police laboratory told her that the mass of crushed candy had contained an unnecessarily large amount of strychnine. The strychnine had been used in an easily available form, a household rat poison. The small openings in the bottoms of the chocolates had been refilled, he believed, by an uncooked mixture of powdered sugar and cocoa. Was that what she wished to know?

Miss Rachel asked him a couple of questions about oak galls. She listened carefully to what he said.

The telephone was in an alcove in the hall. Miss Rachel did not re-enter the living room, where Mrs. Thackley stared at her husband in stony-eyed suspicion, where Mr. Thackley pretended to read a book and where Dorothy watched over Jenny with the anxiety of a mother hen. She went on quietly into the kitchen, snapped on lights, and explored the cupboards. She found several half-used boxes of powdered sugar, a large tin of cocoa and a tube of commercial rat poison. She searched further and came up with a tiny squeeze-gun pastry decorator. She was experimenting with a sugar-and-cocoa mixture, dampened to the proper consistency with cold coffee, and was squeezing out dots of the stuff upon the tiled sink when she heard a step behind her. She turned swiftly. Dorothy Thackley had come in quietly and now stood not three feet away. The lonely, lost expression tightened her mouth, made her eyes bitter. "What are you doing here?" she demanded.

"I wanted to make sure just how the candy had been filled with the poisoned mixture," Miss Rachel explained.

"It wasn't done here."

"Oh, yes, I think so. I never thought it was something a clever criminal would do; amateur, obviously, and needing the sort of tools you'd find only in a kitchen."

Dorothy's lean hands twitched. Her eyes searched over the sink, the drawers, the little box Miss Rachel had brought with her. "I won't let you torment my brother with this insanity. He's had all the worry, the strain, that he can stand."

"There won't be any happiness, any safety, until the truth comes out. By the way, have the police reported anything about the death of Jenny's father?"

Dorothy's jaw set itself. "One of them came in a moment ago and said that the man had been murdered. I don't believe it." Her voice shook. "Why would anyone kill him?"

"For jealousy? Because Jenny might have loved him?" Miss Rachel's glance had settled on the broken cardboard box into which she had put the feathers, the stones, and the little man

made of oak galls. "You see, the truth was much different from
what you three believed, or pretended to believe. Jenny's father
had no wish to harm her. I think actually he loved her very
much."

Dorothy began to back away. The pinched loneliness in her
face gave it the baldness of a skull. She felt behind her for the
door. "I won't stay and listen to you."

Miss Rachel opened the little box and held it toward her. "See
what he brought, soft feathers, downy leaves, smooth little
stones. Things with texture and softness which he knew Jenny
would love because he loved them. You saw how she was with
the jay's feather—"

A spasm of defeat crossed Dorothy's face before she turned
and fled. When Miss Rachel went back to the living room, she
found the woman lying on a couch, her eyes shut, her bleak face
turned toward the wall. Mr. and Mrs. Thackley were listening to
Lieutenant Davis.

Davis was a big, intelligent-looking cop. He was explaining the
murder. "The man was tapped at the rear of the skull with some
blunt tool, not a hard blow nor one which required much
strength. Then he was strung up and allowed to strangle."

Mr. Thackley had his handkerchief out, wiping at his forehead.
Mrs. Thackley said slowly, "The pulling up of that limp body
would have taken strength, though. A lot of it."

"I think the rope was tied to a car. As the car backed, the body
was raised toward the rafters. You're right about the job taking
strength. Even a man might have trouble." His eyes were on
Mr. Thackley, who flinched. "Who used the car around three
o'clock today?"

"I—I did," Mr. Thackley stuttered. "I'd been to see Miss Murdock in the city."

"The car isn't in the garage now. It's in the courtyard," Davis
pointed out. "Where did you leave it?"

"Uh—I'm not sure. I usually put it away." His eyes went everywhere but toward his wife's accusing, suspicious stare. "I
didn't kill the man. I swear it."

"This story about the candy, now." Davis pursed his lips. "You came in a week ago to report the first box, but you declared you had no idea who would send such a thing."

"I was wrong, of course." Mr. Thackley looked down at his handkerchief as though he wished to weep into it. "Quite wrong. My wife thought the man would come out of it, come to his senses."

"I don't think that he ever lost them," Miss Rachel put in. The three turned toward her abruptly. Jenny, playing with the cat in a corner removed from earshot, looked up at the change in attention. "I think he came here, not to do any harm, but to see his child because he loved her. He brought her these little treasures. Whoever killed him scattered and trampled them in the garage." She held out the open box; a couple of downy leaves floated to the floor. Jenny left the cat, crossed the room curiously.

"He loved fuzzy, fluffy things," Mrs. Thackley said dully. "It's a quality Jenny has. I can't break her of it."

"You shouldn't try," said Miss Rachel. "Let her be as she is. And let her remember that her father brought her something, though he didn't live to deliver it." She lifted the toy-man with his Indian crest, and Jenny smiled and reached for it.

"What's that?" asked Davis.

"A toy he made of oak galls. An Indian man." She lifted the little figure suddenly from her palm, stared into her hand critically. "I'd forgotten. Oak galls are a strong source of tannic dye, a kind of natural ink." She raised her glance to Davis while all sound died in the room. "The person who murdered Jenny's father trampled all these little things he brought her—in jealousy, in rage. Why don't you just have a look at these three people's shoes for traces of tannic stain?"

The explosive moment lengthened; its breathless quiet hurt her ears. If she had done right, done it quickly enough and surprisingly enough, one of the three would break. She thought she knew which one it would be; someone whose jealous love had not contained itself, had crossed into madness.

Dorothy Thackley turned on the couch and writhed upright. Her face was set like stone. Only her eyes were alive.

"I don't mean jealousy over the love of Jenny," Miss Rachel explained.

Mrs. Thackley rose from her chair and stumbled toward the hall. She seemed blinded, feeling her way with outstretched hands. "Stop her!" cried Mr. Thackley. "Make her come back here and face it!"

For, of course, Miss Rachel thought, his air of being a little boy afraid of the dark stemmed from his unwilling belief that his own wife had made and sent the poisoned chocolates.

At the door, she flung around. Davis had risen to follow her. He said stolidly, "It won't work. My men are all over the grounds. You'll never get away."

She threw back the lovely shining hair, tugged the black coat higher. "I have a way out. You'll never stop me now."

"Let me see your shoes!" commanded Davis.

She laughed in his face. "Why should I? Of course, they're covered with the dye, or whatever it is came out of the oak galls. I wish I could have broken the thing into a thousand pieces!"

She was tense as a strung wire, her slim body turned, whiplike, against the jamb of the door.

"Wait a minute!" cried Miss Rachel. "There are things that only you can tell us. For Jenny's sake, tell us the truth about the candy. Wasn't it to throw your husband off any suspicion he may have had that you wanted to go back to Jenny's father?"

She laughed again, too high-pitched, too harshly. "He'd never dream that I was counting the minutes until Ted came. Not if I seemed to believe that Ted was sending us poisoned candy."

"Mr. Thackley wanted desperately to believe you," Miss Rachel agreed. "He wanted me to prove your innocence. But, you see, he wouldn't have had me come if he meant to do murder. And Dorothy had been warned. Only you, you see, *didn't know I was coming.*"

She put up a hand to rub her temple. "It wouldn't have made any difference. I went crazy when he told me."

"When he told you what?" begged Mr. Thackley.

"When she knew that it was Jenny he came for, and not her.

Her jealous love for him turned into madness," Miss Rachel said quietly.

Dorothy crept over to Jenny and put her arms about the child and covered the small ears with her hands.

The girl at the door snapped about at the sound of steps. Then she ran with an animal-like fear and swiftness. A door slammed; there were fading steps on the tile path of the patio. Mr. Thackley stood up, braced himself against his chair, looked at Miss Rachel wearily. "Where is she going? There's no escape that way."

"Keep the child's ears covered," Miss Rachel told Dorothy. She met Mr. Thackley's frantic stare. "The sea cliff," she said softly.

His lips moved for a moment before he got words out of them. "It's a horrible drop. More than a hundred feet. She wouldn't try to—"

The scream came, then. Everyone in the room flinched except Davis, who was running in the hall. Mr. Thackley shut his eyes and Dorothy made a muffled, horrified sound against Jenny's hair.

Miss Rachel sat down, shivering as if with a chill.

Mr. Thackley said stiffly, then, "She never did love me. It was all a hoax. A way to get a home for Jenny." He put out a big hand timidly and Jenny, who had been about to cry, clutched it and tried to smile. "I don't mind, once I get used to the idea. Jenny'll always have a home with us."

"I'm sure she will."

The starved look, the tension, was leaving Dorothy's face. She wouldn't have to worry about Jenny's ever leaving.

Miss Rachel bent over the little girl and offered her the tiny box. Jenny accepted gravely. The cat came forward to sniff interestedly at the headdress on the toy-man. There was in the room a sudden feeling of peace, of evil fading away, of hatred and passion burned out and gone.

Jenny giggled. "Your cat likes feathers, too."

"It's as close as she'll ever get to a jay," Miss Rachel explained.

from DETECTIVE WHO'S WHO

MURDOCK, Rachel, cat fancier; b. Los Angeles, Calif., approx. 70 years ago; d. Jefferson D. and Mary (Carlyle) M.; grad., Miss Buxton's Sch.; Greenbriar Academy for Young Ladies. Spinster. Employed briefly as: ingenue in stage production, *Slave Maiden* (1898); tightrope apprentice under Goliath the Great (1901); undefined position in carnival show, one performance (1903); earliest known stunt-woman in motion pictures (1907); retired from theatrical life at request of family. Took up (with sister Jennifer) activities in League for Animal Welfare; Ladies' Aid of Parchly Heights Methodist Church; (without sister Jennifer) recently M. M. M. (More Mystery Movies) Society. Has some private practice as a detective. Home address: 38 Sutter Street, Los Angeles, California.

The most disquieting moment in editing this anthology came when I received the biographical questionnaire filled in by the Mysterious Traveler. In answer to the first blank, born ——, he had simply inserted: ? . And the succeeding answers were equally disconcerting and not in all cases publishable—though I have forwarded a copy to Miskatonic University for its files. Suffice it that no one—not even his nominal creators, Robert Arthur and David Kogan —knows whether the Traveler is detective, criminal, or neither. He is only a sly, insinuating, knowing voice heard weekly over MBS, and here makes his first appearance anywhere in print with a characteristically ironic story of crime and retribution.

THE MYSTERIOUS TRAVELER IN

The Big Money

BY ROBERT ARTHUR

A TRAIN WHISTLES IN THE DISTANCE . . .

Good evening. This is the Mysterious Traveler, inviting you to join me and a gentleman named George Cook on a little journey into the complex and dangerous field of crime. But George isn't worrying about danger, so why should you? George is young, not yet thirty, and very sure of himself. Good-looking, too—if you like that type. Come along with me to a rather elaborate penthouse high over Park Avenue. George is sitting at a mahogany desk and speaking into a dictograph. He seems, if I may say so, just a little agitated. . . .

From *Popular Detective* (published as by Andrew Fell). Copyright 1949 by Better Publications, Inc.

TWENTY minutes ago I had seven million dollars. I had a wife, too. She decided that on her seven million dollars would look good. So now she's gone. And the money's gone with her.

That's a lot of cash for a dame to be carrying off? You don't know the half of it. She took something a lot heavier than money when she went. She took my life with her. If she would just come back, she could keep the seven million. It took me only a month to earn it. I'll be satisfied to get my life back.

But I don't think she's going to come back.

While I try to decide what to do about her, I'll talk. About the seven million and the month it took me to get it. Oh yes, and the murder. You don't get dough like that just for sitting around. You practically always have to throw in a murder.

I'll start with the day they evicted me from my cell up the river. Right in the middle of a housing shortage, too. The warden called me in for the customary good-bys.

"I'm glad you're leaving us, Cook," he said, giving me the firm-handshake routine. "I know you'll go far if you apply your talents constructively."

"Thanks, warden," I said. "When I came here I didn't know from nothing. Now I can pick a lock, short-circuit a burglar alarm, or drill a safe with the best of them."

He reddened, but kept on trying.

"Cook," he said, giving me the old fatherly-reproach tone of voice, "I want to help you. Now, the psychiatrist tells me you still can't remember your past prior to the time you were wounded in the army."

"I remember the shell bursting," I told him. "In Bizerte, that was. It was a ducky flash, warden. Just scrumptious."

He got still redder, but kept on giving it the old college try.

"Cook, you have a dishonorable discharge from the army. You were about to be court-martialed for stealing government property when that shell hit. But still, something might be done for you through the Veterans Administration. Treatment for your amnesia. If you'd like me to . . ."

I yawned, and he stopped.

"Warden," I said, "I bluffed myself out of the army hospital in the first place because I didn't want to remember anything. Growing up in a slum, being kicked around, maybe spending time in a reform school—who wants to remember stuff like that?"

"But your family," he said, still in there trying. He must have had bulldog blood in him. "Your friends."

"They probably forgot me years ago. Maybe I ran away to get away from them. I'm looking ahead, not behind me. Now take the average guy, warden."

"Yes?" he bit.

"He can't concentrate," I told him proudly. "He's distracted by all he remembers—the girls he tried to make and couldn't, the jobs he tried to get and didn't, the lies he told and didn't get away with. Me, I can look straight ahead and stick to business. So good-by, warden, and good luck, and if you ever need a reference, just come to me."

So HALF an hour later I was in the club car of the express, an hour away from the big town, enjoying my first drink in two years. The remains of the going-away five jingled in the pocket of the shoddy good-by suit they had given me.

But I felt fine. I had meant what I said to the warden. I didn't have many memories—but I had something better. A feeling. A feeling the big money was heading my way and that nothing could stop it. Sometimes you get a feeling like that, and know nothing can stop it from coming true. Like a hunch on a horse. This was like that. Only bigger. A million times bigger.

So I relaxed. I knew Fate was on the job. On my side, this time. For all I knew, she had slapped me with that shell for a purpose.

How right I was!

After a couple of minutes, I noticed the two people across from me. A plump, white-haired man ordering bourbon old-fashioneds. And a girl. A girl to make the wolves howl as far north as Nome, Alaska. It was the mink coat that gave her away. No girl could be as blue-eyed, as rosebud-lipped, as radiant with that air of nice, wholesome woman-ness—you know what I mean

—and be on the level in a mink as long, as soft, and as deep as that one.

She was staring at my scar, my Bizerte souvenir. When she caught my eye she turned away at once. After a moment she whispered something to White Hair. After another moment he turned, very, very slowly, and pretended to look at the Hudson River, through the window over my right shoulder.

Then his eyes widened. He leaned forward.

"I beg your pardon." He had a voice like the pastor of a nice, rich church. "I didn't mean to stare, but I have a feeling we're acquainted. But I can't quite bring your name to mind."

"George Cook," I said helpfully.

"Cook . . . Cook." He tasted the word all over. "No, I'm afraid I've mistaken you for someone else. Yes, of course—my old friend, Howard Vincent."

I had never heard of Howard Vincent. He didn't seem surprised. I hadn't expected him to be. But he invited me to join him in a drink and in another minute we were all as cozy as three mice in a cheese factory.

His name with Milo Davenport. His niece's name was Felice. Felice and I got along fine.

I told them all about the Big House—homey little anecdotes like the time a four-time loser went stir-crazy and brained a guard with the heel of his shoe. They loved it. All the time I was talking, Felice and I carried on a little private conversation with our eyes. My face seemed to fascinate her. Maybe the scar made me look virile.

They got off at One Hundred and Twenty-fifth Street. As they left, Milo pressed a card into my hand.

"Come see us, George, my boy," he said, squeezing my biceps like an uncle. "I have many connections. I think I may be able to help you start a new career."

"When you put it like that, Milo," I told him, "how can I say no?"

Felice gave me a smile. One of those this-mustn't-be-all smiles which say things a nice girl just wouldn't put into words—only I didn't think Felice was a nice girl.

Then they were gone, and I was looking at the card.

Milo Davenport
Confidential Inquiries

And an address and telephone number. That was all.

Now why should Milo Davenport, Confidential Inquiries, pick up an ex-con on a train? You tell me. I didn't know. I only knew that Felice had been very, very interested in something about me, and the more I thought of it, the less sure I was it was my manly beauty.

So I went to see them. At two o'clock the next morning.

I had spent the evening wandering around town and lavishly spending the remains of my five. My last dime took me uptown to Milo's address, a nice, substantial private house just out of the high-priced district. I let myself in quietly without disturbing anybody. Why wake up such nice people when I couldn't stay long?

Anyway, I was coming back again. Right now, I hoped maybe I could get a line on Milo's racket. If I knew what his game was, I could come back holding more cards. Besides, I might find a little cash.

So I was going through a mahogany desk in a snug little library when the lights flashed on. And the doctors said I should avoid shocks, too.

THERE behind me was Felice, in an evening gown that began at the floor and ended unexpected. Beside her was Milo, in a smoking jacket. Only he wasn't carrying a pipe. It was a gun.

"Why, George, how nice of you to call so soon," Milo purred.

"I just couldn't wait till morning," I told him. "I'm the impetuous type."

"Admirable," he chuckled. "Felice, you were right. He's our man."

"Of course I was right, Uncle Milo," Felice said, with the voice of a well-bred debutante discussing a choice of dresses. "Now put away that gun or he'll think he's not welcome. I'll bring some brandy and we'll have a talk."

So Milo put away the gun, Felice brought the brandy, and we got chummy again.

"You know, George," Milo said reflectively, "Felice bet me you'd show up tonight. And you did."

"Is that good or bad?"

"Good, very good." And he chuckled again. Milo was a happy man.

"You see, George," Felice put in, and then, seeing I wasn't listening, noticed the shoulder strap that had slipped and pulled it up again without a blush, "you see, Uncle Milo has checked your entire career since we left you. Your army record, your wound, your amnesia, the holdup that sent you to the pen, everything."

"Has a man no privacy any more?"

"It took fast working," Milo put in, "but that's my business, you see. I—ah—hunt for people who have disappeared. Particularly if they have money coming to them."

"Interesting business," I opined. "And do you ever find them?"

"Frequently," Milo chuckled. "More frequently than I have any right to expect."

"Now, Uncle Milo, no boasting," Felice said. "Tell George about Howard Vincent."

"What about Howard Vincent?"

I let her refill my glass.

"I thought he was just a gag."

"He's not a gag, George, my boy. He died six years ago and I've been hunting for him ever since."

"He's dead, but you've been hunting for him? With a Ouija board?"

"George," Milo said reproachfully, "my business is finding the missing heirs to large fortunes. Howard Vincent was the heir to a very large fortune. If I reported him dead, I'd have ceased to receive my retaining fee for keeping up the search."

"Milo," I said dreamily, "you interest me very much. I feel that we have much in common. Tell me more."

But it was Felice who did most of the talking. She had a way of getting to the point of a matter while Milo was busy chuckling.

"Howard Vincent was a typical rich man's son," she told me, in those sweet girlish tones that fascinated me. "He turned out bad. Mean. In 1941 he got into a really bad scrape—hit-and-run, with two dead. He was more afraid of his father than of the police, and he disappeared. Uncle Milo was hired to find him. In the fall of 1941 the Western Racer went off the rails in Wyoming, and Vincent's watch and wallet were found in the wreckage. It was midnight, everyone in a berth, no identification on anyone. There were three bodies unidentified. One of them was Howard Vincent. But Milo reported back that none of them could have been Howard."

"I have a reputation, a very good reputation," Milo said smugly. "So no one doubted my word. I kept on hunting for Howard, therefore, on the theory that he had escaped from the wreck and disappeared again rather than go to jail for manslaughter."

"Fingerprints?"

"Howard was never fingerprinted."

"Convenient."

"Old Terrence Vincent wanted him found, wanted him to serve his sentence, then was going to take him back into his good graces. Only Terrence died in 1943. On his deathbed he forgave Howard and left him his sole heir. Seven million dollars."

Milo rolled those last three words around on his tongue like a tea taster sampling a new oolong.

"So the estate is in the hands of Peebles, Packard, and Penworthy, trustees," Felice cut in. "If Howard isn't found inside another year, he'll be declared legally dead and the estate goes to the commonwealth."

"And Milo stops getting a retainer," I said.

"Not at all," Milo said, rubbing his plump pink hands together. "Howard Vincent has been found."

That's another bombshell for you, isn't it, George, almost as stunning as the one in Bizerte. It takes you a moment to understand Milo's meaning. For a few seconds you're speechless. Howard Vincent found! What have you got to say to that?

I SHOULD have got it sooner. But I hadn't. Sometimes I'm a little dumb.

"He's been found twice before," Felice said. "Better likenesses than you, George. Much better. But the first one was too honest, and the second was too dumb. You're neither."

"I was doubtful about your looks, but Felice has convinced me," Milo said happily.

"He's six years older and been in the army," she said. "That changes a man. Besides, the scar accounts for a lot of difference. And George has amnesia, Uncle Milo, genuine amnesia. If he didn't, we'd have to fake it. And you know how that would turn out."

"I know, I know," Milo said, making a face. "I tried it once, years ago. I prefer to forget the whole affair."

"You haven't," Felice said sweetly, "any objection to being Howard Vincent, have you, George? For seven million dollars?"

"Split fifty-fifty!" Milo hurried to get in.

I'd known it! That feeling had been bubbling and boiling inside me as far back as I could remember. The big money! I'd always been meant to have it, and Fate had been leading me toward it all along. That shell in Bizerte—that was all part of her plan. Suppose I had hung around and let the army cure me?

I'd have been cured right out of seven million bucks!

Shall I tell you how we put it over?

No—you'd get bored before I finished. There wasn't anything romantic about it. No E. Phillips Oppenheim stuff. This was big business, and big business is handled scientifically, everything cut and dried.

Milo did it. He knew his business. I'll give you the outlines, the bare outlines. First I got a job in a garage down on the Bowery. About a week later, Milo "discovered" me. He hurried to contact Mr. Peebles, of Peebles, Packard, and Penworthy. There wasn't any use contacting Packard and Penworthy. They were dead.

Mr. Peebles looked me over. Then he and Milo investigated me. They found out everything about my prison record, my army career, my wound. They discovered I had been inducted from Sausalito, California, where I had worked in a garage. I had blown into town there, no one had known me, no one could trace me back beyond that.

So far, perfect.

Then they broke the news to me that I might—just possibly might—be Howard Vincent. I suspected a gag, a racket, I said they were crazy. That made Mr. Peebles anxious to prove I was wrong. Human nature. Anyway, lawyer nature.

Mr. Peebles was a little man with snow-white hair, wispy as dandelion seeds. But not a dope. Not quite. He hired docs— high-priced brain experts. They tapped my knees, looked into my eyes, gave me word association tests.

Amnesia. Check. Authentic goods.

Brother, was I glad I couldn't remember anything! You can't fake for dough like that!

Milo had a cute theory for Mr. Peebles' sake. I'd got out of the wreck of the Western Racer, he said, and had settled down in Sausalito under the name of Cook, and was waiting for things to blow over when the army had up and inducted me. I'd gone along, figuring on revealing myself when the time came. Then the shell had blown away my memory.

All neat and dovetailed. Everything fitted. I looked like Howard Vincent. I could be Howard Vincent. Mr. Peebles wanted me to be Howard Vincent. Then the clincher. The old sockeroo. The one-two to the body.

Milo has an inspiration. He goes out to the Vincent place on Long Island and examines all Howard's old books. In a *History of Economics*—that was Milo's little joke—he found it! A fingerprint in ink made one night when Howard had been studying at Yale, ten years before.

So we match my finger. Check! It certainly should have checked. Milo had sneaked that book out and we'd made the print a month before.

Mr. Peebles swore with excitement—things like "Dear me!" and "I'll be blessed!" And I was accepted as Howard Vincent.

The old charge against me was squashed, quietly. I was welcomed home, quietly. I started right away undergoing treatments, quietly. That's how money works, quietly. That's the way we wanted it—quietly!

Why, George, you're taking it very calmly, aren't you? You're in the big money at last. Fate has arranged things just the way you always knew she would. And it almost sounds as if you were bored! Or am I wrong?

MAYBE it sounds like I was bored. In a way, I was. It's funny. You have a feeling inside you for years something's coming your way, then when you get it, it's as if you'd always had it. No special kick.

I had a big place on Long Island. A cabin cruiser. Three cars. Servants. A private office—Vincent Shipping and Tin.

And no fear of an upset. The fingerprint had done that. Nobody looked at me cross-eyed. There wasn't any former girl friend to "feel" different, no old friends to say, "How he's changed." Howard Vincent had been a heel without any friends.

That's how I made my seven million dollars in a month.

Then for a while it was like a dream—like one of those dreams I'd waked up from in prison so often. Then it settled down and was solid fact. I had seven million dollars and no one was going to take them away from me.

Correction.

I hadn't settled yet with Milo.

He wanted his. Sure. I didn't blame him.

Only I didn't want to give it to him.

Would you have?

So I kicked it around. I slipped him a few thousand here and a few there, when I could pry them loose without Peebles noticing. I pointed out to Milo how tough it would be to turn over large sums of cash without exciting suspicion.

Milo was reasonable. He waited. He hung awfully close, but he waited. Felice hung closer. Felice draped herself around my neck. I didn't know whether she was watching me for Milo, or for herself. But she was right there.

So we had fun. A cruiser trip to Havana. Night clubs. Things

I'd always wanted to do, that I'd waked up at night wanting to do. And now I was doing them and they were fun, sure, but not as much fun as they should have been.

I was too busy trying to figure how to handle Milo to enjoy them.

It had to look right, just right.

It couldn't smell, not one tiny little bit.

It took me three months. Then I had it.

When I was sure I had it, I invited Milo and Felice to my private office after hours one day, to talk about the settlement. There was no one around, and we had a chummy little discussion. We ended up by me promising Milo fifty thousand a month until his half had been paid off. I didn't care what I promised. I wasn't going to have to make good.

I knew by the way Milo's pale blue eyes gleamed that he didn't have any intention of letting me stop when he'd got his half. So I didn't feel bad about what I was going to do.

The details settled, I suggested they have dinner with me. Swell! Fine! Sure! Milo grabbed his hat. Then Felice decided to go powder her nose.

That was all—just powder her nose.

Because she had to powder her nose, I'm telling you this now.

I tried to slow things down, to hold the pot on the fire till Felice got back. But Milo had already marched across my office to the discreetly blank door of my private elevator.

"A private elevator!" he said, with appreciation. "Delightful are the privileges of wealth, George—I mean, Howard. As I hope to find out some day very soon. I'll ring for the car while we wait on Felice. Automatic, I suppose?"

"So nobody knows when I come or go, Milo," I said. "Here, have a cigar. Special from Havana. More of the privileges of wealth."

But he was already turning the knob of the safety door.

"Funny," he said. "I pushed the button but the car isn't coming. Maybe it's already at this floor."

And he opened the door.

Of course the car wasn't there. What had I spent the whole

afternoon for, carefully removing a cover plate and scrambling the wiring so it would positively look accidental? So the car wouldn't leave the ground, of course, but the door would open.

"That's odd." Milo frowned a little. "The door isn't supposed to open until the car is here. Better report this, Geo—Howard."

For a long second he stood there, frowning down at that hole in the floor, that hole that reached like a black shaft of death twenty floors down. Then it came to him.

"George!" he squeaked. "No!"

HE CLAWED at me and grabbed my wrists. I held the door open with my foot and closed my fingers on his plump throat. He squeaked again and clawed at my hands. I shook him and the squeaking stopped. His pale blue eyes bulged out at me like a lobster's. Little bubbles floated out of his mouth. He tried to knee me.

I gave a shove and opened my fingers. Milo staggered backward like a comedy ballet dancer, pawing the air. He seemed to waltz right across the elevator shaft, eyes bulging, mouth bubbling, hands waving, before he started to drop. Then he went like a slow motion diver, his face drifting away, below the floor level, as if he were a falling feather.

Halfway down, his voice came back to him. The elevator shaft channeled his scream and brought it up to me, adding a voice all its own to the sound. I closed the elevator door quick and hoped his fall wouldn't be heard, that he would go undiscovered until I had finished.

I needed two more minutes.

I had planned for Felice to be there. I had planned for them to go together, clinging to each other, spinning around together the whole twenty-floor drop like dancers in a dream. A horrible accident—my office dark—they had opened the door—Milo had stepped forward before he had seen the elevator wasn't there—he had grabbed Felice—I couldn't do a thing! It was horrible!

I was telling the whole story in my mind when the door opened and Felice came back in.

"All ready, darling," she caroled. "Where's Uncle Milo?"

"In the elevator," I said, and hoped she wouldn't notice the sweat on my face. "We were waiting for you. You get in. I'll get my hat."

"All right, Howard." We had agreed I'd be Howard at all times now. But as I stepped over to the hatrack she didn't move, just stood where she was, looking at me dreamily, like a cat at cream it isn't hungry for, but is going to eat later.

"Well, get in," I said, and tried to make it smooth. "Milo's waiting."

"Aren't you going to open the door for me, darling?" she pouted.

"Sure," I said, "sure." And I grabbed the knob. "Funny, it's stuck. Give me a hand."

"No, Howard," Felice said then, and her voice didn't alter by a tone. "I think I'll stay here. I saw what happened when Uncle Milo opened that elevator door."

"You—saw?"

"I was right outside, just coming back for my compact. I was too far away to interfere, so I watched." She could have been saying, "I was looking at the beautiful sunset." Or, "I'd like a fudge sundae."

"In that case—"

But she was too quick for me. She had the little black automatic out of her bag before I had taken a step.

I stopped. Sometimes I'm dumb, but not that dumb.

"You know, Howard," Felice said then, dreamily, "you've been very foolish. Uncle Milo has a complete account of your impersonation in his safe. In case anything happened to him, it was supposed to go to the police. Luckily, I can destroy it."

"But why?" I asked, staring at her. Meaning, why destroy it? Why not let the cops have it?

"Because, darling," Felice said, ever so gently, oh ever so gently, "you're going to marry me. Then as your wife I won't be able to testify against you. In fact, as a good wife I'll have to help you cover it up. Now won't I?"

Well, that was a surprise for you, wasn't it, George? The last thing you expected was for Felice to agree to help cover up her Uncle Milo's death. Of course, there's a catch in it. But then, there's almost always a catch when you're after the big money, isn't there? So what did you do? Did you marry her?

Sure I married her. What else could I do? I got her point of view. Milo was dead, she couldn't help that, so she might as well cash his chips for him. The easiest way was as my wife, where she could dip into the bank account any time she wanted, with no fuss and no questions, and nobody to get suspicious.

Felice was practical. Oh, you've guessed that?

So practical that she let me know she had drawn up six different complete accounts of the impersonation and my murder of Milo. All of them to be forwarded by different parties to the police if anything happened to her, even an innocent auto accident.

"That makes it a real case of 'till death do us part,' doesn't it, darling?" she cooed to me after the ceremony. "Even if I die of pneumonia you'll . . . But let's not think of that. You're going to take good care of me, aren't you, sweetheart? And we will have fun, too. Because I'm not actually repulsive, am I?"

FELICE wasn't repulsive. She wasn't cold-blooded, either. What's more, she wasn't reticent. In a way, I enjoyed being married to her—when I could stop worrying long enough.

I would have been better off with Milo alive. Then I would have known where I stood. With Felice, I was in a cold sweat every time she went shopping. It's awfully easy to be bumped by a taxi in New York! And there were those documents. . . .

In a way, though, I worried worse about what went on in her mind, behind that sweet, beautifully-trained baby face.

Because she fooled me. She did make a good wife. I had expected her to run up the Jolly Roger and raid the bankroll, but she didn't. She turned conservative. Nothing worse than nice, quite night-clubbing. A few jewels—not too showy. And a penthouse apartment on Park Avenue instead of the place on Long

Island—a simple little shack with nine rooms and a terrace, thirty floors up, where we could sit and watch New York's lights glitter at night like a dowager's diamonds lying in the gutter.

I couldn't figure her. But after six months had gone by, and she hadn't made a wrong move, I began to wonder. Maybe she meant it. Maybe this was what she really wanted.

Yes, sometimes I'm a little dumb.

In June, I slipped and broke my ankle. Fell on the polished parquet floor of the foyer. The perils of wealth!

That meant two weeks lying around. Drinking and thinking. Thinking and drinking.

Felice was the prefect wife. She kept me company. She drank with me, sitting on the terrace and watching the traffic flow by underneath like armies of mechanized lightning bugs. When I was quiet, she was quiet.

The perfect wife.

Too perfect.

I might not have been suspicious if she hadn't been so perfect. Might not have noticed that each night she was urging me to drink a little more. Might not have felt the tension in her voice on the seventh night, when she had Walters, the ultra respectable and veddy English butler she had hired, busy running back and forth with the brandies. Then she had him bring the bottle, and I knew.

I don't know what I knew. But I knew. Enough to start ditching the drinks into the ornamental shrubbery at my side of the terrace.

Because if I'd drunk all she handed me, I'd have been higher than a V-2, I acted more and more blotto. It wasn't hard. I was a long way from sober when Felice leaned over me and whispered:

"Howard!"

I stayed quiet. I could hear her hold her breath. Then:

"Howard! If you're going to fall asleep, don't you think we ought to go inside now?"

I mumbled something. She stood up and shook me, gently at first, then harder.

"Howard! Get up on your feet! I'll help you inside."

I muttered and grunted and stood up, holding on to the chair, her, and everything else in reach. A beautiful picture of a rum-dum hunting for his gutter.

I lurched toward the door, but she caught me neatly and eased me over, sat me on the rail of the terrace, with the street thirty dark floors beneath the seat of my pants.

I lolled there. She had a good grip on my coat.

"Good-by, Howard," she said, and still her voice didn't change. It still lilted as sweetly as the singing of a lark on a May morning.

"I'm saying good-by, Howard!" She shook me a little. "You're going to have an accident—a tragic accident. And I'm going to be the widow of Howard Vincent, inheriting everything. I'm sorry, Howard, truly I'm sorry, that it has to be this way. I'm terribly fond of you. But you keep trying to figure how to be rid of me. And some day you'd find out. So I can't take any chances. I have to do this.

"I'll tell them you tried to stand up, and were drunk. You stumbled and your broken ankle wouldn't hold you. So you plunged over the rail. Isn't that a good story, Howard? Isn't it a lot better than the accident you arranged for Uncle Milo? And Walter will testify to it. He knows you're drunk."

Then she pushed.

She pushed, and I didn't go over. I had my good foot hooked through the openwork of the railing.

"Not this time, baby," I said, and grabbed her wrists.

Felice screamed, in sheer surprise and anger, but I hardly heard her. I was too busy. She was shoving and I was trying to push her away. I had her wrists and she braced herself, butted me with her head, got one hand loose, and clawed at my face, cursing me all the time with language that must have been bottled up inside her all her life.

Felice never liked to have her plans go wrong.

SHE braced herself and pushed and scratched and clawed like a perfumed wildcat. I realized then that I was drunker than I'd thought, and I was only trying to lean forward, to fall on the terrace, where she wouldn't be able to lift me. I heard the brandy bottle fall and break, and it sounded a long way off.

Then the brandy must have trickled toward us, wet the tiles under her feet. She slipped and fell sideways, just as she was lunging at me. Her own momentum took her up on the railing. I still held her wrist, but her weight pulled at me. I heard the wrist bone snap, and heard Felice scream again, as I let go, just in time to pull myself back.

She screamed all the way down, the whole thirty floors. Then a sound like a sandbag being dropped onto cement cut the scream short.

I swayed there, licking blood that was trickling into my mouth from the scratches she had put on my face. And then I saw Walters, standing there with a tray in his hand, his mouth opening and closing like a feeding goldfish.

"Mr. Vincent, sir!" he got out at last. "Mr. Vincent, sir."

"She slipped," I said, and I was thinking of Felice then, not of those documents she had planted away to be turned in to the cops. "She slipped." And I was thinking of those warm soft curves and thirty floors of height and a cold dark pavement. "She slipped and fell over the rail. I couldn't hold her."

Then I saw Walters' eyes and knew something was wrong.

"Mr. Vincent, sir!" That was Walters, the perfect butler to the last. "You pushed her! I saw her struggling with you. You— you murdered her!"

So that's how my wife went, and my seven million dollars with her. Walters loped out of there like a big gray rabbit, ten minutes ago, to call the cops. I'm locked in here in my den, telling this to the dictograph. Why, I don't know. Maybe to keep from thinking of what I'm going to do. Because I've come all the way up a dead-end road. There's Walters to swear I killed her, and there are those documents to prove a motive.

They're outside, hammering on the door now. I have my gun out of the drawer. If I'd had both my legs, I might have run for it. But with a broken ankle. . . .

Well, anyway, Mr. Peebles, I had it. The big money! I knew I was meant for it, and I got it, and that's something most men don't do. I wonder how big a hole a .38 makes. I wonder . . .

No, George, wait! Put down that gun! There's something you don't know. If you'll just wait for the police— Oh, George, you shouldn't have done that. Really you shouldn't. But then, you didn't know what Mr. Peebles could have told you, did you? If you had known, what a difference it would have made! But you remember the old saying, 'Of all sad words of tongue or pen, the saddest are these, it might have been.' Well, let's finish the story. Mr. Peebles has a statement to make.

Statement by Walter J. Peebles: The foregoing is an accurate transcript of my client's last words, as recorded upon a dictograph. I can only add to it that no such documents as he mentions were ever turned over to the police. They did not exist, despite what Mrs. Vincent told him. The reason is obvious.

After Davenport's discovery of the fingerprint in Howard's old textbook—a print I did not know until now was a forgery —I was inspired to hunt further through Howard's former toys. I found a bicycle which he had painted at the age of twelve, and in the paint were dozens of his authentic fingerprints, permanently preserved. These I compared with George Cook's. They matched.

Therefore—and both Davenport and his niece were aware of this all along—George Cook's amnesia was not a result of his war wound. That simply complicated an injury which, it is obvious, dated back to the wreck of the Western Racer in 1941. George Cook was, and always had been, Howard Vincent.

*This is the first of the Nick Noble stories. I can recall why
I started the series: because Ellery Queen had just opened
up a fine new market. I can recall where I got the name
Screwball Division: it was a translation into American of
Carter Dickson's Department of Queer Complaints. I can
recall the model for the Chula Negra: a little Mexican café
on Second Street in Los Angeles, where the staff of a political weekly used to gather to talk about the stories we
were going to write and eat the best lengua en mole I've
ever tasted and drink sherry (which the waitress always
called cherry) at ten cents per water-glassful. But I absolutely cannot recall how I ever conceived the wino-detec-
tive Nick Noble. In fact I don't think I did conceive him
—I think he was always there.*

NICK NOBLE in

Screwball Division

BY ANTHONY BOUCHER

DETECTIVE LIEUTENANT Donald MacDonald, L.A.P.D., was
newly commissioned and inexperienced. He had never been inside a priest's study before. For the matter of that, he had never
seen a murdered priest.

While he listened to the housekeeper, he tried to keep his eye
on the diocesan map of parishes, on the unfinished poster announcing a Baked Ham Dinner with Bingo, on the glaring
chromo of the Sacred Heart; but his gaze kept shifting back to
the body.

From *Ellery Queen's Mystery Magazine*, Sept., 1942. Copyright 1942 by
The American Mercury, Inc. Reprinted with the permission of the author and
Ellery Queen's Mystery Magazine.

"The poor dear old man all alone in the house," the woman was saying. "Father Guerrero off on a sick call, and me hurrying out to the Safeway because we was that near out of flour and he did love his coffee-cake of a morning, the saint that he was."

There was no point in staring at the body. The photographer had taken it from half a dozen angles. The surgeon hadn't got there yet. The body was their business between them. But a black cassock with a stiff white collar, a thin peaceful old face with a fringe of gray hair—these didn't go with murder.

"I'll never forgive myself, that I never will. To leave him alone with the world full of Nazzies and Kingdom People and suchlike!"

MacDonald brought his eyes back to the witness. "And you were gone how long?"

"That I can't tell you, officer, not to the minute. That nice young man at the Safeway, the blond one, he was showing me snapshots of his youngest and—"

"But roughly?"

"Well, say ten minutes. Fifteen maybe."

"And what time was this?"

"I'm not one to look at the clock day in and day out, officer, like my poor sister's husband that never held a job six months in his life, God rest his soul, but it was before dinner, that I know, because it was all in the oven and a good half-hour to go yet."

"And dinner was at what time?"

"Six o'clock sharp, and Father Guerrero gets his sick call five minutes before I left, and he'll come home without a bite in his stomach, the poor lamb, to find his pastor . . ."

The woman had wept before, and it had taken ten minutes to bring her back to the questions. MacDonald hastily interposed, "That would make it about five-thirty you left?"

She gulped a little. "Yes, officer."

"You got back some time around quarter of six?"

The gulp was stronger. "Yes, officer."

"And found Father Halloran . . . ?"

The gulp won. She nodded silently and turned her streaming face away.

MacDonald damned the surgeon's delay and doubly damned the fascination of that hassocked corpse. The housekeeper was huddled in silent sorrow. MacDonald could catch the dry clicking of her lips as the beads of a rosary slipped through her fingers. He forced himself to stare at the body with what he tried to make an impartial and experienced eye, and lined up the facts.

Entrance of bullet below heart to the right. Exit in left shoulder blade. Bullet found in back of chair. Priest had been sitting. Murderer then must have been kneeling to achieve angle of shot. Query: false pretense of confession? Memo: find out mechanics of confessional positions. Time of death: 5:30 to 5:45, pending surgeon's report. Memo: check time with blond Safeway clerk. Time. . . .

Lieutenant MacDonald bent over the corpse and pushed back the black sleeve on the left arm. Wristwatch. A bare chance. . . .

MacDonald rose and looked at the praying woman. There was a new and speculative quality in his stare. The broken wristwatch had registered exactly 7:06.

DETECTIVE LIEUTENANT Dan Barker, L.A.P.D., felt no compulsion to stare at the body on the bed of the seedy Skid Row lodging house. There was more blood on the face of the questioned witness. There was blood on the floor, too, and on the luridly prophetic tracts proclaiming the Kingdom; and the corpse had bled very little.

Barker let another short right jab light on the unshaven jaw of the witness and watched the head bobble on its scrawny neck. "Come clean, friend," he grunted. "You can't get away with it."

The witness tried to stem his nosebleed with what might once have been a handkerchief. Barker slapped his hand down. "Come clean," he repeated.

"Honest to gar, copper, I don't know nothing. I hears the shot and I looks in here and I says, 'Wow! This is where the bulls come in.' So I runs downstairs and I finds Finney on his beat and he takes a gander and calls in you boys. And honest to gar, copper, that's all I know."

Barker looked him over reflectively and decided on the nose.

A light tap jerked the head back and set the blood flowing at a doubled rate: "We've got you cold, friend. Why'd you kill this Marsden jerk?"

The witness leaned over to let the red stream hit the floor. A drop splashed on Barker's right shoe. The officer raised his foot and swung it at the witness' fleshless left shank.

"Keep your blood to yourself, friend." His voice was toneless. "What'd you do with the rod?"

The witness hopped on his right leg and held both hands clasped to his left shin. He moaned. His hopping left bright discs of blood around the floor with spatter-drops radiating from them.

"The rod, friend," Barker went on calmly. "We've got you cold without that, but maybe we could make things easy if you'd help us."

"Honest to gar, copper . . . Oooo . . . !" The witness' voice wavered like an air-raid warning as he hopped about.

"Stand still and on both legs, you yellow-bellied stork."

The witness stood. "Honest, I don't see no rod. I hears the shot and I says, 'Cripes, that screwball next door took the short cut home,' but then I looks in and I don't see no rod, so I goes for Finney just like I says."

Barker smiled now. "You don't see no rod, is that it, friend?"

"Sure, copper. Just like I tells you. Honest to—"

"For gar's sake forget about gar for a while. And you didn't see the murderer come out of this room either, friend?"

"I don't see nobody. Hell, copper, I ain't covering for nobody. If I see 'em, I'd sing. I play ball. You ask Finney."

"I'm asking you. You don't see nobody?"

"Nobody. Honest to—"

Meditatively Barker drove a right against the witness' left ear. The head described a long arc on its skimpy neck and met Barker's left at the end of the arc. The neck stood straight again. The head wobbled and the eyes were glassy. Barker laid a flat palm against the chest to prop up the body, and swore as blood dripped on his sleeve. His other palm slapped the bristly cheeks until a little life came back to the eyes.

"O. K., friend. Now listen to what you've said. This room's at the end of a hall. You're in the next room down. You hear a shot, you think this Marsden creep has killed himself, you run out and look in here. You don't see no rod, you don't see nobody." He mimicked the witness' wavering pipe. "So, my friend, honest to gar, you killed him."

The witness started to open his mouth. A backhand slap closed it and opened his lower lip. Barker had more reasons than vanity for wearing a heavy ring.

"You're listening now, friend," Barker reminded him. "You thought stashing away the gun was smart; they couldn't pin it on you that way. That's where you were wrong. A gun, and it could be suicide. No gun, and it's murder. And you're the murderer, because anybody else would have had to pass you in the hall." Barker paused. "There's one other thing that's phony," he added. "How can you be so cockeyed sure of the time?"

The split lip thickened the witness' speech. "I used to work in a watch factory. Sometimes I do repairs for Joe's pawnshop over on Main."

Barker laughed. "Repairs. O. K. We know Joe's a fence. You alter identifications for him. That'll help you."

The witness decided not to argue. "So I'm setting this watch, see, when I hear the shot. That's how I know what time it is. It's just 7:06 when they get him."

DETECTIVE LIEUTENANT Herman Finch, L.A.P.D., sniffed the aroma of the secretary's obviously custom-made cigarette and lit his corncob defiantly. Twenty years on homicide had still not put Finch completely at ease in any dwelling assessed at over fifteen thousand dollars.

"And you don't know of any threats against the judge?" he puffed.

The young man smiled disdainfully. "Judge Westcott did not move in circles where threats against one's life are a commonplace, lieutenant."

"Social-like, maybe not. But all the same the judge was on the bench. I've never known a court officer yet didn't get threatened some time by some poor sucker."

The secretary tapped his cigarette into a delicate glass ashtray. "Judge Westcott was never threatened. I'm certain that in my confidential capacity I'd have been aware of such a development."

"Horsefeathers!" muttered Finch, whose slang never managed to catch up with the times. He looked around the lavishly furnished room. "What do you know about the judge's will?" he demanded abruptly.

The supercilious youth was unmoved. "I am afraid that's a matter on which you should consult—"

"Sure, formal-like, but you could save me a lot of trouble if you knew."

The secretary shrugged. "Very well. The servants and I receive nominal bequests. The residuary estate is divided among several charities. If you care to know their names . . . ?"

"Later on, for the record. No family?"

"None to my knowledge. Judge Westcott was an orphan and a widower."

Finch poked his index finger into the corncob bowl. "Nominal," he said.

"I beg your pardon, lieutenant?"

"Nominal. What's it mean?"

"What—? Oh, the bequests. As to the servants, I don't know. In my case, as I have gathered from the judge's hints, it means something between five and ten thousand. Surely . . ." He hesitated.

Finch let the silence grow, then drawled out a "Yes?"

"Surely you could not consider such an insignificant sum as providing me with—well, a motive?"

Finch said nothing. There isn't anything you can say to people who call five or ten grand insignificant.

"I'm sorry not to be more helpful."

Finch roused himself. "No way you can narrow the time? Damned doctors always shillyshally—helpful if you can check up on 'em."

"No. The judge regularly spent the hours from six to eight in his study alone. He often dozed off. I found him when I went in to rouse him for dinner."

"Ground floor, French windows, large grounds. . . . I can see how anybody might slip in all right. But how about the noise?"

"The curse of civilization," the secretary sighed. "A shot can be so easily confused with—"

"I know," Finch cut in. "A backfire. Criminenty! If I had me a buck for every time I've heard a witness talk about backfires, I'd be retired and doing right nicely, thank you. But the shot wasn't all. There was pretty much of a brawl in there."

"I heard nothing, and most of the time I was here in this adjoining library."

"You must have heard it. Hell of a rumpus."

"Then it must have happened before I came in here, around six-twenty, or after I went upstairs to dress at seven-thirty."

"Uh-huh." Finch nodded abstractedly and walked over to the study door. The room was a shattered mess. Chairs overturned, ashstand spilled, telephone sprawling, clock . . .

Finch puffed harder on his corncob and strode over to the clock. It was electric, and the struggle had jerked it loose from the wall plug. "Hot ziggety zag!" he murmured. The clock had stopped at exactly 7:06.

DETECTIVE LIEUTENANTS MacDonald and Finch, holders of the newest and oldest lieutenants' commissions on the force, decided on another cup of coffee.

Finch glanced up at the clock in the all-night lunch wagon. "They say the stuff keeps you awake. But when you finish work after midnight, you'll sleep all right."

MacDonald frowned at the counter. "You know," he said, "I had the damnedest thing happen to me tonight."

Finch grinned. "Watch it, Mac."

The younger officer half-answered the grin. "I know. You always say murder's enough in the day's business; keep it quiet after hours. But this is funny. I'd just like to know if it happens much."

Finch stoked up the corncob and said, "Shoot."

"I know it crops up in fiction, but it seems too blamed helpful to be a usual thing. I actually did have a corpse where the wrist-watch broke in the fall and established the time."

"Check with the medical evidence?"

"Close enough. You know doctors. But not with the one witness. Housekeeper claims she found the body an hour earlier, fainted, and didn't get around to calling us for years. Puts me on a spot. I'd like to believe her; I'd like to believe the watch. Did you ever have anything like that?"

"Can happen. Matter of fact, something like it cropped up today. Electric clock pulled out of the wall, stopped at 7:06 sharp."

MacDonald choked on a swallow of coffee.

"Too hot, Mac?"

"No. Only— That's the same time as mine. The wristwatch. 7:06, exactly."

Finch removed his pipe.

"What goes, friend?" a man down the counter called over.

Finch waved a greeting. "Hi, Barker. Damnedest thing. Mac and I were both out on homicide cases today, and there were stopped timepieces in both cases. But that isn't enough: they were both stopped at six minutes after seven."

Barker announced sharply that he would be violated in an unlikely manner.

"Me too," Finch agreed. "Can you tie that?"

"Tie it? Friend, I can make it look sick. I arrested a Skid Row bum today for shooting the crum in the next room. He claims it was an accident and all he did was hear the shot—at exactly six past seven."

"Criminenty!" Finch muttered. MacDonald was speechless.

"Wait a minute, friends," Barker went on flatly. "That ain't the half. While I'm booking this bum, a call comes in from a prowl car squad. They've just dragged a dentist out of his burning office. Toasted up pretty, he was, and a nice handy little smashed wristwatch to show he collapsed at I'll give you one guess what time."

There was a dead silence. Then Finch spoke, and with a certain quiet authority. "Barker, come over here." He lowered his voice when the other approached. "Look. There's something haywire, and if we three play our cards right we can make sense out of it. Four men don't die at exactly 7:06 just for the hell of it. There's a pattern here."

MacDonald nodded, but Barker let out a snort. "Balls," he grunted.

"Look, Barker. I know you're smart. You've got a sweet record of convictions, and we won't talk about how you got 'em. But I've been in this game since you were knee-high to a grasshopper, and I know a screwball setup when I see one."

"Balls," Barker insisted. "It's a chance."

"Four men's too many for chance."

"Friend, nothing's too many for chance. I've been at Padrino's joint when the red came up twenty-three times running, and me with my money on the black all the time till I switch to red on the twenty-fourth. Then bingo! She's black. That cured me. There's no patterns. It's all chance."

"Play in with us on this, Barker, and I'll swear it won't do your rating any harm."

"Deal me out, friends. I got better things to do tonight than play games with you. Or maybe you wouldn't understand about that? Anyway, I've got my murderer, all locked up and softened and ready to sing. So balls to you, my friends."

Finch scarcely glanced after the departing officer. He headed straight for the pay phone and dialed the familiar number. "Finch speaking, homicide. . . . Look, boys, I need some dope. I reported a shooting tonight—Judge Westcott. Has the ballistics report come in yet? . . . O. K., when it does I want it checked with the reports on the cases of Lieutenants Barker and MacDonald. . . . Check. Can you dig up now the report Barker just filed? . . . O. K., read me the high points." He listened, nodding and adding an occasional query. "Thanks. And I want all the dope you can scrape up on a dentist that a prowl car found burned tonight. . . . No, that's all I know; you can dig it out of the records from that. All the details you've got on the man, and an extra careful autopsy. Five'll get you ten there's a bullet in that body; check it against the other three. . . . No, I'll phone back in an hour. . . . Check."

MacDonald started as Finch took his hat off a peg. "Where are you going? I thought we were going to talk this thing over?"

"You're coming with me, Mac."

"But where?"

"Son, I've sort of shown you the ropes, like, around this department. You know all about the vice squad and the chem lab and the ballistics department and the burglary division and God knows what else. But there's one section you never saw before tonight."

"And that's where we're going?"

"On the nail, Mac. We're now headed for the Chula Negra café, sometimes known as the Screwball Division, L.A.P.D."

MacDonald got the picture as a rapid walk took them up North Main Street to the Chula Negra. A scandal and political shakeup in the department a dozen years ago. A captain who was in it up to the neck but pulled enough wires to get clear. A lieutenant who took the rap.

Nick Noble, the lieutenant's name was. He'd broken more big cases than any other man in the department, and half of them some completely screwball setup that usually has the police rocking on their heels. Like the university professor who objected to the existence of one-eyed beggars, and took measures accordingly.

Nick Noble's wife was sick when the shakeup came. She needed an operation badly. She didn't get it. Broke, disgraced, a widower. . . .

"It's no wonder he took to drink," Finch said, "but it's hell he had to do it the way he did." Nick Noble was a wino, the lowest and soddenest kind of drunk that even the Skid Row of Los Angeles can exhibit. Nobody knew where he lived or what he lived on. Nobody knew anything except that he hung out at the Chula Negra and that he could still think.

The one thing that interested him beside his cheap sherry, the one hold life still had on him, was the fascination of his old profession. And he could still give cards and spades to any man in the department when it came to the freakish, the outrageous, and the unbelievable.

Nobody bothered to consult Nick Noble much any more save the old-timers of Finch's generation. The younger men trusted mostly to the laboratories or, like Barker, to their own fists and maybe a rubber hose. "Not that you can't crack ninety-nine of your cases with a lab or a hose," Finch added. "But the hundredth one needs a man like Nick Noble, and Mac, this looks like the one in a hundred."

The Chula Negra didn't run to barflies or juke boxes. It catered to nothing but the single-minded eating and drinking of the local Mexicans. Finch walked over to the third of the ramshackle booths and, motioning MacDonald after him, slid in.

MacDonald had expected a fat and bloated hulk. But alcoholism makes some thin, and Nick Noble was one of these. He was a wizened man whose sharp nose seemed trying to push out of his dead-white skin. His hair and heavy eyebrows were white too, and his eyes so pale a blue as almost to match them.

There was a water glass half-full of sherry before him. He took a long swig and made a swipe at his nose before he saw the officers. "Herman!" he said softly, and looked sidewise at MacDonald. "Friend?"

"Friend. Lieutenant MacDonald, homicide."

"Glad," said Nick Noble, and struck again at his nose. "Fly," he explained. "Stays there." There was no fly.

"I'm afraid," Finch began, "it's up to you again, Nick."

A pale light glittered in the dead blue eyes. "Give," said Nick Noble.

Finch gave.

Nick Noble finished another glass of sherry while Finch talked, and chased the invisible fly away from his nose six times. That nose seemed to grow sharper as he drank, and his pale eyes paler.

"Through?"

Finch nodded. Nick Noble leaned back and rested his head

against the flimsy partition. A film glazed his eyes. He was silent so long that young MacDonald frowned and looked from the empty glass to Finch. But Finch shook his head.

Finally Nick Noble spoke. "Questions."

"O. K., Nick."

"Man on Skid Row. Lige Marsden. Occupation?"

"None, unless you count standing on street corners passing out pamphlets."

"Pamphlets for what?"

"Kingdom something."

"People of the Kingdom?"

"Check."

The pale eyes glazed again. MacDonald remembered the minor sect. The priest's housekeeper had mentioned it. Strange sort of anarchic idealism—civic disobedience as a religious principle. Denial of all rights of authority.

The eyes opened, and Nick Noble asked another question. "Dentist. No name?"

"Not yet. In a minute I'll phone back and check."

"Find out all about him. Especially Draft Board."

"Draft Board?"

"Was he a member?"

Finch nodded. "What else, Nick?"

"Nothing."

MacDonald started. "Aren't you interested? Aren't you going to—?"

"Interested? Oh yes. Pretty problem. Pattern. Thanks, Herman. Proof tomorrow."

Finch grinned. "Don't mind him, Mac. He can't help grandstanding."

"No grandstand. Murders tie together. Motive for time not quite clear yet. Only one murderer possible."

MacDonald half-rose. "You mean we can—?"

"Tomorrow. Don't rush it."

"But if there's a murderer loose— Damn it, Noble, our main job isn't catching criminals; it's preventing crime. And if . . ."

Nick Noble smiled faintly at Finch. "Young," he said. Then

to MacDonald, "All right, boy. No danger. No more murders. Not possibly. Check tomorrow. Now phone, Herman."

When Finch came back, his grin spread from ear to ear. "Criminenty, Nick, you can always pull a rabbit out of the sherry bottle. You've done it again, you son of a biscuit-eater."

"What did you find out?" MacDonald demanded.

"Ballistics check. Same gun killed all four of 'em. And that means the times are phony. Whole damn 'struggle' at Westcott's was probably just to make that clock look plausible. But where Nick comes in with the Noble touch is this: The dentist's name was Dr. Lyle Varney, and he was on his local Draft Board. In fact, he was chairman."

Nick Noble nodded. "Good. Go home. Tomorrow, boys, I'll show you your murderer."

HALF an hour and one sherry later, Nick Noble entered the lodging house on East Fifth Street. His slight figure, his pale worn features, his shabby once-respectable suit all seemed to belong there. The clerk didn't give him a glance. They come and go.

There were two corridors on the second floor. From the end of one came laughter and clinkings. Two rooms at the end of the other were dark, silent. Nick Noble's white hands fiddled for an instant with the lock of the last room. He went in, closed the door, and switched on the light.

The room was any one of a thousand others. All that distinguished it was the absence of ashes and beer bottles and the presence of blood on the floor and the bed. And the pamphlets.

There was a stack of these left undistributed, a stack that reached from floor to table level. Nick Noble picked up the top one and leafed through it. He set it down, then picked it up again, found a page, and reread the heading over a prophetic article:

THE NUMBER OF THE BEAST AGAIN

Nick Noble said "Six" three times, and his eyes glazed. He stood motionless. Then his eyes came alive. He put the pamphlet back, and nodded.

There were steps far down the hall. Nick Noble switched off the light. The steps came as far as the next door and halted. Then they moved on. The door of the dead man's room opened. The beam of a flashlight coursed around the walls, clicked off. The door closed.

Nick Noble crawled out from under the bed. He swatted at the fly that wasn't on his nose and thereby knocked off the cockroach that was on his sleeve. He heard the door of the next room open and shut. He listened, but there was no click of the light switch.

He left the dead man's room without a sound. He paused before the next door, the door to the room of Barker's prisoner. A light came and went in the crack under the door. He drew back to the hinge side.

The door opened in a minute, covering him. Through the crack he saw a man coming out, a man he had never seen before. He carried a flashlight in one hand and something heavier in the other. This man set them both down on the floor and fished a tool out of his pocket, the same tool that Nick Noble had used on the other door.

The strange man closed the door. Nick Noble moved with agility. His hand was on the automatic on the floor when the stranger's right connected.

This time Nick Noble's eyes were glazed somewhat longer.

He was still in the hall when he came to. He felt his way into the dead man's room and doused his head with stale water from the pitcher. He switched on the light and peered into the cracked mirror. The blood had clotted by now, black on his white skin. He looked closer. That was a heel mark on his cheek. His thin lips set tight.

LIEUTENANT MacDonald, reporting for duty next morning, was greeted by Finch. "For once, Mac, old Nick slipped up. He said no more murders. They found Padrino early this morning."

"Padrino?"

"That's right. Maybe you wouldn't know. He runs a bigtime gambling setup. Roulette and the works. Official-like, we don't know about him here. But he was shot sometime between one and three and his watch was broken and set to 7:06. Bullet checks, too."

MacDonald gaped. Finch frowned as he loaded his corncob.

LIEUTENANT Dan Barker was filling out his report on the latest sweating of the bum he had arrested. He yelled admittance when he heard a knock on the door.

A uniformed sergeant came in. "Old screwball here insists on seeing you, lieutenant. Got a minute?"

Barker glared distrustfully at the slight old man behind the sergeant. "All right," he growled.

Nick Noble came in quietly. When the sergeant was gone, he said his name. "Maybe you've heard of me."

Barker's expression changed. "Hell, yes. You're the wino the old-timers tell the tall stories about. What's on your mind?"

"Tried to see Finch or MacDonald. Out. You had the other case. Talk with you."

Barker eyed the heel-bruised old face suspiciously. "O. K., friend. What's the angle?"

"All solved. All the cases at six after seven. No use for me—credit better go to the force."

"You've heard there's another one?"

"Yes. That, too. Want to hear?"

Barker shifted in his chair. "Why not?"

Nick Noble pulled a bottle from his coat pocket and filled the water glass on the table with sherry. "Drink? Sorry. Forget regulations. Well: Look at murders. Pattern. Leave out Padrino now. Just yesterday's. Three deaths timed mechanically. Fakes. One death timed accidentally. Your case. Time true."

"So where does that get you, friend?"

Nick Noble made an attempt on the fly. "Look at men. Three represent authority. Priest, authority of church. Judge, authority of law. Dentist, authority of state. Draft Board. Guessed that. Likeliest kind of authority for professional man. Other man, no authority. Your case. People of the Kingdom. Hates authority."

Barker grinned a lazy grin. "So still what?"

"Look at time. Six after seven. What's that to six?"

"Huh?"

"What's five minutes of seven to six?"

"Six fifty-five."

"And seven sharp?"

"Oh. I get you, friend. Six sixty."

"And six after seven."

"Six . . . sixty-six."

"Six sixty-six. Number of the Beast. Apocalypse. Tied up in all prophecies. Great number with People of the Kingdom. Beast means State, Church, everything they despise."

Dan Barker's heavy body squirmed. The chair creaked. "Smart stuff, friend. What next?"

"Easy. Your man's the murderer."

"The jerk I've got in the can? Hell, he killed Lige Marsden all right, but he didn't kill the others."

"Not him. Lige Marsden. Your corpse. Only motive. Nobody could want to kill him *and* the others, but *he'd* want *them* dead. Other times faked, his real. Crazy gesture in suicide, same time as the phonies."

"Balls! How about the gun?"

"Your prisoner. Hid it in his room. Chance for quick money. Worked with a fence. Won't admit it now; scared of murder rap."

Lieutenant Barker leaned back and eased open the drawer in front of him. "Pretty good, friend. Damned smooth. And crazier'n hell. How about Padrino? Marsden didn't crawl out of the morgue to kill him."

"I know. Why I'm here. No use hounding a dead man. Live murderer now." There was no flicker in Nick Noble's pale blue eyes as he added, "What did Padrino have on you, Barker?"

Barker's hand rested on the open drawer. "You're drunk." His voice was cold with contempt.

"Marsden had to be murderer," Nick Noble went on. "So somebody else killed Padrino. But it fitted the time pattern. Not authority pattern. So pattern faked to shift guilt. Who knew time pattern? Finch, MacDonald, and you."

Barker's hand slipped into the drawer. "Balls. Cops don't murder, friend. Might as well pin it on MacDonald or Finch."

"Cops murder crooks who might talk too much. Lieutenant Becker, New York. And it wasn't Finch or MacDonald I saw coming out of a room on East Fifth Street."

Barker's hand came out of the drawer. It wasn't empty.

Nick Noble sat still. "Keep your head, Barker. You can't kill me here at headquarters."

"Balls," said Detective Lieutenant Dan Barker levelly. "Everybody knows you're a dipso. The worst kind: a wino. You've been brooding all these years about getting booted off the force. You came in here and raised hell to get revenge. I had to defend myself." His trigger finger was tense.

"You were afraid of noise last night when I saw you steal the gun. Besides, you thought I was just another bum, and what was my word against a lieutenant's? Different now."

"Everybody's got his own way of suicide, friend. Yours is being too damn smart. So now you're through."

The crackle of glass blended with the two shots. The sherry, glass and all, hit Barker in the face just as he pulled the trigger. The glass splintered on the floor. The first shot went where Noble's head had been. From the floor Nick Noble saw the second shot burrow into Barker's right hand. Barker's gun lit in the fragments of glass.

Lieutenant MacDonald stood planted in the doorway staring at his service automatic. Shooting a detective lieutenant was something else he wasn't experienced at.

A sergeant put the cuffs on Barker and another sergeant handed a notebook full of pothooks to Finch.

"Hot ziggety zag!" said Finch. "That was a sweet trap, Nick. The Screwball Division pulls it off again."

"Easy. Find the pattern. See what isn't pattern. That's all."

"Horsefeathers! You're the best blame detective on or off the force, and you know it."

"Balls," snorted Barker. The sergeant cuffed him backhanded across the mouth. The sergeant too had more reasons than vanity for wearing a heavy ring.

"I need a drink," said Nick Noble. He fished out the half-empty bottle. It was wholly empty by the time Finch had finished booking Detective Lieutenant Dan Barker, L.A.P.D., for murder.

FROM DETECTIVE WHO'S WHO

NOBLE, Nicholas, unemployed; b. Rockland, Me., 1896; s. Ethan and Anastasia (Joffe) N.; educ. Pasadena High School, U. of Cal. (not graduated). Volunteered U. S. Army Feb., 1917; Sgt. Signal Corps, 1917; Lieut. Signal Corps (cryptanalysis), 1918. Patrolman, L.A.P.D., 1919; Sgt., 1921; Lieut. (Homicide), 1925; dishonorable discharge, 1930. m. Martha Winslow, 1924 (died 1930). Publications: *The New Code of Police Ethics; Crime and Its Patterns; From Bow Street to Bertillon;* and other articles in professional journals of criminology, 1924–1930. Earliest case so far recorded (by Anthony Boucher): the 7:06 Murders, 1941. Relig.: none. Pol. affil.: none. Home address: Unknown. Office: Chula Negra café, North Main Street, Los Angeles, California.

O'REILLY SAHIB IN

The Zarapore Beat

BY LAWRENCE G. BLOCHMAN

"You mean an Indian *chief*," said O'Reilly.

"I mean an Indian *prince*," insisted the precinct captain. "He
ain't one o' these common or Madison Square Garden variety
Indians with feathers and moccasins. He's a—well, elephants.
Pearls. Curry and rice. He's—"

"I got it," said O'Reilly. "A Hindu Indian. And what am I
supposed to do about him?"

"Go up to his hotel right away," said the precinct captain. "The
Prince and the British Consul have been to see the Mayor, and
the Mayor told the Commissioner to assign a cop to look after
the Prince, and the Commissioner passes the buck to the Deputy
Chief Inspector, and the Inspector picks you. I'm damned if I
know why, unless it's because you're six-feet-four and the heavy-
weight champion of the force. Anyway, you're the Prince's personal bodyguard as long as he's in New York. Now beat it."

From *Argosy* (under the title *O'Reilly Sahib*). Copyright 1936 by Popular
Publications, Inc.

Thus did Patrolman Terrence O'Reilly, of the Ninth Precinct Police Station, become attached to Prince Vinayak Rao Bahadur, eldest son of the Maharajah of Zarapore, and heir apparent—so he thought—to the throne of that distant and somewhat obscure Indian state.

Prince Vinayak was on his way back to Zarapore after two years spent at Oxford acquiring social polish, an English accent, and a back-hand tennis stroke. Having mastered these and similar fundamentals fitting him to take his ultimate place among the six hundred-odd rulers of the so-called independent states that make up the India that is theoretically non-British, he should have come home immediately to begin waiting for his father to die. The Prince, however, was something of a heretic; he was unduly interested in the theory of government. He was taking the long way home via the United States of America, to see what those former British colonies were doing in the way of industrial development, municipal hygiene, and state control of utilities. He was even making arrangements to attend lectures on political science at Columbia University, when Patrolman Terrence O'Reilly was ushered into the suite of his Park Avenue hotel.

O'Reilly was surprised at the sight of the Prince. He had expected to see a fat, dark man reclining on silken cushions while many beautiful ladies, dressed—or undressed—in the manner of a Broadway night club floor show, attended him with large feather fans. Instead, he saw a slim, keen-eyed young man in a well-tailored gray business suit, sitting at a desk writing letters. The Prince's skin was really no darker than that of Detective Joe Manelli of the Mercer Street Station, and there was nothing royal about him except perhaps the square-cut diamond as big as an ice cube, which adorned his cravat.

"Howdy, Prince," said O'Reilly. "The Commissioner sent me."

PRINCE VINAYAK looked up. He, too, was surprised—at the towering bulk of O'Reilly. The policeman was roughly triangular, with shoulders that looked as if he had left an oversized hanger in his coat, tapering down to muscular hips and wiry legs. The size of his feet kept him from being top-heavy. You could hang a hat on the corner of his jaw, and somebody had already hung a haymaker on his slightly flattened nose, one night while he was breaking up a free-for-all in a Greenwich Village speakeasy. His hair, the color of a ripe persimmon, topped off a truly impressive spectacle.

"My name's Terrence O'Reilly," said the new bodyguard. "You can call me Terry."

The Prince smiled. "Mine is Vinayak Rao Bahadur," he said with his precise Oxford accent. "You may call me Vinnie."

Then he laughed—an elegant, amused laugh that was completely lost in the great guffaws of O'Reilly as the patrolman joined in the joke.

From that moment O'Reilly and Prince Vinnie were fast friends. O'Reilly slept in the Prince's suite, accompanied him to official receptions, dozed while he listened to college lectures, yawned while he inspected hospitals and waterworks. The nights were less boring, for the Prince had a tremendous curiosity regarding what New York did after dark, which O'Reilly was eminently fitted to satisfy. Since the Prince's European education had been partly devoted to the appreciation of vintage champagnes, their friendship grew warmer over many a cold bottle. It reached a climax with the suddenness of a thunderclap.

One cold, blustery March night, O'Reilly was awakened from a sound, vintage sleep by someone shaking his shoulder. He blinked into the bearded, spectacled face of Sharik, the Prince's Hindu secretary, who continued to shake him.

"Wake up. Wake up, please," Sharik was repeating in a frantic tenor. "Something is happening to His Highness."

O'Reilly sprang from his bed. Faint, strangled cries came from the next room. O'Reilly ran to the door. It was locked. On previous nights it had always been open. It was open, he was sure, when he went to bed. He applied his shoulder, sprung the lock, fumbled for the electric switch.

Light flooded the room. The bed was empty. The window

was open. Three long strides, and O'Reilly was leaning across the sill. Prince Vinayak Rao Bahadur, in silk pajamas, was clinging to a narrow ledge outside, fifteen stories above the street.

When O'Reilly dragged him back into the room, the Prince collapsed into a chair. Drenched with nervous perspiration, he sat trembling for half a minute while the policeman poured brandy into a water tumbler.

"You saved my life, Terry," gasped Prince Vinayak when he had gulped the brandy.

"What happened, Prince?"

"I don't know. I awoke to find myself going out the window. Instinctively I clutched the ledge. How I held on, I don't know. . . . I've never walked in my sleep before, have I, Sharik?"

"No, Your Highness," said the secretary gravely.

"Who locked the door between this room and mine?" demanded O'Reilly, very much the policeman. He addressed the question to the room at large—to the Prince, to Sharik, and to the two turbaned body servants who were bustling futilely about.

"I am finding it locked when aroused by His Highness' cries," said Sharik solemnly.

"If I'm getting to be a somnambulist, Terry," said the Prince with an uneasy laugh, "perhaps I locked it myself."

"Nix, Prince," said O'Reilly. "You ain't no somnam— You don't walk in your sleep. Somebody sneaked in here with a pass-key and just plain chucked you out of the window, that's what."

"Nonsense, Terry. Why should anyone—?"

"Who gets the nomination for Maharajah in case you kick off?" pursued O'Reilly professionally. "Anybody?"

"Yes. My half-brother, Prince Mahmed; but he's a long way off, in India. Besides, our father, the Maharajah, has a good many years to live yet. Unless—" The Prince stopped suddenly. His face went ashen. He half raised himself apprehensively in his chair. "Sharik, what time is it?"

"Ten minutes of four, Your Highness."

"Call the desk." There was dread in the Prince's voice. "Ask if there are telegrams."

"Yes, Your Highness."

SHARIK went to the phone. He looked a little like an owl with his close, curly black beard and horn-rimmed spectacles. He was young—about the same age and build as the Prince. Same deep-set brown eyes, too. O'Reilly thought he would probably resemble the Prince without his beard, spectacles, and the blue turban he wore constantly.

"There is a cablegram, Your Highness," said Sharik, as he hung up. "It came half an hour ago, but the clerk did not wish to disturb Your Highness until breakfast. He is sending it up."

Sharik remained standing by the phone. No one spoke. The anguish of anticipation in the Prince's eyes increased, second by second, until the bellboy knocked on the door.

O'Reilly took the envelope, examined the flap to see if it had been previously opened, then handed it on. The Prince's fingers shook as he tore it open. When he finished reading it, he looked blankly at the wall for a long minute. Then he said in a lifeless voice:

"My father, the Maharajah, is dead."

"Gee, that's tough, Prince. I'm sorry—"

"Terry! I wonder if you're right. I wonder if someone in New York received this news before I did."

"You're doggone right I'm right," said O'Reilly. "And from now on, Prince, you don't leave my sight, night or day."

Prince Vinayak arose suddenly. A ghostly smile of hope crossed his harried face. His voice came to life.

"Do you mean that, Terry? Then you'll come to India with me?"

"What? Me? Why, I couldn't do that, Prince Vinnie. I'm still on the force. I'm due for promotion pretty soon."

"I'll go to the Commissioner for you. I'm sure he'll grant you leave of absence. We will have to start at once."

O'Reilly's blue eyes clouded—with a sort of fear, although he would never have recognized it as such. O'Reilly was not a coward; his record showed that. He once walked into a nest of East Side gunmen single-handed, and had lead dug out of his thigh without an anesthetic. He had cleaned out a dive of thugs in Hell's Kitchen with his bare fists. He had exchanged shots with paroled killers. He knew danger, and therefore did not fear it. But India—well, India was a purely imaginary place, something to read about, not to go to. And for O'Reilly, who had never been outside New York in his life, except for a week in Asbury Park one summer and a trip up the Hudson on the day boat, going to India was a little like dying. . . .

"You see, Prince," he said, "I still got my old lady livin' over in Brooklyn. She depends on me."

"I'll take care of her," said the Prince. "My bank will send her money every week. And I need you, Terry. I need your strength, your courage, and your loyalty. I need someone I can trust. Will you come?"

"Well, O.K., then, Prince," said O'Reilly gloomily. He sat down, a little dazed by the decision he had just made. "Say, how far is it to India? Will we have to stop somewhere overnight, or can we make it in a day?"

THEY made it in thirteen days, thanks to a lucky connection with the Imperial Airways plane in England. It was an unreal fortnight for O'Reilly. Six days of unimagined and ignominious nausea on the Atlantic, a fleeting glimpse of London, then a week flying away from the last blustering days of winter. Like the magic carpet, the plane for India turned gray seas to blue, caught up with the green of spring, left it to dance in the heat that eddied upward from the yellow sands of the desert. Enchanted names passed beneath the wings—Paris, Italy, Egypt, Bagdad— but to O'Reilly they were just names. Landscapes from the air were as impersonal as a page from a geography, and an airdrome, after all, is just an airdrome. O'Reilly spent his time studying New York police regulations. He was due for promotion when he got back.

At Karachi, the sticky heat from the Arabian Sea began to make India a personal matter while he and the Prince and the Prince's small retinue were waiting for the shuttle plane for Bombay. But it was at Bombay that India really began.

In the glaring, sweltering streets of Bombay, teeming with more shades of black and brown than Harlem, more whiskers

than Allen Street, more garish and brilliant costumes than a
Knights of Pythias parade, Patrolman O'Reilly became O'Reilly
Sahib. He put up his police regulations and bought a copy of
Hindustani Simplified. He was outfitted in white drills by a Parsi
tailor with a black oilcloth miter. He bought—with some mis-
givings, as it was twenty years since a self-respecting New York
cop had worn anything resembling a soup-tureen helmet—a *sola
topee.* He also bought a Malacca stick of appropriate strength
and weight to beat off further attempts on the life of Prince
Vinnie. But prospective assassins were conspicuously inactive
while the Prince's party made its way through the tangled traffic
of squawking motorcars, bullock carts, *gharis,* and water buffa-
loes, to the private car which Sharik arranged to have attached to
the Punjab Mail as far as Zarapore.

Aboard the train, the Prince, too, was transformed. Instead of
the natty Western business suit, he wore tight satin trousers, a
long tunic of ivory silk, and a pale pink turban, on the front of
which glittered a diamond, the square-cut diamond as big as an
ice cube. He also wore a frown, which became more and more
worried as the train chuffed over the Western Ghats and rolled
across the sun-baked plains of Central India, past drab mud vil-
lages and parched, dusty peepul trees.

Sharik, the solemn secretary, must have noticed the deepening
frown, for he said: "Perhaps Your Highness would like the private car detached when we cross the frontier of Zarapore State.
We could proceed secretly to Zarapore City by motor."

"Nonsense," said the Prince.

"I was thinking Your Highness was uncertain regarding Prince
Mahmed—"

"Sharik, my name is Vinayak Rao Bahadur. I remind you that
bahadur means 'brave.'"

"Besides," put in O'Reilly, who was smoking a Trichinopoly
cheroot and feeling warmer than he had ever felt in his life,
"there ain't nothin' to be afraid of, as long as Terrence O'Reilly
is on the job. And I don't mind tellin' you, he is."

As O'Reilly spoke, he had a sudden sensation of strange, restless excitement—a feeling that unreasonably recalled a certain

hot July night in Manhattan, when he and Detective Sullivan had cornered two gangsters on a tenement roof, and Sullivan had been shot. He wondered why he should have that sense of impending doom now, the same presentiment of death that came a few moments before Sullivan was gasping out his life in O'Reilly's arms.

There was no reason, of course. It must be the heat—the same sticky heat that hung like a black blanket over New York that July night. He tried to dismiss the whole feeling by drawing deep on his cheroot and blowing a thick blue cloud into a futile, buzzing fan. The smoke came back at him in little puffs—like the puffs from the muzzle of an automatic. . . .

It was after dark when the Mail puffed into Zarapore City. While the train was being shunted onto a siding, where the private car could be detached, O'Reilly looked out the window, fascinated by the color and movement of the station platform. Blazing torches sprayed wavering, orange light over the crowd—*bhistis*, with their glistening black goatskin water bags; bearded food venders; half-naked baggage coolies; brown women with gold ornaments in their ears and nostrils, and bright *saris* wound around their bodies and over their heads. A line of troops kept the crowd away from the center of the platform, green-turbaned soldiers wearing khaki shorts and khaki puttees wrapped above their bare feet.

Prince Vinayak, too, was at the window, scanning faces in the crowd.

"Do you see Prince Mahmed, Sharik?" he asked.

"No, Your Highness."

The train stopped opposite an open space on the platform, where, surrounded by flashing bayonets, stood a group of portly Oriental nobles in silk tunics, ceremonial scarfs, brilliant turbans, and egrets.

"The local lodge is turned out to meet you, Prince," said O'Reilly.

An assistant station-master opened a door of the private car. A band of yellow-robed musicians beat on drums and blew shrieking notes from buffalo horns and interminable silver trumpets. The Prince stepped to the platform. Close behind him were O'Reilly and Sharik.

The turbaned troops presented arms. The silken nobles salaamed.

As O'Reilly's alert glance swept the scene, his eyes paused on the one familiar object in this exotic display: a white face! It was not a very inspiring face, to be sure—thin cheeks, dejected mouth, haunted eyes that peered furtively from beneath the misshapen brim of a grimy, once-white topee. O'Reilly saw it for just an instant before it disappeared behind the turbaned head of a soldier. Then he saw something far more important.

A Hindu in a tattered loincloth broke through the line of soldiers, his naked torso smeared with ashes, his eyes gleaming wildly through a tangle of gray beard. He ran toward the Prince, screaming. His yells were echoed by excited cries from the crowd. He was holding something in front of him, an earthenware sphere trailing a wisp of smoke!

When he saw the smoke, O'Reilly leaped forward.

"Hey, Prince!" he shouted. "Duck!"

Before Prince Vinayak could move, O'Reilly had committed *lèse majesté* by tackling the heir apparent to the throne of Zarapore and throwing him to the ground. He scrambled over the Prince's recumbent body to get at the screaming fanatic with the earthenware sphere. Before he had taken a step there was a deafening explosion.

O'Reilly suddenly found himself sitting on the ground. His hands, instinctively before his face, were bleeding. He coughed violently from the acrid fumes that filled his lungs. When he got to his feet he was engulfed by a yelling, fighting crowd that had surged forward in instant confusion. The Prince was gone!

THE half-naked Hindu who had carried the crude bomb was spread-eagled on the station platform, motionless beneath the bare feet of running, shouting soldiers. Men near him sat on the ground moaning.

"Hey, Prince!"

O'Reilly charged through the yelling, milling, panic-stricken mob, seeking Vinayak Rao Bahadur. Grunts and howls followed him as he cleared a path with his elbows, tramped on bare feet with a trip-hammer tread. Faces swam before him in the shimmering torchlight—bearded faces, fear-contorted faces, brown faces, the determined faces of the soldiery. Once he caught a glimpse of the haunted face of the white man with the grimy topee, the man he had seen from the train window. The white man was slinking away into shadow. But nowhere did he see the pink turban of Prince Vinnie, nor even the blue turban of Sharik, the owl-faced secretary. The earth had apparently swallowed Vinayak Rao Bahadur.

"Hey, Prince!"

The confusion was lessening. Little by little the Hindu soldiers were driving back the crowd with their rifle butts. At last O'Reilly found himself almost alone on the station platform, looking into the tiny cruel eyes of an Oriental almost as big as he was.

"You are O'Reilly?" queried the Oriental.

"You guessed it, mister," said O'Reilly, scrutinizing his inquisitor. The man was half a head shorter than he was and about fifty pounds heavier—excess weight which almost hid his small, glittering eyes and billowed under his long black alpaca tunic. He had a little, silky, black mustache and wore a lemon-yellow turban.

"Come with me, please," he said.

"Yeah?" said O'Reilly. "And who the hell are you?"

"I am Major Kobi Khan, Minister of Police for the Sirkar of Zarapore."

"So there's a minister runnin' the police force in this town, is there?" declared O'Reilly, folding his arms. "I mighta known it, from the lousy protection you gave the Prince. You oughta go back to your church."

"Come with me, please," repeated Major Kobi Khan.

"Let's put it the other way," said O'Reilly. "I happen to be special bodyguard to the future Maharajah o' Zarapore that your imitation cops just lost in the shuffle. Suppose you come with me while we find out what happened to the Prince."

"*Havildar! Idhar ao!*" shouted the Major over his fat shoulder. A squad of soldiers with fixed bayonets responded, surrounding O'Reilly. "Come with me, please," repeated Kobi Khan to the red-headed giant.

O'Reilly came, muttering. He was convoyed through a murmuring crowd, through the station, into the hot darkness of a street lined with trees aglitter with fireflies, and finally into an imposing building surmounted with domes which made silhouettes like inverted turnips against the stars. Here he was left to perspire in a smelly room full of soldiers who could not understand him.

He was impatiently considering the most expeditious means of exit when a door opened and someone called: "O'Reilly Sahib."

O'Reilly was ushered again into the presence of Major Kobi Khan, who was now seated at a table beside a florid gray-haired European. The white man was introduced as Mr. Leonard Henderson, British Political Officer for Zarapore.

"Howdy," said O'Reilly. He started to extend his hand, but Mr. Henderson dismissed the introduction with a curt nod. He made a distinguished picture in his tussah silk suit, if somewhat cold and preoccupied.

"Mr. Henderson wishes to know what you are doing in Zarapore?" demanded Major Kobi Khan.

"Me? Why, I'm just a pal o' Prince Vinnie's. You see, in New York, me and the Prince—"

"Please tell us what you know about the plot."

"Plot? What plot?"

"You were seen to attack His Highness. You knocked him down."

"Sure. That's the natural move when a mug heaves a pineapple. Offer the smallest target possible—"

"When informed that you were accompanying His Highness," interrupted Major Kobi Khan, "I had your antecedents investigated. You seem to have been once a reputable person. How did you become involved in this conspiracy?"

"Say, what is this? A frame?" O'Reilly flushed indignantly.

"Why don't you ask that fuzzy-face secretary where's the Prince? Why don't you ask that guy Sharik about a plot? Where is Sharik, anyhow?"

"Sharik," said Major Kobi Khan, "is in jail. He will be shot in the morning."

"Shot?" exclaimed O'Reilly. "What for?"

"Negligence. Neglecting the safety of a sovereign is treason in Zarapore. Ten men will be shot for treason at dawn: The Risaldar of the State troops, seven of his subordinate officers, the assistant station-master, and Sharik."

"That's pretty dumb," said O'Reilly. "Why bump off a lot o' witnesses before you find out what happened to the Prince? Bring these birds over here, and let's work 'em over a little. I bet I can sweat a story out of 'em."

"Your advice," said Major Kobi Khan, "is not required."

"Listen, Mr. Henderson," O'Reilly appealed to the Britisher who was watching with calm detachment. "Prince Vinnie's a friend of mine, and I'm just the guy to go to bat for him. I put in time with the Missin' Persons Bureau. I been with the Explosives Squad before they stuck me in the Ninth Precinct. I—"

"As Political Officer of the Viceroy," said Henderson, "my capacity in Zarapore is purely advisory. I have no authority to interfere in strictly internal affairs. This, as I see it, is a police matter. Moreover, I fail to see how you could be of value to the investigation, beyond telling Major Kobi Khan what you know. You are a stranger here. . . ."

"A good cop," said O'Reilly, "is a good cop anywhere."

"The first train leaving Zarapore," said Major Kobi Khan, "is the Bombay Mixed Passenger at six o'clock in the morning. You will please take it."

"So you're running me out o' town?"

"Not at all. My idea originally was to have you shot with the others. Since you are an American, Mr. Henderson suggests that we avoid possible complications. So you are free—at least until six o'clock tomorrow."

O'Reilly stared at the Minister of Police for a long moment.

His rough-hewn features were perfectly solemn. He saluted gravely—and winked at Leonard Henderson.

"O.K., toots," he said.

HE WALKED from the Ministry of Police swinging his Malacca cane like a night-stick, his square chin high, his stride as confident as though he were starting out to take over his beat on Avenue A from Monahan. There was nothing synthetic about O'Reilly's confident manner, either. He was not a man given to bluster. He was simply unaware of the enormous handicaps which lay before him in the task he had set himself. A foreigner in a strange land? Not O'Reilly. The land might be foreign and the people strange, but O'Reilly was a New York cop. New York was the greatest city in the world, wasn't it? Therefore a cop who knew his job in New York should find any other city a minor problem.

True, O'Reilly was a trifle mystified by the disappearance of Prince Vinayak Rao Bahadur—at least by the actual mechanics of the disappearance. He was not fooled in the least by the bomb explosion. The crude earthenware pineapple had been chiefly noise and smoke. Any well-made bomb, or even a first-class grenade, would have killed dozens in that crowd, notably Terrence O'Reilly. As it was, the only casualty had been the ash-smeared fanatic who was hugging the bomb close to his naked stomach; and his death had probably been an accident.

No, the explosion was evidently designed to promote sufficient panic and confusion to cover the abduction of the Prince. He had been kidnaped, of course. And kidnaping was certainly not beyond the ken of a New York cop. The routine was simple. He had only to keep his eyes and ears open and ask questions.

O'Reilly walked toward that part of Zarapore that was still lighted. Where there was light, there would be people. In ten minutes he had reached the bazaar streets—crooked ant-runs between whitewashed buildings, swarming with yellow turbans, purple pugarees, red fezzes, green *hajji* caps, and wagging beards. Flares burned before striped awnings, and oil wicks flickered inside cavernous open-front shops. Here and there were signs in ungrammatical English, and O'Reilly entered to ask questions.

He described a man he was seeking, but the few shopkeepers who understood could give him no information.

Several hours passed in useless interrogation. Wooden shutters went up in front of shops, for it was long past midnight. Rayots trickled into the bazaars from the country, bringing produce for the next day's markets: two-wheeled carts dragged by nodding, hump-backed bullocks; a string of dusty donkeys, no bigger than dogs, piled high with earthenware chatties.

O'Reilly mopped his brow as he watched a shopkeeper take down his display of bright, spangled slippers with turned-up toes, hanging in bunches like bananas. He began to feel disheartened. He was a little giddy, too, from breathing the strange, humid scents of the hot night—the mingled spicy fragrance of saffron and jasmine, with unpleasant overtones of rancid ghi, sweat, and bullock dung.

Then he saw his man.

HE HAD been looking for the furtive European in the grimy topee, the man he had seen slinking away from the railway station immediately after the explosion. At first glimpse O'Reilly had spotted the man as a familiar type—the sort of person he would pick up if he found him loitering on his beat, to be fingerprinted on a chance that he might be wanted somewhere, to be questioned if there had been any unsavory incidents in the neighborhood. Now the man in the grimy topee was still slinking, walking stealthily along the opposite side of the narrow street, hugging the buildings, looking behind him every dozen steps. O'Reilly backed into the gloom until the man had passed.

The man disappeared around a jog in the crooked street. O'Reilly, trying to hurry his steps, found himself knee-deep in a flock of black goats that a naked ten-year-old boy was herding through the bazaar. By the time he reached the corner, the man with the grimy topee was nowhere to be seen.

Not yet having heard of the Hindu Rope Trick or the Great Mango Tree Illusion, O'Reilly did not ascribe the disappearance to an Oriental miracle. Instead, he began examining the closed shutters of the first shops at hand. He looked at nine before he

found one with light glowing between the boards. He put his
eye to a crack. Instantly a deep chuckle of satisfaction stirred in
his throat. His man was inside.

He was seated at a table with three Orientals—a pot-bellied,
three-chinned Bunya; a gray-whiskered Punjabi; and a coal-black
Singhalese with a semi-circular comb stuck into the knot of long
hair at the back of his head. Light from a kerosene lamp glistened
on four perspiring foreheads bent over an object lying in the
palm of the white man's hand. The object was a square-cut diamond, as big as an ice cube and flashing cold fire. It was the
diamond of Prince Vinayak Rao Bahadur.

O'Reilly retreated a few steps, lowered his shoulder, and
charged. The dry wood of the shutter splintered into kindling.

The four men about the table sprang up in alarm. The man
with the grimy topee thrust the diamond into the trousers pocket
of his crumpled white suit.

O'Reilly advanced into the dim, odorous recesses of the shop,
brushing himself off.

"Evening, gents," he said.

The quartet stared at him in hostile silence until he had
reached the table. Then the Bunya said in a quavering tenor:

"Good evening, O'Reilly Sahib."

O'Reilly blinked in surprise. "Where'd I ever meet you before?" he demanded.

"Nowhere, Sahib. Bazaar talk has wings. And how could we
mistake one so tall and strong, with such magnificent scarlet
hairs?"

"What's your name?" O'Reilly pointed his stick at the man
with the grimy topee.

The European did not answer.

"You are doubtless stranger in India," whined the Bunya after
a pause. "From Calcutta to Bombay people know Jan Van
Laar. . . ."

"Van Laar, eh? Dutch?"

"Yah," said Van Laar.

O'Reilly's forehead creased in a pensive frown. He had arrested four Dutchmen once, during a diamond cutters' strike.

"What's your business?" he asked.

"Oh, a liddle uff ever't'ing," said Van Laar. "Anyt'ing to make a liffing."

O'Reilly noticed that Van Laar still had one hand in his pocket, the hand that held the Prince's diamond.

"Ever been a diamond-cutter?" he asked suddenly.

Van Laar began to stammer. "No. . . . Dat is, I used to was a diamond-cutter . . . but . . . years ago when I was young . . . in Amsterdam. . . ."

"And you cleared out two jumps ahead of the police." O'Reilly shook his head knowingly. "Hot ice, eh?"

Van Laar did not reply. His lips quivered slightly.

A poor crook, O'Reilly thought. No nerve. The sort of petty criminal that turns stool-pigeon.

"You was at the station tonight," said O'Reilly. "What happened to Prince Vinayak?"

There was a long pause. Insects buzzed and thumped about the kerosene lamp. Finally the Bunya spoke again.

"Anyone can guess, Sahib. Prince Vinayak is dead."

"Yeah?" exclaimed O'Reilly. "Why?"

"Because his greedy and ambitious half-brother, Prince Mahmed, wants to be Maharajah."

"Does Major Kobi Khan know this?" queried O'Reilly.

The Bunya, the Punjabi, and the Singhalese laughed softly. Only Van Laar did not laugh.

"Of course," smirked the Bunya. "Kobi Khan will be Prime Minister when Mahmed is Maharajah."

"Then why'n hell is Kobi Khan havin' ten men shot for not protectin' the Prince?" pursued O'Reilly.

The Bunya smiled pityingly. "Men to be shot are friendly to Prince Vinayak," he said. "Mahmed and Kobi Khan are destroying possible enemies."

"And is this guy Henderson in on their game?"

"Henderson Sahib is learned man," said the garrulous Bunya. "Henderson Sahib is making new translating of *Mahabharata* from Sanskrit. But his eyes are too deep in books to see what goes on in court and bazaars of Zarapore. . . ."

"Suppose he found out? What'd happen?"

"Who knows, Sahib?"

"Well, who the devil knows for sure that Prince Vinayak is dead?"

No answer.

"You, Van Laar!" O'Reilly poked the European in the chest with his cane. "Was the Prince dead when you grabbed the diamond off his turban?"

Van Laar paled. "Vot . . . vot diamond?" he faltered.

"The sparkler you got in your pocket."

"You must be mistooken," Van Laar began, "I got no—"

His speech ended in a whimper. O'Reilly reached out one hand, grabbed Van Laar by the back of his soiled collar, lifted him clear off the floor, and shook him until his teeth chattered. Suddenly he dropped him. He saw something glitter in the hand of the Punjabi.

O'Reilly's cane swished through the fetid air. A knife clanged to the table. Then O'Reilly's left fist, with two hundred-odd pounds of New York policeman behind it, smacked into the Punjabi's hirsute face. A chair clattered over as the Punjabi fell backward and lay in a limp heap on the floor.

"And now," said O'Reilly, buttoning his coat, "let's quit foolin'. Where is that diamond?"

Van Laar no longer hesitated. His trembling hand placed the sparkling gem on the table. O'Reilly picked it up.

"I—we found it," said Van Laar.

"That's a lie," O'Reilly declared.

"No, I swear."

"Don't give me those," said O'Reilly.

"He is speaking truth," whined the Bunya. "We found it."

"Where?"

"Between railway station and qaibkhana."

"Come again?"

"Between station and jail."

"Now we're gettin' some place," announced O'Reilly, sitting down and taking out a Trichinopoly cheroot. "How'd you happen to find it? Follow the Prince?"

"No, no," protested Van Laar frantically. "We did not know

it was Prince Vinayak. After bomb explode, I see some men carrying somet'ing heavy between cars of train—jail is on odder side of tracks from station—so when train leave, I follow. Just before jail, I find *burra hira*—dis diamond."

"That's funny," mused O'Reilly. He lit his cheroot and squinted into the smoke. If they were going to kill the Prince, why hadn't they killed him outright, blaming it on the bomb? Why had they packed him off to jail? Maybe they were afraid a crude murder might bring investigation by the British Political Officer. Maybe they were making sure in some way that Prince Vinayak would be obliterated without an incriminating trace. How? And why the jail? And why, of all things, had they got rid of this diamond? The diamond could not merely have dropped off, since it was firmly fastened to the front of the Prince's pink turban.

O'Reilly puffed furiously on his cheroot. It was possible, of course, that Van Laar was lying, although O'Reilly's policeman's instinct, born of years of contact with liars, told him that this trembling, sniveling beachcomber was speaking the truth. O'Reilly leaned back in his chair, looked at the glowing end of the cheroot, and thought back to that night in New York when someone had tried to push Prince Vinnie out the hotel window. . . .

Suddenly he sprang to his feet.

Van Laar cringed before an expected blow.

"What time is it?" O'Reilly shouted.

"Half past four of morning time," said the Bunya.

O'Reilly stuffed the diamond into his pocket and grabbed Van Laar's arm.

"Come on," he said. "Show me the way to this bird Henderson's house—in a hurry."

O'REILLY banged on the door of Henderson's bungalow for five minutes before he aroused a sleepy *durwan*. Between yawns, the *durwan* explained drowsily that under no circumstances could he awaken his master at this hour. Whereupon O'Reilly awakened the *durwan* with a sharp blow of the heel of his palm under his brown chin. As the Hindu started over backward, O'Reilly caught him, tucked him under his left arm, and entered the dark house. The outraged *durwan* squawked, kicked, and yelled as O'Reilly strode across book-lined rooms. The *khansama* and two other servants came to the rescue, added their voices to the uproar.

At last the Political Officer himself appeared.

"You!" he exclaimed, as the luminous cone of his flashlight picked out the New York policeman.

Leonard Henderson was the first man O'Reilly had ever seen who looked dignified in a nightgown.

"Get your duds on, Mr. Henderson," shouted O'Reilly, unceremoniously dropping the squalling *durwan*. "We're going to stop a massacre."

"My dear fellow, I've already told you that this is a purely internal—"

"Listen," O'Reilly interrupted. "You're Political Officer, ain't you? Then rotten politics is right up your alley, ain't it? Well, where I come from, they invented rotten politics, Mr. Henderson, and I know the smell. Look here."

He showed the Prince's diamond, briefly told his story.

"Extraordinary!" agreed the Political Officer. "Perhaps I *had* better go with you."

"Right away!" said O'Reilly.

The sky was already beginning to pale in the east as O'Reilly helped Henderson's heavy-eyed syce hitch a horse to his victoria.

Henderson was still tying his cravat when he jumped into the carriage, and ordered: "*Jeldi jao!*"

The syce's whip cracked, and the horse leaped into a canter. In front of the Ministry of Police, the brakes clamped shrieking against the wheels.

A *pahare-walla* on duty said that Major Kobi Khan was not there. He had already gone to the prison for the executions.

Again the syce urged the horse into a gallop. The victoria bounced and clattered over the railway tracks. Ahead, at the foot of a gentle slope, the bulging domes of the prison loomed black against the brightening sky.

There were crowds of people on the road, too, despite the hours—straggling groups of Hindus and Moslems heading for the prison, drawn by some common morbidity, by the universal fascination of foreordained death. Apparently the executions were to be public, on the sun-baked field outside the prison walls, for a troop of mounted guards was deployed there, green pennants hanging limp from their lances in the calm of dawn.

The mounted guards stopped Henderson's carriage, and there was a heated parley in Hindustani as to whether it was to be allowed to go on. In the meantime the prisoners were being led from the prison. O'Reilly could see them marched through a gate, flanked by soldiers and torch-bearers whose flares paled at the advance of day. He heard a sudden blare of sound—the ominous beat of drums, the mournful bellow of Hindu horns, and the squeal of gourd instruments. A little band of turbaned musicians in gaudy uniforms followed the prisoners, pouring out strange dissonances as a last salute to the men about to die.

"Achcha, Sahib!"

The mounted guards were convinced. The Political Officer's carriage started rolling again.

O'REILLY could see the firing squad, now—a double rank of green-turbaned soldiers. Opposite them the ten condemned men were being lined against a wall. Eight of them stood erect and unafraid. One was gesticulating and talking wildly. The tenth, whose blue turban, horn-rimmed spectacles, and close-cropped black beard proclaimed him as Sharik, was slumped against the wall.

Major Kobi Khan half turned in his saddle at the approach of the victoria. When he saw the Political Officer, he beamed with pleasure. When he saw O'Reilly beside him, his expression changed. Turning back abruptly to face the officer commanding the firing detail, he gave an order.

"Banduq chalao!"

"Stop!" Henderson exclaimed. "They mustn't fire, Major! They—"

"It is the hour set for the execution," said Kobi Khan.

Then Terrence O'Reilly went into action. With a single bound he landed in the driver's seat, almost in the syce's lap. Snatching up the reins, he snapped them with the sound of a pistol shot, stung the horse into a gallop.

Kobi Khan shouted something as the victoria dashed past him, past the firing squad.

O'Reilly tugged at the right rein as though he wanted to pull the horse's head off. The carriage veered, tottered, and then went careening across the field of death, throwing up showers of stones and clouds of dust between executioners and condemned.

Henderson leaned over the driver's seat, his face white, his lips determined.

"You're mad, O'Reilly. They'll kill us."

O'Reilly stole a backward glance. The voice of Kobi Khan boomed above the confused roar of the crowd.

"They won't dare shoot the Political Officer," said O'Reilly. "And as for Officer O'Reilly—"

He yanked the left rein. The horse reared, shied, then made the turn. There was a scraping of wheels.

O'Reilly jumped. Without looking behind, he ran the few remaining steps to the ten prisoners backed against the wall. He went directly to the limp, black-bearded man in the blue turban, who toppled over when touched. O'Reilly picked him up tenderly, listened anxiously for his heartbeat. The man gave a queer, guttural gasp.

Inexplicably the fatal volley still hung fire.

Leonard Henderson, who had stopped the victoria, came running up beside the red-headed giant.

"Hear that snoring noise he makes, Mr. Henderson?" panted O'Reilly. "Concussion. They musta cracked him on the onion when they snatched him. . . . Grab that blue turban off, Mr. Henderson. And them glasses . . . while I peel off these phony whiskers. Look. Crepe hair, Mr. Henderson!"

O'Reilly stripped tufts of false beard from the pseudo-Sharik.

"Extraordinary!" exclaimed Henderson. "It is Prince Vinayak. How will Major Kobi Khan explain this?"

BUT Major Kobi Khan had not remained to give any explanation. While he was more than eager to murder his own people for the sake of his ambitions, he was not ready to risk the wrath and might of the British Empire by shooting a Viceregal representative. Hence he had left the firing squad to shift for itself, while he departed hurriedly for the Zarapore palace to inform Prince Mahmed and the genuine Sharik, who was hiding there, that a long voyage would be good for their health, and that he would be glad to accompany them on the Bombay Mixed Passenger leaving at six o'clock. . . .

Prince Vinayak Rao recovered consciousness late that night. O'Reilly and Henderson were at his bedside.

"What happened?" he asked.

Leonard Henderson told him briefly, and Terrence O'Reilly told him at length. O'Reilly explained that his suspicions had been first aroused when the name of Sharik was included in the list of friends of the Prince scheduled for execution. Since the incident of the cablegram and the sleep-walking in New York, O'Reilly had had a pretty good idea that Sharik was by no means a friend of the Prince. The finding of the diamond by Van Laar suggested that the Prince's pink turban had been torn violently from his head. Why—since it was not for the purpose of stealing a gem as big as an ice cube? Something more important. What? Well, it must have been for a quick change, to replace the pink turban with a blue one, to disguise Vinayak Rao so that he could be shot, killed right under the nose of the British agent, and buried under another identity, which would balk investigation.

"An extraordinary bit of police work, Your Highness," commented the Political Officer, "for a man who has been only a few hours in Zarapore, who doesn't know the language, who—"

"Baloney!" interrupted O'Reilly, holding up his huge, authoritative hand as though he were directing traffic in Times Square. "A good cop is a good cop anywhere."

FROM DETECTIVE WHO'S WHO

O'REILLY, Terrence Patrick, police officer; b. New York, N. Y., March 17, 1910; s. Michael Terrence and Mary (Mulvaney) O'R.; grad., P.S. 41, Washington Irving H. S., New York. Patrolman, N. Y. Police Dept., 1931; on leave July 1936–July 1941, to serve as Marshal of Personal Safety to His Highness Vinayak Rao Bahadur, Maharajah of Zarapore, Central India (see O'Reilly Sahib, Whole Hog, The Mad Yogi of Zarapore, Midnight Train, Bringing Up Babu, recorded by Lawrence G. Blochman). Sergeant, N.Y.P.D., 1942. U. S. Army (C.B.I. Theater), staff sergeant, Military Police, 1943–45. Now acting lieutenant, N.Y.P.D., 13th Detective Squad, 327 E. 22nd St., Manhattan. Organizations: Knights of Columbus, Holy Name Society, American Legion. Home: Brooklyn, N. Y.

Stewart Sterling has few rivals in piling up what Pooh-Bah called "corroborative detail added to lend verisimilitude to an otherwise bald and unconvincing narrative." Not that there's anything bald or unconvincing about Sterling's narratives themselves; but they do gain a great deal in verisimilitude through their enthralling detail on the intricacies of running a large hotel, on the special problems of the harbor police, or, as in this story, on firefighting and arson investigation.

FIRE MARSHAL BEN PEDLEY IN

Never Come Mourning

BY STEWART STERLING

IT SEEMED futile to hunt through that steaming jungle of twisted metal and charred wood. A screen of blackish water dripped from the warped girders above. A veil of smoke hung sluggishly over the smoldering wreckage. Searchlights, shooting up from the street, cast grotesque shadows through the gutted hotel. Yet the man in the soot-smudged gray raincoat and the sopping gray felt hat moved steadily up the stairwell behind his flashlight.

As he followed the fat python of canvas which coiled up the staircase around the steel bones of the elevator shaft, he appeared to be methodically following another, more obscure, trail through the clutterment. His eyes, reddened from too much exposure to acrid fumes, held the bleak bitterness of a boy helpless to prevent the agonies of a pet dog. A dark smudge across one of his high

From *Detective Book*, Winter, 1948. Copyright 1948 by Fiction House, Inc.

cheekbones, where a dangling wire had lashed him across the face, added to the small-boy resentment on his long narrow face.

He moved, cautiously, focusing the cone of light here on a lump of fused glass, there on the drooping angle of a buckled pipe. The melted metal of electric fixtures held peculiar interest for him; he inspected the alligatoring of charcoaled wood with the attitude of a surgeon observing an open wound.

On the landing between the third and fourth floors, he flattened against wet brick to permit gangway for a helmeted pair clumping streetward with a limp burden. It didn't seem to disturb them when the head of the sagging figure they were lugging banged against a beam.

The man with the flashlight asked, "Many more up there?"

"Plenty on nine and ten, marshal." One of the laddermen had recognized him. "Ain't any hurry about getting 'em out, now, though."

His partner cursed in corroboration; they clumped on down. Chief Fire Marshal Pedley went up.

He left the stairs, moved slowly down the corridor of the fourth floor. The boards became suddenly springy beneath his feet. He went down on hands and knees, distributing his weight.

It was slow work, crisscrossing the corridor from door to door, creeping over jagged shards of glass, slivers of metal. The drenched woodwork was still blistering. The planking grew spongier underneath him. He kept on, hacking lightly at the inside and outside of each door with his emergency ax. All the chips showed a greater depth of char on the corridor side than on the room side, until he reached room 441.

The blackened fragments from that door showed the room side burned much more deeply than the exterior. He started into the room. There was a sound like ripping canvas; the floor sagged, tilted away from him.

He spread-eagled, as he would have on ice too thin to support him, then inched on.

His fingers touched fibrous jelly interlaced with coiled wire— what was left of the mattress. Two-thirds of the way across the bed, the drenched pulpiness became greasy residue, where the mattress-filling had burned away. This was where the blaze had started. . . .

With infinite caution, he worked his way around the room. The front legs of the bureau had burned first, tipping the glass top and what had been on it forward onto the floor. Women's things. Hairpins. A long nail file. The fused back of what had been a silver hair-brush. A compact.

The beam of his flashlight glinted on a thin, round neck of glass. The remnants of a liquor bottle. Beside it, flat pieces. An ash-tray that had cracked in two, folded over on itself as if made of cardboard. Between the two segments was the sopping stub of a cigarette, unburnt, the paper stained tobacco yellow. He fished it out of its place of protection with a pair of tweezers as if he were extracting the fangs of a cobra.

Below in the street, gongs clanged as pumpers and combinations rolled back to their stations. Pedley remained for long minutes in room 441, wriggling across the insecure floor, putting shoe-eyelets into envelopes, scooping up ashes with a spatula, scowling. . . .

By the time he had descended to the lobby, only the big quad and the hook-and-ladders remained in the street, their long fingers pointing accusingly up at glassless windows. Hosemen were uncoupling. Police were forcing the fire lines back toward the avenue. The bloodshot eyes of ambulances glared at shiny black rubber and crisp white jackets moving among the rows of tarpaulin covers stretched along the curbs. . . .

Inside the lobby, firemen, policemen, and a few individuals in civilian clothes milled about wearily. One of the latter, a blocky man with a raw-hamburg complexion, signaled to the marshal across the wreckage of the room clerk's desk:

"Those babies're raising hell, Ben. They want out of here, bad. That manager's ready to blow his fuse. Says he's going straight to the Commish . . ."

"Tell him to go to hell. This fire was set. He's partly responsible. Before we get through with him, he'll wish he was lying out there on the sidewalk with the others." Pedley's voice was a gritty file on rough metal. "I'll take 'em in the manager's office. One at a time. That floor patrol, first."

THE DEPUTY MARSHAL pushed a heavy-set, white-haired man into the manager's office. The man's puffy face was shiny with sweat, his eyes dull with shock. The absence of his left eyebrow and part of his hair on the left side gave him a lopsided appearance. The port sleeve of his light blue uniform had been slashed off at the elbow; his wrist and hand were encased in a bandage.

"Doc says this gent has to hustle to Polyclinic for treatment," the deputy explained. "He hung out one of them seventh-floor windows twenty minutes before they got the big ladder up to him. That's a second-degree burn on his duke. He got a bellyful of fumes, too."

"Don't fret about him, Ed." Pedley wasn't impressed. "Plenty of others aren't getting to the hospital, either."

"Yeah. Name's Lester Harris. Here four years. Okay record." The deputy went out, closed the door behind him.

"You phoned the alarm, Harris?"

The floor patrol nodded glumly. "I'm up on the ninth, see? I smell this smoke. So I beat it for the hand extinguisher down the end of the hall. When I get down there I see smoke's comin' from the stair door. Comin' up from eight. So I run down there an'—"

"What time was this?" Pedley cut in.

"Only a couple minutes before I phone in. Don't know exactly. I just punch my clock on nine when I get that whiff of smoke. When I get down to eight I still can't tell where it's coming from. I figure it ain't safe to delay any longer. So I push in 802—that's a vacant they're repapering—and grab the phone."

"Been making your regular tour up to that time?"

"Yes, sir."

"Where'd you start?"

"From the mezz."

"When?"

"Midnight. Maybe a little after. Clock'll show."

"The alarm hit the Telegraph Bureau at 1:07. How long's it take you to cover a floor?"

"Suppose to be around five minutes. They allow an hour for me to cover ten floors."

"Why'd it take you sixty-seven minutes to inspect eight, then?"

"Chrissake!" Harris coughed. "I don't generally gallop up them stairs. An' I took out for a personal. On six, that was."

"Didn't notice anything out-of-the-way on any of the lower floors when you came through?"

The floor patrol's glance flickered for a split second.

"No, sir."

"Know the party in 441?"

Harris repeated the number with a rising inflection.

Pedley consulted a card. "Register says it was occupied by a Mrs. Doris Munson, Danbury, Connecticut."

"She's a permanent." Harris fumbled at his bandage, showed his teeth in a grimace. "Works here. On the switchboard. Day side."

"Know anything about her?"

"A blonde. A nifty. Thirty or so." He rubbed his bald eyebrow. "Why? What's she got to do with it?"

"Fire started in her room."

The floor patrol's eyes grew round. "Holy cats!"

"Smoking in bed, looked like." Pedley's face told nothing. "Was she much of a boozer?"

"Not that I hear of. But—" Harris didn't finish whatever it was he had been going to say.

"But what?"

"Nothing."

The marshal took two quick steps, wound his fingers in the cloth of Harris' uniform coat at the second button, jerked the shorter man up on tiptoe. "This blaze put twenty people in the morgue! Twice that many in the hospital!" He put his face close to the other's, growling, "If you know one damn thing about how it started, spit it out! Fast! Or you'll have a long time to wish you had!"

"I don't know," Harris looked as if he were about to sneeze, "if I *do* know anything—"

"Let me decide." Pedley released him.

"This Mrs. Munson. She's kind of . . . uh . . . friendly . . . with Check Wayner . . ."

"Who's Wayner?"

"Bell captain. Night side."

"Keep pouring."

"He goes up to her room once in a while. He ain't supposed to; it's strictly against house rules. I doubt if anybody else knows it. But I seen him coming out of 441 a couple times when he didn't know I was around. He was in there tonight."

"You see him go in?"

"No, sir. I hear him. When I'm comin' along the corridor on four. They're havin' some kind of argument."

Pedley eyed him stonily. "So you listened at the door."

"I'm suppose to see nobody roams around in rooms where they don't belong," the patrol protested. "Mrs. Munson was a single."

"What were they battling about?"

"You couldn't prove it by me. I only horn in on it a minute. I figure it's one of them things and none of my business. Except I wonder how Check gets away with bein' off his desk so long."

"What were they talking about?!" Pedley stepped in close again.

Harris retreated a step. "Near's I can make out from the little I hear," he muttered defensively, "Check is bawlin' her out for fidoodling around with some other joe. An' she's tellin' him to peddle his papers, she'll do like she pleases."

"That all?"

"Well, Check gets pretty sore, from the way he sounds. I figure he's about due to come bustin' out of the room. So I mosey along. Last thing I hear him say is, '*I'd rather see you dead than living this way, Doris!*'"

PEDLEY waved brusquely at the short, dapper youth in the snappy bellman's uniform. "Sit down, Wayner."

Check Wayner didn't make any move toward the straight-backed chair beside the manager's desk. "You got no right to hold me."

"Get the idea out of your mind, fella. I've the right to hold you, arrest you, try you and convict you—right here and now. At the scene of a fire I'm cop, prosecutor, judge, and jury, all in one. You better take my word for it, but it won't make a damn bit of difference whether you do or not. What you know about this blaze?"

"Nothing."

"Still alarm came in at 1:07 A.M. Fire had a ten-, maybe a fifteen-minute start by then. Where were you, around ten minutes to one?"

"Taking a bucket of ice up to somebody, chances are."

"Your call sheet doesn't show any entries after 12:25."

"Then I was in the lobby."

"Weren't up on the fourth?"

"No." Wayner's eyes became wary.

"Not in 441, maybe?"

"No."

"When was the last time you were up in that room?"

"Don't the call sheet tell you that, too?" the bell captain inquired sullenly.

"You were up in Mrs. Munson's room about quarter past twelve. How long'd you stay?"

"I don't remember. . . ."

Pedley looked unhappy. He got up from the chair behind the desk, shucked his coat. "I'll lay it on the line, kid. This hotel was torched. The fire started in Mrs. Munson's room. It was set so it would look as if she'd been smoking in bed and fell asleep. . . ." He rolled up his sleeves; Wayner watched him, worried.

"A lot of people got killed," the marshal went on. "A lot more got hurt, some of 'em so bad they'll die. Most of 'em were guests in this hotel, but some of them were firemen. Friends of mine." He stared down at his big hands, flexing the fingers slowly. "I'm going to find out who touched off this blaze. I don't know whether it was you, or not. But you know something. I'm going to get it out of you, one way or another. Up to you, how I do it. . . ."

Wayner spoke through set teeth. "You think I'd start a fire that put my sister in the hospital?"

"Mrs. Munson your sister?"

"Yes. I got her the job on the switchboard here."

"What were you quarreling about, tonight?"

"We weren't."

"Les Harris says he heard you when he came past 441 on his twelve o'clock tour."

The bell captain snarled, "He's a liar."

"He says he heard you tell Mrs. Munson you'd rather see her dead than living the way she was. What was that all about?"

"Why don't you ask her?"

Pedley turned, tapped the telephone. "The doctors just told me she wouldn't be answering any questions, Wayner."

"She's dead?" He breathed it, as if it hurt him to speak.

"Not yet. She's going to die."

The youth whirled for the door. Pedley caught him.

"If you want to see her before she goes, you better loosen up, kid. I can't let you go until you do."

Wayner's lips trembled; he stared blankly at the carpet, his head rocking from side to side in misery. "All right. She was fooling around with the manager here and—"

"Broodman?"

"Arnie Broodman, yuh. Doris"—tears began to stream down his face—"she was in love with the crumb. He tells her he's going to marry her, all the time he's got a wife an' a couple of kids out on Long Island. He keeps sayin' he's going to get a divorce so he can marry Doris, but I know better. He don't intend to do nothing of the kind. I been trying to get her to break it up, quit her job, move out of the hotel. She tells me to keep out of it, she's old enough to know her own mind. Maybe she is, but she don't know Arnie's . . . and now—" He closed his eyes and lifted his face toward the ceiling.

"Was your sister drinking heavily tonight?" Pedley didn't ease the pressure.

"Some. Arnie'd been up to see her around eleven an' he brought her up a fifth of brandy. To celebrate the good news, he says. He was feeding her a lot of yatadada about the hotel closing down for six months—repairs or something—an' him going down to Miami to run another place so that's when he'll split up from Mrs. Broodman an' marry Doris. I tell her she's feeble-minded if she falls for an old line like that, but she laughs me off. Finally I ask her how long she's going to stand for the run-around an' she says if Arnie doesn't file suit or whatever as soon as the hotel closes here an' he goes to Florida, then she'll know he isn't on the level an' she'll raise plenty of hell with him." He opened his eyes, staring fiercely at Pedley. "Y'know what I think? I think she told Arnie that, too—an' he hadn't any idea of bustin' up his home, so he was afraid of what Doris might do an' he beat her to it, tonight. *That's what I think!*"

"You didn't see him go up to the fourth again, after you left?"

"I didn't see the crumb at all!"

"Not after the alarm went in?"

"No. Soon's I heard those sirens I grab one of the service elevators and run it up to take people off the eighth—that's where Harris says the fire is. . . ."

"You don't know where Broodman was, from the time you left your sister's room until the apparatus began to come in?"

"No." Wayner's mouth hardened. "But I know where he'll be when I get my mitts on him! I'm going to—"

"Go out in the lobby and sit down and keep your mouth shut. Understand me?"

"You said you'd let me go to see my sister."

"I'll tell you when you can go." Pedley rolled down his sleeves, put on his coat, opened the door.

"Ed?"

"Yeah, Ben?"

"Keep an eye on this kid. Send Broodman in."

ARNOLD BROODMAN was a tall, gaunt, sandy-haired individual with deep frown-creases slashing the bridge of his nose; he had a golf-course tan and a slightly disheveled look about him, as if he had dressed hurriedly.

Pedley didn't ask him to sit down. "A week ago," the marshal read from a tissue carbon, "the Bureau of Fire Prevention wrote you as follows:

Arnold J. Broodman
Resident Manager, Hotel Grolier

You were directed by the Fire Commissioner on . . . March 7, 1947 . . . to:

1. Equip with steel doors all exits from all floors,
2. Install acceptable fire breaks on floors 2 to 10, inclusive,
3. Satisfactorily enclose two elevator shafts,
4. Erect an additional fire escape on the Forty-fifth Street side of the building,
5. Provide for an automatic smoke alarm system within . . . 60 days . . . at the premises occupied by . . . the Grolier Operating Corporation (leased) by you, said premises being considered dangerous to life and property and in its present condition a violation of law.

Having failed to cause the ordered re-equipping to be done within the . . . 60 day . . . period, I am required by law to notify you that the said premises are hereby ordered to be . . . vacated.

"That notice was signed by John M. Bresnahan, Deputy Fire Commissioner, City of New York."

Broodman laced and unlaced his fingers wretchedly, but said nothing.

"Three days after you received that notice, your lawyers obtained a two-week stay of ejection from Judge Potter. In your application for this deferral, you promised to cease operating this building as a hotel within ten days; you pleaded inability to get labor and materials with which to make the required alterations to date."

The manager sweated it out in silence.

"A couple of days ago you attempted to obtain an additional policy of fire insurance to the tune of forty thousand dollars—"

"To cover the improvements on the property," the hotel man interrupted.

"The companies turned you down. After checking with us. Anyhow, failing to get your additional coverage, today you began to give your employees their week's notice. And tonight you have a fire."

"Nobody can feel worse about this than I do." Broodman combed his hair nervously with his fingers.

"A hell of a lot of people feel a hell of a lot worse!"

"The corporation won't attempt to deny its responsibility."

"You won't, either."

"You're not suggesting—?"

"I'm making a flat statement, Broodman. This blaze was incendiary. You . . . and your other stockholders . . . are the only persons who could profit from it."

The manager's tan became a muddy gray. "As far as profit is concerned, every cent I have was in this hotel. The insurance won't cover sixty per cent of the loss. I'm wiped out . . . even if the corporation wasn't liable for damage suits. Don't talk to me about profiting from a ghastly business like arson. I'll sue you for defamation of . . ."

"After I get through with you, you won't have any character that could be defamed, mister. The fire started in Mrs. Munson's room. You were up in her room tonight. She was liquored up. You supplied the liquor. You were in a jam with her. Now she's going to die, you think you're out of that jam. Well, you're in another, and it's a lot worse. They electrocute people for first-degree arson in this state, in case you didn't know."

Broodman scowled. "You sure the fire started in Doris' room?"

"I can make it stand up in court."

The manager sat down suddenly in the straight-backed chair, buried his face in his hands. After a minute he groaned:

"I guess you're right, saying I'm responsible. But not for arson. Only because of Doris."

"Trying to say the girl deliberately burned herself?"

"That's what she *would* do, marshal—what she must have done. She threatened as much, though she didn't say anything about . . . setting a fire."

"When was this?"

"Tonight. Half-past eleven or so. We'd been threshing the thing out—apparently you know about it . . .?"

"Only what I got out of Harris and Wayner."

"Well . . . I told her I had to shut the place up . . . was going south to run a hotel there. It would take a while for me to get a divorce and so on. She wanted to know how she was going to live in the meantime. Couldn't she go with me and so on. Finally I got sore. Told her if she wasn't satisfied to play it my way, we'd call the whole thing off."

"And then . . . ?"

"She bawled and got hysterical, the whole damn rigamarole women put on. But I'd had enough of it by then—I suppose worrying about the shutdown made me kind of jumpy—and I told her we were all washed up. Finally she said she'd kill herself; she'd make me sorry for treating her that way if it was the last thing she ever did." Broodman chewed at his lower lip. "That's the kind of break I get—for her to be so badly burned she can't tell you the truth of it. You could ask her . . ."

"I will," Pedley said. "She might come to and talk a little before she signs off."

Broodman shivered.

THERE were more reporters than firemen in the lobby when the marshal left the office; more photographers than interns, in the street. The crowd had thinned; the fire lines were permitting traffic on the opposite sidewalk. Pedley spoke to a haggard man in a white helmet:

"How about Maxie?"

"Died on the way over, Ben." The Battalion Chief spat. "Rest his soul. He was a good man."

"He was." Pedley nodded, walked to the red sedan. Maxie Rhine had been in the old Engine Eleven Company with him when they were probationers. They had rolled to many a bad blaze together; once Maxie had waded through the acid-loaded water of a drug warehouse cellar to drag Pedley out from under the I-beam that had pinned him. Now Maxie had taken a gust of flame from a back draft up on the tenth floor of this firetrap and they'd be sounding the four 5's for him in the morning. And there were three other wearers of the Maltese Cross who'd never answer the gong again, though Pedley hadn't known them as well as he had Maxie. There'd be those who'd miss every one of them. . . .

At the hospital the doctor confirmed what Pedley had learned on the phone. Doris Munson had been seriously burned about the breast and throat; was suffering from shock and smoke inhalation; barring pneumonia setting in, she'd recover. The matron said it was all right for the marshal to talk to her, long's he didn't excite her. He said he'd try not to.

The girl on the cot in Ward C couldn't have been identified as a blonde; there wasn't enough of her hair left. She looked up at Pedley out of bandages swathing her like a mummy.

"First thing I remember," she mumbled, "was someone at the window yelling 'Water!' "

"Had you been smoking in bed, Mrs. Munson?"

A negative shake of the head; her throat ached when she spoke.

"Were you feeling pretty good—you know, hit the cork quite a bit—before you turned in?"

Another negative. "I only had three little drinks," she added with an effort. "I was feeling terrible. I'd just found out something that would have sobered me if I'd drunk a gallon."

He told her what Broodman had said. "Is that true?"

Doris nodded, her eyes widening with horror. "Oh! Arnie thinks I . . . started the fire!"

"You could have."

She struggled to sit up. He put a hand on her forehead, forced her back onto the pillow.

"*Maybe I did!*" she whispered. "If I did, I hope I don't live. I couldn't bear to know I'd . . . caused all *that!*"

"Take a sleeping pill to get you to sleep?" He knew there must have been something to make her doubt her own actions.

"I took . . . six."

"Yeah." Not enough to kill her. Enough to scare Broodman if he'd learned about it. "You wash your face before you went to bed?"

"What?"

"Wash your face? Or use cleansing cream?"

"No." She was puzzled. "Why . . .?"

The nurse came in. "Phone for you, marshal."

He took it out in the corridor.

"Ed, Skipper. I been keeping an eye on Wayner, like you suggested."

"So . . ."

"He didn't head for the hospital at all."

"Know he didn't. Where is he?"

"Seven fifty West Twenty-eighth. Rooming house. No savvy if he lives here or not. Name isn't on the mailbox. That don't necessarily mean anything at a flea-bag like this."

"Where you calling from?"

"Candy store. Across the street."

"Stay there till I get down."

He didn't bother to go back to the ward. The red sedan made it in four minutes, with the blinkers but without the siren.

Shaner stopped devouring a chocolate bar long enough to say, "Must be in one of the back rooms, Ben. None of the fronts have lighted up since he went in."

"He could be rooming with somebody," Pedley said.

"Or he could be calling on somebody. Better let me go in with you."

"You go back, sit on Broodman's neck. I want him handy when the grand jury meets, in the morning." Pedley went across the street, into a hall that smelled of cabbage and pork and carbolic. In the front of a black tin mailbox was a cardboard with a dozen names printed on it; a couple of them had been crossed out. *Harry Lester, 6-C*, hadn't been crossed out; the marshal thought it was close enough to Les Harris to be worth casing.

He went up a staircase where the paint flaked off the walls like skin off sunburned shoulders; he made no particular effort to be silent about it.

On the third floor, lights showed under two of the doors,

none under 6-C. He walked on up to the top floor, opened the door of the common bathroom, closed it. Then he took off his shoes, went down one flight in his stockinged feet.

He listened at 6-C long enough to make sure somebody was opening a window inside, quietly, in the dark. Pedley set his shoes down carefully, took out his flashlight. He tried the knob, turned it noiselessly. The door wasn't locked.

He pushed it open suddenly, swung his flashlight in an arc covering as large a segment of the room as possible.

A washstand. A bed, rumpled up. The toe of a shoe just behind and beyond the open edge of the door. Pedley reached around the jamb for the switch. The movement took his head and shoulders into the doorway for an instant.

Long enough for a gun butt to smash down across the crease of his hat. . . .

THE room was still dark, but dull red flashes pulsated before the marshal's eyes. It was some seconds before he realized they came from a neon sign high on a building in the next block. The ruddy reflection from a polished shoe-tip was the thing that made him recognize it.

He reached out, touched the shoe. There was a foot in it; the foot didn't move when he felt it. Pedley pulled himself up by the bedpost, found the light switch, snapped it.

The foot in the shoe belonged to Les Harris, who lay on his back with a small scarlet worm wriggling down from a dark spot in his right temple. There was a purplish lump an inch above his right eye. The body was still warm. An automatic lay on the grass matting of the floor about eight inches away from the dead man's head.

The marshal looked at his watch: 4:42. He hadn't been out more than ten minutes or so.

He felt in the pockets of the floor patrol's uniform. Nothing but a fistful of silver coins and a couple of keys. No bills, of any denomination. But on the chair beside the bed was a strange collection.

Six wrist watches; two men's, the others the tiny diamond

doodads women go for. Four rings; one wedding, two solitaires, a pinky set with what looked like real rubies. A black opal brooch. A gold comb. A platinum cigarette case with the initials K. T. M.

Pedley stripped a pillow-slip off the bed, tilted the chair so the jewelry slid gently into the white sack. He lifted the gun by sticking a pencil in the muzzle, deposited it on the loose end of the pillow-slip, wrapped the surplus fabric around the weapon.

He retrieved his shoes, put them on. When he left 6-C, he took the key from the inside of the door, locked the room.

"Every arsonist has a twisted mind." The marshal stared coldly across the manager's desk at Broodman. "I don't mean pyros, either; they're psycho cases, anyhow. But every firebug is so snarled up in his mental processes that he figures a fire has to be set by some tricky method . . . and it always backfires on him." He opened a flat metal case, like a child's paint box. "This one used a cigarette, hoping it would look as if Mrs. Munson had fallen asleep smoking and set the bed on fire. But he forgot the lipstick."

Broodman leaned forward to peer at the brown-stained stub. "I don't see—"

"There isn't any. Would have been if Mrs. Munson had been smoking it—no matter how water-soaked it had gotten. She used lipstick, of course; she hadn't wiped it off."

The hotel man sighed. "She didn't start it, then."

"No. She was hurt enough to do it, maybe. But her mind didn't run to endangering other people's lives—only her own. She took an overdose of luminal. Not enough to kill her. But enough to keep her from waking up until the blaze had a better start than the firebug ever intended it should have."

"Who—?"

"He opened the door with a master key, after Mrs. Munson had gone to sleep—say twenty minutes to one. After he made sure she wasn't awake—he probably assumed she was drunk— he tiptoed in, took the lighted cigarette out of his mouth, laid it on the edge of the ashtray that was on her bed-table, put the

ashtray and cigarette on the bed so the burning stub would fall
off and ignite the mattress. He thought Mrs. Munson would
wake up after the mattress started to smolder and filled the room
with smoke. She didn't; the sleeping pills prevented her from
waking up until the flames from the burning blankets began to
sear her."

"What was the idea . . . if he didn't mean to burn down the
building?"

"To cause a panic. Get people running around the corridors
in their nightgowns and pajamas, half scared to death. With the
corridors filled with smoke, the apparatus rolling in with bells
clanging and everybody screaming 'Fire!,' it was easy for the
bug to go through the guests' rooms on the pretext of routing
them out and starting them for the elevators and the stairs."

"For God's sake! Why?"

Pedley slid the contents of the pillow-case out onto the desk-
top. "So he could loot their rooms, their clothing. Most people
don't lock up their money or jewels when they go to bed. They
leave their money in their purses and wallets, their rings and
watches on the bureau. With a hotel employee yelling at them
to get out of their rooms in a hurry, with those sirens and the
smoke stampeding them, not many would take time to go for
their valuables before they rushed out into the hall."

"Wayner!"

"There's another screwy thing about firebugs." The marshal
shook his head. "They always have to have an alibi. In twenty
years I haven't run across one who hasn't claimed he was somewhere else when the fire was set—who didn't try to prove he
couldn't possibly have been around when the fuse was lit. Now
your bell captain didn't have any alibi, any more than you did."

"That damned Harris!"

"Sure. He kept impressing me that his patrol clock would
show by the times he punched it, on each floor, that he couldn't
have been down on the fourth at the time the place was
torched."

"But why—?"

"Your fault, partly. You gave him his notice today. He didn't know where to get another job, probably. By the room he was living in, I'd say he didn't have much money saved up. He saw a way to get even with you for firing him and to get his hands on a lot of valuables, at the same time. Only the thing got out of hand; he didn't know it until it was so late he got cut off, up on the eighth, and nearly lost his own life before the boys brought him down."

"They should have left him up there," Broodman said grimly. "Did you get him?"

"Somebody did." Pedley stirred the heap of jewelry with his fingers. "He's dead. It was supposed to look like suicide. He was shot with his own gun. But he'd been slugged before he was lit up."

"Ah . . .!" Broodman waited.

"One of my deputies trailed Wayner over to Harris' rooming-house, called me, and I went down there. When I went in the room, somebody was hiding there. I didn't see him; he crowned me with a gun-butt and got away while I was out cold. My deputy trailed your bell captain back here to the hotel, collared him and found a big roll of bills on him. Nearly a thousand bucks. Wayner'd slugged Harris, taken the money which couldn't be traced and left the jewelry because it would be risky to pawn it."

"Check Wayner shot Harris?"

"No. You did that."

The manager didn't deny it. He appeared to be too dazed by the accusation to attempt an answer.

Pedley felt of the bump on the top of his skull. "Wayner wasn't the person who crowned me. He isn't tall enough to swing a gun down on the crease of my hat. Harris wasn't, either. But you are. And you sneaked out of the lobby right after I left for the hospital."

"For coffee," Broodman admitted. "I had to have some coffee. I was dead on my feet."

"Harris was, anyway. You doped it out just the way Wayner had. Only your bell captain wanted the money he guessed Harris had stolen; you wanted to get even with Harris for ruining you.

If you hadn't been afraid the whole business about your entanglement with Mrs. Munson would come out, if Harris had been forced to defend himself in court, you might have had him arrested and tried for arson. But you didn't want your own dirty linen hung up for everyone to see, so you took his punishment into your own hands. . . .

"You followed Wayner to the boarding-house, waited in the hall until the bell captain had slugged Harris and taken over the dough. When he came out, you went in. You were still in there when I arrived. Wayner was down in the hall somewhere—anyhow, he left the rooming-house before you did. My men trailed him—didn't see you!" The marshal walked around the desk. "We better be rolling downtown."

Broodman said stolidly, "You don't think you can prove any of this."

"No," Pedley admitted. "But I know it."

"Then . . .?"

"I'm not booking you for murder," the marshal said harshly. "I'm taking you in for criminal negligence in connection with the deaths in this fire. You'll have the better part of the next ten years to wish you'd spent the dough to make those changes the commissioner ordered. At that," he gripped the manager's arm roughly, "it won't be as long as a lot of other people will have, to regret what happened tonight. Come on. . . ."

from DETECTIVE WHO'S WHO

PEDLEY, Benjamin Tilmon, Chief Fire Marshal; b. N. Y., N. Y., Jan. 4, 1913; s. John T. and Louise (Sparrow) P.; pub. schs., N. Y. C., 1919–1931; Fire Dept. College, L. I. City, 1936–37. Entered NYCFD, Sept. 13, 1931, as probationer, assigned as ladderman to H & L Co. 61; transferred to Truck 12, Oct. 1932; served as tillerman 1933–35; promoted to acting Lieut. 1936; entered Bureau of Fire Investigation as Deputy Marshal June 1937; appt'd Ass't. Chief Marshal 1941–2; Chief Fire Marshal 1923. Departmental Citations: 1934; 1936 (2); 1940. Instructor, Chemistry of Combustibles, Columbia U., 1942, '43, '44. Lecturer: "Modern Methods in Arson Investigation," Stevens Institute, Hoboken, N. J., 1945; "Fighting the Fire Bug," U. Chicago, 1946. President, Nat'l. Ass'n. Municipal Fire Marshals, 1948–9. For extended biographical data, consult published works of Stewart Sterling. Res.: Hotel Metropole, W. 23 St., N. Y.

> Nature abhors a vacuum—at least, apparently, a temporal
> vacuum of more than four years. It was in 1903 that a great
> man abandoned a private inquiry practice in Baker Street;
> and in 1907 another commenced his practice in Praed
> Street—a man singularly like his predecessor in method, in
> speech, in character, and even, at times, in stature. Other
> types of detective may come and go; but this type must for-
> ever flourish in London, whether the Avenging Archetype
> moves under the name of Holmes or Pons.

SOLAR PONS IN

The Adventure of the Purloined Periapt

BY AUGUST DERLETH

WE HAD BEEN talking about the science of deduction that
noon hour, when we turned into Praed Street not far from our
lodgings, and Pons touched my arm with a gesture designed to
direct my attention to a young man walking not far ahead of us.

"Now then, Parker, let us see what you make of that fellow
going there. You know my methods; apply them."

"He seems a perfectly ordinary young fellow," I answered at
once. "Like thousands of others."

"Yes, indeed. But do not speak so hastily. Look again."

I saw that the object of our scrutiny walked along with occasional glances at the numbers, and said that manifestly he was
looking up an address.

"Elementary. Anything more?"

"He seems to be of modest means; he is not yet thirty years
of age; he is obviously English."

From In Re: Sherlock Holmes. Sauk City: Mycroft & Moran, 1945. Copyright 1945 by August Derleth.

"You see nothing further?"

"Nothing but the obvious details relative to the color and make of his clothes." I glanced at him. "I suppose you are about to tell me a host of incredible conclusions to which you have come in these few steps."

"No, no, you overrate my poor powers, Parker. I was about to add only that he is unmarried; he lives in the suburbs of London; he cycles to work; he is very probably a bookkeeper; and he is employed in our immediate vicinity. Moreover, he is not imaginative, but rather prosaic; he is precise and methodical, but sparing at the expense of neatness, and he is at the moment doing without his luncheon in an effort to accomplish something which has nothing to do with his work, for he is too conscientious to take time away from his work to pursue an inquiry into what is a purely personal matter."

For a moment I was too astonished to reply. Then I protested. "Oh, come, Pons—I have every respect for your use of the science of deduction, but I cannot follow you in all that."

"I assure you it is all extremely simple, my dear fellow. Surely no wife would permit her husband to go to work in such unpressed clothes, any more than she would allow him to wear a shirt which carries on the cuff the kind of inkmarks commonly found on the cuffs of those engaged in bookkeeping? By the same token, the fellow is sparing at the expense of neatness, for he has not had his suit pressed, nor his shirt washed; yet he dresses rather well, if in singular dreariness of color, betraying a lack of imagination."

"He cycles, you said."

"Surely that mark on his trousers' leg is nothing other than the mark of one of those clips designed to keep the trousers free of the wheel."

"I missed that. But how, then, do you know he lives in the suburbs?"

"Because a cycle is the readiest way to work from the suburbs, if one is employed in the heart of the city and is at the same time of such modest means that a certain care in spending money is advisable."

"Very well, granting that—I fail utterly to understand how you can say with such positive assurance that he is employed in our vicinity."

"Ah, but surely that follows inevitably. If he cycles to work, obviously he has his cycle at hand. Since he does not use it to look up an address which I fancy will turn out to be our own, certainly it is not too much to deduce that his place of employment is so close to the address he seeks that it would be superfluous to use his cycle!"

I shook my head. "I am afraid I am destined always to fall short of your kind of observation, Pons."

"But you have your diagnoses to uphold, Parker, and they should be your primary concern." He smiled. "Ah, see; it is as I thought. He has reached number seven; he pauses; he is going in. Now we shall soon learn what it is that troubles him to the extent that he is willing to depart from what is doubtless a long-established routine in order to bring the problem to us."

As we entered the outer door to our lodgings, we were seen by Mrs. Johnson, who had answered the bell.

"You're in luck, Mr. Harris. Here they are now." She smiled in our direction and raised her voice a little to say, "Here's a gentleman to see Mr. Pons!" and then vanished discreetly into her own quarters.

"Come along, Mr. Harris," invited Pons, as we ascended the stairs to our own lodgings on the second floor.

"Thank you," replied Mr. Harris soberly, and set out after us with an expression of intense gravity on his serious young features.

In this prosaic fashion began one of Solar Pons's favorite adventures, for Mr. Sidney Harris had come to consult Pons about the loss of a jeweled amulet, to which he referred constantly as "my uncle's periapt." He was a young man whose demeanor gave evidence of every deduction Pons had made of him; he readily admitted that he was employed as a bookkeeper for the firm of Chasins and Abramson only three streets away from our lodgings, and he told his story with simple precision.

"I live with my sister, who keeps house for me, and there are living with me my father, who is in ill health, my brother, who is occasionally employed as a clerk in a tobacconist's shop, and my cousin, Richard Murchison. We live in South Norwood, and I cycle to work every day, since my salary does not permit of unnecessary expense in traveling to and from the place of my employment. About three months ago my uncle died; he was Teale Murchison."

"Ah, the publisher of religious books."

"Yes, Mr. Pons. The firm still carries his name, though he was no longer actively associated with it at the time of his death. He was my mother's only brother, and he lived in the country south of London."

"A wealthy, charitable old man," observed Pons. "How does it come that his son lives with you?"

"He has a small annuity, and contributes modestly to the household expenses. We do not own the house; I take it by the month. The fact is, Mr. Pons, Mr. Murchison thought his son a wild boy because he had an unfortunate affair with a young lady, and he cut him off with but a modest allowance."

Pons's interest kindled. "To whom, then, did Mr. Murchison leave his wealth?"

"To charity, Mr. Pons."

"His house?"

"I am his heir, in accordance with the terms of his will. Unfortunately, the house has been put up for sale; it is a large, rambling structure, and there is simply not enough left from my uncle's estate to enable me to keep the house up. We had no knowledge of my uncle's doings. Mr. Murchison was a very religious man, but he was also a very crotchety one, with a ready temper and a sharp tongue, which he regretted many times thereafter. I felt very badly about his action in regard to his son, for Richard is not wild in the sense his father had it, and he did not deserve the treatment he received. Mr. Murchison had always had a fondness for me; he believed that I was a 'steady' young man." He said this with an apologetic grimace, which made him instantly more likable.

"I had hoped to be married on some part of my uncle's

wealth, but now I shall have to put that off until after the house is sold, for, of course, I intend that my cousin Richard shall share whatever can be realized on the sale of the house. I had intended, as soon as I learned of the terms of the will, that Richard should share with me. However, when we went to my uncle's bank after the will was read, we discovered that he had only two months previous to his death converted all his cash reserve, all his stocks and bonds, into gold pieces, and had then gone about London bestowing his wealth upon various charities. We traced some of it, but naturally made no attempt to trace it all, since my uncle had constantly spoken of giving everything he owned to charity, and it was, finally, no surprise to learn that he had done so. However, he thought very well of me, as his only sister's first child, and he left his house and furnishings to me. Among the possessions he bestowed upon me was a valuable little periapt of beaten gold, set with four emeralds and a single ruby. I have no idea as to its worth, but it was set apart in the will as mine, with my uncle's instructions that I follow his precept and carry it more or less as he did, in the nature of a good-luck piece. I accepted my uncle's periapt, and have carried it ever since."

"How large was this amulet?"

"About two inches in diameter. I believe it was handmade, except for the settings."

"A plain gold piece set with jewels?"

"Not quite, Mr. Pons. My uncle had had some religious verses inscribed into the back of it."

"Let us come now to the incident of its loss."

"That took place this morning. I did not have to reach my desk this morning until eleven o'clock, since I had worked overtime last night. As a result, I departed from my usual custom of taking a steam-bath near my place of work, and took a bath at home. As far as I know, I was alone in the house, except for my sister, who rapped on the bathroom door while I was in the tub, to say that she was going marketing. Since I meant to change clothes, I had emptied the pockets of my suit, and had ranged their contents on my bureau. Among them was my uncle's periapt. About ten minutes after my sister had gone out, I came out of the bathroom and went into my own room. Almost instantly I discovered that my uncle's periapt was missing. I thought I had mislaid it, or that it had fallen from the bureau; but it did not reappear. In my agitation, I forgot to put on the fresh clothes I had laid out, and came away again in my old suit, as you see me. I thought the matter over in the hour before my luncheon, and determined to put the problem before you."

"The door was not locked?"

"Neither back nor front door, Mr. Pons. My sister had not gone far away; I was in the house; I suppose she did not consider it necessary to lock the doors."

"So that anyone could have walked into the house and taken the periapt?"

"I am afraid so."

"Did very many people know of your having this trinket apart from the members of your household?"

"Not more than half a dozen or so in the neighborhood, and perhaps one or two people in the office."

"Yet a child, who had no previous knowledge of it, could have walked into your room and made off with it."

"I am afraid that is the case, Mr. Pons. Perhaps the problem affords nothing in the way of evidence, but I hesitated to go to the police and have the pawnshops watched, because I do not really know that my uncle's periapt has as much actual value as it has intrinsic value to me. It is rather a matter of sentiment than of actual monetary worth. I would like to have it recovered and, while I cannot afford much additional expense, I am sure we could come to some agreement about your fee."

Manifestly Pons had made up his mind to find the purloined periapt, for he smiled and suggested, "Perhaps we ought just to run out to your home and look around a little in the hope of discovering the lost amulet."

Harris looked gravely at his watch and shook his head. "I am sorry, but I cannot come along. I would be late to my work if I did so. However, I will send a message to my sister to expect you. I am sure I wish you luck, Mr. Pons, for your luck is mine. But I know my uncle's periapt was on my bureau when I went into the bathroom, and it was not there when I came out. That is the long and short of it."

Immediately after luncheon Solar Pons and I set out for South Norwood.

Mr. Harris' house appeared to be one of a great number built in the same plan, in a somewhat undesirable neighborhood, for living space was obviously crowded, and the street outside the house was occupied by a great many urchins of both sexes. We were admitted to the house by a tired and harassed-looking woman whose features plainly and unmistakably identified her as our client's sister. Tired as she was, however, she was in good voice.

"You're the gentlemen Siddie telephoned about. 'Agatha, I'm sending two gentlemen out to look around a bit,' he says to me. 'Whatever for?' I asked him, but he did not answer."

Nor did Pons volunteer any information, though she paused pointedly.

"He said I was to show you right to his room, gentlemen, and here it is, just as he left it. I ain't had time to put his clothes away, that he was to wear and forgot. Seems to me Siddie gets more forgetful every day."

I confess that at this point, with the vision of our client as a forgetful young fellow, I began to feel that the adventure of his uncle's stolen amulet was certain to turn out to be one of the most trivial of all those exploits upon which I had had the good fortune to accompany my friend, Solar Pons. And our almost instant discovery on entering Harris' chamber came as confirmation of this conviction, for there, in plain sight on Harris' bureau, lay the object of our search!

Pons closed the door behind him, shutting out our client's curious sister, and went directly over to the periapt.

"Ah, I fancy this is what we want."

"And more of a wild goose chase I have never seen," I said in disgust. "That fellow simply mislaid it, and his sister found it and put it back."

"Slowly, slowly, Parker! How delightful and how empty life would be if all things were so simple! But I fear it is not so. You will reflect that his sister has only just now told us she had no time to put Harris' clothes away; it is not too much presumption to believe that she had no time to clean this room, either; there is no evidence of it. Furthermore, the actual reappearance of this periapt is not adequate grounds for adducing that our client did not know what he was talking about. No, you may depend upon it, Parker, our client meant and believed and knew just what he said; as he put it, the long and the short of it is that the periapt was on the bureau when he went to take his bath, and it was not there when he came back; now it is some three hours, almost four, since that time, and here it is back on the bureau once more. Yet it was gone, it had been taken. But manifestly it had not been stolen because of its monetary value."

"Unless no pawnbroker would accept it," I protested.

"In less than four hours, the thief had poor faith indeed if he gave up trying to dispose of it so quickly." He picked it up. "Besides, it has a good value. The jewels are real enough, and if I am any judge, the piece is solid gold. I fancy any pawnbroker would be happy to lend a modestly substantial sum on this piece. Let us just examine it."

He bent over, turned it about, smiled with a most quizzical expression in his eyes, and handed it to me. "What do you make of it, Parker?"

I took it and scrutinized it closely, aware that something about it had caught Pons's interest and imagination. The face of the amulet was not particularly attractive; indeed, I should have said it was singularly unattractive; its ruby was set squarely in the center, and four little emeralds framed it in the shape of a cross. The entire face had a rough appearance, as if it had been pounded and worked by hand, and it badly needed burnishing. I turned it over and discovered that the back of the piece was burnished and carried the religious "verses" of which Harris had spoken. *Ask, and it shall be given you: seek, and you shall find: knock, and it shall be opened to you. Numbers: 8, 2.*

"It appears to be quite valuable," I said, handing it back.

"Nothing more?"

I smiled. "If there is anything more to be learned from that piece, I should be delighted to be instructed."

"Ah, forgive me, Parker; I am your humble servant. I should say only that it is possible to draw a conclusion or two from it. The late Murchison was a wise old bird, who, though he fancied his nephew, did feel that he lacked imagination and was altogether a little obtuse in matters pertaining to his own best interests. Plainly, too, he was a man who believed that one ought to merit his just deserts."

"My dear Pons! You are having me."

"Not at all. It is all written here as plainly as this quotation from the Bible."

"I fail to see it."

"Look again."

He returned the periapt to my hand, and I examined it once more. I could not see what it was that gave Pons any reason to make the deductions he had just made. I said so, with some heat.

"Ah, well, ponder it. Perhaps it will come to you."

I shrugged, a little nettled. "Well, this must certainly go down as our most unimportant and most quickly solved puzzle."

"On the contrary, it has only begun. I daresay we shall have a little excursion before we are done. Come, we are finished here. Let us just go back into the city and surrender the periapt to Mr. Harris."

So saying, he opened the door of the chamber and stepped out just as our client's sister made a show of being busy not far away. It was clear that she had been listening at the threshold. We bade her good afternoon and set out for Chasins and Abramson's, to deliver his amulet to Mr. Sidney Harris.

Our client was soberly pleased at Pons's discovery, though a little nervous at having been summoned from his work to take time for Pons's questions. He strove to settle upon a fee, but Pons would not ask one.

"By no means, Mr. Harris. I found your little puzzle instructive, and our discovery of the periapt was due to no acumen of mine."

"I cannot understand it," said Mr. Harris for the third time. "I know it was not there, it was not in the room—I searched for it carefully."

"Ah, it is strange how objects can elude one. Tell me, Mr. Harris, do you have the key to your late uncle's house?"

"Yes, Mr. Pons. Would you like to look at it?"

"I have for some time been entertaining the thought of buying or renting a house in the country. It may be that your uncle's home is in the nature of what I had in mind. Do you think we might go down to look it over?"

"When I can get away."

"Ah, but I would rather not lose time. I should prefer to go down within a short time. If you will but lend me the key."

"I think that will be all right, Mr. Pons. You can bring the key back to me here tomorrow."

He detached the key from a ring in his pocket, and gave it to Pons.

"By the way, your late uncle was a Roman Catholic, was he not?"

"Yes, sir. Our family belongs to that faith."

"You mentioned your family this noon. Would it be too much to ask you to describe them to me? Your sister, of course, we have seen."

Harris looked apprehensively toward the clock on the wall of the receiving room, but nevertheless set forth upon the details Pons had asked of him, with such precision that in a remarkably short time he had brought his father, his brother, and his cousin to vivid life, so that it seemed to me I should be able to identify any one of them at sight.

"Ah, that is splendid, Mr. Harris. Is it my impression that your uncle carried this periapt as a kind of good-luck charm?"

"So he said."

"Of some years' standing?"

"That was our belief."

"Well, thank you, Mr. Harris. Good day."

As we were walking leisurely back toward our lodgings, Pons beckoned one of the street gamins to us; I recognized him for the son of a locksmith who had his little shop in the vicinity. The boy came running up, a bright-eyed lad of ten or thereabouts, touched his cap, and stood with his arms akimbo before Pons.

"Alfred, my lad—do you think you might find three boys and come 'round to 7B posthaste?"

"I think so, Mr. Pons."

"Capital! I have a little mystery to solve. Be off with you now."

The boy cut away and vanished into an alleyway; in a moment his voice sounded at a distance, raising a hue and cry for a companion. Pons looked after him with a whimsical smile.

"Are you taking to the children to assist you now, Pons?" I asked.

"I have used these lads before your time, Parker. And no doubt I shall use them after. They are remarkably alert. I call them my Praed Street Irregulars." He glanced at me quizzically. "Did not something in Mr. Harris' conversation give you pause, Parker?"

"Oh, nothing but his fidgeting. Why, the man carried on as if he feared he would be summarily dismissed if he took time to answer your questions."

"Yes, yes—but it was not that I had in mind. Did it not seem to you a little strange that a man like Teale Murchison should carry a good-luck piece?"

"Many people do."

"True. But surely it is inconsistent with the tenets of the Roman Catholic faith to put any trust in such charms and amulets as this?"

"I believe it is."

"And since we know that the late Murchison was a religious man, a manufacturer of Bibles, no less, this tale of his good-luck charm does not ring quite true."

"What are you getting at?"

"I submit that Mr. Harris' periapt was not designed as a good-luck charm at all."

Somewhat impatiently, I retorted that very clearly it was meant to be coin of the realm.

"Strange you should say so, Parker. Now, I had the distinct impression that the amulet was made up of two gold pieces, melted down—somewhat crudely, to be sure. Moreover, I submit that the amulet is not more than four months old at the most, and that it was made out of two of those gold pieces the late Murchison removed from his bank."

"How can you possibly make that assertion?"

"Ah, it is a simple matter of deduction, Parker."

"Well, it is quite beyond me."

"Indeed, it is so elementary I hesitate to mention it."

But he offered no explanation, and I did not ask one, for it was manifest that he believed anyone alert and observant should have recognized his premises. So it was in silence that we mounted the steps of number seven and went up to our rooms.

We had hardly removed our light coats before there was a rush and a clatter on the stairs, coupled with Mrs. Johnson's indignantly raised voice; the door was thrown open without ceremony, and young Alfred burst into the room, followed pell-mell by a trio of grinning urchins.

"Here we are, Mr. Pons!" cried Alfred, closing the door and marching up to the table, followed by his companions, who ranged themselves in a row beside him.

"So I see," replied Pons. "It is a mystery to me how you can manage to act so quickly, Alfred—even to the extent of having a little bread with jelly before you came. Yes, there at the corner of your mouth, my boy."

While he spoke, Pons went about gravely taking from his pocket four guineas, which he placed in a neat row at the edge of the table. Four pairs of bright, eager eyes watched him with keen interest.

"Now, then," continued Pons, standing before them. "How many of you have cycles?"

Two hands went up.

"Good. Two will carry the four of you. I have a little errand I want you to do. For the next three hours I want you to watch a house in South Norwood. There are four people of interest to me. The fifth I know. I want you to watch everything these people do, put down where they go, and come back here by six o'clock. Then these guineas will belong to you. Listen to me carefully."

Thereupon he repeated almost word for word the excellent description of his relatives given us by Mr. Sidney Harris, our recent client; and, so armed, the boys descended the stairs with the same clatter and banging which had accompanied their arrival. Pons, appearing well pleased with himself, rubbed his hands in satisfaction and gazed over at me with a twinkle in his eyes.

"The lads are far less likely to excite suspicion than you or I might be. And these are onerous details."

"It would seem to me that Harris might have told you what you wanted to know."

"Not he. No, no, Parker, he is too trusting. He sees no evil, hears none, and plainly believes little. We must have some unbiased comment on these people, and I am sure we shall get it from the 'Irregulars.'"

Promptly on the hour set, the boys returned.

As their acknowledged leader, Alfred instructed them, one after the other, to make their reports. The smallest lad, a red-haired boy called "Pinky," had been detailed to observe Harris' sister, who had emerged once in late afternoon to go to market. Pinky did not have a high opinion of the lady, for he observed that she quarreled with the green-grocer about the price of vegetables. She was also seen to manifest her insatiable curiosity by peering into windows of the neighboring houses. She gabbled for a long time with another woman out marketing, and the boy had crept close enough to overhear the two ladies energetically gossiping about a third. The second lad kept his eye out for the old man, Harris' father; he had come home from the house of a friend, and was clearly enough an ailing man. A husky lad had pushed him home in a wheel chair, and the old man had given him a coin of some kind; he had seemed very friendly and bore very well the immediate scolding set up by his daughter.

The third lad had watched for Richard Murchison, who had arrived home from his work shortly after four o'clock. He was a boyish young fellow, and shortly after he had gone into the house, he came back out once more carrying a letter, which he read. "It was a love letter," said the lad scornfully.

"Ah, indeed! How could you tell, Peter?"

"'E 'ad such a silly grin, 'e did, all the time 'e was a-readin' it. Then 'e picked a flower and 'eld it under 'is nose, 'e set down on the kerb and read the letter twice over."

"Ah, observant lad! Poor Richard is a second time bitten in the same place."

Clearly the lad had no good opinion of Richard for his being in love.

Alfred, however, had the longest tale to tell. He had watched Harris' brother, whose name, he had discovered, was Charles. Charles had been at home when the boys arrived, but he did not stay there long. He went down the street some distance to a pub; there he sat for some time scribbling on the back of an envelope. Then he went to a library in the neighborhood and came out whistling. He went back to the pub and set them up for the three or four men in the place at that time. He did a little more figuring and writing on the edge of a newspaper. He crumpled up one of the papers on which he had been writing and threw it away as he came out of the pub; Alfred had rescued it, and now handed it to Pons, who took it eagerly and unfolded it.

"Ah, Mr. Charles's new suit is ready, his tailor writes, 'but please, sir, to come with the money to pay for it in advance.'" He looked up. "Evidently Charles is living on his future."

"That's all, Mr. Pons," said Alfred.

"Well done, boys! And there are your guineas. Now be off with you."

There was a chorus of "Thank you, sir!" and once again that mad clatter on the stairs, followed by Mrs. Johnson's portentous sighs, made pointedly loud from below, so that Pons and I would be sure to hear.

"Mrs. Johnson bears her cross well," observed Pons. "Well, Parker, what do you make of it?"

"Frankly, nothing."

"Oh, it is not as bad as that. I fancy Charles is the man we want. I have no doubt he overheard his brother say he meant to have a bath, and slipped back into the house to take the periapt while Sidney was in his bath. He had begun to wonder about the periapt. That he did not get it back before Sidney came out again was very likely a miscalculation on his part."

"Oh, come, Pons! How is it possible from these lads' tales to deduce that?"

"Why, it is a process of simple elimination. Harris' father and sister are clearly out of it; his cousin is in love, and between his work and his romance—his addiction to romance, you will remember, was responsible for the rift between his father and himself—he has little time for such calculations which plainly occupy the mind of Mr. Charles Harris."

"What are those figures on the envelope?"

"They are calculations concerning the probable state of Mr. Charles Harris' finances, if he can riddle himself into riches. He does not seem to be a poor man, for all that there is no evidence of his having saved money." He threw the letter carelessly to the table and got up. "But come, Parker, we have but an hour or two until darkness to get on with it."

Mystified, I got into my topcoat, and set out with Pons for the street below, where we walked for a short distance before Pons managed to hail a cab. We got in, and Pons gave the driver the address of our destination. It was not South Norwood. It was beyond London, past the outlying districts of the city.

"I thought it was Charles we were after," I said pointedly.

"Dear me, no. Charles is the man who purloined the periapt. We are done with him unless he has more wit than I credit him with. As to that, we shall see in good time. We are off to look over Mr. Teale Murchison's country house."

"Yes, that is a matter I meant to ask about. What the devil did you mean by telling such a fabrication to Harris?"

"Ah, you know my methods, Parker. Ponder them."

Pons sat back and relaxed, his eyes half closed. Swallowing my chagrin, I did likewise.

In a little over an hour, we were delivered at a fine old country estate, clearly at one time the property of a wealthy man. Pons instructed the driver to wait, and we walked up a flag-stone path under a gracious avenue of trees to the front door, a heavy, paneled piece with bronze finishings. Pons fished from his pocket the key Harris had given him, inserted it into the lock, and opened the door.

"I take it you are looking for something specific," I said as we entered the house.

"Capital, Parker! Indeed I am. I am looking for a seven-branched candelabrum. Or perhaps seven lamps. But I rather fancy it will be a seven-branched candelabrum, after all."

My astonishment did not permit me to reply.

"Let me see—where are we most likely to find such an ornament? The study, perhaps, or the library. Let us just look around."

We went down the hall, peering into one room after another, Pons somewhat in the lead.

"Hm! Surely this looks like it, does it not, Parker?"

We entered a small library, packed with books on all walls save the wall to our left as we entered; that wall opened on to a fireplace, and, above the mantelpiece, one on each side, were affixed two seven-branched candelabra, wired for electricity. I gazed in amazement, for I knew that Pons had never before entered this house, nor had Harris in any way described it except in the most general terms.

"I fancy this is the room we want," said Pons tranquilly.

"How in the devil did you know these candelabra were here?"

"Oh, I did not know they were in this room, Parker. You credit me with too much knowledge. But it was almost inevitable they were somewhere on this estate; surely that was manifest from the beginning!" He turned to look at the candelabra. "I daresay that switch over there controls the lights. Try it, Parker."

I did so, and the candelabra glowed with a soft, yellow light.

"Excellent!" murmured Pons, turning on his heels, his back to the candelabra. "And here on this wall, I fancy, we will find what we are looking for. Let us just examine these books a bit. The light falls here, well above the floor."

He stood back from the shelves and looked the books over

without touching them. The contents of the shelves before us were what one might expect of a manufacturer of Bibles; they were ancient, worn tomes of considerable size, and certainly of great weight, apparently of no especial value save as curios, for they were, on closer examination of their scarcely legible titles, old variations of, and commentaries on the Scriptures. Without further study, Pons moved forward, opened the case, and began to turn over the books, taking them from the shelves until he came to a set of four of the largest books which were especially encased and were among those quaint old books which bore locks.

"Ha!" he cried. "I fancy we shall want these, Parker. If you will take two of them, I will take the other two."

I picked them up, and found them as weighty as I had expected. "I am by no means anti-religious, but these Scriptures are as heavy as lead."

"Spoken like a true sinner, Parker."

I laughed and carried on.

Pons carefully locked the door. We got into the cab, and rode back to London, reaching our lodgings before ten o'clock. Pons lost no time in going at once to the telephone and asking our recent client, Sidney Harris, to step around. Then he went calmly to the wireless and turned on the news, to which he listened with unbroken attention for the next half-hour, thus effectively keeping me from asking the questions that welled up inside me with insistent urgency.

In less than an hour, Mr. Sidney Harris arrived. He had cycled over, and he rang our doorbell with an uncertainty that reflected his feelings. Pons stepped to the door, opened it, and called down to invite Harris up. He entered the room with perplexity plainly evident on his features; he was completely at a loss to know why my friend, Solar Pons, had sent for him, and there was manifest also some apprehension, very possibly because he feared Pons had decided after all to ask a fee for his services.

"Come in, come in, my dear Mr. Harris! I have a little matter that requires your attention. First of all, the key to your late uncle's house. I believe the house would be far more suitable for occupation by your bride and yourself."

Harris goggled at Pons as he took the key and mechanically attached it once more to his key-ring. "I'm sorry," he managed to say. "We are hoping to sell it."

"I fancy that will not be necessary." Pons walked with a catlike agility around the table, took up one of the ponderous tomes he had brought from the Murchison house, slipped it from its case, and pried open the lock. "Pray overlook the liberties I am taking with your property, Mr. Harris, but I believe your uncle intended you to follow this course."

As he spoke, the book fell open with a dull sound, and there lay revealed not an orthodox book at all, but a cleverly made dummy, into the pages of which had been laid row on row of gold pieces!

"My Lord in Heaven!" exclaimed Harris, staring open-mouthed.

"Ah yes, these gold pieces are quite real, believe me, my dear fellow! There are four volumes of them. I discovered them precisely where your late uncle said they would be."

Harris, who had taken a tentative step or two forward, hesitated once more and stared at Pons with that strange mixture of uncertainty and respect which my friend never failed to command by these casual announcements of his remarkable deductions.

"My uncle?" he said, passing his tongue over his dry lips.

"Indeed, yes. He left the word for you as plainly as he could in his determination to tax your ingenuity. I fear he had no very great respect either for your knowledge of Scripture or your imagination. I fancy, too, he had a good time exercising his own ingenuity and wit by setting out to distribute his wealth and ending up by concealing the bulk of it for you to find. Your inheritance was precisely where the late Mr. Murchison wrote that it would be—opposite the seven-branched candelabrum, where the light fell on the north wall of his library."

Harris sat down nervously. "I am afraid this is quite beyond me, Mr. Pons. I am all a-tremble."

"Dear me! Pray pull yourself together. You are wealthy, Mr. Harris. No more will you need to cycle to work daily, and no longer will you need to put off your wedding. But, come, let me explain the puzzle to you. Have you your uncle's periapt?"

Wordlessly, Harris produced the curious object.

"Herein lies the solution of the matter," continued Pons. "I apprehend neither you nor my estimable companion knows his Scripture well. Attend me: *Ask, and it shall be given you: seek, and you shall find: knock, and it shall be opened to you. Numbers: 8, 2.*" He looked up, his keen eyes narrowed. "Now, then, think: what is the source of that quotation?"

Harris swallowed and answered uncertainly. "It is not from the Sermon on the Mount?"

"Capital! Capital! Of course it is, Mr. Harris. But what, then, is it doing in *Numbers*, which is in the Old Testament?"

Harris began to look a little foolish, and I have no doubt I too looked as foolish as I felt.

"There you have it. The quotation is from Matthew: 7, 7, the Douay version, which is the version of Scriptures preferred by members of the Roman Catholic faith. Clearly, then, Mr. Murchison meant you to seek and find, and he told you at least initially where to look. Let us turn to Numbers: 8, 2."

As he spoke, he lifted from his shelves the Bible in question, turned over a little more than a hundred pages, and read aloud:

"*Speak to Aaron, and thou shalt say to him: When thou shalt place the seven lamps, let the candlestick be set up on the south side. Give orders therefore that the lamps look over against the north, towards the table of the loaves of proposition, over against that shall they give light, towards which the candlestick looketh.* Surely that is plain enough!"

At that, Mr. Sidney Harris found his voice. He came to his feet, seized Pons's hand, and began to shake it in the sudden expression of his joy. "Mr. Pons, I owe you more than I can pay you. You have given me a new life, indeed, you have!"

"On the contrary, my dear fellow—it is I who owe you a debt of gratitude for bringing to my attention one of the most intriguing problems in many months. And, by the way, if I were you I should not permit natural generosity to make it unnecessary for brother Charles to get himself a suitable position and learn to work."

FROM DETECTIVE WHO'S WHO

PONS, Solar; b. Prague, circa 1880; s. Asenath, consular official at Prague, and Roberta (McIvor) P.; younger brother of Stoneham, in His Majesty's Service; pub. sch. edu., matriculated Oxford summa cum laude, 1899. Unmarried. Member: Savile; Diogenes; Athenaeum; Cliff-dwellers; Lambs. Estab. private inquiry practice at 7B Praed Street, 1907. British Intelligence, World War I. Monographs: *An Inquiry into the Nan-Matal Ruins of Ponape* (1905); *The Varieties of the Criminal Method* (1911); *A Logical Approach to the Science of Ratiocination* (1917); *The Chess Problem and the State of Mind* (1919); *The Inductive Process* (1921); *On the Value of Circumstantial Evidence* (1925); *An examination of the Cthulhu Cult and Others* (1931). Widely traveled. Residences: New York; Chicago; Paris; Vienna; Prague; 7B Praed Street, London, England.

*Some years ago Ellery Queen (the editor) announced that
Ellery Queen (the author) was readying a new and different series of stories about Ellery Queen (the gentleman detective)—a kind of criminous calendar, deductive duodec-
alogue, 'tec twelvemonth, in which each story of the cycle
should deal with a crime which could happen only in one
specific month of the year. The project has not yet been
completed; but here you may read one of the very few
Queen stories never before printed in hard covers—the
monthly murder for March.*

ELLERY QUEEN IN

The Ides of Michael Magoon

BY ELLERY QUEEN

IT WAS PASSED in the third session of the Sixty-fifth Con-
gress and approved as of 6:55 P.M. on the twenty-fourth of Feb-
ruary, 1919, and its title is Public—No. 254 [H.R. 12863].

Nor is there anything alarming in its subtitle, which happens
to be *An Act To provide revenue, and for other purposes.* The
fifth word may raise a few scattered goose pimples, but hardly
more.

It is necessary to read on.

Nothing will be clear until you come upon the phrase, "on or
before the fifteenth day of March."

Then everything will be clear, clear as the clap of the tocsin.
There is only one calamity which befalls America, *urbs et suburbs,* on or before the fifteenth day of March, and that is the
income tax.

Before going on to Michael Magoon and his unusual tax problem, it is tempting to take a short detour into the statutes, which concern not Mike alone but very nearly all of us. There was income-tax legislation before the Revenue Act of 1918, and there has been income-tax legislation since, but Public—No. 254 [H.R. 12863] bears a curious distinction. It was the first income-tax law which pronounced the annual Judgment Day to be March the fifteenth. Its predecessors designated March the first.

Why the change in dates?

There is a reason, of course, and it is not the reason your tax expert, for all his awful knowledge, can give you.

Someone—perhaps it was Mr. Secretary of the Treasury, or a Gentleman from Indiana or Ohio, or even some lowlier lackey of the People with a finger in the legislative pie—someone with a frightening lack of humor remembered great Caesar and the bloody daggers. Someone remembered the signs and the portents and the gathering crimson thunderheads over the full Capitoline moon. He may even have recalled that *postridie idus.*, the day following the Ides, was held by the ancient Romans to be unlucky.

And who among us, after rendering unto Caesar, will deny on any given March the sixteenth that the Romans were right?

THE whole thing was certainly unlucky for Magoon.

Mike was what the fancy boys like to call a private "op," or "eye." These fascinating terms inevitably materialize a slim-hipped, narrow-eyed, cigarette-dragging character in a Finchley custom-drape, a Sulka tie, and a thirty-five-dollar Dobbs, who is greased-death on the draw, kills five thugs and one mastermind on every case, is as irresistible with dames as a fox in a hen-coop, carries a self-refillable flask of Scottish dew on the other hip, and speaks, when he speaks at all, in insolent monosyllables—something out of Chandler by Bogart.

Alas, Mike Magoon was a sagging sixty-three with a forty-eight waist, very large flat feet, and blinky brown eyes covered by tortoise shell glasses, which gave him an air of groping astonishment. He wore Adam hats, suits from Barney's, and shoes by W. L. Douglas. And he neither smoked nor drank—asthma barred the one and, as for the other, his good wife had the nasal infallibility of a beagle. He had never manhandled a lady client in his life; not that he lacked a libido, but he cherished his license more. And in the sudden-death department, he had discharged his police positive exactly twice since resigning from the force four years before, and one of those times he was cleaning his pistol on the fire escape when a neighbor's pride and joy whanged his shooting hand with a well-directed B.B. shot.

No cases came Mike's way involving mysterious fat men with inscrutable eyes, or Maltese falcons, or gangster chieftains in luxurious penthouses. For the most part he spent his time trailing thirtyish ladies for suspicious husbands or putting the grab on shop clerks allergic to the boss's till. On those Saturday nights when he was not working, he took his wife to the movies. On Sundays, after church, there was always The Little Ukraine on Fordham Road—Mike was mad about *shashlik* and *borscht* with sour cream. And on Wednesday nights, bingo.

The first three years Mike was a private eye he operated out of his three-room Bronx flat to cut the overhead, picking up what cases he could through tips from old friends in brass buttons. Then he and Mrs. Magoon decided that a front and a midtown telephone number might pay for more bingo games, so Mike sublet one room of a four-office suite in a Forty-second Street office building, sharing the premises with a public stenographer, a commercial artist, and a little bald man with a gold tooth who had four phones which were always ringing. A week after *Michael Magoon, Confidential Investigations* had sprouted in gilt on his pebbled-glass door, Mike opened it to admit Mrs. Clementa Van Dome, the kind of client the Magoons of this world lie awake nights praying for—the client who pays an annual retainer for continuous services rendered. It was a klep case in which—but more of Mrs. Van Dome anon.

Three times since that gold-letter day the Ides of Martius came and went, and Caesar was satisfied. And then came the fourth time.

The fourth time it was Mike who went, hurrying as fast as his asthma and flat feet would permit, to the Queen apartment.

A DETECTIVE consulting a detective struck Nikki's funnybone. And poor Mike's manner as he looked around at the Queen walls somehow made it even funnier.

But the best was still to come.

"Ellery," said Mike, blushing, "I have been robbed."

"Robbed," said Ellery with a straight face. "Robbed of what, Mike?"

"My income tax return."

Nikki excused herself heroically. When she came back, Ellery was putting his handkerchief away.

"Forgive me, Mike," he was saying. "My old pleurisy. Did you say your tax return has been stolen?"

"That's what I said, and you're healthy as a horse," said Mike Magoon doggedly. "Oh, I don't blame you for goin' into hysterics. But it ain't funny, McGee. Today's the fourteenth of March. How am I gonna make the March fifteenth deadline?"

"Well, your—hrm!—return can't be terribly complicated, Michael," said Ellery gravely. "Get another blank and fill it in, and so on."

"With what, I ask you!"

"With what?"

"You gotta have data!"

"Well, certainly. Don't you have data?"

"No!"

"But—"

"Listen, Ellery. All my papers and records—everything I was usin' to make out my return—it's all been swiped!"

"Oh."

"It was in this brief case, the whole business. It'd take me weeks to round up duplicates of my records! Meanwhile what do I say to the Collector of Internal Revenue?" And Mike, because he was an old stable-mate of Inspector Queen's and had known Ellery when he was a cigar in the inspector's pocket, added: "Wise guy?"

"Ellery, that is a nuisance," said Nikki, glancing over at the table to make sure that her own records and return were still there.

"Records and all. . . . Where were the contents of your brief case stolen from, Mike?"

"My office. You been up there, Ellery—you know there's three other tenants—"

"And you all use a common reception room," Ellery nodded. "Were you in your office at the time, Mike?"

"Yes. Well, no—not exactly. Look. I better tell you the whole thing, just the way it happened. It's got me loopin'."

It HAD happened around six o'clock the previous day. Mike had been working on his tax return. Just before six he had decided to give up the struggle for the day. He had collected his canceled checks, memoranda, receipted bills and so on and had put them, together with his return, into his brief case.

"I'd just put on my overcoat," said Mike, "when Mrs. Carson —she's the public steno who leases the suite and rents out the offices—Mrs. Carson comes runnin' into my office yellin' there's a fire in the reception room. So I run out there and, sure enough, the settee's on fire. Somebody'd dropped a match into a waste-paper basket right next to it, and it blazed up and the settee caught fire. Well, it wasn't much—I put it out in five minutes— then I go back to my office, pick up my hat and brief case, and amble on home."

"And, of course," sighed Ellery, "when you got home you opened your brief case and your return and records were gone."

"With the wind," said Michael Magoon bitterly. "Cleaned out and a newspaper stuffed inside instead."

"Could the transfer have been made, Mike, en route from your office to your home?"

"Impossible. I walked over from the office to the garage where I park my car, with the brief case under my arm. Then I drove home, the case next to me on the car seat."

"You're sure this is the same brief case?"

"Oh, sure. It's an old one. It's my case, all right."

"Then it wasn't a wholesale substitution," said Ellery thoughtfully. "Someone opened your case on your office desk, removed its contents, substituted a newspaper, and closed the case again, all while you were putting out the fire in the reception room."

"It must have been that Mrs. Carson," said Nikki, wondering how the obvious could have escaped even such a pedestrian sleuth as Mike Magoon.

"How about it, Mike?" asked Ellery.

"Not a chance. She ran out in front of me and stayed with me in the reception room, runnin' back and forth from the water-cooler to the settee with a vase she keeps on her desk. Didn't leave my sight for a second."

"Who else was in the suite, Mike?"

"The two other tenants. One of 'em's a commercial artist named Vince, Leonardo Vince, a screwball if I ever saw one. The other's a little crumb calls himself Ziggy, Jack Ziggy. He thinks I don't know it, but he's a bookie."

"Didn't Vince and Ziggy run out of their offices when you and Mrs. Carson tackled the fire?"

"Sure. But they didn't help put it out—just stood around givin' advice. I didn't pay any attention to either of 'em."

"Then it's possible one of *them*—?"

"It's possible. But I can't be sure. Anyway, I drove right back down to the office again last night, thinkin' maybe I'd left my tax stuff on my desk or somethin'—"

"But of course it wasn't there."

"I didn't sleep last night," said Mike miserably, "and if I could have slept, the old lady's jawin' would have kept me awake."

"Have you been to the office this morning, Mike?"

"No. I came right down here, Ellery."

"Well." Ellery rose and began to fill his pipe. "A very unusual problem, Mike."

"Huh?"

"Unusual!" said Nikki. "All right, Mr. Queen, I'll bite. What's unusual about it?"

"Why should someone steal a man's income-tax return—the return of a man like Mike? To find out what Mike's income was last year? With all respect to your industry, Michael, that could hardly interest anyone; and more to the point, if that was what the thief was after, he wouldn't have to *steal* the return—a quick look would tell him what he wanted to know."

"Then why," asked Nikki, "did he steal it?"

"That," replied Ellery, "is what makes the problem interesting. Mike," he eyed Mike sternly, "have you been up to anything illegal?"

"Illegal!"

Ellery chuckled. "Routine question, Michael. Of course, if you were finagling, you'd hardly report it to Uncle Sam. No." Ellery puffed on his pipe. "The only thing that makes sense is the source of your income."

"I don't get it," complained the eye.

"Now, now. After all, Mike, you're a private dick. Your own shingle advertises the confidential nature of your work. Tell me: Which paper or papers in your brief case referred to a client or case in which secrecy is of the essence?"

Mike looked doubtful. "Well, all my cases are what you might call confidential—"

"Mike, I'm willing to bet your tax against mine that you have at least one client who's extremely wealthy, who came to you under a pledge of absolute secrecy, and whose records, or a record of whose case, were in your brief case yesterday."

"Mrs. Van Dome," said Magoon, gaping.

"Mrs. Van Dome," said Ellery briskly. "Sounds as if I've hit the jack pot, Mike. Nikki—notes!"

AND Michael Magoon told the story of his very best client, Mrs. Clementa Van Swicken Van Dome.

Mrs. Clementa Van Swicken Van Dome, had she been either a Van Swicken or a Van Dome, would have occupied a position of high altitude on the social pyramid. Being both a Van Swicken and a Van Dome, she reigned alone at the very apex, surrounded by the stratosphere and God. She was so far out of sight of mere earthlings that Nikki, who was Ellery's Almanach de Gotha, had never heard of her, whereas Ellery had. She considered Park Avenue gauche, and the D.A.R. upstarts. A Van Swicken had helped build Fort Amsterdam in ye Manhatas, and a Van Dome had led the trek to Gowanus Bay nine years before he became restless and moved on to establish a settlement which was named Breuckelen. The measure of Mrs. Clementa Van Swicken Van Dome's social standing was that she was invited to all the most exclusive functions in New York and never went to any. She herself gave one party each year; her guest-list was more carefully scrutinized than the personnel at Oak Ridge, Tennessee, and only those were invited whose forefathers had settled in the New World before 1651 and whose fortunes had not been tainted by trade for at least six generations.

Mrs. Van Dome was a widow, and she had one child, a daughter.

"You ought to see this Margreta," said Mike Magoon. "Skinny as a pretzel-stick, pimples all over her map, forty-five if she's a day, and she's a poetess."

"A what?" said Nikki.

"She writes poetry," said Mike firmly.

"Under the name of Hollandia," nodded Ellery. "Brutal stuff. I take it, Mike, mama consulted you about Margreta?"

"That's it."

"Just because she writes bad poetry?" said Nikki.

"Because she's a klep, Miss Porter."

Nikki looked excited. "What's that? It sounds—"

"Relax, Nikki," said Ellery. "Mike means a kleptomaniac. It all begins to be too, too clear, Michael. Stop me if I'm wrong. If there's one thing Mrs. Van Dome fears, it's scandal. The unlovely Margreta does not merely commit the crime of writing bad poetry, she also develops a yearning to take things belonging to other people. There have been polite complaints, perhaps, discreetly made to mama. Mama pays, but begins to worry. Margreta shows no signs of reform. The habit grows. It will soon be in the papers. Mama comes to a relatively unknown private detective—no doubt after checking your personal reputation, Mike, with your old pals at Headquarters—and puts Margreta into your hands on a one-hundred-per-cent hush-hush basis."

"That's it, that's it," said Mike. "My job is to protect Margreta from arrest and publicity. I trail her whenever she hits the street. When I see her take somethin', I quietly pay for it after she drifts on. Mrs. Van Dome gives me an expense account—which, believe me, she looks over with an eagle eye! I get an annual retainer—not a heck of a lot, but it's good steady dough."

"And among your income tax records," nodded Ellery, "were the various accounts, receipted bills, *et cetera*, pertaining to the misadventures of Margreta."

"Somebody," cried Nikki, "trailed Mr. Magoon or something, saw what was going on, then stole his income-tax records to . . ." Nikki stopped. "To what?"

"To make use of them," said Ellery dryly. "Obviously."

"*Blackmail!*" roared Mike, jumping up as if he had just been given the hot-foot. "By cripes, Ellery, with those receipted bills, and correspondence, and stuff—whoever it was could blackmail old lady Van Dome till she was—was black in the face! She'd pay anything to keep that yarn from gettin' out! That's it!"

"Somebody," said Nikki. "Who's somebody?"

Mike sat down.

But Ellery, knocking his pipe out on the fire screen, said: "Mrs. Carson."

"Mrs. Carson?" said Mike, blinking.

"But Ellery, Mr. Magoon says she couldn't possibly—"

"Nikki. A fire starts in a wastebasket which ignites an office settee which sends Mrs. Carson running into Mike's office yelling for him to—what? Run out—with her. Mike does so. And Mrs. Carson sticks with him." Ellery shrugged. "By the same token, Mike sticks with Mrs. Carson—while Mrs. Carson's accomplice slips into Mike's office and, having no time to winnow the Van Dome papers from the rest, lifts the entire contents of Mike's brief case, puts a newspaper stuffing in their place, and slips out. Mike," said Ellery, setting his pipe into the mantelpiece rack, "let's go down to your office and give that public stenographer a little dictation."

So COLLECTOR of Internal Revenue v. Magoon was a simple business after all.

Only, it wasn't.

When they opened Mrs. Carson's door they found Mrs. Carson taking dictation from a higher Authority.

"FEELING better now?" asked Ellery, drinking the rest of the bourbon in the paper cup.

"Oh, Ellery," moaned Nikki. "That dead woman."

"—Is a dead woman."

"But a dead woman without a face!"

"I should think you'd be used to that sort of thing by now, Nikki."

"I suppose that's why you finished my drink."

"I was thirsty," said Ellery with dignity; and he strolled through Mrs. Carson's doorway waging a heroic battle with his stomach.

They were standing around the typewriter desk staring down at Mrs. Carson's ruins. Nobody was saying anything.

"Oh, Ellery."

"Dad."

"Six inches," said Inspector Queen in a wondering voice. "The rod was fired not more than six inches from her pan."

"There's no question but that it's Mrs. Carson?"

"It's her, all right." Mike was slugging it out, too.

"Mrs.," said Ellery, looking at her left hand. "Where's Mr.?"

"In Montefiore Cemetery," said Mike, still swallowing powerfully. "He kicked off six years ago, she told me."

"How old was she, Mike?" Funny how hard it was to tell a woman's age when her face was not there for reference.

"I'd have said around thirty-six, thirty-eight."

"Ever mention a boy friend?" asked the inspector.

"Nope. And she never seemed to have a date, inspector. Always workin' in here late."

"Michael, Michael," said Inspector Queen. "That's why she worked in here late. Only she wasn't working. Not at a typewriter, anyway."

Through the greenish overcast, Mike looked puzzled.

The old gentleman said impatiently: "We know she decoyed

you with that fire she set herself; we know somebody lifted the Van Dome stuff from your brief case during the fire. And who was here at the time? The other two tenants. So one of *them* was the Carson woman's accomplice. Does it fit? Sure, Mike. When she was 'working late,' she was playing hoopla with either Leonardo Vince or Jack Ziggy right here in the office."

"But then," muttered Mike Magoon, "who plugged her last night? You mean Vince, or Ziggy . . . ?"

The inspector nodded.

"But why, inspector?"

"Michael, Michael."

"The double-cross, dad?" asked Ellery, not skeptically—just asking.

"What else? She helps him swipe the documents he can blackmail Mrs. Van Dome with, so then he rubs the girl friend out. He's got it all to himself, and no blabbermouth to worry about besides. Ellery, why you looking as if you smell something?"

"He must be very stupid," said Ellery.

"Sure," said his father cheerfully. "They're only smart in the fairy tales you write. Now if this were one of your mystery plots, Ellery, you know who'd be the criminal?"

"Mike," said Ellery.

"*Me!*" Mike immediately looked guilty.

"Sure, Mike," chuckled the inspector. "By the way, what time was it when you got back here last night? Your return trip, Mike —when you came back to see if you'd left your papers behind?"

"So that's it," growled Mike. "Listen here, inspector . . . !"

"Oh, don't be an ass, Mike," said Ellery irritably. "What time was it? Was she alive? Was her light on? What?"

"Oh. Yeah, sure. Must have been a quarter of eight or so. She was workin' in her office here. I says Mrs. Carson did you find any papers of mine around from my brief case and she says no Mr. Magoon I didn't. I says where's Ziggy and that nut artist and she says oh they went home long ago. So I says good night and goes back home myself."

"How did she seem to you at the time, Mike?"

"Okay."

"Not nervous?"

"Hell, I don't know. She was always nervous."

"Well." The inspector scratched his head. "The best Doc Prouty can give us is that she was killed between seven and nine last night. The cleaning woman's no help—she was through giving the offices a lick and a promise by seven o'clock, she says, and she says Mrs. Carson was here alone. So, Mike, if you left her alive near eight, then she was bopped between eight and nine."

"By one of these two characters," said Sergeant Velie from the doorway.

The first man was a tall, frayed, decaying-looking fellow with prehensile dirty fingers and half-slices of lemon under his eyes. The second was a little bald-headed man with a very gold tooth. Their eyes bugged at the thing lolling on the typewriter and they both back-pedaled fast. But Sergeant Velie was leaning in the doorway, licking a cigar.

The tall man went over to the window and opened it and stuck his face out into the cold March air-stream. The small man went over to Mrs. Carson's wastebasket and bent over, almost embracing it.

"How can you stand it? How can you stand it?" the tall man kept saying.

"Arrrgh," said the little man.

"That's Vince the artist," said Mike. "That's Jack Ziggy the bookie," said Mike.

"I didn't kill her," said the tall man. "I'm an artist. I'm interested in life. I couldn't kill a spider crawling up my leg. Ask anybody. Don't think you'll make me say I did it. Cut pieces out of me—" Leonardo Vince was getting worked up, blood in his musty face again.

"You've made your point, Vince," said the inspector mildly. "I suppose, Ziggy, you didn't kill her either."

The little bald man raised his head to reply, but then he stooped quickly again and repeated: "Arrrgh."

Sergeant Velie drawled, "Inspector."

"Huh?" The old gentleman did not glance at him.

"The night man here says Vince and Ziggy both came back to

the buildin' last night. He can't remember the exact times but he says they came separate, and they came between eight and nine."

MRS. CARSON was a pall, definitely. Even Sergeant Velie sucked on his cigar with more enjoyment when she floated out of the office between two Welfare men.

Leonardo Vince shut the window, shivering, and the little bookmaker straightened up with the wastebasket, glancing around apologetically. The inspector nodded to a detective and Jack Ziggy went out holding the basket high and wide.

"Cobalt blue," said the inspector to the artist. "You were saying . . . ?"

"You can't make it out red or ocher or any damned thing but what I say it was," said Vince wearily. "It was cobalt blue. Go into my office and see if you can find the tube. You can't. It's not there. I took it home last night. That's why I came back. I may serve commerce during the day, and damn the shriveled souls of all agency men!—but my nights are dedicated to Art, gentlemen, with a capital and profitless A. I got home, had a bite, went to my easel, and found I had no cobalt blue which I happened to need for a purpose which would be far above your vulgar understanding. The supply stores were closed. I returned to the office here for a tube of—"

"Cobalt blue," said the inspector, nodding. He stared at Vince hard. Vince stared back, with hate. "And Mrs. Carson was—?"

"Am I supposed to contradict myself?" asked the artist bitterly. "But how could I? A child could repeat this story *ad infinitum*. I didn't even see Mrs. Carson. There was a light on in her office but the door was shut. Don't bother to ask the next question. It was about eight-fifteen. No, the homunculus wasn't here—I refer to the creature who calls himself Ziggy—at least, I didn't see him. And I have no idea if the woman was alive or dead; I heard not a whisper from her office. And lastly, I am a woman-hater. Now what do I do—say it all over again?"

On the heels of this remarkable soliloquy came the homunculus, with the detective but without the wastebasket.

"And me," whined Ziggy, "me, I don't know—"

"Nuttin."

"—nuttin. But from nuttin."

"You had a couple of parties to ring up," prompted Inspector Queen politely, "and—?"

"Yeah. Private calls, see? Confidentially, some of my clients owe me some back dough and they been tryin' to sucker me, so I come back at eight-thirty to use my own phone, see? More private, like. And I don't remember a thing, not a thing. No light, no Mrs. Carson, no nuttin. I don't remember nuttin. I don't see nobody, I don't hear nobody—"

"Oh, hell," said the inspector. "Ellery, have you got anything?"

"I see no reason," said Ellery absently, "to hold these two men any longer."

His father frowned.

"You've established no connection between these fellows and Mrs. Carson, beyond a common tenancy. The woman was obviously killed by someone else. Get them out of here, dad—I'm sicker of them than you are."

When Leonardo Vince and Jack Ziggy were gone, the old gentleman said: "All right, Master Mind. What's the great big plot?"

"And why'd you warn us not to say anything about Mike's income tax stuff on Mrs. Van Dome bein' swiped?" demanded Sergeant Velie.

"Suppose," said Ellery, "suppose thief-killer-potential-blackmailer is in desperate need of ready cash." He looked at them.

"He wouldn't dare," breathed his father. "Not now."

"Maestro, he's hot!"

"He doesn't know we've made the least connection between the theft of Mike's records and the murder of Mrs. Carson."

Inspector Queen trotted around the office, pulling at his mustache.

Then he stopped and said: "Mike, phone that Mrs. Van Dome. I want to talk to her."

THE next morning, when Ellery hung up, he said to his audience: "It's a curious experience, speaking to Mrs. Van Dome. Didn't you find it so yesterday, dad?"

"Never mind how I found that snooty, upstaging, cop-hating old battle-ax," grunted the inspector. "What did she just say, Ellery?"

"Like a dream-trip through outer space. It leaves you with an exhilarating memory of indescribable grandeurs and only the vaguest sense of reality. Mike, does she really exist?"

"Never mind the fancy stuff," growled Magoon. "What did she say?"

"She received the note in the first mail this morning."

"Really, Ellery," said Nikki, "your omniscience is disgusting."

"I better ankle over there," said Sergeant Velie, "see Her Nibs, get the note, and arrange for—"

"You will not be received," said Ellery dreamily. "Mrs. Clementa Van Swicken Van Dome has just passed a Law. It is to the effect that if she wants to pay blackmail, she'll pay blackmail, and if the City of New York sends so much as one policeman or detective to the rendezvous, she'll sue said City for a large number of millions."

"You mean—" cried the inspector.

"She's afraid that you'd scare off the blackmailer, dad. Then he'd give the full and documented story of Margreta's little vice to the newspapers. To prevent that, she's ready to pay ten thousand dollars, and so on. She was quite nasty about it in an imperial sort of way."

"So our hands are tied," groaned the inspector. "If only we knew what was in that note!"

"Oh, that. I have it here on my pad, word for word."

"She *read* it to you?"

"It seems that I," said Ellery, "am a gentleman—of a lower order, to be sure—but still . . . Oh, you heard my line. Here's the note: 'Mrs. Van Dome. I have the proof your daughter is a crook. Be in the south Waiting Room at Penn Station at eight o'clock tonight. Bring ten thousand dollars in nothing bigger than twenties. Wear a black hat with a purple nose-veil. Wrap the dough in red paper, hold it under your left arm. Don't tell police. If there's any sign of gumshoes or cops tonight I'll see to it every paper in town gets the lowdown—with photostats—on how your daughter's been lifting stuff from New York department stores for years. Be smart. Play ball. I mean business.' No signature."

"It sounds like that gold-tooth man," said Nikki, but doubtfully.

"I think it's Vince," said Mike excitedly.

"Might be either," grunted the inspector. "Ziggy being extra-careful about his English, or Vince being purposely sloppy. Good work, son. We'll be there and—"

"Oh, no, you won't."

"You think I won't?"

"City. Suit."

His father ground the inspectorial jaws.

"Besides," said Ellery, "I gave Mrs. Van D. my word as a gentleman that no policeman or city detective would be at the rendezvous tonight."

"Ellery," groaned his father.

"On the other hand, I'm not a policeman or city detective, am I? Nor is Mike. And certainly Nikki isn't."

"Ellery!"

"Mike, you don't look pleased."

"Pleased! Today is March the fifteenth," said Mike through his teeth, "the rat won't show till eight o'clock—the deadline for income-tax returns is midnight—and he says I don't look pleased."

"Why, Michael," said Ellery soothingly. "That gives us all of four hours."

"To collar this skunk, find out where he's hid my tax stuff, get 'em, finish workin' out my return, and have it in the mail—all between eight and twelve!"

"Cinch," said Ellery. "Michael, my boy, it's as good as in the bag—the mail bag—right now."

PROPHECY is a perilous art.

At twelve minutes of eight o'clock on the evening of March fifteenth a large stout woman wearing a black hat and a purple nose-veil, carrying a fat parcel wrapped in red paper under her left arm, appeared suddenly in the entrance to the south Waiting Room at Pennsylvania Station.

Mrs. Clementa Van Swicken Van Dome surveyed her fellow-Americans. There was an expression of excitement on those remote features. So these were the People, it said. One gathered that this was at least as great an adventure.

The People stared back, rather uneasily. The steamfitter jaw bunched, and Mrs. Van Dome swept regally to the nearest bench. A Negro soldier moved over to make room for her. On the other side a young mother was struggling to diaper a kicking, screaming infant. Mrs. Van Dome was seen to take a long, deep breath. Then she sat down, and she sat rigidly. She grew red in the face.

She was trying not to breathe.

At twelve minutes of ten she was still seated there. By now her neighbors were an old man without a tie who was carrying a paper bag, and a girl in a mink coat and no hat who was smoking a cigarette.

The three watchers crossed glances over their newspapers.

"All this excitement," muttered Nikki, "is killing me—" she stirred tenderly, "—and you know where."

"He couldn't have spotted us," mumbled Mike. "Ellery, he couldn't have."

"It's unlikely," said Ellery. "Unless he was here at six o'clock and saw us enter the station. If he wasn't, it's even unlikelier because, from where we're sitting, we're invisible unless you come *into* the Waiting Room, or at least stand in the entrance. That's why I picked this spot."

"But then we'd have seen *him*," winced Nikki.

"Exactly." Ellery rose. "We've either been gulled, or he got cold feet at the last moment."

"But what about Mrs. Van Dome?" asked Nikki.

"Let her stay here inhaling the odors of America," said Ellery. "Do her good. Come on."

"My income tax," groaned Mike Magoon.

AND the first people they saw when they entered Inspector Queen's anteroom at police headquarters were Leonardo Vince and Jack Ziggy.

"Ellery—" cried Nikki; but then she saw the inspector's face, and she stopped.

"Ah, here's a man who'll be interested in your yarn, Mr. Vince," said the inspector genially. "Ellery, guess what.—Oh, by the way, son, did you have a good dinner?"

"Disappointing."

"You can't always tell from those fancy menus, can you? As I was saying, at seven-thirty this evening Mr. Vince marches into headquarters here. Mr. Vince, tell my son what you told me."

"I was home, painting," said Leonardo Vince wearily. "About a quarter of seven my phone rang. It was Western Union. They read me a telegram. It said: 'Want to commission daughter's portrait. Am leaving town tonight but will have few minutes discuss it with you before train time. Meet me eight tonight south Waiting Room Penn Station. Will be wearing black hat and purple nose-veil and carrying red parcel.'"

"Signed," said Inspector Queen, "'Clementa Van Swicken Van Dome.'"

"Have you—?" began Ellery.

"Sure, Maestro," said Sergeant Velie. "That's the copy I myself got from the telegraph office this evenin' when I checked. The message was phoned in to a midtown station in the middle of the afternoon. They can't tell us who phoned it in. They had instructions to deliver the wire to the addressee at a quarter of seven tonight."

Then Ellery turned to the artist and asked pleasantly: "Well, why didn't you keep the appointment, Mr. Vince?"

The artist bared his woody-looking teeth. "Oh, no," he grinned, "not little Leonardo. You develop an animal instinct for danger when you've been hunted in this world as long as I have.

Riches descend on me the very same day I become a suspect in a murder case? Ha, ha! I came straight to Inspector Queen."

"And he's been here," said Inspector Queen dryly, "ever since."

"Can't get him out of the office," complained the sergeant.

"It's such a nice, safe office," said Leonardo Vince.

"And Mr. Jack Ziggy?" asked Ellery suddenly.

The little bookmaker started. Then he said: "It's a frame. I don't know—"

"Nuttin," said the inspector. "Mr. Jack Ziggy, Ellery, was picked up at seven-thirty this evening in a routine raid on a big bookie joint on Thirty-fourth Street and Eighth Avenue."

"When the boys found out who they had," said Velie, "they brought him right here." He looked baleful.

"Where he's been keeping Mr. Vince company. Velie, stay here and entertain these gentlemen. We're going into my office."

"My income tax," muttered Mike Magoon.

"THE way I see it," said the inspector comfortably, putting his feet up on his desk, "is that this is pretty smart stuff. Vince is our baby. He's a cutie. He knows we've connected the theft and the murder. Or he suspects we have, maybe because we haven't handled Mike as a suspect, too. He decides to play it safe."

"Sends that letter to Mrs. Van Dome," said Nikki, "making the appointment at Penn Station—then today he wires *himself* to keep it!"

"And, of course, promptly comes hotfooting it down to me with it instead," nodded the inspector. "Effect? He's an innocent man being framed for theft, intended extortion, murder—the book."

"But then," protested Mike, "how's he ever figure to blackmail Mrs. Van Dome? I thought that was the whole idea!"

"I said he's a cutie, Mike," replied the inspector. "He weighs relative values. Decides his original hunch was a bad mistake and this is his way of covering up while he backs out. How does it sound to you, Ellery?"

"Admissible, but rather on the involved side, don't you think?"

Ellery scowled. "There's an alternate theory which is much simpler. Mr. Jack Ziggy. Mr. Ziggy, too, develops chilled feet. Mr. Ziggy therefore decides to give us a fall guy. Writes the note to Mrs. Van Dome, sends the wire to Leonardo Vince."

"Maybe he even heard a rumor about that raid," cried Nikki, "and purposely went to that bookie place to be picked up before the eight o'clock meeting tonight at Penn Station! With Vince meeting Mrs. Van Dome, and himself arrested on a minor charge—"

"What's wrong with that, dad?"

"Not a thing," snarled his father. "Two theories. Why couldn't there be just one?"

"My income tax," moaned Mike. "Ain't anybody interested in my income tax? Look at the time!"

"Oh, there are more than two theories, dad," said Ellery absently. "I can think of at least two others—either of which would satisfy my plot appetite considerably more. The trouble is—" But then Ellery stopped. He was staring at his father's feet.

"What's the matter?" said the inspector, sighting along his legs. "Hole in my shoe?"

"That brief case you've got your feet on," said Ellery.

"What?"

"That's mine," said Mike. "You remember, Ellery, the one I brought when I came to you."

"We took it from Mike after we got down to the offices," said the inspector. "Routine. Here, Mike, we're through with it."

"Wait a minute, Mike," said Ellery. "You know, come to think of it, I never did examine this brief case while you were at the apartment, and finding Mrs. Carson dead at the office as soon as we got there— Dad, may I have that?"

"Sure. But it won't tell you anything."

"Is this the newspaper that the thief stuffed into it?" asked Ellery, drawing out a rather crumpled copy of *The New York Times*.

"Lemme see," said Mike. "Yeah. I remember that tear just over the 'T.' "

"You're sure, Mike."

"Sure I'm sure!"

"What are you looking so eagle-eyed about?" sniffed Nikki, peering over Ellery's shoulder. "It's just a copy of yesterday's *New York Times*."

"And there isn't an identifiable fingerprint on it," said the inspector.

"So now tell us you've made a great big blinding deduction."

Ellery opened his mouth, but something else opened simultaneously—the door to Inspector Queen's anteroom. Sergeant Velie stood there.

"Her Highness," said the sergeant, "is back from the front—madder'n hell."

"Ah, Mrs. Van Dome!" said Ellery, jumping to his feet. "Come in, come in—you're just in time."

"I imagine, Mike," said Ellery, "that your original plan didn't include the concept of an accomplice at all."

"What's that?" said Mike. "What did you say, Ellery?"

"When you set fire to the reception-room settee, it was in a less involved plot. You would smell smoke, you would come running out of your office raising an outcry, Ziggy and Vince and—yes—Mrs. Carson would dash out of *their* offices to see what was the matter, you would put the fire out yourself, and meanwhile any of the three—yes, including Mrs. Carson—might have been the 'thief' who slipped into your office and stole the Van Dome kleptomania-case records. You would have given us three red herrings instead of two—a more nourishing diet."

"What are you talkin' about, Ellery!"

"But something went wrong. In fact, Mike, the most interesting part of your plot to extort money from Mrs. Van Dome is that it never really got started. Something went wrong at the outset. Since Mrs. Carson is the one you murdered, it takes no great intellect to infer that it was Mrs. Carson who threw the monkey-wrench. What was it, Mike? *Did Mrs. Carson accidentally see you set the fire with your own hands?*"

Mike sat very straight in the honored chair beside the inspector's desk. But then, all at once, he sagged.

"Yes. She saw you do it, Mike. But you didn't know that till you came back to the office that evening ostensibly to 'see' if you hadn't left your tax records there by mistake. You found Mrs. Carson there alone, you asked her about the tax records—and she told you she had seen you set the fire. Did she also perceive dimly that you had taken your own property? I think so, Mike. I think Mrs. Carson accused you of skulduggery, and I think it was then and there that you gave up all thought of bleeding Mrs. Van Dome of considerably more than she was paying you to protect her daughter's name. You took out your gun and shot Mrs. Carson to death. Very stupid, Mike. Lost your head. But that's the way it is with honest men who go wrong. You'd have been better off to let Mrs. Carson talk. The worst that would have happened is that you might lose your license—you had still not committed any crime! And even if you had already tried to extort, would Mrs. Van Dome have prosecuted? No, indeed. Your very plot in its origin—setting up a straw man who 'stole' your tax records and so got into the position of being able to blackmail Mrs. Van Dome—was predicated on Mrs. Van Dome's willingness to do anything rather than let the story of her daughter's kleptomania come out.

"All this must have been obvious to you—and still you shot Mrs. Carson. Mike, Mike."

The inspector was sitting there with his mouth open.

"The rest," said Ellery, scowling, "followed logically. Having killed, you then had to direct attention away from yourself. You'd already made a beginning with the fire. The killing made it look as if Mrs. Carson had been murdered by an 'accomplice.' The 'accomplice' was what you had to work with. And you worked it to death, winding up with a frame of Leonardo Vince—who was supposed to take the rap for you, but—so unpredictable are plots, Mike—who refused to fall into the trap. That was another bad mistake, Mike—picking Mr. Vince. But you made a mistake that was even worse."

The inspector tried twice to speak, nothing coming out but a bray and a croak. The third time he made it. "But, Ellery, this is all speculation! You haven't *deduced* anything. It's guesswork!"

This was the most repulsive word in the Queen lexicon.

"Wrong, dad. There's a clue which, taken at the source, leads on to the logical conclusion. This newspaper." Ellery waved *The New York Times* from Mike's brief case.

Even Mike looked curious at that. Out of the stupor into which he had fallen he roused himself to blink and lick his lips and glance uneasily at the paper.

"Nikki," said Ellery, "what day is today?"

Nikki jumped. "Day? Why, March fifteenth."

"And what is the date on this newspaper?"

"Why, you saw it yourself. And I remarked on it. Yesterday's paper, I said."

"Yesterday's. Then it's *The New York Times* of March fourteenth. When did Mike come to consult me?"

"Yesterday morning."

"The morning of March *fourteenth*. When, according to Mike's story, had the theft of his income-tax records taken place —the fire, the theft, the substitution of a newspaper for the records in his brief case?"

"Why, the evening before that."

"March *thirteenth*. And what did Mike say?" cried Ellery. "That the fire and substitution of newspaper for records had taken place around six o'clock—six o'clock on March thirteenth! How could a *New York Times* dated March *fourteenth* have been put into Mike Magoon's brief case at six o'clock on March *thirteenth*? It couldn't have been. Not possibly. No morning newspaper comes out that early the previous day, not even the tabloids. And certainly not *The New York Times!* Then Mike Magoon lied. The substitution hadn't been made the previous day at all—it had been made on the morning of the fourteenth —just before Mike came to see me—obviously by Mike himself. Then Mike's whole story collapses, and all I had to do was re-examine the known facts in the light of Mike's duplicity." Ellery glanced at the clock. "There's still time to send your tax retur to Uncle Sam, Mike," he said, "although I'm afraid you'll hav to change your address."

———————————

Mr. Anthony Boucher
Mystery Writers of America, Inc.
408 West 14th Street
New York 14, N. Y.

Dear Tony:

Your plea for an autobiographical sketch finds me sympathetic bu temporally disabled. I'm crawling on my hands and knees in and ou of a case which seems to call for the talents of Theseus; my publishe is crawling about after me prodding the *derrière* of my conscienc with our Next Novel Contract and reminding me that it is later tha I think; and of course there's always EQMM, bless its bloody hear

Nevertheless, because my whole soul goes out to anyone trappe in an editorial job, I comply as follows:

I was born, I have lived, and I'm going to hang on as long as I car

The above, it seems to me, gives every fact essential to an aut biography and has besides the very rare merit of economy.

I give it to you free and unencumbered, for whatever dark uses yo may have in mind, in perpetuity.

Yours,

EQ/np

Ellery

Not only does Michael Shayne have a tougher mind and a greater capacity for brandy than most of his rivals among hard-boiled private operatives; but he exhibits a believable vigor and vitality which most of them sadly lack. The reason why Shayne is one of the few of the private eyes to emerge as an individual character may lie in his peculiar relationship to his author—which is a story in itself, fully as interesting as many of his cases.

MICHAEL SHAYNE IN

Michael Shayne As I Know Him

BY BRETT HALLIDAY

I IMAGINE that most of my readers are familiar with the dramatic first meeting between myself and the man who was later to become the central figure in a series of mystery novels featuring a red-headed, fighting Irishman whom I call Michael Shayne. This first meeting, which occurred on the Tampico waterfront more than a quarter of a century ago, was described in a nationwide radio broadcast from WOR in New York in 1941, and subsequent events made a news story that was printed throughout the country.

But for the benefit of those who may have come in late, I will briefly summarize the details here.

I was a youngster then, working as deck hand on a Pan American oil tanker, and on a stopover in Tampico a bunch of us spent the evening ashore in a tough waterfront saloon.

I noticed him before the fight started, and was intrigued by him even then. A big rangy redhead with lines already forming on his face, he sat alone at a table in the rear, surrounded by lights and music and girls who were offering themselves to any takers. There was a bottle of *tequila* on the table in front of him and two water glasses. One of the glasses held ice water— and he was drinking straight Mexican liquor from the other.

I don't know how the fight started, but it turned into a beau- tiful brawl with half a dozen unarmed American sailors slugging it out on uneven terms with twice as many natives who all seemed to have knives or guns on them.

We were doing all right, as I recall, making what you might call a strategic retreat and almost out the door, when I got a crack on the head that sent me under a table.

I remember lying there and wondering dazedly, "What next, little man?" when I heard the crash of a rear table overturning and peered out to see the redhead sailing into the fracas.

He was a fighting man and you could see he loved it. Three or four Mexicans went down in front of his fists before he reached me, dragged me out from under the table and tossed me out the door bodily.

That's all of that. I got back to the ship somehow, and we sailed next morning, and I didn't know who the man was or what he was doing in that saloon or why he came to the rescue of a fool kid whom he didn't know.

I still don't know any of those things, though I believe I now know him better than any man alive.

It was four years before I ran into that red-headed Irishman again. A coincidence? Sure. This story is full of crazy coinci- dences—the sort that happen in real life but no writer would dare put between the covers of a book.

It was in New Orleans and I was four years older and maybe a little wiser. I was broke and jobless, and I wandered into a Rampart Street saloon on a foggy night and there he was.

Sitting alone at a rear table again, with a bottle in front of him and two water glasses. One of them was half full of ice water, and he was sipping cognac from the other.

He didn't recognize me, of course, but he did remember the fight in Tampico, and he grinned and gave me a drink of cognac when I thanked him for that time. He didn't talk much, but did say he was working as a private detective. He was friendly and we were getting along fine until a girl walked in and stood at the bar looking the joint over.

I saw his big frame stiffen and the lines in his cheek deepen into trenches as she walked toward our table. His left thumb and forefinger went up to rub the lobe of his ear as she stopped beside our table and leaned forward and said, "Hello, Mike," in a throaty voice.

That was all. He didn't reply, and in a moment she turned away and went swiftly out the door. Two men had followed her inside, and they began to move slowly toward us—casually but purposefully.

That's when he leaned forward and told me swiftly to get out of town fast and forget I'd seen him.

He stood up before I could ask any questions, strolled forward and the two men closed in on each side of him. They went out in a group and disappeared in the swirling fog of Rampart Street.

That was our second meeting. I knew his name was Mike, and I knew he was a private detective. I didn't know who the girl and the two men were, nor why Mike walked out with them so quietly.

I still don't know, though I have a feeling that things happened then that had some bearing on the feud between him and Captain Denton of the New Orleans police—a feud which flared up anew during a case described in the book I titled *Michael Shayne's Long Chance*.

It was years later that the next act occurred. I had begun writing books (not mystery novels) and was living in Denver, Colorado. I had never been able to put the memory of the redhead out of my mind, and there was a network radio program originating in New York which offered people a chance to broadcast an appeal for information concerning relatives or friends with whom they had lost contact.

Planning a business trip to New York to see my publishers, I wrote the manager of the program and asked to be allowed to tell my story over the air.

I did so, with an astonishing and completely unforeseen resul
A few days after the broadcast I was informed from Denver tha
a man named Connor Michael Shawn, ex-actor, theatrical ma
ager, and private detective, had tuned in my broadcast on h
deathbed and declared to his wife that he believed himself to b
the man I was describing over the air.

Connor Michael Shawn died the next day, and when I re
turned to Denver a few days later I immediately visited his wif
and discussed the situation with her. Many of the facts of h
life as she knew them checked with the dates and places of m
story. The photographs she showed me were not conclusive.
felt that Shawn *might* have been my "Mike"—but I couldn't b
positive.

I wasn't positive until more than a year later when I was hole
up in a one-room log cabin at Desolation Bend on the Gunniso
River in Colorado trying desperately to write three novels i
thirty days (which I did, incidentally).

Mike turned up one day in a cabin near mine on the rive.
That was when I learned his real name (which isn't Shayne)
He gave no explanation for his presence except that he was o
vacation from a lucrative private detective practice in Miam
Florida.

This meeting, I now believe, was not so much of a coincidenc
as it appeared at the time. From small things he has let slip ou
since then, I believe he had heard about the radio broadcast an
being in the neighborhood, had taken the trouble to look me u
out of curiosity.

At any rate, that was the beginning of an intimate friendshi
that has now endured more than a decade and the writing o
twenty books about his cases.

We drank cognac together in his cabin and mine during th
long lazy evenings that followed my stint at the typewriter, an
talked about his work as a detective and my unrealized dream o
writing mystery stories. There was no real compact reached be
tween us at that time, but when he left for Miami I had an ir
vitation to visit him there whenever I wished.

I followed him south a couple of months later, and he seemed pleased when I turned up at his modest apartment on the north bank of the Miami River, overlooking Biscayne Bay.

That night, over a bottle of Martel, he told me he had fallen in love for the first time in his life—with Phyllis Brighton, whom he had just cleared of a charge of matricide.

Mike was a lonely and brooding man that night. He had sent Phyllis away, gently but firmly, a few days earlier and he honestly did not hope ever to see her again. She was too young, he told me over and over again. Too young and sweet and trusting to waste herself on a man like him.

I didn't argue with Mike that night. Nor point out any of the obvious things. I did draw him into a discussion of the case just ended, and before the sun rose over Biscayne Bay he had agreed to turn his notes on the Brighton affair over to me for fictionalization in a book which I called *Dividend on Death*.

Before this book was published, he had met Phyllis Brighton again (as related in *The Private Practice of Michael Shayne*) and before that case was ended, Mike had capitulated to the intensity of Phyllis' love.

I was best man at their wedding, and saw them installed in the larger corner apartment above Mike's old bachelor quarters, which he kept and fitted up sketchily as an office.

The next few years, I am positive, were the happiest Mike has ever known. Phyllis worried him sometimes by insisting on acting as his secretary and getting herself mixed up in some of his cases, but there was perfect companionship and understanding between them, culminating in a long-delayed honeymoon trip to Colorado, where Mike managed to get himself mixed up with murder in the old ghost town of Central City (*Murder Wears a Mummer's Mask*).

Back in Miami, there was one more adventure together before that black night when I sat with Mike in the hospital waiting room, sweating it out with him while the baby, which Phyllis so ardently desired, was being born.

I went back to his apartment with him at dawn, and sat across the room from him in a deep chair while he wept unashamedly. Both Phyllis and the baby were gone, and the doctors didn't know why.

He swore, at that time, he would never touch another case that dealt with death, and I think he might have kept that resolution had he not received that telephone call in the night that sent him out on the trail of a vicious gang of black marketeers (*Blood on the Black Market*).

I noted a subtle change in Mike's inner character after Phyllis' death. In some ways he became more ruthless and driving and demanding of himself, but the hard outer shell of assumed cynicism was cracked, and for the first time in his life he wasn't afraid to let traces of gentleness and pity shine through.

I was glad when he closed his office and went to New Orleans (*Michael Shayne's Long Chance*), and gladder still after that case was ended and he had met Lucy Hamilton and acquired a new secretary.

People ask me now if Mike and Lucy are likely to be married. I have to answer honestly that I simply do not know. I am sure they understand and respect each other, and that Mike loves her as much as his memories of Phyllis will allow him to love any woman. They are happy together in the companionship and intimacy of dangerous work, and that appears to be enough for them both at the moment.

About the man himself . . . I know of little I can add to what I have written in my accounts of his cases. I think his most important attribute is absolute personal honesty. He not only does not lie to anyone else—what is more important, he does not lie to himself.

I think the most important characteristic in his spectacular success as a private detective is his ability to drive straight forward to the heart of the matter, without deviating one iota for obstacles or confusing side issues. He has an absolutely logical mind which refuses to be sidetracked.

He acts. On impulse sometimes, or on hunches; but always the impelling force is definite logic. While other detectives are wandering aimlessly about in a maze of conjecture and doubt,

Mike selects a certain path and drives forward inexorably in one direction until he is proved right—or wrong. When he makes a mistake, he wastes no time in idle repining, but adjusts his sights and turns just as inexorably in another direction.

At various times readers have complained to me that Mike seems to seek danger needlessly; that he seems to take an almost masochistic pleasure in thrusting himself into a situation which inevitably results in physical pain to himself.

To those readers I can say only that I fear they have not followed the published accounts of his cases carefully. I have never heard Mike say, "Had-I-but-known." In every instance he calculates the risk involved carefully, weighing the results that may be attained by a certain course of action against the probable lack of results if he chooses to move more cautiously. Once convinced that a risk is worth taking, he moves forward and accepts the consequences as a part of his job.

It is this driving urgency and lack of personal concern more than any other one thing, I think, that serves to wind up most of Mike's most difficult cases so swiftly. In time, few of his cases consume more than one or two days. Readers have complained that he doesn't seem to eat or sleep while on a case. He does, of course, but only if there is nothing more important to do at the time. He drinks more cognac than any man I have ever known, but I have never seen Mike drunk. Actually, while relaxing between cases he is a very moderate drinker.

This sums up Michael Shayne as I know him. The hardest work I do in writing my accounts of his cases is attempting to make my readers see Mike as he is, to feel what Mike feels, to know the man himself as I know him. Insofar as I succeed in this, my books are successful. Certainly, no writer ever had a better subject with whom to work.

Ed Hunter and Uncle Am, the detectives in Fredric Brown's novels, are highly colorful characters. Even more colorful are the characters (including at least one detective) who enliven his science fiction and fantasy stories. But it's doubtful whether any of these can handle a case with quite such neat dispatch as colorless Henry Smith—or turn such a neat profit at the same time.

HENRY SMITH IN

Mr. Smith Kicks the Bucket

BY FREDRIC BROWN

MR. HENRY SMITH, dapper little agent and investigator for the Phalanx Insurance Company, smiled at the girl at the reception desk, took off his gold-rimmed pince-nez spectacles to look at her better, and then put them back on.

"I wish to see Mr. Thorwald, your program manager, please," he said.

The girl looked doubtful. "The Bucket of Gems program goes on the air in just a few minutes and Mr. Thorwald's in charge of it. I don't—"

"Yes," said Mr. Smith. "It is concerning that program that I wish to see him. Ah, you may take this in to him with my card."

The object which Mr. Smith took from his vest pocket made the receptionist blink. It was almost two inches in diameter, red, transparent, and many-faceted.

She gulped once and then went into Thorwald's office with the red object in one hand and Mr. Henry Smith's card in the other.

From *Detective Story*, Aug., 1944. Copyright 1944 by Street & Smith.

She came out almost immediately. "Mr. Thorwald will see you."

The program manager looked up at Mr. Smith with harassed eyes. "This looks like the Kent ruby."

"It does," admitted Mr. Smith. "Ah, I understand, Mr. Thorwald, that you are starting a series of programs sponsored by the Jewelers' Mutual Co-operative Association, each program to present, in dramatized form, the history of a famous jewel. The writer of the best essay on some topic concerned with gems will receive a prize known as a 'bucket of gems,' from which the program takes its name, the Bucket of Gems program. Ah, may I sit down?"

"Do sit down. Is this the Kent ruby?"

"Thank you," said Mr. Smith. He sat down. "I understand that, whenever possible, you plan to have, for the audience to see, the jewel whose history is being dramatized. Of course, the radio audience, as distinguished from the studio audience, cannot see it, but they will obtain vicarious satisfaction from knowing that it is present at the studio. Is that correct?"

"Yes, except that we're going to have the featured jewel at all programs. We'll feature only jewels we can get hold of, not the Kohinoor or the Cullinan. Ones we can borrow, like— Now, damn it, is this the Kent ruby?"

"Ah, no," Mr. Smith murmured. "You see, the Phalanx Insurance Company, my company, has insured the Kent ruby. For that reason I have been quite interested in it. You recall, at the World's Fair, the exhibition of paste reproductions of famous jewels? This was one of them, and because it became badly scratched, I was able to acquire it for practically nothing. A pity, of course, that it is damaged, but one must look closely to see the scratches."

Thorwald looked closely. "Yeah, I see them. Can't a real ruby be scratched?"

"Yes and no," Mr. Smith replied judiciously. "A diamond is ten on the scale of hardness, a ruby is nine. So one could scratch a ruby with a diamond. Now about your program, Mr. Thorwald. When precious stones are moved and handled, there is always danger of theft. I came to quote you on a policy that would cover your liability in case a theft occurred, either of the featured stones or of the stones in your award, the 'bucket of gems.' "

"We don't need insurance," said Mr. Thorwald. "With the guards and precautions we've arranged, the borrowed stones will be as safe as houses. And the 'bucket of gems' isn't worth . . . uh . . . isn't sufficiently valuable to justify— Well, look for yourself. There they are."

On a table at one side of the room was a neat array of fifteen jewel cases, each containing a small jewel. Behind them stood a small bucket, about eight inches in diameter and five inches high, which would obviously be filled to overflowing with the jewel cases.

Mr. Smith walked over and looked down at them.

"Half-carat diamond?" he asked.

"Yes. Unflawed. Ruby and emerald are the same size. Good stones, but not extraordinary ones."

"And the others are larger, but less precious. An opal, a zircon, a garnet— But even so, there must be five hundred dollars' worth of gems here, at retail."

"At retail, yes," said Thorwald. "The Jewelers' Mutual doesn't buy them at retail."

"Of course," Mr. Smith murmured. "I grant it would be hardly worth while to write a policy on the 'bucket of gems' alone. But what would it cost you if the Kent ruby were stolen this evening?"

Thorwald grunted. "Why would it cost us anything? Didn't you say your company already had insured it? Mr. Carmichel couldn't collect from both of us."

"But you agreed, did you not, to be responsible for the full declared valuation of a hundred thousand dollars? Our policy is for thirty thousand. Mr. Carmichel could, and would, hold you legally liable for the difference. A matter of seventy thousand dollars."

The program director whistled softly. Then he sighed. "O.K., so we'd lose seventy thousand. And I'd lose my job. But, man, we've got four armed guards! Say, why'd you send in this hunk of paste with your card? Just to get my curiosity so I'd see you?"

Mr. Smith smiled gently. "I fear I must confess to some such motive, but in a good cause." He picked up the red stone from the desk and replaced it in his pocket.

"A very interesting stone, the Kent ruby," he said. "Too bad that it is very slightly flawed or it would be worth—well, any figure you might name. Because of that, and because it is not properly shaped, too thin for its diameter, we insured it for only thirty thousand. But when one considers its bloody history—"

The buzzer on Mr. Thorwald's interoffice communicator interrupted. He flicked the switch.

"Mr. Carmichel is here, sir, and the four detectives."

"Send them in," Thorwald said. "And . . . uh . . . Mr. Smith, if you will be so kind as to leave now, I'll—"

"To leave? But, Mr. Thorwald, my company requested me to remain here until the program is over and Mr. Carmichel has been escorted home. We have a thirty-thousand-dollar interest, you see. They delegated me to . . . ah . . . protect the jewel."

The program manager looked at the mild-mannered, dapper little man across the desk from him, and only good breeding kept him from snorting aloud.

Two private detectives came in first. Mr. Smith knew them both; Waters and Powell of the Argus Agency. Powell was a tall, gangling youngster not many years out of school; Waters was middle-aged, middle height, middle everything, so inconspicuous one had to look twice to see him. The best shadow cop in town, Mr. Smith knew.

Then came Mr. Carmichel, hanging tightly on to a brief case. Mr. Smith knew him only by sight, as a moderately wealthy confectioner whose money, made from bonbons, went into jewels for his collection.

After Carmichel came two men whom Mr. Smith recognized as police detectives and he nodded approvingly of Thorwald's choice of an escort. Krasnowicz and Lieutenant Brady were both good men. And the rivalry between the police and the private detectives from the Argus Agency would keep all of them on their toes.

Thorwald glanced at the clock on the wall. "Just in time, Mr.

Carmichel. Twenty minutes to go. You . . . uh . . . brought the ruby?"

Carmichel took a jewel case from the brief case. He opened it and said, "The Kent ruby, Mr. Thorwald."

The program manager gazed reverently, and the others craned their necks for a glimpse before the box snapped shut. Thorwald said, "Thank you, Mr. Carmichel. We'll take good care of it." He put the case on his desk.

Brady had strolled over to the table that had the smaller gems on it. He said, "Nice stuff here," and held up the case containing the half-carat diamond. "This'd go nice in a ring."

Thorwald nodded. "Time to put those cases in the bucket. When you've looked at that one, lieutenant, just close it and put it in."

He followed suit by walking over to the table and closing another of the jewel cases and putting it into the small bucket.

Carmichel, looking at the opal, said, "Nice stones, but pretty small, aren't they, Thorwald?"

"Of course, but, after all, we're giving them away. Darn few programs give prizes worth as much as this bucket. It's worth more than any prize given regularly on any other program."

Powell said, "Me, I think it's a swell prize. Got flash."

The bucket was full now, and Thorwald said, "We'd better go up to the studio. I'll take the bucket. You bring the ruby, Mr. Car—"

His hand was almost on the handle of the bucket when it happened. A sudden hissing noise and then a flash of light that shone almost intolerably bright down within the bucket of gems, showing blindly between the edges of the cases.

Then flame and smoke as the tinderlike jewel cases caught fire.

It was Mr. Smith who moved first. He lifted his foot and knocked the bucket off the table onto the tile floor.

Jewel cases scattered. Some of them flaming, some smoldering, a few that had been on top, untouched. Some of the cases came open, others stayed shut.

And out of the bucket, too, came a tiny cylindrical metal thing, still burning with dazzling brightness.

"Incendiary," Brady snapped. "Let it alone. Get the stones out of the cases, quick."

There was momentary bedlam that gradually straightened itself into order. Less than a minute later the incendiary had burned itself out and was a mere bit of white ash in the center of a very black spot on the tile floor.

Several of the jewel cases, kicked into a pile in one corner, still smoldered and smoked. But they were all empty. On the table where the bucket had stood lay all fifteen of the jewels. A few were dark and blackened, but most of them were unharmed.

Thorwald sighed and wiped his forehead with the handkerchief he had used to handle several burning cases, leaving a smear of black from temple to temple. "Thank Heaven, we've got buckets in the safe upstairs ready for several programs ahead."

He bent over the jewels lying on the table. "Garnet's ruined, and the opal. That little black thing used to be a pearl. Others are all right, although some of them will have to be repolished. Not much loss."

"How much would you say?" Waters asked.

Thorwald shrugged. "Not more than a hundred dollars. Even counting the cases and replacing a few tiles in the floor."

Lieutenant Brady was bending over the ash where the incendiary had burned itself out. "Something like an incendiary pencil in miniature. Only an inch or so long. But who put it in there?"

"One of us," said Mr. Smith.

Brady turned to stare at him. Mr. Smith nodded. "The bucket was empty five minutes ago. I picked it up and looked at and in it. As to which of us put it in— Well, we all had an opportunity. All of us were helping to close the jewel cases and to put them in the bucket."

Thorwald said impatiently, "I'm afraid this will have to wait. The program goes on in five minutes. I'll have to get another bucket of gems from the safe, and then we'd better—"

"Just a minute," Mr. Smith broke in. "Before anyone leaves this room, wouldn't it be a good idea to check on the safety of the Kent ruby? Nothing was accomplished by that incendiary, unless possibly it was placed there to cause a distraction."

Thorwald stared for a long moment at Mr. Smith and then whirled and grabbed the black case containing the Kent ruby. He opened it.

It was empty.

Lieutenant Brady took two steps to the door and put his back against it. He took a deep breath and seemed to get taller, his voice assumed new authority.

"All right," he said. "Guess I'm in charge. And the ruby has to be in this room, so nobody's leaving. Thorwald, you use the telephone if you want to. Tell them to get that other bucket for the program, and that they'll have to put it on without the Kent ruby, unless we find it in time. How long we got?"

Thorwald looked dazed. "It was to be shown near the end of the program, after the dramatization of its history. We've got almost half an hour."

"We'll find it then," Brady said. "It's got to be in this room."

Brady waited until Thorwald had phoned. Then he said, "No use calling headquarters till we've got the ruby. Unless somebody objects to being searched without a warrant. In that case, we'll get a warrant. Anybody object?"

Nobody spoke up.

"And you won't object, Mr. Thorwald, to our searching the office?"

Thorwald's voice was grim. "Tear it to pieces if you want."

"It's in this room," Brady repeated. He said it emphatically, as an article of faith. "Krasnowicz can search me, then I'll search Krasnowicz. Then we'll go over the rest of you, one at a time. If it's on anybody, we'll find it. If we don't, we'll take the office apart. But we'll find it."

"I don't think you will," Mr. Smith put in quietly.

Brady glared at him. "If we don't, we'll all go over to headquarters, and there's an X-ray machine there."

Carmichel nodded approvingly. "I was going to suggest that. A stone that size would be dangerous, but not impossible, to swallow."

Waters asked, "Isn't a ruby transparent?"

"Not to X ray," said Carmichel. "Even a diamond shows up."

"Yeah," confirmed Brady. "Well, now that we got the program laid out, anybody want to save us the trouble?"

There was a deep silence and then Mr. Smith coughed deprecatingly and reached into his vest pocket. "I fear that I'd better account for my having this object, before you find it. It was not stolen from the case."

Brady grabbed for it, and his face turned almost as red as the object in his hand. He said, "Is this a gag? The hell that ain't the Kent ruby! Did you—"

Mr. Smith sighed. "I fear I shall have to call on Mr. Thorwald to corroborate my story. And to vouch for me on my possession of the imitation before the original came into this room. He examined it before you gentlemen entered the office."

Thorwald nodded. "That's right. And he explained how he acquired it and— Is that stone scratched?"

Brady looked closer. "Yeah, a little."

Thorwald took the stone, glanced at it, and handed it back. "That's the same one. I can identify the marks on it."

"I would suggest," said Mr. Smith, "that you put it aside and proceed. Later, at any time, you can check with the Phalanx Insurance Company on my possession of—"

"All right, all right," Brady broke in impatiently. "Then this ain't it." He started to put it into his pocket and then, apparently remembering he was to be searched first, put it on Thorwald's desk blotter.

Then he raised his arms slightly from his sides and said, "O.K., Krasnowicz. Go ahead."

Krasnowicz stepped forward.

Mr. Smith took off his gold-rimmed pince-nez and breathed gently first on one lens and then on the other.

"Really," he said, "this is quite unnecessary. I mean, the Kent ruby is not concealed upon the person of anyone in this room."

"Yeah?" said Brady. He didn't lower his arms.

"Yes," repeated Mr. Smith, "and I might further say that it will be equally unnecessary to search the room. It is not concealed anywhere in the office."

He smiled gently. "In fact," he added, "Mr. Carmichel did not bring the ruby here this evening at all."

"Yeah?" said Brady. Then he lowered his arms and said, "Huh?"

"Yes," said Mr. Smith. "Much as I regret to expose Mr. Carmichel's duplicity, he did not bring the ruby here tonight because he no longer had the ruby. Some time recently—I don't know just when—Mr. Carmichel's house was broken into, and the ruby stolen."

"Huh?"

"Exactly," said Mr. Smith. "Mr. Carmichel did not, I regret to say, report the loss either to the police or to us."

Brady looked at Carmichel and then back at Mr. Smith. "What reason could he have for not reporting it?"

"We had insured the ruby," Mr. Smith went on patiently, "for the sum of thirty thousand dollars. Had Mr. Carmichel reported its loss, he would have received just that. But he already had arranged to lend his ruby for tonight's radio program. Now do you understand?"

"No," said Brady. "I think you're nuts."

Mr. Smith sighed. "The studio had agreed to be responsible for the gem while it was here, and at its full value, declared by Mr. Carmichel, of a hundred thousand dollars. If it were stolen, or appeared to be stolen, here tonight he could recover seventy thousand dollars from the studio besides the thirty thousand from us. A net gain of seventy thousand dollars."

"You mean," said Brady, "he brought a phony tonight instead of the real ruby? And he put the little incendiary in the bucket to distract attention while he took it out of the case?"

"Exactly," said Mr. Smith.

"But what the hell? The imitation he brought—we all saw there was something in the case—will have to be on him or hidden in the room here. He couldn't have got it out of the room, and it would give away the play if we found it."

"Quite true," said Mr. Smith. "He would certainly have anticipated a search, however. And I think I can make a sufficiently accurate guess as to how he disposed of the imitation ruby that was in the case."

"How?"

"In moving picture comedies," said Mr. Smith, "you have undoubtedly seen people break glasses and bottles over one another's heads, not to mention dishes and other articles?"

"Sure."

"Those articles do not injure because they are made of spun sugar, instead of glass. An imitation ruby could be made of colored spun sugar and if enough care were used in its making, it would stand superficial examination. Mr. Carmichel just gave us a quick glimpse when he opened and closed the case. It would probably have stood even a slightly closer examination; Mr. Carmichel is a confectioner, you know."

"But—"

"Exactly," Mr. Smith murmured. "I suggest that while the excitement over the burning bucket of gems was at its height, Mr. Carmichel took the imitation ruby from the case."

"And—"

"*And ate it*," Mr. Smith finished. "The sugar would digest, of course, and leave no traces for the X ray. But, if I am right, proof can be found by making a microscopic examination of the lining inside the case. Surely minute traces of colored sugar would remain on the nap of the silk. A substance which certainly could have no other logical reason for being there."

Brady said, "I'll be a—" And turned to look at Carmichel. "Well, Mr. Carmichel, is he right? I mean, when we examine the case, will we find what he says?"

The confectioner met his stare for a few seconds, and then nodded slowly. "He wins. But I don't see how he guessed."

Mr. Smith sighed. "I had to guess, Mr. Carmichel, only at the method. You see, I already knew that the stone had been stolen from you. So I knew you couldn't bring it here tonight. The burglar who took the stone came to the Phalanx Company, knowing from the newspapers that we'd insured it, to try to make a deal with us. But we do not make deals with criminals. We turned him down, and one of our detectives managed to tail him to his room when he left."

"The hell!" said Brady. "They get him?"

"I regret to say, no. He left his room almost immediately, be-

fore our operative could arrange to have him arrested there, and
a few blocks off he discovered he was being followed. He ducked
our man in a subway station. But our detective returned to the
man's room, found the jewel, and reported in with it. The police
have been notified and are now watching the room for his re
turn."

Thorwald glanced at the clock, and groaned. "Then I suppose
we've got to go through the program without the Kent ruby.
Your office is miles from here and there won't be time to send
for it. The stone would have to be upstairs in ten minutes."

"I fear there would not be time," admitted Mr. Smith. "But
about that policy, Mr. Thorwald. Do you now see the advisability
of complete protection?"

"Damn it, yes. Have your office write one up, and I'll sign it."

"Excellent," said Mr. Smith. "But I anticipated that after what
might happen here this evening, you would be ready to sign with
us. I have the policy application right here."

He put a paper on Thorwald's desk.

"But you will not wish to sign it without reading it, of course,
and there is hardly time for that if you wish to take the Kent
ruby up to the studio for the end of the dramatization. Mr
Brady, if you will be so kind as to take that red stone from the
desk and rub it briskly with your handkerchief, the scratches will
come off. They are . . . ah . . . external, applied with a jewel
er's marking pencil."

Thorwald's eyes bulged. "You mean that *that's* really the—"

"Exactly," murmured Mr. Smith.

from DETECTIVE WHO'S WHO

SMITH, Henry, insurance salesman; b. Athens, Ohio, April 13,
1892; s. Everett W. and Elsie
(Wheeler) S.; grad., Athens Public
Sch., 1906; Hughes High Sch., Cincinnati, Ohio, 1910. Started work
as office boy for Phalanx Insurance
Co., Cincinnati Branch Office,
1910; asst. bkpr., 1911; salesman,
1913; transferred Springfield, 1922
as asst. branch mgr., resigned offic
in 1923, preferring selling to offic
work; recd. gold button for 25 yrs
with Phalanx, 1935; spec. award
as best salesman in territory, 1932
1938, 1946. Single. Hobbies: mu
sic, chess, insurance, and criminol
ogy.

One of our more prolific creators of series detectives, George Harmon Coxe has used the longer forms of novel and novelette to tell the sagas of his photographer-sleuths, and the short story for excerpts from the case-book of medical examiner Dr. Paul Standish. And (with no disrespect to photographers Murdock and Casey) Dr. Standish's neatness of thinking and depth of feeling can make such a short story as this more memorable than many novels.

DR. PAUL STANDISH IN

Death Certificate

BY GEORGE HARMON COXE

IN THE two years that Dr. Paul Standish had acted as the city's medical examiner he had become acquainted with death in nearly all its violent forms, but not until the night Dr. Cheney was found dead had it ever occurred to him that the performance of his duty might some day become a personal matter.

The call from the telegraph bureau awakened him shortly after two-thirty that morning. By the time he had dressed, a police car was waiting at the curb, and he rode along deserted pavements to the north side of town near the river. Here, in a street of grimy loft buildings and tenements, another police car had been backed around so that its headlights focused into an alleyway.

One of the officers gathered there spoke to Standish and he answered automatically, having no preparation for what came next, yet knowing in his first glance that the man who lay sprawled on the dusty cobblestones had been murdered. The back of the head was broken and bloody, and because he had become accustomed to approach each case as a diagnostician and view it with a clinical eye, he noticed the nondescript character of the worn suit and topcoat, and found them in keeping with the telegraph bureau's announcement. An unidentified man, the bureau had said, and that was what Paul Standish had expected until he turned the body over and realized that this man had once been his friend.

Recognition was swift and left him shaken and sick inside. The night air was suddenly cool and though he heard one of the officers speak, it was some seconds before he could recover from the shock and think reasonably.

"We went through his pockets as well as we could without moving him," the officer said. "Looks like he's clean. We figure some muggers slugged him on the walk and dragged him in here out of sight."

Standish forced himself to concentrate. He made sure about the pockets as he made his preliminary tests for *rigor mortis*. He knew then that there was nothing more to be done here; he knew that insofar as his job was concerned, his work, which was to determine the cause of death, was finished. Yet now, as his thoughts went back to the Dr. Cheney he had known ten years before when he was a young interne at City Hospital, he knew that it was not enough to write a report which said that this same Dr. Cheney had been murdered by a blunt instrument, and he turned to ask whose beat this was.

"Mine, sir," said a uniformed husky. "My flashlight picked him up when I turned it in here at two-fifteen on my way down the street."

"Did you turn it in here on your previous round? At what time?"

"One-fifteen, sir. And there was no sign of him."

Standish straightened, a moderately tall man with good shoulders and a well-boned face that looked lean and angular in the glare of the headlights. For another moment he stared beyond the body, his eyes obscured and his normally easy mouth a tight grim line; then, speaking quietly, he asked if anyone was here from homicide.

"I am," a voice said. "Sergeant Wargo."

Standish recognized the man as an assistant of Lieutenant Ballard's. He had hoped Ballard would be here; he needed him now but he did not ask about the lieutenant who was his friend. He merely nodded as he heard the ambulance draw to a stop in the street, and asked the sergeant to wait.

Five minutes later, when the body had been removed, they stood on the sidewalk and Wargo, a young man of intelligence and ability who had not yet asked a question nor offered an opinion, said, "We're pretty sure he was dragged into the alley, doctor."

"Yes," Standish said. "But he wasn't killed on the sidewalk. He'd been dead at least three hours when I examined him."

Wargo whistled softly. Then, as though held by something in the doctor's manner that he did not understand, he said, "Do you know him?"

Standish nodded and took time to marshal his thoughts, knowing now that he would not be going back to bed and knowing also that he would need help. "Ballard's not on call?"

"Not tonight," Wargo said. "The captain told him to get some rest because he's been going steadily ever since yesterday morning when Frankie Montanari jumped his bail. So has everybody in the department." Wargo grunted softly. "Even homicide, because I guess they figure when they find Frankie, it'll be a homicide job."

Dr. Standish had no interest in Montanari, who had been about to be sentenced for bribery in a gambling case when he disappeared. The newspapers had intimated that the length of the sentence would depend on whether or not Montanari disclosed the real boss of the gambling syndicate that employed him, but Standish felt only annoyance that such a case should rob him of Lieutenant Ballard's help.

"I'm going to the morgue," he said, and then, standing beside the police car, he told Sergeant Wargo what he wanted him to do.

Dr. Cheney had as his office and living quarters the lower floor of a two-family house which stood on the east side of town in a neighborhood no more than a cut or two above the slums. There was a police car out front when Standish arrived and Sergeant Wargo was sitting on the steps waiting for him.

"The guy upstairs owns the place," Wargo said. "I got the key from him. This coupe"—he indicated a battered car in front of the police sedan—"is Doc Cheney's. There's no doctor's bag in it and I didn't find any in the office. You can have a look if you want."

Standish went into a poorly furnished waiting room overlooking the porch. He inspected the adjoining private office and the living quarters beyond, finding no signs of prosperity and knowing finally that the bag, without which Cheney would never have made a professional call, was not here. Then, because he did not understand this any more than he understood the dead man's empty pockets, he examined the appointment book on the desk.

"He made his last call at five."

"The guy upstairs saw him come in around six," Wargo said. "He thinks he went out around nine."

"What makes him think so?"

"He heard the doorbell ring, heard the doc answer it. He thinks he went out."

It was nearly six o'clock when Paul Standish reached his apartment and though he undressed, he did not go to bed but sat by the window and tried to find some reason for a murder that on the face of it seemed utterly senseless. That it was not his job to do so, did not occur to him at all until Lieutenant Ballard put it into words at eight-thirty that morning in his office at police headquarters, when Standish showed up there.

They had worked together often, these two, though it was generally Ballard who yelled for help and Dr. Standish who maintained it was not his job to do detective work. This time the shoe was on the other foot and though the lieutenant heard him out, he offered no encouragement, nor even agreement with the doctor's theory.

"Sergeant Wargo thinks it was a hold-up job," he said. "And I've got to go along. A couple of young punks jumped Cheney and maybe he gave them an argument and they sapped him—too hard."

"Three hours before he was found?"

"So what? Maybe it happened in their neighborhood and they got scared and went back and moved him. Hell, I can think of a dozen answers to that one."

Standish tried to be patient. "Someone called for Cheney at nine o'clock, otherwise he would have taken his car. He took his bag with him because it wasn't in his office. He's not found until three hours after he's killed and there's no bag, no identification on him. If I hadn't known him, he might have lain in the morgue for days before we knew who he was, and I say that doesn't shape up as a mugging job."

Ballard ran his fingers through his sandy hair and his shrewd gray eyes were troubled. He recognized sound reasoning when he heard it but he was a harried man just now, conscious of pressure from above that demanded he and every man on the force find a missing gambler named Frankie Montanari, an assignment which was a little out of his line.

"Look, Paul," he said, "right now I can't agree with you. I think a couple of thugs did the job and you know how we catch guys like that. We add some men to the district and keep our eyes open and the punks keep trying the same racket until we catch up with them. Before we get through, we'll know what jobs they've pulled. This Cheney thing will turn out to be one of 'em." He took a breath and said, "But even if I'm wrong, what do you want me to do?"

Paul Standish started to speak, then checked his reply when he realized it was inadequate. He took a moment to think, aware that if Ballard was right there was nothing more to be done. But if Ballard was wrong, there could only be one answer: that Cheney had been killed deliberately and for a definite and clear-cut reason.

He wanted to know what that reason was. Like any good diagnostician, he wanted to know why. Yet when he spoke of this, it sounded silly, even to him.

"I want to know why."

Ballard sighed heavily and threw up his hands. "Find Montanari and I'll put twenty men on it. Maybe they can answer you. I can't." He paused, gray eyes half-closed. "Who was this Cheney, a brother of yours or something?"

MARY HAYWARD asked Paul Standish a similar question at eleven-thirty, after the last of his office patients had been taken care of. Mary, his nurse, secretary, and Girl-Friday, had medium-blond hair and green eyes and a nicely-modeled figure. She was jealous of Standish's time and quite possibly of his affections. She believed he was wasting his talent as medical examiner, arguing that he would be much further ahead if he put this time into his own practice. And because she was young and forthright she spoke not too kindly about Dr. Cheney.

"I can't understand why you bother," she said. "I've heard you speak of him. I thought he was a bum."

Standish eyed her somberly, but because he was used to her ways and understood in some measure what was behind them, he took no offense at her words.

"He was no bum, Mary. He was resident physician at City Hospital when I was interning. He was a very nice guy."

"Ten years ago."

"He was a nice guy today. Weak, maybe. That's the worst you could say about him. You could call him a failure—a lot of people did—but he was a good doctor and I don't believe he ever consciously did a dishonest or unethical thing in his life."

He hesitated, no longer seeing Mary as his mind turned back. Speaking more to himself than to her, he told how Dr. Cheney had left the hospital to give all his time to his own practice and how, the following winter, a truck had skidded out of control and killed his wife and the two-year-old son she had been carrying across the street.

"Some people can take a thing like that and others can't. Cheney couldn't. It took the heart out of him and he closed his office. I don't know what was in his mind or what he wanted to do; I do know that it was the best thing that ever happened to those people in his neighborhood when he turned his back on the society he knew and opened that east side office. He collected enough to live on and if you wanted medical treatment you got it from Cheney no matter who you were."

The quiet sincerity of the young doctor's words impressed the girl and her eyes were soft and concerned. She said she was sorry, that she hadn't understood, and she remained that way until Standish glanced at his watch and stood up. When he said he was going to the morgue, and from there to the district attorney's office, Mary said, "Don't forget your two o'clock appointment with Mr. Lane."

Standish frowned. "Cancel it. Call him up and—"

Mary interrupted him, her voice horrified and then indignant. She said that Mr. Lane was rich and that the thorough physical check-up that Standish was to give him would bring more of that kind of business to the office.

Standish was adamant. He said tomorrow or the next day would do just as well, that Mr. Lane would understand if Mary told him the doctor had been called out on an urgent matter.

"Urgent?" Mary was still indignant. She would have argued further if Standish had not opened the door and walked out.

ONE of the duties of the medical examiner's office was to see that a copy of all autopsy reports was sent to the district attorney and, in the case of Dr. Cheney, Paul Standish delivered this report in person.

John Quinn, the district attorney, was in conference when Standish arrived and he had to wait a half-hour in the anteroom before the door finally opened and a thick-bodied, hard-jawed man with small, deep-set eyes and not much hair came out. His name was Mike Darrow and he was still talking.

"I'm getting a little fed up with this," he said to Quinn, who stood in the doorway. "If you want to see me again, you'd better subpoena me. . . . Hi, doc. How's it going?"

Standish stood up, making no reply, and started towards the private office. Quinn followed him in, his face flushed and his eyes angry behind the shell-rimmed glasses. He swore softly a moment before he glanced at the report Standish handed him, finally put his mind on it as the doctor told his story.

Standish knew the news was bad even before he finished. He could see it in Quinn's face and he had to listen while the other spoke of a budget that always kept him short-handed and made him dependent on police efforts.

"What exactly did you have in mind?" he said.

"I don't think Cheney was mugged," Standish said. "And if I'm right there has to be a reason. I thought you might know some things I don't know, that you might think of some reason."

Quinn said he was sorry. He could think of no reason for any deliberate attempt on Dr. Cheney, but maybe Standish could help him. "Where," he said, "would be a good place to hide a body?"

"Montanari's? How do you know he didn't run out on you?"

"I'll tell you," Quinn said, and he did, starting with Mike Darrow and going back to prohibition days when Darrow had been a strong-arm man and hijacker. He enumerated a record of arrests that ranged from extortion to murder, commented profanely on the lack of convictions, and brought the record up to date by explaining the ramifications of Darrow's gambling syndicate, which had branched out into sporting events and made a mistake in trying to bribe certain college basketball players.

"When those kids told their story," Quinn said, "we dug back and found a couple of boxers who sang the same song. Montanari is the lad who offered the bribe and Darrow is his boss, though we can't prove it. And Montanari knew what the score was. I had his wife down. I told her he'd get only two years if he co-operated and gave us the goods on Darrow, and I promised to put in a word when he came up for parole. I told her he'd go away for ten long years if he refused to tell the truth. And then I got a break."

Quinn leaned across his desk. "His wife is going to have a baby in about six months. She hadn't told Frankie, but she did tell him after I talked to her, because yesterday when he turned up missing she came down here to see me. She said Frankie had promised her he would sing and I think he made the mistake of telling Darrow so." Quinn sat back and said, "That's why we're looking for a body. It's the sort of thing Darrow would do because he knows that Montanari's testimony would put him away for a long, long time."

Quinn stood up and shrugged. "I'm sorry, doc. I don't know how I can help you. Until we find Frankie I won't even be able to think about anything else."

IT WAS nearly five when Paul Standish returned to his office and Mary Hayward, who was checking records at her desk, took one look at his face and wisely made no comment when he went into his own office and closed the door.

It was, Standish realized as he shed his hat and coat, a mistake to have wasted any time on Quinn. And because he felt tired and beaten, it seemed now that it had been a mistake to concern himself with the Cheney death at all. He had spent hours accomplishing nothing and now he was through; in the future he would confine his efforts to those covered by the statutes governing his office.

At least, that is what he told himself. That is what he thought for a few minutes as he straightened his desk and busied himself with other matters. The trouble was he was a stubborn man when confronted by a problem, medical or otherwise, and his mind kept going back, probing, testing, weighing the bits of information at hand. And finally, not realizing it, he was thinking of old Doc Lathrop who had given him the job of assistant medical examiner at a time when Standish needed the work to pay his office rent.

It was Lathrop who had told him that through the experience gained by such work he would add to his knowledge as a diagnostician, and as he remembered some of the advice the grand old man had given him, one oft-repeated remark kept coming back. *The truth always rings true.* That was what Lathrop liked to say when faced with a difficult problem, and though it had sounded corny at times, Standish realized that this was all he needed now: The truth.

If Cheney had died at the hands of ordinary thugs, as Ballard maintained, he could be satisfied; if not, he had to know why—he had to know the truth.

He stood up, dark hair tousled and fatigue lining the angles of his eyes. He walked round the desk and sat down again, lighting a cigarette and then playing absently with his lighter. Just what made him think of Dr. Cheney's missing bag he did not know, but suddenly the idea was there and he reached for his own bag, wondering with new hope if the murder could be traced to something that Cheney had carried.

With his own bag open, he pawed through its familiar contents. He removed the stethoscope and saw the hypodermic kit, and though this gave way to further speculation he continued his search, taking out his pad of prescription blanks and then another, larger pad, his glance inspecting the printed form and then narrowing into a hot bright stare.

For another minute he sat quite motionless, his mind racing; then, not daring to hope that he had an answer, but desperately, like a man grabbing at straws when all else has failed, he sat erect and reached for the telephone.

He got his number without delay, spoke briefly in quick, urgent accents. When he hung up there was new brightness in his eyes and that gleam was still there ten minutes later when he strode down a corridor in the City Hall and opened a door marked Department of Health.

The assistant he had spoken to was waiting behind a counter and as Standish thanked him for keeping the office open, he pushed a slip of paper across the counter which was a duplicate of the form Standish had seen in his bag. Across the top of the form were printed the words: Death Certificate. And this one had been filled out and signed by Dr. Edward Cheney.

"Is there anything wrong?" the assistant asked, held by the intentness of the doctor's inspection.

Standish said no, but he had a pencil out now as his glance took in the details and he wrote down the cause of death as stated by Dr. Cheney. Chronic gastric ulcer, hemorrhage into gastro-intestinal tract, spontaneous, is what Cheney had written, and Standish saw now that the deceased was one Charles Judson and that the certificate was dated the day before yesterday.

He had other questions to ask before he left and then he went out to his car and drove swiftly crosstown to Dr. Cheney's flat, the excitement riding him now in spite of his efforts to hold his hopes in check.

The two-family house looked even more depressing by daylight but Standish found the office unlocked, and the middle-aged woman who had been Cheney's secretary answered his question about Charles Judson and let him inspect Cheney's records. When he saw there was no card for Judson and was sure the secretary had no knowledge of the name, he again turned to the telephone, this time calling Lieutenant Ballard at police headquarters.

"I have a lead on the Cheney murder," he said. "I want to call on a fellow named Earle Jennings." He mentioned an address and said, "Can you meet me there in ten minutes?"

"No."

"Why not?" Standish said, surprised and a little annoyed at Ballard's curt reply.

"Because I'm up to my ears in this Montanari thing and I've got to go into a meeting with the captain and the commissioner and I don't know how long I'll be. Call me back in an hour."

"An hour?" Standish said, outraged. "An hour?"

And then all the tension and the lack of sleep and the fatigue that he had been battling became too much for him and his normally even disposition dissolved abruptly, leaving his voice irascible and hard. He said that since two-thirty that morning he had been working on a murder that was really none of his business, and he finally had a lead, and if Ballard didn't want to know about it, it was all right with him. He had no intention of waiting an hour, or even fifteen minutes, and what did Ballard think of *that*.

Ballard finally interrupted him. He said wait a minute and to take it easy. "What makes this Jennings guy important?" he said. "Who is he, anyway?"

"He's an undertaker," Standish said, and hung up.

By THE time he had parked his car and walked along the street to the colored, opaque window bearing the inscription, *Earle Jennings—Funeral Director*, Paul Standish was ashamed of his outburst and no longer so sure that his hunch was right. He stood for a moment looking at the narrow-front shop, sandwiched in between a stationery store and a bakery, aware that this was a run-down neighborhood, and tempted to go on by; that he did not was due not only to pride and native stubbornness but also to a well-entrenched and ever-present desire to know the truth.

Having come this far, he could not quit, and so he opened the door and stepped into a long, narrow room with somber walls, wicker furniture, and a threadbare rug. At the far end, near a curtained doorway, was a desk, but there was no one in the room so he walked on, past the desk, parting the curtains and finding himself in a short hall leading to a room in the back. As he stepped into this room, the man working over the casket heard him and wheeled.

A somberly-dressed, shifty-eyed man, as tall as Standish but thinner, he had a heavy screw driver in his hand and his glance was both startled and apprehensive.

"What's the idea?" he said.

"Are you Earle Jennings?"

"Yeah, why?"

"The Department of Health issued you a burial permit for a man named Charles Judson."

"Sure." There was defiance in the voice now but the eyes remained shifty. "We buried him this afternoon."

"Did you?" Standish glanced about, aware that the room was a sort of display room and noting the open doorway leading to the preparation room beyond. He moved slowly then, up to the table supporting the casket, then reaching for a handle and testing its weight. "I doubt it," he said. "Open this up and let's see."

Jennings swore viciously. He demanded to know who Standish was and when he found out, there was fear in his glance. He tried to bluster and when Standish started for him, he backed away, his manner changing.

"All right, doc," he said. "You're off the beam but if you want to look, O.K." He stepped up to the casket, unfastened the catches, and lifted the lid. As he moved aside, Standish took a quick look, then stopped to stare.

For there was a dead man inside the cheap, shallow box—a thin, almost undersized man. His name was Frankie Montanari and as Standish leaned forward he saw the bullet hole in the side of the head just above the hairline.

But even as he noticed this, he knew he had made a mistake. Sheer surprise had already robbed him of a vital second or two, and then it was too late. He tried to duck, sensing rather than hearing the sudden movement behind him, but even as he moved something smashed solidly in back of his head and pain exploded inside his brain.

The floor heaved and the room spun about him. He went down slowly, dizzily. He was on his knees. Then Jennings was tugging at him and he was helpless to resist the pressure that dragged him across the floor until vaguely, as from a great distance, he heard a door slam and blackness engulfed him.

Never quite losing consciousness, it took Paul Standish a while to find the strength to stand. By that time he knew he had been locked in some closet, and though he hurled himself at the door he had little room and could not get enough momentum in his charge to do any good.

Realizing finally that he could not break out alone, he began to think, and presently the pattern of Dr. Cheney's murder became clear. He knew now what had happened, and why. He also knew about what to expect and was ready for it when the door opened a few minutes later and he stepped out to find Mike Darrow standing there, a gun in his hand, Jennings beside him.

Darrow's blocky face was grim and uncompromising. "You had to stick your nose in, huh?" he said flatly.

Standish glanced about, weighing his chances and not liking the odds, knowing now that the district attorney's guess had been right when he said Montanari had made the mistake of going to Darrow.

"Frankie came to see you," Standish said. "To tell you he was going to talk."

"With a gun in his pocket," Darrow said. "This gun." He gestured with the automatic in his hand and laughed abruptly, an unpleasant sound. "I took it away from him."

"And after you'd shot him, you were stuck. It was a murder you hadn't planned. You had no alibi, and a body to get rid of and you thought of a way." Standish hesitated, his bitterness at Darrow's cleverness erasing any immediate fear for himself. "You needed a death certificate and that meant a doctor, preferably a poor one, without a family. Someone crooked if possible—like Cheney."

He took a breath and said, "But Cheney was no crook. You found that out and you knew, once you'd tipped your hand, that you'd have to kill him. But that didn't matter to you because you'd already killed once and had no further penalty to pay. I guess Cheney knew, too."

He paused again, his bitterness festering as he realized what must have happened to the man who had once been his friend. Cheney had to sign or be killed, and even if he signed he must have known that his chance of survival was slim. But he had taken that chance because it was all he had, and in doing so had left behind one clue for whoever might be curious enough to make a search for it.

"The first certificate he made out," Darrow said, "he put down some funny words as the cause of death. I was afraid he was trying to tip off the health department. I made him write out another with words I could understand. What put you wise?"

"What difference does it make?"

"None." Darrow flattened his lips and his little eyes were implacable. "Tomorrow morning Frankie gets buried as Charles Judson and nobody's ever going to know what happened to him. Only now we need a deeper casket, doc. To hold you too."

He spoke over his shoulder to Jennings but Standish did not

hear him. His lean face was shiny with perspiration and his hands were damp. As he tried to think of some way out, he saw Jennings leave the room and come back lugging two saw-horses; then Darrow was prodding him with the gun, directing him through the preparation room to the storeroom in the back, forcing him to lift one end of a deeper casket while Jennings took the other.

Standish did not notice the weight of this burden; he was thinking about Ballard. He knew Darrow would not get away with his plan, since Ballard knew that Standish had come to see Jennings. When Standish turned up missing, Ballard would move in and eventually find out what had happened; but he could not expect Darrow to believe it.

Nevertheless, he tried. As they trudged back into the second room, he had his say and Darrow laughed at him, and now he knew that no matter what happened, he had to put up a fight, and quickly, before time ran out on him. Having nothing further to lose, the problem became simply a question of method, and he wasted no time feeling sorry for himself.

For they were putting the casket on the saw-horses now, he and Jennings, and Darrow was on the other side, and suddenly Standish's nerves were quiet and he knew what to do.

Feeling poised and ready now, not watching Darrow, he wedged his thigh under the edge of the casket as Jennings tried to adjust it and then, in one continuous movement, heaved mightily, tipping it towards Darrow.

What happened then took no more than a brief second, but to Paul Standish each detail was clear-cut and exact. He heard Jennings yell as the casket teetered and started to fall. He saw the gun flash and heard it hammer twice as Darrow fired wildly in his belated effort to jump clear; then the casket crashed and the floor shook, and above it all came Darrow's scream as his leg snapped under the casket.

After that, things were a little hazy for Paul Standish. He remembered seeing the automatic spin from Darrow's hand; he saw Jennings dive for it. He scrambled over the casket, aware that Jennings would reach it first but hoping he could get close.

He watched the man scoop it up and straighten, knowing as i
leveled that he would not be in time.

He saw the scared white face behind it and, still movin
watched the trigger finger tighten. Then the gun thundered an
only when he saw Jennings's torso jerk did he realize that it wa
not this gun that had fired.

He stopped short then, hearing Darrow's moans, and h
grabbed the gun from limp fingers as Jennings started to sag
Then he turned, unbelieving, and found Sergeant Wargo in th
doorway to the hall, a short-barreled service revolver in his hand

Jennings crumpled a joint at a time and fell over on his face
Darrow stopped groaning and the room was suddenly stil
Wargo moved up, lowering his gun. He walked past Standis
to glance at Darrow, who had fainted, and then at Montanari'
casket.

Standish realized he was holding his breath and let it out,
little surprised that he could still move. He started to speak an
had to clear his throat before any words came out. When h
started to hand Wargo the automatic, he saw that his hands wer
trembling, and an odd weakness crept up the back of his legs a
reaction hit him.

"Where," he said finally, "did you come from?"

"I was outside." Wargo motioned Standish to help him lif
the casket from Darrow's leg. "This guy's going to the chair witl
one leg shorter than the other," he said and then, continuin
with his answer, he added, "Ballard said the way you talked t
him over the phone anything might happen and I'd better com
out here and keep an eye on you. When I saw Mike come in,
thought I'd better have a look."

LIEUTENANT Ballard got the rest of the story a half-hour late
after Mike Darrow had been shipped to the hospital and Jen
nings had been removed. And because he was still shocked b
what might have happened to his friend, his remarks wer
pointed and profane until he thought of something else; then h
shrugged.

"What the hell," he said. "What am I crabbing about? W

got Montanari and Darrow, and we know you were right about Doc Cheney. You got a good scare, and it served you right for not telling me the truth over the phone."

"I didn't know then," Standish said. "I didn't know I was going to find Montanari in the casket. All I knew was that Cheney would never have signed that death certificate of his own free will."

Ballard frowned, not understanding. He wanted to know why not. "Don't people die from ulcers and hemorrhages?"

"Certainly. There was nothing wrong with the wording."

"Then what tipped you off?"

Standish took his time because he wanted to make things clear. "Look," he said. "The law says that when a man dies suddenly, the death certificate must be signed by the medical examiner—unless there is a doctor in attendance who is familiar with the case. The laws reads something like this: *Attending physicians will certify only to such deaths as those of persons to whom they have given bedside care during the last illness*, etcetera."

"I still don't get it," Ballard said.

"The death certificate said the hemorrhage was spontaneous. And due to chronic gastric ulcers. A physician *who had just been called in* could not know of that condition; he would have to be familiar with a case to make any such diagnosis."

"So—"

"So when I read that, I went to Doc Cheney's place and examined his records. He never had a patient named Judson, never called on one. If he *had* been called in and if there *had* been a man named Judson, and Cheney *had* found him dying, he would not have signed a death certificate. It would have been unethical and illegal."

Standish tipped one hand, let it fall. "And so I knew that the only way anyone could make Cheney sign such a certificate was by force. Because he was that kind of man. I don't believe he ever did a dishonest thing in his life, and he always did the best he could to make the truth ring true."

Ballard looked at Paul Standish and deep down in his eyes there was respect and approval. He seemed about to say some-

thing, checked himself. He took the doctor's arm and turne
him towards the door.

"When you have faith in a guy," he said, under his breath
"you go all the way, don't you?"

Standish heard only part of Ballard's words and he was to
tired to pay much attention to those. He wanted mostly a drin
and something to eat. "What?" he said.

"Nothing," Ballard said. "Let's go see that good-looking se
retary of yours that's always bawling you out. I've got an ide
she's going to be sort of proud of you. Are you buying the drink
or am I?"

Standish said it didn't matter. He said either way was all righ
so long as they drank first to Dr. Cheney.

from DETECTIVE WHO'S WHO

STANDISH, Paul E., physician; b. Chandler, Mass., June 23, 1922; s. Andrew W. and Martha Lee (Cowens) S.; grad., Chandler High Sch., 1939; B.S., Cornell U., 1943; M.D., Cornell Medical, 1946; postgrad. work, College Physicians & Surgeons, 1947. Intern, Presbyterian Hospital (N. Y.) and Uniontown (Conn.) Hospital, 1947– 1948. In private practice sinc 1948. Member: American Medica Ass'n.; State Medical Soc.; Sigm Xi; Sigma Nu. Congregationalis Republican. Unmarried. Clubs Cornell Club (N. Y.), City (U iontown). Contrib. articles to mec journals. Home: 423 Elm St. O fice: 102 Lake St., Uniontown Conn.

*Readers who know the career of Timothy Trant may think
they detect, in this never-before-published story, a resemblance to one of his already-recorded cases. The facts of the
matter are as follows: A timid magazine editor, fancying he
saw an analogy with another case then in the papers, insisted that this shipboard episode be completely rewritten
and set in an Alpine chalet—a rewrite job which Q. Patrick
completed overnight, and astonishingly well. But here, for
the first time, you may read the original statement of one
of Trant's deftest cases.*

LIEUTENANT TIMOTHY TRANT IN

Girl Overboard

BY Q. PATRICK

YOUNG LIEUTENANT TRANT of the New York Homicide Bureau sat in the lounge of the S.S. *Queen Anne*, feeling bored.
Around him passengers were chattering and dancing in a mood
of mid-Atlantic festivity. After a month's vacation in Europe,
Trant was tired of frivolity. His one authentic enthusiasm—his
passion for murderers—had been starved.

He watched the dancers, hoping rather wistfully that one of
them would drop dead under mysterious circumstances.

The lounge steward brought the drink he had ordered. "Here
we are, sir."

"Thanks, Jimmie."

The steward, with his sun-bleached hair and lazy smile, was
the dream boy of the female tourists and knew it. He was also
colorfully informed as to ship's gossip. Trant, who took an un-

357

orthodox interest in the backstairs of life, had made the York-shire-born steward his particular crony.

"How's our girl friend and company tonight, Jimmie?"

He nodded across the lounge to a corner table where two young men and two girls with suntanned backs were making a stormy but striking quartet.

"Miss Marriner's party, sir?" Jimmie's speech and manner would have done credit to a duke. "They seem a little edgy, sir. I'm afraid trouble may be brewing again."

"Trouble," remarked Lieutenant Trant, studying the blonder of the two backs appreciatively, "is something which Miss Mavis Marriner carries around like a pocketbook."

Jimmie grinned. "She is a bit of what you might call a magnet, sir."

"A magnet for males."

Trant alerted, for at the other side of the lounge the blonde had risen in apparent pique and a cloud of turquoise taffeta. Turning the suntanned back contemptuously on her companions, she skirted the dancers and made her way to Trant's table. She sat down and gave him a blinding smile which she then switched to Jimmie.

"Jimmie, darling, be an angel and get me a drink." As the steward hurried off, Mavis Marriner, England's newest, prettiest, and probably least talented movie star, moaned: "Darling, be nice to me. I'm having a foul evening and you're the only bearable male on the ship."

Lieutenant Trant, whose taste in women was also unorthodox, felt a certain weakness for Mavis Marriner although, apart from a torrid physical appeal, she had nothing to recommend her. She was both silly and selfish and, although she worked overtime to make every man in love with her, she remained—he was sure—technically as virtuous as a police matron. He found it hard to tell why she moved him. Perhaps it was her youth or perhaps in her he saw the classic example of a murderee.

"What's the trouble tonight, Mavis?" His lean young face was mildly amused.

She shrugged. "My dear, so positively stupid! Just because

that divine Larry Howard—he's a great Hollywood producer now, you know—happens to be interested in my career, Armand smolders, my dear, as if he was the Bull of Bashan. And that revolting Claire Howard! Really! She thinks I'm trying to steal her husband. So absurd, I mean!"

From this rambling statement, the experienced police officer in Trant deduced that Mavis Marriner, who was engaged to the French movie actor, Armand Bardou, had been vamping the multimillionaire playboy, Larry Howard, thus infuriating both Howard's recent fourth wife and her own fiancé.

This was, in fact, a typical Mavis Marriner evening.

"Really," continued Mavis, batting her huge lashes and looking almost unbearably luscious, "jealous people are so dismal. Darling, let's dance."

Mavis' dancing was an expert seduction. Sinuous in Trant's arms and headily perfumed with *Tantalizing*, she murmured:

"You really are intriguing. So mysterious. I'm sure you do something frightfully fascinating."

Trant, who knew he was being exploited merely to make Armand Bardou and the "divine" Larry Howard that much more dismally jealous, grinned at her affectionately.

"I'm a mere nobody. Clay in the potter's hands."

They went back to the table. Jimmie had brought Mavis a menthe frappé. Mavis dazzled at him.

"Jimmie, you're a duck. And don't forget the milk tonight. With just a spoonful of brandy as usual. At one o'clock."

Jimmie, all ducal gallantry, said: "Of course, Miss Marriner."

Mavis turned to Trant. "Jimmie's so sweet. Every night he leaves a glass of milk and brandy outside my stateroom—like a gnome. It helps me sleep. Darling, let's dance again."

Mavis danced long and shamelessly enough with Trant to drive her companions, one after the other, from the lounge. Having achieved her objective, she withdrew in pursuit of other game. It was just after two when Trant finally escaped to his cabin from a relentless chess game with the captain. As he climbed into bed, the boat, which had been quiet all evening, gave an eccentric lurch, toppling his traveling clock onto the floor. He bent to pick it up and thought of Mavis as a stormy sea, toppling everyone she met off balance.

Soon he drifted into pleasant dreams of suntanned backs and *crime passionelle*. . . .

He awoke next morning at nine to a voice booming eerily over the loud-speakers:

"Miss Mavis Marriner. Miss Mavis Marriner, report to the bridge at once."

A moment later the chief mate appeared anxiously to announce that the captain wanted him in Mavis' cabin. When they reached it, they found the captain alone, looking grim.

"I think I'm going to need a policeman's help, Trant. She's gone."

He told Trant what he knew. The stewardess who brought Mavis' morning tea at seven had found the cabin empty and locked. She was familiar with all of Mavis' clothes and was sure that none of them were missing except the black silk pajamas in which she slept. A discreet search of the liner had not yet located her.

The captain dismissed the mate, saying: "Tell Mr. Spiwack on the bridge that, if there's no word in ten minutes, he's to turn the ship around and retrace our course." He added to Trant: "Regulations. Naturally we'll never find her if . . ."

Trant, silent but bright-eyed, was gazing around the cabin. The bed was neatly made. The cover of the aft porthole was loose, flapping slightly back and forth. The turquoise dress in which Mavis had danced the night before was slung over a chair. There was an overpowering—even for Mavis—odor of *Tantalizing*. A glance at the dressing table showed a bottle of perfume almost empty. Intrigued, Trant traced the odor to an area by the bed where it seemed at its strongest. He dropped to his knees and observed a faint stain on the flowered carpet. It was still a trifle damp.

"Blood?" queried the captain melodramatically.

"I don't think so. Mind if I ruin the company's rug?" Without waiting for the captain's consent, Trant produced a pocket-knife and cut a small circular patch from the carpet.

The purser came in and announced: "The entire ship has been searched, sir. No trace of her."

Trant folded the piece of carpet into one of the company's envelopes, which he took from the desk, and moved to the porthole.

"The cover was this way when the stewardess brought the tea?"

"Nothing's been touched."

Trant hooked back the loose cover and studied the port. He gave a little grunt.

"Look."

At his shoulder, the captain peered. Caught on the metal edge was a scrap of black fabric.

"Black silk," said the captain, awed. "Her pajamas. So she's overboard. Suicide."

Trant put the shred of material into another envelope, feeling a cosmic pity for Mavis Marriner and all other foolish young women who reap what they sow. He also felt guilt at having had his frivolous wish of the night before so speedily granted.

"Unfortunately, it's not suicide. No girl could have squeezed herself through that porthole with the heavy cover flapping loose. Try it yourself. She couldn't have unhooked it by accident, either, as she went through."

The captain stared. "So it's murder?"

"I'm afraid it is," said Trant sadly.

But only part of him was sad. The other part was musing on Mavis Marriner's murderer as a hungry owl might muse on a mouse. . . .

At that moment the chief steward appeared with a fraught-looking middle-aged stewardess. He said to the captain: "Mrs. Kuzak, the night stewardess, has something to report, sir."

In an explosive Polish accent, Mrs. Kuzak affirmed: "Last night at one-thirty flickers the call light of Miss Marriner. I come to this cabin. I knock. Answers a man's voice: 'Is all right. Only Miss Marriner has trouble with the porthole. Now is fixed.' I said: 'Okay.' I leave."

"One-thirty." Trant watched her. "What was the voice like?"

"From a foreign land. Not of English. Heavy with accent."

The captain whistled. "She was engaged to that Frenchman."

Trant made no comment. He stepped out into the corridor and glanced at the little ledge by the cabin door. A full glass of milk stood there. He sniffed it and smelt the odor of brandy.

"Get Jimmie, the lounge steward," he said to the hovering purser. "And if he's got a cabin mate, bring him too. To save time."

The purser returned shortly, accompanied by Jimmie, who looked sleepy with ruffled blond hair, and a large dark man with tattooed forearms.

Trant said: "When did you bring the milk, Jimmie?"

"At one, sir. Like always, sir."

"Did you knock?"

"Yes, sir."

"And Miss Marriner answered?"

"Yes, sir. She told me to leave the milk on the ledge as usual and said good night, sir."

"You heard no other voice in the cabin?"

"No, sir."

"Did Miss Marriner sound at all different from usual?"

"No, sir."

"What did you do after you'd left the milk?"

"My work was over. I went to my cabin, sir."

Trant glanced at the dark cabin mate. "You check that?"

"Yes, sir. I woke up when Jimmie came in, sir. We sat a while talking."

"What time was it?"

"Just after one, sir." He glanced at a large silver watch on his tattooed wrist. "I looked at my watch when I woke up."

"Since she never came out to get the milk, her visitor must have come very soon after one. Almost certainly she was dead before one-thirty and certainly the voice Mrs. Kuzak heard was the voice of the murderer." Trant reflected. "I'm going to need an assistant, captain. Can I have Jimmie?"

"Naturally."

Trant patted Jimmie's arm. "Rout out Mr. and Mrs. Howard

and Mr. Armand Bardou. Tell them the captain wants to see them in his cabin. And use that well-known tact. . . ."

The ship was futilely retracing its course as Trant and the captain questioned the three principal suspects. Trant seemed to find the interviews boring.

Mrs. Claire Howard, a vivid red-headed ex-actress with a knife for a tongue, said:

"I'm prostrated by grief. I couldn't be sorrier if the python at the Bronx Zoo kicked the bucket."

Although she made no effort to conceal her resentment of Mavis' behavior with her husband, she was firmly alibied by the testimony of an elderly Italian prima donna who swore she had been telling Mrs. Howard's fortune in the Howard stateroom between one and one-thirty.

Larry Howard was more conventionally distressed than his wife. He fussed with his hand-painted tie, looked more like a movie idol than any of the stars on his payroll and kept repeating: "So tragic—such a lovely girl—such a talent—"

He too had what seemed like a perfect alibi. After leaving the lounge the night before, he had run into a Hollywood script writer and had spent the significant time period in the writer's cabin, discussing an idea for a supercolossal Marriner vehicle— which now would have to be tailored to suit another star. The script writer corroborated this.

After these two had apparently cleared themselves, Armand Bardou was pitifully without defense. The elegant, mournful-eyed French actor denied having been in Mavis' cabin but had absolutely no alibi. All he could say for himself was that, humiliated by his fiancée's shameless flirtation with Larry Howard, he had paced the upper deck for hours in an attempt to console himself.

"But Mavis was my heart," he announced with Gallic fervor. "You cannot accuse me of murdering my heart."

After he had gone, Trant no longer looked bored. In fact, there was a gleam of pleasurable anticipation in his eyes. The captain said: "Well, I suppose we're left with Bardou. No alibi —foreign accent."

"Foreign accents can be assumed," suggested Trant mildly. "And it's too early to talk of alibis."

"You mean we're not restricted to the suspects we've questioned? Anyone else on the boat could have killed her?"

"They could have killed her," agreed Trant, "but they didn't."

"Trant, you're not telling me you know who did."

"Oh, yes," murmured Trant with an exasperatingly casual shrug, "I've suspected it for half an hour. Now I'm sure—"

The captain, who was a long-suffering man, fell in with Trant's requests. They were simple. First the lieutenant wanted to inspect the ship's log. Having done so, he wanted to interview the three suspects individually in Mavis' cabin. While the purser went off to arrange this, Trant stationed Mrs. Kuzak, the Polish night stewardess, in the little pantry opposite the half-open door of the stateroom. He told her to listen to everything that was said in the cabin and to break in if she heard the foreign voice she had heard the night before. Once she was at her post, Trant and Jimmie went into the cabin. Trant sat down by the bed, lit a cigarette and offered one to the steward.

"Mr. Howard's coming first, Jimmie. Before he arrives, I want you to duck into the bathroom. Don't come out till I call."

"Okay, sir."

Trant's gray eyes moved to the porthole. "Jimmie, you've had plenty of experience with women crossing the Atlantic. You can help me on a point of psychology. A lot of them throw their bonnets to the sea breezes, don't they?"

Jimmie grinned. "They're apt to be in a holiday mood, sir."

"Exactly. But Mavis was different. That's the point about her. She vamped like Salome but when the time came to crash through, it's my hunch she went colder than a Pilgrim Mother."

"That's how we crew members had her summed up, sir."

"All right, Jimmie, before Mr. Howard arrives, let's assume for a moment that I'm the murderer." Trant smiled contentedly at this hypothesis. "Miss Marriner certainly hurled her all at me last night. Suppose I'd taken her up on it and come here to the cabin expecting a Big Romantic Moment. What would I have got? The old don't-touch-me-you-nasty-man. Suppose I was vain, used to easy conquests. Suppose I got rough. Suppose she rang for the stewardess. Suppose I realized what an awkward spot I'd be in if the stewardess reported an attempted assault to the captain. Say I struggled with Mavis trying to keep her from calling out when the stewardess knocked, planning to reason with her later and calm her down. O.K. The stewardess came. I invented some trouble with the porthole to explain the ring and to get rid of her. But later—after the stewardess had gone—I realized to my horror that I had been rougher than I thought. I had strangled Miss Marriner."

Trant looked meditatively at his own hands as if they were the hands of a strangler.

"There was Miss Marriner lying on the bed—dead. I hadn't intended to kill her, but it was done. I got into a panic. I thought of the porthole. Surely, if I pushed the body through the porthole, they might think it was suicide. I carried her to the port and pushed her through. But I was nervous. As I brought my hands in, I unhooked the porthole cover without noticing it. All I wanted to do was to get the heck away from the cabin as fast as I could. I hadn't been a very smart murderer, but then I hadn't planned to be a murderer at all. How's that fit, Jimmie?"

Jimmie's blue eyes had widened. "It fits, sir. But what about the foreign accent?"

"Oh, I left out a couple of details. The accent, for example— and the spilled perfume." Trant nodded to the little hole in the carpet. "The perfume's simple. There was a stain on the rug, a most incriminating stain. Although the murderer was rattled, he knew he had to remove it. He thought that perfume, with its alcoholic content, would be more effective than water so he tried to wipe it away with *Tantalizing*. I'm afraid he didn't succeed. When we reach New York, a laboratory analysis will show what it was."

"What was it, sir?"

Lieutenant Trant rose. Suddenly he seemed depressed.

"Milk," he said.

"Milk?"

"Milk and brandy brought in by the murderer. I'm afraid he

was a rather vain murderer. As the glamour boy of the *Queen Anne*, he was used to conquests. He thought that Mavis, with her 'darlings' and 'angels,' should be as much of a pushover as the others. It must have been humiliating when he came into this cabin last night as a Don Juan to find that Mavis just thought of him as a fresh steward. It was frightening, too, to know that she was going to report him to the captain. That would have meant a quick end to his career."

Jimmie sprang to his feet.

"I know what you're going to say," continued Trant quietly. "The glass of milk on the ledge outside proves that you never came into this cabin last night. Unhappily, it doesn't prove that. The ship's log reports that we ran into a violent squall last night at two. The boat rolled. In fact, it toppled the clock off my dressing table. If you'd actually left that glass of milk on the ledge at one last night, it would certainly have spilled."

He studied Jimmie with a thoughtful expression. "You put the new glass of milk there this morning. Last night's glass was spilled on the carpet in here while you struggled with Miss Marriner to keep her from calling out to the stewardess. You thought you were being clever planting the second glass on the ledge. I'm afraid your cleverness backfired.

"And I'm afraid your neat alibi can be broken too. Your cabin mate said he woke up when you came in. He woke up because you deliberately awakened him, didn't he? But before you awakened him, you switched the hands of his watch backwards. It was easy to stay awake yourself until he fell asleep again and then to turn the hands forward to the correct time."

It was painful to see Jimmie collapse under this swift, deadly attack. The young steward's ducal composure fled and with it his elegant accent. He was a frightened little mill boy again and, lapsing into a broad Yorkshire dialect, he cried:

"Yer caan't say thaat a' me, zur. She war crazed fur me. She aasked me ter coom oop. Ah didn't knaw— Ah didn't meean ter—"

Mrs. Kuzak burst into the cabin. "That's it!" she announced. "Is the same foreign voice I hear last night."

Jimmie swung to her. "Eh, wumman, ye caan't—"

"That's all we needed," interrupted Trant quietly. "People almost always revert to their natural dialect when they're rattled, Jimmie. No wonder Mrs. Kuzak thought that Yorkshire brogue of yours was a foreign accent."

He nodded the stewardess out of the cabin. Alone with Jimmie, he felt a twinge of sadness. The hunt was always exciting; the kill never so. Particularly when he was fond of the murderer.

He said: "You didn't mean to kill her. I'm sure of that and I'll do everything I can. . . . I'm sorry, Jimmie. I set a trap for you. I feel like a heel."

Jimmie had managed to turn himself into the perfect steward again. He smiled a ghost of his engaging smile.

"That's all right, sir. After all, it's your job, sir."

There were times when Lieutenant Trant took a low view of his profession.

This was one of them.

FROM DETECTIVE WHO'S WHO

TRANT, Timothy Tregaskis, police officer; b. 1914; s. T. R., M.D., and Ellen (Tregaskis) T.; Educ.: East Kent School; Princeton University, Phi Beta Kappa, Class 1935. Entered N. Y. Police Force, Homicide Division, 1935. Hobbies: Italian art; collecting neckties. Peculiarities: Sartorial elegance; fondness for murderesses. Most famous cases (chronicled by Q. Patrick): *Death for Dear Clara* (1937); *Death and the Maiden* (1939). Less complicated cases, chronicled briefly as "White Carnations" (1944); "Footlights and Murder" (1947); "Murder in One Scene" (1948); "Who Killed the Mermaid?" (1949); "Laura, Woman of Ice" (1949); several others.

Since Dashiell Hammett's Nick and Nora Charles (or even earlier, since Agatha Christie's Tommy and Tuppence Beresford), the Bright Young Couple has been a staple of detective fiction. Among the few genuinely likable and unstrained BYC's are Jeff and Haila Troy, whom you'll now meet in a prize-winning story from a recent EQMM contest, never before published in book form.

JEFF & HAILA TROY IN

Two Over Par

BY KELLEY ROOS

JEFF STEPPED BACK from teeing up my ball and handed me the family driver. I kept my head down and swung. The ball, obviously a faulty one, curved into a thicket not far away. Jeff teed his ball, kept his head down, and swung. His ball sliced into the same thicket. The Troys, as they say around the club, were in the rough.

"Are you sure," I said, "that you're really supposed to keep your head down?"

"I don't know," Jeff said dismally. "But I couldn't raise mine now even if I wanted to. I'm too ashamed."

"Those are our last two balls."

"Yeah." Jeff picked up our bag, slung it over his shoulder. "If we didn't spend so much money on balls we could afford a caddy."

"Couldn't we alternate? Hire a caddy one day, use balls the next?"

"Women," Jeff said, "shouldn't be allowed on a golf course."

We trudged toward the thicket and plunged into it. We separated and began looking for our balls. It wasn't very interesting work. Perhaps I had done too much of it in this week since we had taken up golf. I kicked aimlessly at the thick grass as I walked around, I—

"Jeff!"

"Did you find your ball?" Jeff yelled.

"No," I said. "No, I—I found a caddy!"

Then Jeff was at my side. He saw what I had seen. He crouched down beside the young man, reaching for his wrist. But he didn't test his pulse; he didn't need to. As Jeff touched the arm, the body rolled onto its back and we saw the bullet hole in Eddie Riorden's head.

I turned away. "I'll go back to the clubhouse. I'll phone—"

"Wait," Jeff said.

He moved deeper into the thicket. I had taken one step after him when he stopped. I saw his shoulders go rigid. Then he turned and came back to me.

He took me by the arm and led me out onto the fairway.

"Jeff," I said, "what is it? What did you see?"

"Eddie was caddying for Mrs. Carleton."

"For Mrs.— Oh," I said.

"Yes. Just like Eddie. Shot through the head."

I NEVER got it straight just what Joe Hinkle's official title was—chief of police, sheriff, constable, what? But when murder was committed at the Ocean Country Club on Long Island, Joe Hinkle was the man who represented the law. He was a pleasant, large-faced man. He seemed a little put out that there had been two murders; he seemed to feel that somebody had overdone it.

Joe talked to Jeff and me in a private dining room off the club's bar. He kept looking over our heads toward the bar. I got the impression that Joe would have liked to forget the whole thing and have a drink, then another, followed by a few more—even though it was still only nine-thirty in the morning.

Joe Hinkle sighed and put the palms of his hands on the bare dining table. He looked at us.

"You found the bodies," he said.

"We're sorry," Jeff said.

"That's all right." The policeman sighed again. "If you hadn't somebody else would have. You two play golf pretty early in the morning."

"We're self-conscious about our golf," I explained.

"Was there anyone else on the course while you were playing?"

"We didn't see anyone," I said.

"What difference would that make?" Jeff asked. "It looked to me as though Mrs. Carleton and Eddie had been lying there all night long."

"Yeah, that's right," Joe said. "Doc Grandle says they been dead about twelve hours or so. That's what I figure, too. It get dark around nine these nights. So Mrs. Carleton was playing her round of golf some time before then. I expect to set the time of the shooting pretty close by asking questions around the club. wish whoever did it would confess."

"I wouldn't bank on that," Jeff said.

"No, I guess I shouldn't. If I killed two people, I wouldn't admit it." Joe slouched down in his chair and closed his eyes. "Mrs Carleton and Eddie Riorden—who would have a motive to kil them two? I figure nobody would. I figure that the killer sho Eddie, then had to shoot Mrs. Carleton, too, because she was a witness to Eddie's murder. Or vice versa. By that I mean, there i the alternative that Mrs. Carleton was the intended victim, and Eddie the innocent bystander. How does that sound to you Troy?"

"Logical," Jeff said.

"I'm glad to hear you say that. You've had some experienc with murder cases, I understand."

"A little," Jeff admitted.

"Well, that's more than I've had. Thank the Lord."

Jeff said, "Did you find anything interesting in that thicket?"

"We found Eddie's cap. And Mrs. Carleton's golf bag. That' about all so far."

"You must have found a lot of balls. Mrs. Carleton and Haila and I aren't the only ones with a slice around here."

"You're right. We did find some balls." Hinkle extracted three balls from his jacket pocket and rolled them across the table to Jeff. "Maybe one of them belongs to you."

"This one is Haila's. Mine isn't here." Jeff looked closely at the third one. "This ball's monogrammed. L.K."

"Yeah, probably Louis Kling. I'll see he gets it. All Mrs. Carleton's balls are initialed, too—J.T.C. We found two of them in her bag, still wrapped in tissue paper."

Jeff said, "You didn't find the ball she was playing with?"

"Not yet. We haven't had much time to do any real looking around in that thicket. I'm having the place roped off for a hundred yards around the spot the bodies were. I plan to have the boys go through it with a fine-comb."

"That's the idea," Jeff said. "With a fine-comb."

"I hope we find more than a bunch of golf balls." Hinkle heaved another of his sighs. "I wish we'd find a gun with the killer's fingerprints on it. I'd like that—that'd be nice, wouldn't it?"

"It would even be rather surprising," Jeff said. "Did you know Eddie Riorden?"

"Sure. Everybody knew Eddie. He was our high school football hero four of five years ago. Eddie must be about twenty-two now and as far as I know he never did a lick of work except enough to keep him in cigarette money. Caddying, pin boy—that kind of stuff. Nice kid, though, just lazy. Well, I got to go over and talk to Mrs. Carleton's husband. I want to get that over with. If there's anything you can do for me, Troy, I'll let you know."

"Thanks," Jeff said.

Jeff and I walked back to the cottage that was teaching us never again to rent a cottage for the summer. Automatically, with our minds still in a thicket on a golf course, we started on our morning chores. I made the bed while Jeff put fresh adhesive tape on the screen door. Jeff tried to talk the hot-water heater into justifying its existence while I spray-gunned the joint. I was about to start my daily campaign against the ants in the icebox when the girl slammed into the house.

"I'm Fran Leslie," she said. "Where's your husband?"

"Jeff!" I yelled.

I had seen Fran Leslie around the club. She was a pretty girl, in a rather wild, excited way, who seemed continually to be in motion. I finally realized the reason for it. Fran considered herself too sophisticated for the younger set, but she found the older set a bit stuffy. So she spent most of her time shuttling between sets. This, however, seemed to be good for her figure. It was, in fact, developed far beyond her mind.

Impatiently, she said, "This is terribly important!"

I shouted for Jeff again. He came into the room, saw Fran Leslie inside our cottage, then looked at the screen door as if he were reproaching himself for having put adhesive tape in the wrong places.

"Hello," he said.

"Mr. Troy!" Fran said. "How much do you charge?"

"Different prices," Jeff said. "Three dollars for fixing a flat, five for taking down an old Christmas tree, six—"

"I mean for your services as a detective!"

"Is it you who needs a detective?" Jeff asked.

"Yes."

"Why?"

"Because I'm going to be arrested for killing Janet Carleton, that's why! You've got to save me, Mr. Troy. I didn't kill Janet— or that caddy, either; but everyone on Long Island has thought for years that some day I would—kill Janet, I mean."

"Sit down, Miss Leslie," Jeff suggested.

"Please, Mr. Troy!" Fran turned to me in exasperation. "I'm practically on my way to the electric chair, and the man asks me to sit down!"

"All right," Jeff said. "What's your motive?"

"Oh, I've got one—and a jury would just eat it up! I wouldn't stand a chance. Janet stole the man I love. I've been insanely jealous for ages."

"A fairly good motive," Jeff said unenthusiastically. "The man you love is Mr. Carleton?"

"Yes. Tom Carleton. Tom's always been my man, if you know what I mean. Then, four years ago, Janet came along—glamorous, exciting, beautiful Janet! You can see how much I hate her! She took Tom. He never looked at me again."

"Fran," Jeff said, "how old are you?"

"Seventeen. Why?"

"Then Janet took Tom Carleton away from you when you were thirteen."

"Yes! That's how ruthless she was! She knew Tom and I couldn't get married right away and—"

"I suppose," Jeff said, "that your parents insisted you finish grammar school first."

"I knew that I would mature quickly," Fran said. She threw back her shoulders to prove it, and she did prove it. Jeff modestly lowered his eyes. "Tom is only twelve years older than I am," she said, "and we have so much in common."

"What?"

"Well, for one thing—"

"Go on," Jeff said.

"Well, for one thing, we both belong to the Country Club."

"Oh," Jeff said. "Frannie, could you see it in Tom's eyes that some day he would marry you?"

"He would have married me, he would have!" Fran cried. "And I've wanted to kill Janet for years! Everybody knows that! Mr. Troy, you've got to save me by finding the real murderer. I'll give you five hundred dollars!"

"Frannie, why don't you go to a movie or something?"

"If you won't take this case, you know what I'll do? I'll—"

"Stop," Jeff said. "Don't even tell me what you'll do. I'll take the case. I'll try to prove, Frannie, that you didn't commit two murders."

"Oh, thank you so much!"

"Good-by, Frannie," Jeff said.

She pouted. "Aren't you going to ask me about my alibi?"

"All right. Where were you at the time of the crime?"

"I was walking on the beach, alone."

"Did anybody see you?"

"Not a soul!" Frannie said happily. "I absolutely cannot prove that it wasn't me who committed those murders! I have no alibi!"

"Good-by, Frannie," Jeff said sternly.

A little later I asked Jeff if he really meant to take Fran's five hundred dollars. He thought that he might as well. She would probably just spend it on bubble gum. I told him I thought that he was underestimating a woman of seventeen. At seventeen a woman has all her faculties; that is, she's a woman. He said he agreed with me but, he said, let's not discuss this any further, let's go and see Mrs. Carleton's husband, Tom.

We found Tom Carleton sitting on the steps of the side porch of his big, year-round house. The fears we had that he might rather see us at some later time he quickly dispelled. He needed someone to talk with, someone, preferably, who was not a friend of the family paying a duty call. We filled his need admirably, he insisted.

He said, "Joe Hinkle told me about you. He's glad you're around. Shall we sit here on the steps? Or would you rather—"

"This is fine," Jeff said.

We sat down with Carleton. He was lean and tall and very attractive in a strong, rugged way. The wrinkles of good humor and laughter stood out now in his pale, somber face like tiny, drained stream-beds. He was in complete control of himself. It would be he who would console his wife's friends, not they him.

"I might have prevented it," he said.

Jeff said, "Almost anybody can always figure out that they—"

"No," Tom said, "this is real. You see, I haven't played much golf this year—in the past month none at all. I just went sour on it. Yesterday Janet tried to talk me into playing a round with her before dinner. We used to do that all the time. But I said no, and I wouldn't let her talk me into it. To tell the truth, she got pretty sore about it, in her funny way. Humorous way, I mean. She made some remarks about me and my fishing and fish in general that were classics. Lately, you see, I'd rather fish than golf. So Janet went to the club alone. When she didn't come back for dinner I didn't think anything of it. She often stayed at the club, especially when she was a little sore at me. I went to bed about nine. To get to Montauk Point for fishing by five, I have to be on my way at four. So I slept in my study—as I always do when I'm getting up early and don't want to waken Janet when I roll out of bed. That's how I got out of the house this morning without knowing she wasn't at home. I'd left my car in front of the house; I took for granted that Janet's was in the garage. But what I started to say was . . . if I'd played golf with her as she wanted me to . . . but I see your point, Troy. It's no good—that kind of figuring."

"I don't suppose," Jeff said, "you've had any time to think about who might have killed your wife."

"Yes, I have. It doesn't take very many minutes to do a lot of thinking about a thing like that. Nobody could have wanted to kill Janet, no one had any reason to. Nobody had anything to gain in the way of money or anything. And as far as anyone hating her—well, Janet lived an ordinary, suburban life. You don't make enemies living like that. She ran the house, she played golf in the summer, bridge in the winter—she never did anything that would have made an enemy for her."

"What about Fran Leslie?"

Tom Carleton looked at Jeff and smiled wanly. "I think," he said, "that's a foolish question."

"So do I, but I had to know that you thought so, too."

"Frannie's been an embarrassment to me for years. I realize that you should take adolescents and their emotions seriously. But Frannie—there's nothing deep or psychological about her. She's a good, healthy extrovert. I spanked her when she was fourteen and if she hadn't enjoyed it so much, I would have kept on spanking her. No, Troy, nobody wanted to kill my wife."

"I think," Jeff said, "I know what you mean."

"Yes. I mean that someone must have been gunning for Eddie Riorden. And Janet was killed because she saw who murdered Eddie."

"Do you know where Eddie lived?"

"No. But the caddy master at the club would know."

"We'll ask him—and thanks."

JAMESTOWN, Long Island, was as Colonial American as anything you saw on the way to Boston. There was a white church, a cannon in the square, a Town Hall beside the Super-Market. The Riorden house was on the edge of the town—a two-story frame building, a yard without a lawn in front of it, a collection of shabby sheds and coops behind it. Eddie's sister answered Jeff's knock. She was a little younger than Eddie, a beautiful girl with shining black hair, dark eyes, an appealing mouth. There was no doubt she was Eddie's sister.

Jeff said, "We'd like to talk to you about Eddie—for just a moment."

"Are you from the police?" She looked at me. "Or a newspaper . . . or what?"

"We're working with the police," Jeff said.

"I suppose you want to know who Eddie ran around with . . . things like that?"

"Yes."

"I'll have to tell you what I told the rest of them. We don't know. We hardly knew Eddie any more. He wasn't ever home, except to sleep. He just—well, drifted away from us lately. We didn't see him much, he never brought any of his friends home."

"Who were his friends?"

She shook her head. "I don't even know if there was anyone special. I—I don't like to say this, but it's true. Except for the country club in the summer, Eddie spent more time in Andrew's Bar than he did at home. I wish I could help you, but . . ."

"You have helped us," Jeff said.

Andrew's Bar took up half the ground floor of a tourist hotel that apparently had never lived up to its original owner's hopes. There were only three cars in the parking space meant for twenty or thirty. The bar was not filled with vacationists sopping up before-lunch cocktails; four male natives were spending dimes on beers.

When the bartender placed our beers before us, Jeff said, "My name's Troy, I—"

"Troy," the bartender said. He glanced down at his group of our customers. They all looked at Jeff. "Troy," the bartender said again. "I've heard about you. You're helping Joe Hinkle with he murders."

"Yes," Jeff said. "News travels fast around here."

"Yes, it does. A little place, Jamestown, but a nice place."

The tallest of the four beer drinkers said, "We've just been alking about it, the murder."

"I guess you all knew Eddie," Jeff said.

"He was in here every night," the shortest drinker said.

"He missed once a week," the third one said. "The night of he midget auto races."

"He came in then. Late, though," Shorty said.

The third one nodded. "After I went home, I guess."

"Well, more or less you could just about say," the bartender aid, "that Eddie was in here every night." He turned to Jeff. 'What's that got to do with the murder?"

"You've just been talking about the murder," Jeff said.

"Naturally," the bartender said.

"Eddie was a popular boy, wasn't he?"

"He was a sweet kid," Shorty said.

"A sweet kid," the third man said. "A great ball player, any ind of ball. He was going to go places if he ever got a break. He ad everything to live for."

"Everybody liked Eddie, I guess," Jeff said.

A moment died away. Then, carefully, the bartender said, Yeah, everybody liked Eddie. I can't think of a single exception o that rule."

For the first time the fourth man spoke up, and he spoke up ngrily. "The hell with it!" he said. "I can think of somebody vho didn't like Eddie!"

"Now, wait, Mel," the bartender said. "Take it easy."

"The hell with it!" Mel said. "Listen here, Troy. George Carey lidn't like Eddie and everybody here knows it!"

"George Carey," Jeff said. "You mean the golf pro at the Country Club?"

"That's right. I've no idea what it was between Carey and Eddie, but—"

"Mel," the bartender said, "I'm not sure it's up to you to—"

"Eddie's dead, murdered! Listen, Troy, for the past month or so Carey used to come in here—to see Eddie. They'd go back there to the corner table and talk—no, not talk, argue! We never could hear what it was all about and Eddie would never tell us, but it wasn't good. They got pretty hot, the two of them, Eddie and Carey. Well, the other night was the blow-up. For a minute it looked like they were going to start swinging at each other. When Carey went out of here he looked just about mad enough to—"

"Now, take it easy, Mel," the bartender said.

"Mad enough," Jeff said, "to kill Eddie?"

"Yes, blast it! That's what I was going to say and I am saying it! Mad enough to kill Eddie! And Eddie was killed."

WE HAD seen George Carey around the club, of course, but we had never said more than hello to each other. He was a genial, nice-looking fellow in his forties. When Jeff and I walked into his little office in the caddy house, he knew at once why we were calling on him. He wasn't the sort of person you had to handle with care, and Jeff went straight to the point.

"We've just come from Andrew's Bar," Jeff said. "We heard that you and Eddie Riorden nearly slugged it out a couple of nights ago. We didn't hear what it was you disagreed about—or maybe that isn't important."

Carey thought that over for a moment. "It is important," he said, "because I'm sure you're not going to find anyone else, anyone at all, who ever tangled with Eddie in the slightest degree."

"Everybody loved Eddie," Jeff said. "He hadn't an enemy in the world."

"That's true—literally."

"But the other night you were ready to take him apart. That could mean that Eddie had one enemy in the world."

"Yes," Carey said. "That's why it's important you understand why I was fighting with Eddie."

He opened a drawer of his desk; he found what he was looking for. He slid the letter out of its envelope and handed it to Jeff. Jeff held it so that I could see.

It was a short note, written without the aid of a secretary, on the stationery of Randall College, Randall, Ohio. It said: "Dear George; I've got everything set for your boy, Eddie Riorden. He'd better be as good as you say he is. In haste, Carl."

"That's Carl Moss," Carey said. "He coaches football at Randall."

"He got Eddie an athletic scholarship," Jeff said.

"Yes."

"But Eddie didn't want to go to college," Jeff said. "No matter how much you tried to persuade him, he wouldn't agree to go."

"That's it," Carey said. "I've known Eddie since he was caddying up here in his bare feet. He was quite a kid. He was the best high school athlete I've ever seen. For the last three years I've been after him to go to college. But he was tired of school, he said. Actually, he was lazy. I'm afraid Eddie was well on his way to being a bum. I decided finally to go ahead and get him a scholarship at my old school . . . I thought maybe that would turn the trick. But it didn't. Eddie'd been slopping around for so long that his ambition was all gone. He used to avoid me here at the club. The only place I could corner him was at that bar. I talked myself hoarse to him, and the other night I lost my temper. It made me sore to see a boy like Eddie turning into a bum."

"But you still liked him," Jeff said.

"How could I help it? How could anybody not like Eddie?"

"Well," Jeff said, "I guess that's that."

"Even if it isn't," Carey said, "I'll have to leave you now. Joe Hinkle seems to be holding a little meeting that I'm invited to."

"We'll go with you," Jeff said.

Hinkle was holding his meeting in the same room where we had seen him that morning. The meeting was a small, intimate affair. Carey, Jeff, and I joined Hinkle, Fran Leslie, Tom Carleton, and the club's woman champ, Arlene Miller. The meeting didn't look as though it had started; Joe Hinkle didn't look as though he wanted to start it. He was a morose, discouraged man.

"Troy," he said, "tell me something."

"Sure," Jeff said.

"Tell me who killed them. So we can all go home."

"I know how you feel," Jeff said. "Did you find anything more in the thicket?"

"We found a lot. The two halves of a broken niblick, some empty bottles—mostly half-pints—a couple of old tin cans, a dozen or so tees, a watch that Mac Small lost seven years ago, a fifty-cent piece, and nine golf balls."

"Did you find Mrs. Carleton's ball?"

"Not yet. We had to knock off because it was getting dark in the thicket. But, frankly, I think we found everything there is in it."

"But of course," Jeff said, "you'll look some more tomorrow."

"Of course. I'm nothing else, but I'm thorough."

"Mr. Carleton," Jeff said, "is there any chance that Mrs. Carleton wouldn't have been playing with one of her own balls?"

Arlene Miller gave a short laugh. She said, "Janet Carleton would no more think of using any ball but those special ones of hers than she would think of using someone else's clubs. Janet was a real golfer, not a Sunday player."

"I see," Jeff said. He turned back to Hinkle. "Have you found anyone who saw Mrs. Carleton playing her first nine holes?"

"Her last nine holes," Arlene Miller said.

Hinkle cleared his throat. "I been all through that, Troy. Mr. Carleton says that, considering the time his wife left home, she would have been lucky to get much more than nine holes played before dark. It seems like she was the last one to start around. Nobody seen her park her car or tee off."

"That isn't unusual," Carey said. "At that time of day everybody at the club is either in the dining room or the bar. There's as much drinking as golf around this place, you all know that."

"Anyway," Hinkle said, "nobody saw her. She must have walked straight from her car to the first tee, or whatever you call it. Eddie must have met her there. He always caddied for her. He was probably waiting for her."

"Somebody," Jeff said, "the last person who left the club last night must have noticed Mrs. Carleton's car was still here. Why didn't they worry about her?"

"That was Al Frost," Hinkle said. "He admits seeing the car. He also admits that after an evening at the bar here he never worries or wonders about anything. Nice fellow though, Al."

"Well," Jeff said, "I won't hold up your meeting any longer."

"I wish you'd stay, Troy."

"No, I couldn't add anything to the proceedings. Call me to-morrow, will you, if you find Mrs. Carleton's ball?"

"Why don't you come and help us?"

"I will," Jeff said.

It was beginning to grow dark when Jeff and I left our cottage that night. It was very dark when we walked through the empty parking lot of the locked-up, deserted clubhouse. I followed Jeff through the gap in the hedge, then I stopped.

"Darling," I said, "I won't go another step until you tell me where we're going and why."

"Haila, if I told you, you wouldn't go with me. Come on now, quietly."

I went on, quietly. We walked across the start of the fairway of the first hole. We went another fifty yards and we were crossing the ninth hole's fairway. Then, in another minute or two, we were groping our way into the thicket. I could touch Jeff, but I couldn't see him. I held on to his jacket and shuffled blindly forward. Jeff stopped and sat down; he pulled me down beside him. He put his arm around me. But he didn't kiss me. I still didn't know what we were doing in this hell-black hole.

"May I smoke?" I whispered.

"No. From now on don't even breathe unless it's absolutely necessary."

We sat there for so long that I began to be convinced that I had slept through a day and was now sitting through my second night. I was uncomfortable, cold. I was something else. I found Jeff's ear and whispered into it.

"I'm scared," I said.

"Naturally," Jeff whispered back.

That reassurance did me a lot of good. I wasn't cold any longer, or uncomfortable—I was just frightened. Jeff's hand touched my wrist and tightened on it. I stopped breathing. I had heard it, too.

Through the thicket something was moving toward us. It might have been slithering along on its stomach, it might have been edging along on two feet, or more—but it was coming toward us. Now a piece of foliage brushed my face as it moved back in place. The shuffling sound came closer, and then stopped.

I felt Jeff move. I heard the click of his flashlight and saw a beam of light shoot through the blackness. For a moment it searched wildly, then it hit and held. I saw a man's outstretched arm, his hand six inches above the ground. Clutched in the hand was a golf ball.

Jeff pulled the light up the man's arm until it flashed full in his face. Tom Carleton straightened up. I saw his arm back out of the ray of light, then swing forward through it. . . .

WHEN people regain consciousness, they usually start life again by asking a silly question. My question didn't seem silly to me at the time, but that's exactly what it turned out to be. I looked at Jeff and Joe Hinkle for a moment before I spoke.

I said, "How could Tom Carleton find his wife's golf ball in the dark like that?"

"He didn't find it," Jeff said. "He was losing it."

"Oh," I said. "Where am I?"

"In our cottage," Jeff said.

"Where is Tom Carleton?"

"In my jail," Joe Hinkle said. "Are you all right, Mrs. Troy? He hit you with a golf ball, you know."

"Yes, I know, Mr. Hinkle. But I'm fine. That's just what I needed."

"Well, then, Troy—"

"Sure, Joe, listen. You and your boys couldn't find that ball—because there was no ball. There was no ball because Mrs. Carleton wasn't playing golf. Eddie Riorden was not her caddy—he was her lover."

"Eddie and Mrs. Carleton . . ."

"That thicket was their rendezvous. If anyone had wandered into it unexpectedly, Eddie would have gone through the motions of caddying for a lady with a bad slice. It was a nice setup while it lasted. And it lasted until Tom Carleton got wise."

"So I was wrong," Joe said, "when I figured that one of them got killed because he saw the other one murdered."

"Everybody liked Mrs. Carleton," Jeff said. "Everybody loved Eddie. Nobody had a reason to kill either of them. But maybe, I thought, somebody had a reason to kill both of them. And then, when you couldn't find the ball Janet Carleton should have been playing with . . ."

"Yeah," Joe said. "I guess that proved it to you. And when Tom heard you talking about the ball this afternoon, he figured he'd better get one there in a hurry."

"Oh, now I see," I said. "He didn't find that ball. He was putting it there."

"That's right. I'm sorry he hit you with it, Haila."

"Oh, I don't mind. That's a hazard of the game, getting hit. But I don't think it was very sporting the way he did it."

"What, darling?"

"It's a rule, Jeff! You're supposed to yell 'Fore!' "

FROM DETECTIVE WHO'S WHO

TROY, Haila Rogers, housewife; b. Columbus, Ohio, Oct. 4, 1919; d. Whitney and Mildred (Atkins) R.; grad., Nightingale-Thompson Sch. for Girls, 1938; m. Jeff Troy, Nov. 23, 1941. Jobs: Acted in touring company, *You Can't Take It With You;* New York companies, *January Thaw, Green Apples;* photographic modeling. Member: Actors Equity Association; Twelfth Night Club. Res.: 39 Gay St., N. Y.

TROY, Jeff, photographer; b. Niagara Falls, N. Y., May 25, 1916; s. Albert and Robin (Simpson) T.; grad., Boston Latin Sch., 1934; Dartmouth College, 1938. m. Haila Rogers, Nov. 23, 1942. Jobs: Good Humor Company; Fuller Brush Company; Standard Oil Service Station; Thomas Advertising Agency; Photo-Arts, Inc. Member: Betty Grable Fan Club. Address: 39 Gay St., N. Y. C.

One of the first and still one of the best of spinster sleuths, *Miss Hildegarde Withers* saw her shorter exploits collected three years ago in the notable The Riddles of Hildegarde Withers—a paper-backed book already almost as scarce a collector's item as her own book of poems, All That Glisters ("attractive slim volume"—Pasadena Star-News). This later episode, not included in the collected riddles, offers one of the most ingenious clues that even Hildegarde ever encountered.

HILDEGARDE WITHERS IN

The Riddle of the Tired Bullet

BY STUART PALMER

"Oops, EXCUSE ME!" Like a ruffled Buff Orpington, Miss Hildegarde Withers backed hastily out of the inspector's private office, where she had just surprised him in the embrace of a pretty red-head.

The spinster schoolma'am was deeply engrossed in a study of some old "Wanted for Murder" posters on the wall when Oscar Piper finally emerged to usher his fair visitor toward the corridor. She was thanking him effusively in a weak, brave voice. "And I'll take your advice, inspector."

When the tap of her heels had died away, the inspector came back toward Miss Withers, mopping his brow sheepishly. "Women!" he sighed.

Her sniff was pointed. "And at your age, too."

"And why not?" His Irish flared up. "You're jealous, maybe?"

Copyright 1947 by The American Mercury, Inc. Reprinted with the permission of the author and *Ellery Queen's Mystery Magazine*.

"For some years," the schoolteacher told him gently, "my interest in you has been purely academic. I barely noticed the woman, except to see that she has suspiciously red-brown hair and that she was wearing a last-year's suit made over at home. Not exactly young, but still pretty if you like the type." Miss Withers paused for breath, and then noticed that the inspector had turned back into his inner office. She rushed after him so fast that her hat, which resembled a bon-voyage basket a day after sailing, slid rakishly over one eye. "Wait, Oscar! Is it a new murder case?"

Oscar Piper poked painstakingly through his ashtray for a cigar butt recent enough to bear relighting. "Not yet it isn't," he admitted. "But the little lady was crying on my shoulder because she thinks she's going to be a widow."

"Something she dreamed, no doubt. Or is it astrology?"

"More to it than that. I had to agree with her that Ernest Hawkins is The Man of the Week Most Likely to Decorate a Marble Slab. Don't you recognize the name? Well, you'll be hearing more about him. Hawkins was secretary to old Amos Bigelow, ex-Senator Bigelow, of the Bigelow Buddy Fund Committee."

"But of course. They set out to raise money to send packages to the men in the armed forces, during the last year of the war. I was even asked to help them solicit, but the Gray Ladies work took up my spare time."

"Just as well. The Committee never got around to announcing how many packages ever got to the boys in uniform. The grand jury started to investigate them last week, and Hawkins blew the lid off when he promised to testify, under a promise of personal immunity."

"A tattle-tale, eh?"

"None of your brats down at P.S. 38 are in his class, though. He did the stool-pigeon act up brown, dragging in a lot of supposedly important citizens. He also admitted that fifteen or twenty thousand dollars of the money stuck to his own fingers, but he claims he dribbled it away in the night clubs and gambling."

"Fast women and slow horses, no doubt?"

"Yeh. He even named the bookie who took his bets, so now a tough Broadway character known as Track-odds Louie is out of business and under indictment. Which makes a sizable group of people who would like to cut Mr. Hawkins's throat."

"Oscar, something must be done at once!" Miss Withers nodded. "Think of his poor little wife."

"You think of her. Rena ought to be able to take care of herself—she used to be a tap dancer around the Fifty-second Street spots before she married Hawkins and settled down. I told her that she ought to go home and look up a good private detective agency in the phone book if she wanted protection—the homicide bureau is only interested in murders after they've happened."

Miss Withers stood up suddenly. "But Oscar, you're like a doctor who doesn't try to cure his patient because he's so interested in how the autopsy comes out!"

"Now, my dear Hildegarde—"

"I'm not your dear anything. If you'll excuse me, I think I'll break our date for dinner and the movies tonight. I prefer the company of my tank full of tropical fish—they're so much warmer-blooded!" And she flounced out of the office.

In spite of what she had said, Miss Withers had no time for her aquarium and its miniature jeweled fish that evening. She dined very sketchily on what she would have called "cold nothings" out of the refrigerator, and then went out to sit through most of a double feature. But somehow between her and the screen drama there kept popping up the figure of little Rena Hawkins, who knew that her husband was going to be killed. "It's as bad as King Charles' head," Miss Withers murmured. The woman beside her turned blankly. "*David Copperfield*, by Dickens," the schoolteacher explained, and then fled in the midst of a chorus of annoyed hisses.

It was after ten o'clock, and she knew that she ought to go home and mind her own business. But somehow she was impelled to hurry through the drizzling rain to the nearest telephone booth, and then down into the bowels of the subway.

The house, when she finally located it on the wrong street in the wrong part of Queens, was a narrow three-story brick, stuck between a chain grocery and a used-car lot. It was dark and quiet, so quiet that the ringing of the doorbell under her thumb made the schoolteacher jump. But nobody answered, in spite of her repeated ringing.

Miss Withers went down the steps, hesitated a moment, and then picked her way back toward the alley, past the rusting heaps of unsold and unsalable automobiles. From the rear the residence of the Hawkins family was even less attractive than from the front, and she paused to thank her lucky stars that she had never been inveigled, in her early days, into matrimony and a life amid these drab surroundings.

There was, however, one sign of life here—from a third-floor window a lace curtain fluttered in the breeze and a soft light was shining. Someone must be at home, after all. Well, she had come miles and miles to bring aid and friendly counsel to a fellow human being in desperate straits, and she was determined to make delivery.

She turned in through the creaking back gate, past the looming bulk of ashcans, garbage containers, abandoned summer furniture and sagging clotheslines. The rain splattered on rusting tin and there were other sounds, like soft scurrying feet, which she tried not to hear. Hurrying a little, Miss Withers went up the steps and knocked on the door. There was no answer, nor had she expected any. Neither had she expected the door to swing silently inward.

In a way it was an invitation, like the bottle in *Alice* with the label on it that said "Drink Me." So she entered on tiptoe, and then jumped as the door closed quickly behind her. The beam of a flashlight caught and held her impaled. "Hel-lo!" cried a man's high nervous tenor. Then the kitchen light was turned on, and she blinked at a beefy, curly-haired man in his shirt-sleeves and stocking feet, an athlete just beginning to run to fat. There was the strap of a shoulder holster across his chest, and in his fist a businesslike revolver. He looked jittery, competent, and—finally, puzzled.

Miss Withers heard her voice, breathlessly explaining that she had only come with the best of intentions and that if he would only dial headquarters instead of shooting, why somebody would vouch for her, and if he himself was Mr. Hawkins then—

The man with the gun relaxed just a little. "Mr. Hawkins is asleep upstairs," he said, in a tone which plainly indicated that all other respectable citizens should be likewise. "And so is his missus. My name is Johnny Brannigan, from the Onyx Agency on Fourteenth Street."

"A private eye!" she cried impulsively.

"A *what?*" Brannigan stared at his prisoner with growing distaste. "Lady, you got a bad case of too many movie thrillers. I'm just an ex-cop that got out of the marines a couple months ago and come back to help start up a new private agency. My job is to see nothing happens to Ernest Hawkins."

"I'm sure you are competent, but—" Miss Withers shook her head. "I learned about the situation quite by accident and got so worried that I just couldn't stay away. But nobody answered the door—"

He sighed. "Lady, would you answer a doorbell if you were in my shoes?" He caught her glance, and flushed slightly. "Anyway, I heard you out front. I heard you coming around to the back, so I left the door open and got ready—"

"So I see. And now that I'm here, could I have a word with Mr. Hawkins?"

"They both turned in for the night, lady. It's almost eleven o'clock, and I got orders not to bother them. They're paying me fifteen bucks a day and expenses to carry out orders."

"Of course. But—"

"Look," said Brannigan, with sarcastic patience. "Let's settle it this way. You leave me do my job, and you get back on your broomstick and fly away home, huh?" He held the door invitingly open.

She had no choice but to flounce out into the night and the rain, angry as a boil. But the anger was mostly at herself, for getting into a ridiculous situation. "Men!" she muttered, as she picked her way toward the alley. Then all of a sudden the night exploded, and she was paralyzed by a blinding light and a racking roar of sound, which turned out to be nothing more than a suburban train swinging around the curve of the railway embankment, which bordered the alley on the far side, a dike of dirt and cinders as high as the telephone poles.

"My nerves!" protested Miss Withers. Then she stopped, and looked up at that lighted window. It was odd that a frightened man would lie in a room with an open window and a fluttering curtain. The curtain must be soaked with rain, too. The schoolteacher took a deep breath and then began to pick her way up the steep side of the embankment, at considerable damage to her dignity, her shoes, and her gloves. But she finally made it, and then turned to look directly into the lighted window. She stood still for a long moment, and then started headlong down. . . .

Across the street from headquarters stands the Criminal Courts Building, one wing of which is devoted to the activities of the district attorney. In a reception room, furnished with uncomfortable modern chairs and decorated with photographs of municipal projects, six people were waiting—six nervous, unhappy persons guarded by an impersonal policeman.

Though the members of the group did not know it, they were at the moment being carefully studied through a one-way mirror set in the wall of Assistant D.A. Tom Minor's office. Minor himself was uneasier than any of them. "I still think we've overplayed our hand," he was saying. "These people are big shots, and they can make a lot of trouble."

"I'm used to trouble," Inspector Piper told him. "Who is which?"

"The old man with the jowls and the flowing hair is ex-Senator Bigelow, professional do-gooder. The hag in mink and pearls is the actress, Maylah Raymond, who used to have Diamond Jim Brady drink orange juice out of her slipper back when she was the toast of Broadway. The fat man in tweeds is General Hector Fleming, National Guard, formerly a famous armchair hero. The tall guy with the lovely gray toupee is Waldemar Hull, world-traveler, author, and lecturer at women's clubs. Facing him is

Matthew Gruber, used to be legal counsel for the Watch and Ward Society up in Boston. They say he has the world's finest collection of pornography. That's the entire Bigelow Committee. . . ."

"What about the headwaiter with the big cigar, sitting all by himself?"

"Louis Margolis, the bookmaker. They say he has twenty dinner jackets."

"He may trade 'em for prison gray," Piper said. "Well, Tom, which is your candidate? Who looks like a potential murderer?"

Minor hesitated. "Well, now, inspector . . . this was your idea, not ours."

"Okay." Piper looked at his watch. "Five of eleven. Not bad work, considering the order to pick 'em up didn't go out until ten. Come on, let's give 'em the business."

A moment later they faced the group and Tom Minor cleared his throat apologetically. "Ladies and gentlemen," he began, "you have been asked to come down here—"

"Asked!" shrieked Maylah Raymond. "I was dragged!"

Minor held up his hand. "—to come down here in connection with certain threats said to have been made against the life of one Ernest Hawkins." Behind him the door opened and a uniformed man came in to hand a teletype to Piper, but the assistant D.A. did not notice it. "You will be allowed to return home very shortly, as soon as you have put up a peace bond. But first I want to introduce you to a gentleman who has a few words to say. Inspector Oscar Piper, of homicide. . . ."

Minor paused, and waved his hand. He felt a crumpled sheet of paper shoved into his sweating fingers, and heard the door slam. Then he too read the message, and gulped. "The—the inspector asks me to apologize for him," he continued automatically. "He's just been called to take over the investigation into the murder of Ernest Hawkins. *Hawkins!*" he repeated, staring blankly at the six people who had every reason in the world to want that name on a tombstone. And they all stared back at him. Somebody in the room—was it Margolis the bookmaker?—let go a long, heartfelt sigh.

By THE time the inspector reached the Hawkins house, the complex machinery of homicide investigation was already whirring. The place was blazing with lights, and everywhere detectives, uniformed officers, ballistics, fingerprint and cameramen scurried like ants in a disturbed ant-hill. It was a picture to bring satisfaction to the heart of any homicide squad skipper, with only one jarring note—the gaunt and unhappy figure which rose to greet him on the front porch.

"Oscar!" cried Miss Hildegarde Withers. "They won't even let me inside, and I'm the one who discovered the body!"

He blinked at her. "But how—"

"I just happened to be climbing the railroad embankment across the alley from the rear of the house, so I could take a peek into the third-floor bedroom window. I looked in and saw a man lying in bed, under a reading-lamp. Only he wasn't reading at all —his face was covered with blood. Quite dead, I could see that. So I turned in the alarm."

She followed him inside, still talking about her adventures of the evening. "Wait here, will you?" he said finally, and left her. When he returned his face was very grave.

"The body—?" she began hopefully.

"Dr. Gavin, the assistant medical examiner, is upstairs now," Piper said. "If he needs your help he'll send for you."

"But Oscar—"

"This case has been a headache from the very beginning," he snapped. "Come with me." And Miss Withers found herself hustled unceremoniously into the living room, where Mr. Brannigan, the private detective, was sweating copiously under the stern gaze of a headquarters sergeant. On the couch lay Rena Hawkins, her reddish hair disheveled and her eyes looking like two burnt holes in a blanket. She wore a man's woolen bathrobe.

"Oh, it's you," the woman cried, when she saw the inspector. Her voice was thin and brittle. "Didn't I tell you so? Didn't I beg you to do something? You and your advice to go look up a good private detective—as if this clumsy ox was any protection —" She gave the private detective a look that could have curled his hair.

"Hold it," Piper said. "Brannigan, according to your story somebody tried to sneak into the house last night just before eleven o'clock?"

"Yes, sir." Brannigan pointed accusingly toward Miss Withers. "It was *her*. I figured she was just a harmless nut, so I let her go."

"Why, of all things, when I was merely trying—" Miss Withers was gasping. "How dare you say that?"

"Okay, okay, I'll ask the questions," Piper said wearily. "Brannigan, after you got rid of the lady, what next?"

"I began to worry about Mr. Hawkins. I tiptoed upstairs to see if he was all right, and there was a streak of light under his door. Only he didn't answer my knock. I went and tried to wake up his wife, only she was dead to the world. I got really worried then, because he was locked in and I didn't have a key. So I kicked in a panel of the door, and there he was, stiffer'n a mackerel. It looked like a .45 caliber hole in his head."

"The medical examiner bears that out. What did you do next?"

"Me? I went downstairs to let the police radio car boys in, before they smashed the door down. Somebody already called 'em. . . ."

"What was the last time you saw Hawkins alive?"

Brannigan frowned. "Shortly after I got on the job, about nine-thirty, when he went up to bed."

"And you stick to your story that you didn't hear the shot?"

"Not even a loud noise. Nothing."

"How do you account for a man in this house being killed with a large-caliber pistol and you not hearing it?"

The man shook his head miserably. "Honest, inspector, I don't."

Piper's face wore an expression of deep disgust, but he turned quickly to Rena Hawkins. "Well, are you deaf too?"

She was dry-eyed, but Miss Withers thought the woman not far from hysteria. "I didn't hear a thing," Rena said dully. "But there were two doors between me and Ernest. I was in our regular bedroom on the second floor front. You see, I just had to get some sleep, and Ernest has been tossing around so much at night,

I made him go upstairs to the spare bedroom where he could lock himself in."

Miss Withers whispered in the inspector's ear. "Oscar, I have an idea! Suppose we make a test—I'll lie down in Mrs. Hawkins' bedroom and you close the doors and then fire off a pistol in the murder room, to see if I can hear it?"

He was unimpressed. "No good, unless we had the same gun."

"Oh, yes!" said the schoolteacher happily. "*The same gun!* I wonder if it could have been the weapon Mr. Brannigan was waving in my face earlier this evening? He wore one of those gangster strap things around his shoulder—"

The private operative flushed beet-red. "Ask Sergeant Mertz about that," he said sulkily.

"Sure," said the sergeant. "We took the roscoe off him when we got here. Ballistics has it now, but I can tell you beforehand that it's a new .38, never fired, and too small for the hole in Hawkins' head."

Rena Hawkins said, through dry lips, "There wouldn't be any use in the test of whether I heard the shot or not, unless Miss Whatshername here took a couple of stiff slugs of whisky and a double dose of veronal, like I did when I went to bed last night."

"She was still groggy when we got here," Mertz put in. "The radio car boys say they had to pour water on her to wake her up."

"Okay for now," the inspector said. Rena Hawkins subsided upon the couch, biting her handkerchief, but Brannigan stood up hopefully. At the look in Piper's face he sat down again. Miss Withers felt herself impelled out into the hall.

"Oscar," she cried hopefully, "I have another idea! Couldn't somebody have sneaked into the house and picked the lock of Hawkins' bedroom, or else climbed up to the window on a ladder and then shot him using a silencer?"

Piper shook his head wearily. "A silencer is no damn good except on a rifle, though the general public doesn't know it. Moreover, there's a Yale-type lock on the bedroom door, practically unpickable. No ladder marks in the soft mud of the yard, either."

She shrugged, "Well, I was only trying—"

"Trying to make a mystery out of what must be a simple

inside job. That Brannigan fellow is lying like a rug. Only—"

"Only why should an ex-policeman, with so much experience along these lines, and with intelligence enough to start his own detective agency when he left the service, tell such an obvious lie?"

It was close enough to nettle the inspector. "Maybe—"

"And with all those people on the Bigelow Committee wanting Hawkins dead—"

Wearily the inspector gave a résumé of his evening. "I was only trying to follow your suggestions," he said. "Preventive detection, and all that. But we can cancel out the lot of them. Dr. Gavin says that Hawkins died shortly after ten. None of the suspects could have been out here murdering Hawkins and got home in time to be picked up when the order went out. So forget it."

"But Oscar," she cried, "there must be some mistake—"

"You're making it," he snapped. "Nobody asked you to come out here and solve the mystery of the locked room. You're off base. Suppose you just sit here a while and let men do men's work, huh?" He pointed to the bench, and hurried upstairs again.

When the inspector finally came back downstairs, he found her studying the pile of tattered phone books on the bench. His mood, she sensed, had mysteriously improved. "Trying to look up the answers in the back of the book, Hildegarde?"

"Not quite. But I did have an idea. Only none of the suspects seems to live out here on Long Island. Of course, these phone books are a year old. They're titled *Summer-Fall 1946*, and people might have moved."

"So what?"

"The murder was committed between nine-forty, when he went to bed, and a little after eleven, when I first saw the body. The medical examiner says shortly after ten. Suppose the killer lived only a few minutes from here—he could have still got home in time to be picked up. Maybe he was laughing up his sleeve, or quaking in his boots, down in the district attorney's office?"

"Relax," Piper told her. "They all live in Manhattan. But we're way ahead of you. Now that the case is all over but the shouting, come on up and I'll show you how it was done."

"And by whom?"

"That part'll be easy. You see, Dr. Gavin says Hawkins was killed by a .45 bullet that only went an inch or so into his brain."

" 'Not so deep as a well, nor so wide as a church door, but 'tis enough,' " she quoted. "Shakespeare."

"You don't get the point. The shot couldn't possibly have been fired in the bedroom at all, or it would have gone through him and buried itself in the wall. A gun that size can put a bullet through four inches of hardwood. The slug that killed him was a spent bullet, just about at the limit of its effective range." They came to the third floor and along the hall, through the door with the smashed panel and into the room where at the moment Ernest Hawkins was posing for his last photographs. Miss Withers took another look at the lifeless, sagging body, one hand still loosely holding a copy of *Turf and Paddock Magazine*, sniffed at the empty brandy bottle on the bedside table, and then turned quickly away. It was a relief to rejoin the inspector, who was pointing out the window.

"Nobody heard the shot," he said, "because it wasn't fired inside the house. What noise there was drowned out by the roar of a passing train. You see that the embankment is almost at this level? The eastbound trains go by like a bat out of hell, but the ones headed toward Manhattan have to slow down along here for a signal block ahead. The killer must have been standing on the rear platform, where he'd be alone. Luck was with him— it was a good two hundred and fifty feet, but you yourself know how the open window and the bed-lamp made a target out of the victim. And if the shot had only winged Hawkins, it would still have scared him out of testifying at the trial."

Miss Withers admitted all that. She had more to say, but the inspector was suddenly called downstairs to the phone. A few moments later he came back up the stairs, his face wreathed in a wide grin. At the landing he stopped, frowned, and then turned back and went into Rena Hawkins' bedroom, where he surprised Miss Withers poking around among the boxes and bottles on the vanity table.

"Look, Oscar," she cried, displaying a sphinx-marked box. "She does use henna!"

"Okay. So you were right about one thing, anyway! But you have no business to go snooping around. What do you suppose you could find that we didn't notice when we officially searched the place, huh?"

She hesitated. "Sometimes I think that the police only see the things that are there, instead of noticing the things that should be and aren't." She gestured, vaguely.

The inspector looked at the bottles and jars on the vanity. "Looks like ordinary dime store stuff to me."

But Miss Withers had turned her attention to the heavy, steel money-box on the bureau. "Oh, if that's it, I've got the key," Piper said. "Wanta peek?" He opened it, dumping out a sheaf of old pari-mutuel tickets. "Proving that Hawkins made some very unlucky fifty-dollar bets when he went to the track. Probably saved them so he could prove his losses against his gains, for the income-tax people."

With feminine contrariness, Miss Withers had lost interest in the strongbox and was peering into the closet. "Bedroom slippers, three pairs of oxfords, a pair of opera pumps run down at the heel, and one pair of overshoes," she enumerated.

"No Seven-League boots?"

"I was thinking," Miss Withers announced cryptically, "of glass slippers—the kind that Cinderella wore to the ball."

The inspector said he had had enough of fairy stories and urged her toward the door. "I've got work to do," he said.

"You have your work cut out for you, if you're going to try to prove that theory about the shot being fired from a train," she insisted. "I've been thinking it over and—"

"And the shot that killed Hawkins was fired from a westbound train which passed this point at exactly ten-five," he told her.

"Just got a report that a maintenance man in the Pennsy yards stumbled on a .45 automatic, recently fired, one shell gone, on the rear platform of a suburban train that ended its last run at ten-fourteen. I'll bet you all the tea in China that the slug in Hawkins' head fits that gun."

Miss Withers was opposed to betting. "I don't see why you're so elated, Oscar. That puts us right back where we started. Because any of the suspects could have been aboard that train, perhaps as a round-trip passenger, and still have had time enough to get home to his residence anywhere in midtown Manhattan and be picked up by your detectives at ten-forty or before. It re-opens the case—"

"Sure. But now we've got some things to work on. We've washed out the possibility of an inside job. The shot was fired from outside, and neither Brannigan nor Rena were outside last night, because I personally looked for traces of mud on their shoes. We've got the murder gun and we'll start checking it. We know the killer was a good shot, and that he was on that train. We'll have men check with every ticket-seller, every conductor, every taxi driver. . . ."

"It sounds like a lot of trouble," she said. "But I've noticed that nothing is too much trouble for the department—*after* a murder is committed. Except to sit down quietly and think about things."

He grinned. "You mean the things that aren't there?"

"Perhaps I do. Oscar, are you still holding the members of the Bigelow Committee?"

"Only for the nitrate test. And the killer was probably smart enough to hold the gun with a glove and then toss it overboard immediately after the shot. First thing in the morning we'll comb the right of way, naturally."

"Naturally." Miss Withers started down the stair. "Oscar, will you excuse me? I hate to remind you, but it'll be daylight soon."

"Huh? So it will. Come on." They came down into the lower hall of the Hawkins house. Miss Withers peered into the living room, where Rena Hawkins was alone, sleeping sprawled out on the couch and snoring faintly.

Miss Withers gently drew the dressing gown over the woman's knees and turned out the glaring overhead light. "I suppose you have already released Mr. Brannigan?" she asked.

"Sure. He was glad to get out of it, even if she wouldn't give him his pay for the job. Last thing he said was that he thought

· he'd try to get back on the force, and I'll help him." Piper
turned. "Hey, Sam!" After a short wait Sergeant Mertz came
toward them from the kitchen, wiping his mouth. "Sam, will
you be a good guy and run Miss Withers home? She has to teach
geography to a bunch of little hoodlums tomorrow."

"Sure!" the sergeant said. "Glad to."

"Thank you," said the schoolteacher. "But it's just that I want
to get away from all this confusion to some place where it's
quiet." And she stalked out of the door.

PROMPTLY at nine o'clock next morning Miss Hildegarde Withers accepted the two red apples which were her day's offering,
and then called to attention her third-grade class at P.S. 38. At
nine-ten the last of her pupils disappeared down the hall, headed
for an unexpected half-holiday. " 'All work and no play,' " she
said to herself, and reached for her hat again.

But it was rising noon when she walked into the office of her
old friend and sparring partner, to find the inspector taking as-
pirin and chasing it with black coffee out of a paper cup. "Oscar!"
she cried. "I just dropped in to congratulate you. Because it says
in the afternoon papers that the police have the Hawkins case
well in hand and an arrest is expected any moment!"

"Don't rub it in," he said bitterly. "As you very well know,
that's the standard press handout when we are completely up a
tree."

"Dear me! You mean to tell me that even with the entire
Bigelow Committee as ready-made suspects, you haven't arrested
anybody? Do they all have perfect alibis?"

Slowly Piper shook his head. "Worse than that. They don't
have any alibis that you can check. They all had motive and opportunity—at least opportunity to be aboard that train, though
the railroad employees don't seem to be able to identify anybody. We've more or less narrowed it down to General Fleming,
Waldemar Hull, and Track-odds Louie, just because an army
officer, an explorer, and a gambler should each have had some
experience with firearms. But they all deny it. No luck tracing
the pistol, either—it was listed as stolen eleven years ago."

"How sad," she murmured, "to have the wonderful, efficient, infallible detective machinery bog down."

"We found the glove, anyway!" he blurted out. "On the right of way, not fifty feet from the Hawkins house. Only—"

"Only it was probably cheap cotton, untraceable, and large enough to fit any suspect, man or woman?"

Piper nodded, his shoulders sagging. "I guess that was to be expected." Then he cocked his head, suspiciously. "All right, why are you needling me this way? What are you up to?"

"I? Why, nothing at all. I just gave my pupils a half-holiday this morning, so I could play hooky. I made several phone calls, too. One of them was to the Onyx Agency, after I first got the number from Information. Mr. Brannigan answered the phone, and I asked if he remembered me. He said he didn't think he ever could forget, but that he would try. Very bitter, he was. But he did brighten up when I asked him to help me solve the Hawkins case, and told him my theory. . . ."

"Wait a minute," put in the inspector testily. "Whose side are you on?"

"I am," she said, "interested only in getting at the truth, through any available door. That was why I made another phone call this morning—to Mr. Margolis, the bookmaker. Did it ever occur to anybody to ask just how much money the late Mr. Hawkins lost playing the races?"

"No, and I don't give a hoot."

"But you should. I did ask, and I found that Hawkins didn't lose—he won. Thousands and thousands of dollars. The devil takes care of his own, they say. Anyway, his winnings must have constituted the money that was in the strongbox in the Hawkins bedroom, before the murderer took it and substituted old pari-mutuel tickets. There had to be something for you to find inside."

"So what?" Patience had never been the inspector's long suit. "Will you get to the point of all this, if there is any point?"

"By all means. I made still another phone call—to Rena Hawkins. I wanted to ask her who it was that suggested the Onyx Agency to her."

"She said she looked it up in the phone book—" Piper began.

"I know she said that. But the phone book was put out a year before the agency was opened. I wanted to ask Rena if maybe she hadn't known Brannigan when she was a dancer around the hot-spots, and when he was a policeman assigned to the Times Square area. In fact, I did ask her, but she only hung up on me."

The inspector was rigid. "Brannigan!" he whispered.

"An inside job," Miss Withers agreed. "And you have no idea just how much of an inside job it was."

Piper wasn't listening. "Brannigan," he said again. "Somebody got to him, hired him to do the job. Why, that—"

"We really ought to make Mrs. Hawkins answer the question," Miss Withers suggested again. "Perhaps if we went out there—?"

"Never mind that. Brannigan—and you actually phoned him and tipped him off?" Without waiting for an answer the inspector pressed the switch of the interoffice communicator, roaring orders to pick up Thomas Brannigan on a charge of murder.

It was some time before Miss Withers could repeat her request for a trip out to Queens. "That can wait," Piper told her. "Lucky thing we've got a man stationed in the Hawkins house." He reached for the phone, and dialed a number.

"No answer?" Miss Withers nodded. "It doesn't surprise me at all." The inspector grabbed his hat and headed out of the office, but she kept close behind him. The departmental sedan, siren screaming, cut across the bridge and eastward into the depths of Queens County. During a lull Miss Withers said gently, "Oscar, if you shot somebody from the rear platform of a train what would you do with the gun? Would you put it down gently beside you, or would you hurl it as far as you could? Also, why couldn't the gun have been tossed onto the train, by someone standing on the embankment out in back?"

He didn't answer. Finally they drew up before the Hawkins house and for a while everything was confusion. The door had to be forced and then they found the policeman on duty there. He had not left his post after all, but he lay on the kitchen floor cold as a Christmas goose, a lump on his head and a broken beer bottle beside him. Of red-haired Rena Hawkins there was no sign whatever.

The inspector was on the phone, directing the laying of a dragnet, the complicated operations of a manhunt that would extend all over the metropolitan area of New York. "And put all available men on the railroad stations, the bus depots . . ."

Miss Withers plucked at his sleeve, but he jerked away angrily. "You and your meddling," he growled.

"Shh," she whispered. "Watch your language. Little pitchers, you know—"

He suddenly realized that she had brought a veritable horde of small boys into the house with her, thirty or more round little faces staring at him, smiling through missing teeth, breathing heavily. . . .

"My class," she explained. "But Oscar, before you hang up, I suggest that you forget about the stations and the airports and look for a 1931 gray Maxwell coupé, probably headed south for Mexico."

He only stared at her.

"You see," she hastily went on, "while you were running around in circles in here I went out and had a chat with the nice man who runs the used-car lot next door. I had noticed that one car that was there last night was missing now, and it occurred to me that if somebody was in a hurry to hide some money last night, in a safe place *outside* the house—"

"Are you saying Rena stole the car?"

"Oh, no. The man said it was sold over the phone this morning, to a Mr. Smith. It's being delivered to him out in Jersey City right this minute—the buyer promised to pay cash and I wonder if perhaps he doesn't plan to pay it out of the money that was stuffed under the cushions or somewhere last night just after the murder was committed?"

The inspector was already giving quick orders over the telephone, orders that were eventually to result in the New Jersey state police swooping down on their motorcycles to pick up Brannigan and Rena Hawkins before they had even had their first flat tire. Which was a good thing, because there was no air in the spare tire—only eighteen thousand dollars, in a neat package.

"They're guilty, all right," the inspector was saying. "But we've
no valid case against them. Because neither one of them left the
house last night, to fire the shot or to stash the money. I checked
their shoes—"

"Feet," pointed out Miss Withers, "were made before shoes.
I mean bare feet. And moreover, I keep trying to tell you—the
shot wasn't fired from outside, either from the platform or the
railroad embankment. It was fired *in the bedroom!*"

"And I keep trying to tell you," Piper shouted, "that it
couldn't have happened that way, because the bullet would have
gone right through Hawkins' head at close range!"

The thirty little boys still waited. Miss Withers pushed two of
them forward. "Inspector, this is Sigismund and this is Walter—
two of my best pupils. When I gave my class a half-holiday, I
suggested that they might use their bright little eyes in searching
the alley and the railroad tracks back of this house. Boys, please
show the nice inspector what you found."

Walter nudged Sigismund, who gulped and then started to
prospect in the recesses of his clothing. With some assistance
the urchin finally produced a piece of oak two-by-four. "There,
you see?" cried Miss Withers, in modest pride. "That will do,
boys. The inspector will reward each of you with a dollar, and
everybody else gets money for ice cream."

In a daze the inspector found himself paying off. The little
boys disappeared, whooping like Comanches.

"This piece of wood," Miss Withers promised the inspector,
"is worth every cent it cost you. Do you remember saying to me
that the gun which killed Hawkins could shoot through a four-
inch plank? Well, it immediately occurred to me that if there
actually had been a plank held against the forehead of a sleeping man, and if the muzzle of the gun were pressed tight against
the plank . . ." She gestured.

"Judas Priest in a whirlwind!" muttered the inspector. He
rubbed his thumb against the powder-blackening on one surface
of the two-by-four, and then poked a finger into the hole drilled
clean through the wood.

"It was a spent bullet, Oscar, just as you said—*even though it
had to travel only a few inches.*"

The inspector had to admit that she was right. He wrapped up the piece of wood in his handkerchief and put it into his pocket. "This will be Exhibit A in the case of the State of New York versus Thomas Brannigan and Rena Hawkins."

Miss Withers nodded. "Hell," she said, "hath no fury like a wife who finds that while she has been sitting home her husband has been gallivanting around the night clubs. Exhibit B should be a pair of new evening slippers."

"Huh?" Oscar Piper blinked. "What slippers?"

"The ones he never bought her," said Hildegarde Withers.

FROM DETECTIVE WHO'S WHO

WITHERS, Hildegarde Martha (witherz), educator; b. Dubuque, Iowa, April 7, 189–; d. William Ellery, D.D. (pastor, First Unitarian Church) and Penelope (Revere) W.; student, Central High Sch., 1910–1914 (valedictorian and class poet); A.B., Iowa State Teacher's College, 1918; grad. work, N. Y. State Teacher's College, 1919–20; M.A., Columbia, 1928. Teacher, elementary grades, N. Y. Pub. Schs. (Jefferson and P.S. 38) 1918–1947, retired. Technical adviser, Paradox Pictures, Hollywood, on *Life of Lizzie Borden* (released as *Passion's Pawn*) 1940. Regional Director, Gray Ladies, 1942–46. Secretary, N. Y. SPCA, 1938. Clubs: Fortnightly; Central Park West Civic. Unitarian. Liberal Republican. Hobbies: Criminology; tropical fish; semantics; dianetics. Author: "Hoodlumism in Children Six to Twelve" (*National Educator*, May 1947); *Basic Arithmetic* (MacCauley, 1926); *All that Glisters* (poems, Dorrance, 1922), out of print. Home: 32 West 74th Street, New York City.